THE DOCTOR'S FORBIDDEN TEMPTATION

AND

FROM PASSION TO PREGNANCY

BY
TINA BECKETT

D0550350

MILLS
BOON

Hot Brazilian Docs!

*Sizzling Brazilian nights with the hottest docs
in Latin America!*

The hotshot docs of Santa Coração Hospital
are all top-of-their-class surgeons—
and Adam and Sebastian are no exception! But handling
a medical emergency is nothing like falling for the
two feisty, sexy women who stumble across their paths.
Suddenly these Brazilian docs are further out of their
depth than they've ever been before!

The **Hot Brazilian Docs!** duet by Tina Beckett
is available from September 2017

Adam's story:
The Doctor's Forbidden Temptation

Sebastian's story:
From Passion to Pregnancy

And if you missed them earlier:

Marcos's story:
To Play with Fire

Lucas's story:
The Dangers of Dating Dr Carvalho

THE DOCTOR'S FORBIDDEN TEMPTATION

BY
TINA BECKETT

Published in Great Britain 2017
By Mills & Boon, an imprint of HarperCollins*Publishers*
1 London Bridge Street, London, SE1 9GF

© 2017 Tina Beckett

ISBN: 978-0-263-92664-4

Printed and bound in Spain
by CPI, Barcelona

Dear Reader,

Best friends! They're wonderful to have! You do everything together: share experiences, celebrate victories and losses…and stay adamant about remaining bachelors. Yep, Adam Cordeiro and Sebastian Texeira are childhood buddies, and they are both determined to remain unattached. But what happens when one best friend falls for the other best friend's kid sister? *Oh my!*

That's exactly what happens to Adam after catching Natália Texeira in her barely-theres. Natália is even less inclined to tie the knot—especially since she's always had a little crush on the hunky Brazilian doc. But when the kindling is ignited it turns into a blaze that nothing can extinguish…not even Sebastian's blatant disapproval.

I loved these two characters. Natália's vulnerability struck a chord with me, and I so wanted to give her the happy ending she deserved.

Thank you for joining Adam and Natália as they struggle to overcome deep emotional issues from the past. And maybe—just maybe—this special couple will decide that love is worth fighting for. I hope you love reading about their journey as much as I loved writing about it.

Enjoy!

Love,

Tina Beckett

To my family. As always. I love you!

Three-times Golden Heart® finalist **Tina Beckett** learned to pack her suitcases almost before she learned to read. Born to a military family, she has lived in the United States, Puerto Rico, Portugal and Brazil. In addition to travelling Tina loves to cuddle with her pug, Alex, spend time with her family, and hit the trails on her horse. Learn more about Tina from her website, or 'friend' her on Facebook.

CHAPTER ONE

THE VIEW WAS SPECTACULAR. At least from where he stood. And not at all what Dr. Adam Cordeiro expected when he opened the door to the exam room.

Instead of eighty-seven-year-old Delfina Benton, who was confined to a wheelchair, the figure in front of him stood on her own two feet. Although all he could see of the person at the moment was a pair of frilly fuchsia panties. And since she was facing away from him and bent over at the waist, trying to force her foot into a pair of black jeans…

Meu Deus do céu.

He glanced at the electronic file in his hand. Room 206. And the placard on the wall beside him read…204. Damn. Wrong room.

Slowly backing away, he was just getting ready to close the door when the figure straightened and then whirled around with a couple of hopped steps until she'd moved far enough to look at him. Her face turned the color of that lacy undergarment. "Adam! What are you trying to do? Give me a heart attack?"

Him? Give *her* a heart attack? He didn't think so.

"You are very lucky it wasn't Sebastian who opened this door."

"I thought I locked it."

One leg was still half-buried in the leg of the jeans, while the other impossibly long limb was completely bare. And sexy.

And…hell, no!

Where was the pale, skinny little girl he'd practically grown up with? Not here, that was for sure.

The woman standing before him was all feminine curves and dark-lashed eyes. And…

Off limits.

Completely off limits. His comment about Sebastian wasn't totally misguided, because if someone happened to come into this room and see them, both he and Natália would have a whole lot of explaining to do. Besides being his best friend, Sebastian Texeira was pretty damn protective of his little sister. With good reason.

"Well, you *didn't* lock it." Realizing the door was still open, he swung it closed, shutting off the view to anyone else who might happen by. It took more strength than he expected, but he somehow managed to pivot to face the door. "You might want to finish what you started."

Except what she'd started was a small fire in the pit of his stomach that was growing bigger by the second. And higher.

Shuffling sounds behind him told Adam that she was taking him at his word. "Thank you for at least turning around."

"There is a staff dressing room, you know."

There was a pause. Then her voice came from behind him. "I was in a hurry. And the floor was practically empty."

Speaking of empty, he was supposed to be seeing a patient right now. "Anyone could have walked in on you, Nata."

Why had he never realized that the shortened version of Natália meant "cream" in Portuguese? And hell if it didn't fit her perfectly right now. A thought that made him brace his hand against the doorjamb.

"Good thing it was you, then."

If she could read his thoughts, she might not be so blasé about saying that. Because while she might view him as an annoying big brother, kind of like she saw Sebastian, Adam wasn't feeling very brotherly right now. Instead, his reaction was something quite...different.

He gritted his teeth. "Are you done yet?"

"Almost."

He tried not to let his brain wander down any more side roads.

This was Natália, Sebastian's baby sister, damn it! But his mind just would not let go of the picture of Nata standing there in a pair of tiny skivvies and a matching bra that barely held her curves at bay. Well, they were even then, because Adam was barely holding some things at bay himself.

He waited a second or two longer, and then she murmured, "It's safe."

It wasn't. Not by a long shot. But that didn't stop him from turning around to face her once again. This time she was fully dressed, her close-fitting jeans topped with a dark green tunic that she'd belted around her waist. Her sleeves came down past her elbows, a habit she'd adopted in her teenage years and still preferred, even on the hottest days of summer. Her hair was a dark disarray of curls that bounced past her shoulders, and he knew from memory that they slid all the way down to the slope of her lower back. She'd always kept those dark locks long.

And he'd never thought of that as sexy before. Until now.

He was in trouble.

"Is Sebastian here?"

Natália glanced around, eyes wide in what had to be fake fear. "I don't know. Did he come sneaking in too?"

"I didn't come sneaking. And you know what I mean."

"No. I really don't." She slung a purple bag over her shoulder, the silver chain matching the color of the belt links. "But I never knew you were the peeping Tom type."

"I'm not." He scowled to cover the fact that he'd done exactly that for the first five seconds after entering the room.

No, you tried to leave as soon as you realized what was happening.

And if Natália had been doing something other than changing? This time it was his face that was growing hot. Not in embarrassment, but in anger. He'd never even seen her hanging out with a man, much less caught her in the act of getting it on with one.

Why would he even care?

Because Sebastian wouldn't approve.

And you, Adam? Would you approve?

Hell and double no. He and his friend had always tag-team protected Nata.

"Well, if you'll excuse me, I have a date."

A date? Adam swallowed. Was that why she had on

those sexy undergarments? Because she had always seemed the type to lean more toward utilitarian selections when it came to clothes. Or was he just remembering Nata as a kid and forgetting that she was now a grown woman?

She had a date.

Well, good for her. Adam might not have found happiness at the altar of so-called love and matrimony, but that didn't mean that someone else couldn't find a partner who would honor their vows.

Or at least not cheat on him with someone from the same hospital.

Priscilla had remarried almost before the ink had dried on the divorce decree.

Bile washed into his gut. If someone tried to do that to Natália after everything she'd been through, he would put a fist down their throat.

"Adam?"

His gaze jerked to her face to note that her head was tilted and she was staring at him as if he'd grown horns. "Sorry, did you say something?"

"I was asking if you were going to keep blocking that door." She tugged her left sleeve down just a little bit lower. He'd always hated it when she did that.

Despite her veiled request, he didn't move right away. And he almost didn't move at all. He wanted to know where she was going in all that pink lace. "So you have a date, do you? Does Sebastian know?"

"Yep and no. My plans for tonight are none of my brother's business." The smile she threw him was one he recognized all too well. Full of mischief and laughter, it said she wasn't about to tell him what he wanted to know. Instead she arched her brows in a very femi-

nine move that Adam would have never pictured her
doing. Before panty-gate, anyway.

Panty-gate? Oh, brother. He rolled his eyes and
stepped to the side, gripping the door handle and pulling the door open in one swift move designed to let
her out so that he could finish his day and see his last
patient. And try not to think about what else he had
seen or what Natália was going to do that she didn't
want her brother to know about. In the meantime, he
was going to mind his own business and forget—or
at least try to forget—that this unfortunate encounter
had ever happened.

Natália Texeira swished down the hallway, trying to
look a lot more confident than she felt. In reality, her
legs were shaking and her heart was pounding. A date?
Well, that was a great line.

Not so great was the look of shock on his face. Did
he think she couldn't get one? Well, he could just go
and…

Better not to even think that. Because while he
might have been surprised about her so-called date
night, his reaction to seeing her undressed had been
totally masculine.

And totally hot.

She'd dreamed about him looking at her like that
for most of her teenaged and young adult years. But
since he was six years older than she was, he'd always
thought of her as a little kid. Those days were long
gone. They were both adults now. He'd been married
and divorced. They'd moved past childhood infatua-
tions.

Not that Adam had ever had a crush on her.

She wanted to look behind her. Was dying to know if he was still staring at her. There'd been something in those deep brown eyes that had made her insides sizzle. Of course she'd kept her scarred arm facing away from him, although she had no idea why. He had to have seen it at some point over the years. More than once, despite all her efforts to keep it hidden.

"Nata? Did you forget something?"

His voice sounded from right behind her. Not only was he looking. He'd followed her. She couldn't imagine what he was talking about. Heart in her throat, she spun around to face him.

In his hand he held something brown and shiny and… Her barrette.

The tiny zing of anticipation died a hard death. Ugh. What had she thought he was going to say? That she'd forgotten to kiss him goodbye? Not in this lifetime.

"Thanks." She forced a smile, hoping it was bright and cheery. She gave her sleeve a tug and then held out her hand for her errant hair ornament. In her haste to get away from him, she hadn't realized she'd left her hair down.

"Why do you keep doing that?"

She blinked. "Doing what?"

"Pulling at your sleeve. Is your arm hurting you?" His brows puckered in… Concern. *Oh, God, no. Not again.*

Her smile disappeared. "No. This shirt is just snug."

Liar. Her top was a stretchy, flowy material. The opposite of snug.

"When was the last time you had it checked?"

"Are you kidding me, Adam?" This time it wasn't anticipation that tingled up her back until it hit the base of her skull but raw anger. "I'm a doctor. I think I would know if my prosthesis was giving me trouble."

His wince was unmistakable at her bald words. Well, what she'd said was true. Her prosthetic device might not be visible to the world, but it was there just the same. And for him to ask her about it after the encounter they'd just had was almost unbearable. So much for feeling sexy and confident. He'd just transported her back to when she was sixteen and woken up in a hospital bed with seven inches of her left humerus gone, replaced by a shaft of metal. She found herself bending her elbow, a subconscious response to thinking about the osteosarcoma that had almost taken her arm. If she'd never gotten sick, her life would be very different now.

And maybe Adam would have looked at her through different eyes.

But it was what it was.

"I'm sorry."

The man actually looked penitent, something she couldn't normally say about the handsome orthopedic surgeon. He'd had a reputation as a playboy back in high school, college and for most of med school. All that had changed when he'd gotten married and then divorced a couple of years later. Women still threw themselves at him, but from all accounts those advances were ignored with a quick smile as he went on his way.

Except the way he'd looked at her in that exam room… If she'd wrapped her arms around his neck would he have rebuffed her?

Um, yes, if this conversation was anything to go by. And she would be mortified to have him set her aside like a child. She wasn't a child. And she was going to show him that once and for all.

Only she had no idea how. Or why.

Up went her chin. "You and my brother need to get it through your thick skulls that I do not need protecting. I'm a big girl with big girl panties, and I've been wearing them for quite some time."

"So I've seen." The words were muttered in a low pained tone. At first she thought she'd misunderstood him, but since he was now avoiding her eyes like the plague, she was pretty sure she'd heard him correctly.

Well, then. Maybe she hadn't been wrong about his adult male reaction after all. "That's what you get for walking in on someone—"

"In an unlocked exam room. What if I'd been the hospital administrator?"

"You weren't. Karma wouldn't do that to me."

At least she hoped not. She tried to be nice to those around her. Except when a certain overprotective brother and his hunky cohort started to meddle in her affairs.

Not that she had any affairs worth meddling in.

"Oh, I think karma has a pretty twisted sense of justice."

Was he talking about his divorce? She'd heard his ex-wife had not only married another doctor but she'd gotten a hefty settlement during the divorce trial. Due to some ridiculous lie about how he withheld himself from her emotionally after she'd told him she didn't want children.

Adam was no cold fish. And surely his wife had known how much he wanted a large family. Natália remembered him always talking about wanting lots and lots of kids. Of course, he would tweak her nose as he said it, adding something along the lines of hoping all his little girls were as cute as she was. Only that was never going to happen. Not now. And unlike his ex-wife, it wasn't because Natália didn't want children. "Maybe it does, since you happened to be the one who caught me. Someone who is practically family."

The dig was meant to get a reaction out of him, but she was sorely disappointed. He merely nodded.

She flexed her elbow again, then stopped mid-movement when his eyes followed the gesture. "It's fine. Just a bad habit."

Kind of like her crush on Adam had been. A bad habit that she'd had the hardest time breaking. But she had. Finally.

Right?

Absolutely. Maybe karma really did have a twisted sense of justice. She couldn't give him what he wanted. In more ways than one.

"If you're sure," he said.

"I am."

He glanced at her face, lingering there for what seemed like an eternity before his gaze brushed down her nose…across her lips. She swallowed, then his index finger came up and tapped under her chin. "I like your hair down, by the way. I don't think I've seen it that way in…well, a long time."

Her mouth popped open, but before her sluggish brain could even think of a response he'd dropped his hand to his side with a lopsided smile. "I'd better go. I have a patient to recheck before I clock out. And you evidently have a hot date."

That's right. She was supposed to be going out on

a date with someone besides a bowl of yakisoba from a nearby takeout joint. If her food was hot, it counted, right? Why had she ever concocted that lie? Maybe because she'd been so flustered to have been caught there in her underwear by the very man she'd fantasized about for so many years. "Yep. I'd better go and get ready then."

He started to say something, and then gave his head a brief shake. He took a step or two in the opposite direction and then threw a single line over his shoulder without looking back. "Call me when you get home from your date."

What? Oh, no!

She would be home in a half-hour. Forty-five minutes, tops. And then she would have to come up with a plausible reason why her "date" hadn't lasted longer than it had. She could ignore his order. And have him call Sebastian and very possibly the police?

Not if she could help it. A slow smile curved her lips. That was fine. She'd call him. But she'd wait a couple of hours and make him sweat a little.

He rounded the corner, leaving her standing alone in the hallway with nothing more than her thoughts— which were now running wild with all sorts of possibilities.

But one thing she did know. When she finally put that call through, she was going to have a tale to tell that beat all tales. Of being wined and dined long into the night. She could pick up a bottle of wine with her takeout and watch a romantic movie. So it wouldn't be a total lie. Right?

And he would stay on the other end of that line and listen to the whole darned thing. After that, it was doubtful that Adam Cordeiro would ever try to play big brother to her again.

She was stranded.

Dammit. She turned the key in the ignition of her small car again, only to hear the same ominous click she'd heard for the last five minutes. She'd tried to call three of her girlfriends, including Maggie, but so far two of them had gone to voicemail. The other was working the graveyard shift and Natália hadn't had the heart to ask her to leave the nurses' station right after she'd gotten to work.

She could call Sebastian. And have him give her a lecture about having her car serviced regularly? She tried to remember when the last time had been. But life was so busy with all these hot dates and everything...

She rolled her eyes. Natália had had one serious relationship in her life. And in reality she was too self-conscious about her scar and the questions that would invariably come up. Plus the fact that her chemo treatments meant she could develop lymphoma at some point in her life. And, really, how did one bring up subjects like that with someone you were just getting to know? And yet to not talk about the realities she faced seemed dishonest somehow. To let someone fall in love with her and then suddenly spring it on him: "Hey, I had cancer. And chemo. And a complicated surgery that included having most of my arm bone removed. Oh, and by the way, I'm sterile and might not live to a ripe old age."

Her lungs went tight all of a sudden at the thought of not ever having a baby. *Dammit, Nata, you hold babies every single day.*

But it wasn't the same. She sighed in exasperation.

So, yeah, she never could figure out how to deal with any of that so she just did the next best thing. She didn't date. Or at least she rarely dated. Her boyfriend hadn't even lasted long enough for her to think about The Talk. Maybe because she'd been an uptight neurotic mess the whole time they'd dated. Undressing in the dark had been a huge turnoff for him, and she hadn't wanted him to see her scars so that she didn't have to go into explanations… And, well, it had just been too exhausting to keep up the act.

It was easier just to deal with eating takeout and sleeping alone.

She was going to have to do what she'd vowed not to do. But at least she had the great story she swore she'd have before she talked to him—she had her bottle of wine right next to her. Ugh! She could just catch one of the many buses that came through the area, but in São Paulo, leaving a car unattended was just asking to have it stolen. Or at least stripped down to almost nothing.

Kind of like she'd been in that exam room.

That got a smile out of her.

He *had* told her to call him, right? And she *had* wanted to make it uncomfortable for him, hadn't she? Well, what could be more uncomfortable than having to come and give her a ride back to her apartment—after calling for a tow truck to have her car transported to her place, at least until she could find a service station that had time to fix it.

Securing the carton of yakisoba behind her purse on the seat so it wouldn't dump out all over her floorboards, she fished out her cellphone. She didn't bother wondering if his number had changed since the last time she'd called him, because she was pretty sure it hadn't. Adam had had the same phone number for the last several years. He didn't deal well with change.

So his divorce had probably not been the easiest thing for him to deal with. But he'd survived. Just like she'd survived a life-changing illness. His ex had been bad news. In Natália's book he was much better off without her.

She took one deep breath and then two, her lips moving as she went through the story she was going to give him when he answered the phone. Then she found his number in her list of contacts and hit the dial button. The phone rang. And rang. And rang again before clicking to voicemail. Natália ground her teeth. Okay, so maybe Adam wouldn't get the satisfaction of rescuing her after all. There was no choice. She had to call Sebastian. Just as she punched in the first two numbers, the cellphone began to ring. She glanced at the screen.

Adam.

Only now she was all frazzled, the planned words swept away.

"Hello?"

"Hi, Adam, it's me, Natália."

"I know who it is. Sorry, I was in the shower and didn't hear the phone right away."

The image of Adam standing on a bathmat with water streaming down his chest was something that made her brain freeze even further. "I know I said I'd call you when I got home, but I'm…um…kind of stranded."

"Stranded? What do you mean, stranded?" There was silence for a second or two, then his voice came back. "*Meu Deus do céu.* I want a name, Nata."

The low quiet tone held a wealth of menace. How humiliating was this? But she'd called the man. She could hardly pretend she hadn't said the words. "I'm at the yakisoba place down in Santo Amaro."

"I'll be there in a few minutes. But I'm still waiting for a name."

She gulped. "Okay. Palácio de Yakisoba."

"Not the name of the restaurant. The name of your date."

The name of her…

Deus!

That's right, where was that story you thought up?

Not in her head, that was for sure. She did not want to admit that she didn't have a date after all. For some reason she thought he would be far too pleased with that news. And the last thing she needed was for Adam to turn into Sebastian and go all big brother on her. She didn't need two of them. So she decided to hedge.

"It doesn't matter. I just need to be jumped."

Another pause. Longer this time. "Jumped?"

"Yes."

"I don't understand."

Did she have to spell it out? "My car died at the takeout place. I think it's the battery."

A low chuckle came through her phone. "I see. For some reason I thought jumped meant…"

"You thought it meant what?" Natália was thoroughly confused.

"Never mind. So you were the designated driver this evening?"

Well, since she'd designated herself to drive to the restaurant, this question she could answer fairly truthfully. "Yes, yes, I was. It didn't work out quite like I was hoping."

"I'm glad he didn't just leave you without transportation. Not that I approve of him leaving you there with a car that is *quebrado*. Did he find another way home?"

She gulped. "There is definitely something wrong with that picture, isn't there?" Mainly because it wasn't true. Not at all.

"Don't worry, Nata. I will be there in fifteen minutes. Don't go anywhere."

Exactly where was she supposed to go? Her car was stuck here and so was she. "Please don't say anything to Sebastian about this."

"Your brother has a right to know."

"Um, not really. I'm a grown-up, remember?"

"Then you should be grown-up enough to tell him yourself."

Her brother would freak out if he thought some man had abandoned her at a restaurant. She was going to have to tell Adam the truth, dammit. But it could wait until just before she closed the door of her car and left the parking lot. She didn't want to have to endure the expression on his face. Or listen to some kind of quippy comment. Yes, that would be the best route. "Don't worry. I'll let my brother know you turned into my knight in shining armor."

A low dark sound tickled her ear. "I'm no knight, Nata. Remember that. I'll see you soon."

With that he was gone, and she was left standing next to her useless car with an even more useless sense of longing. Why could Adam never see her as an adult?

Maybe because they'd grown up together. Maybe because she had been someone he'd had to be careful around because of her cancer. Whatever it was, he had never seen her as an equal. Even after coming back to Brazil after furthering his training in orthopedic surgery in the United States. That had been after his marriage had taken a wrong turn.

If anything, Adam was more cynical and guarded now than he'd been as a young adult. Who could blame him? His wife had cheated. None of it could have been easy for him.

Shaking her head, she opened the door to her car and got back in. If she could just get the darned thing started, she wouldn't have to face him at all. Her momentary thrill at having gotten a reaction out of him in that exam room had changed to flat-out embarrassment. She'd been mistaken about the expression on his face. She had to be. Her conversation a moment ago confirmed that.

She turned the key in the ignition and heard the same sluggish growl the vehicle had given for the last half-hour. Something was definitely wrong with it.

Another car pulled up beside her. It wasn't Adam, and the young man seated in the passenger seat made her slightly uneasy. Dark hair and hard eyes surveyed what he could see of her, from her hands clenching the steering wheel to the window that was half-open to let in a little cool air. Maybe she should have waited in the restaurant rather than sitting around in the open with her car in obvious trouble. This wasn't a particularly dangerous part of São Paulo, but there were always people out there who were willing to take advantage of a vulnerable situation. Her parents had been robbed at gunpoint twice while stopping at night at a traffic light. People had learned to just run the lights if it was late at night, rather than risking a problem.

"Precisa ajuda?"

His words were nice enough, asking if she needed help.

"No, I'm good. I have someone coming. They should be here any minute."

Instead of discouraging the man, his door clicked open and one scrawny leg appeared followed by another as the man stood. "Maybe I should take a look at it."

"No, I really am okay. I think I'll just—"

Her words were cut off when another car pulled up between them, the sleek front bumper coming within inches of the intruder's knees. The man's head turned so fast that strands of his lank hair fell over his forehead as he shouted, *"Oi, cara, quase me atropelou."*

Oh, damn. That was probably the wrong thing to have said to the owner of this particular vehicle, whose occupant emerged, one hand resting on his door, the other on top of his sports car. "You'll get a lot more than run over, if you take one more step toward her."

The driver of the original vehicle called to his buddy, who scowled for a second or two before ducking back inside. The two then peeled out of the parking lot, a cloud of burning rubber filling the air.

Adam slammed the door to his car and crossed the few feet until he was standing next to her little clunker. "If I try the handle to your door, I will find it locked, will I not?"

Her fingers itched to punch the button that would do just that, but he would hear it. "No, because I was just trying to start it one more time before going back into the restaurant. And I have a pretty powerful scream, if you remember."

One side of his mouth lifted, the anger in his eyes dimming. "I do at that. I also remember how you used to like to shriek right in my and Sebastian's ears."

"Only when you were being really mean. Like setting my dollhouse on fire."

His smile widened. "You never liked that dollhouse."

She shrugged. "It didn't matter. Besides, if anyone was going to burn it down, it was going to be me."

Instead, her parents' fighting had burned down her whole childhood. Sebastian's too. She had made the decision that she would not marry someone unless they could be friends outside of the passion. The problem was finding the right balance. It was either friend/friend. Or passion/passion. So far the terms seemed to be mutually exclusive. Maybe she was looking for a unicorn—something that didn't exist.

"You never did, though." His grin faded just a little. "So, now that the excitement is all over, what seems to be wrong with your car?"

"I think it's the battery. Sometimes it acts like it wants to turn over, but other times it just clicks."

"Try it now."

Natália obliged, turning the key and giving it her best shot. She had no better luck now than just before those thugs showed up. "See? Do you think a jump will work?"

"No. I bet it's your starter, which means it will have to be towed to the shop."

She groaned. "I have to work tomorrow, how am I supposed to get there?"

"We do work at the same place."

No. That was not an option. "I can take public transport."

"Have you seen the subways at rush hour?"

"Yes. I used to ride them to school. We all did."

"That should be reason enough for you to want to avoid them." He motioned for her to give him a minute and then held his phone to his ear. Once he started talking, it was obvious he had a mechanic on the other end of the line.

Perfect. This was all she needed. Her day had gone haywire from almost the moment she got up that morning.

He was off the phone within seconds. "I have a friend who's sending a truck. He said he should be able to have it fixed by tomorrow afternoon."

Not soon enough to avoid having to ride into work with Mr. Tall, Dark, and Ridiculous. Why was he taking over and making decisions for her? "What if I had my own mechanic?"

"Do you?"

"Not really." The misery she felt must have shown on her face because he reached down and opened her door. "Come on, Cinderella. We'll leave your keys with the owner of the restaurant and I'll take you home."

"Public transport." But the words came out as a sullen mutter, because she already knew it would do no good to suggest it. There was nothing to it but to let Adam take her home.

But if she had her way, it was going to be the shortest trip in history.

CHAPTER TWO

"WHY DID YOU tell me you had a date?"

Taking a long pull of the beer Nata had offered him, he leaned back in his chair and studied her. With her hair now piled on top of her head and held with a clip, she had a sheepish look on her face that almost made him laugh. Almost. Because the wave of fury that had churned to life in his gut when he thought she'd been abandoned by some nameless jerk had shocked him. Sebastian would have been mad too. But his anger would have been because Nata was his sister. What was Adam's excuse?

Something he'd better not examine too closely.

"I have no idea. It just kind of came out. I didn't expect my car to break down or for anyone to find out."

"I bet."

Natália glared at him over her glass of wine. They had split the container of takeout food, Natália saying it was the least she could do to repay him for arranging for the tow and bringing her home. He could have refused to share her meal. Probably should have refused.

He'd been feeling out of sorts for most of the day. Sitting across the table from her wasn't helping.

"You and Sebastian have always tried to run herd

on me, and I didn't want you taking up where you left off before you…"

She didn't finish the sentence. What had she been about to say? Before he divorced? Before he left for the United States? Before he'd caught her in her "barely theres" in that damned exam room?

"Your brother and I were worried about you, that's all."

"You babied me. From the moment I got my diagnosis. It was irritating."

"If Sebastian had been diagnosed with cancer, what would you have done?"

Her brows puckered for a few seconds. Then she took a deep breath. "I probably would have done some of the same things. But not to the ridiculous extent that you both went to."

"I'm pretty sure I remember you flipping out when Sebastian broke his arm, threatening to 'flatten' whoever had tripped him in the school hallway that day."

"Someone told me the person did it on purpose."

"See? You were protecting him." He took another drink of his beer. "The same way we both protected you."

Her jaw lifted to a dangerous angle. "We? There's a difference between you and Sebastian. You are not my brother. And I'm not your sister."

She didn't need to tell him that. Not any more. But it stung that she'd just put him firmly in his place…as an outsider. "Maybe not. But I'm your brother's friend."

And that brother was fiercely protective of his sister. He'd never approved of any boy…or man…who'd been attracted to her. It was probably a normal sibling reaction. Adam had always been careful to keep on the right side of that barrier, never allowing even the slightest hint of interest to show in his words or actions. Not that there'd been any interest between him and Sebastian's sister. They were too far apart in age and too close in other ways. And Adam did not have a good track record when it came to relationships.

Like his high school girlfriend? He'd messed up big that time. Or how about his ex-wife?

Not a good track record at all.

Much better to stay friends with Natália than to ruin things forever.

"Yes, well, that doesn't give you a license to criticize my choices."

"Whoa." He held up his hands. "Exactly how did I criticize you?"

"Well, you…" She swirled her drink in her glass. "I'm sure you would have if I'd actually had a date there in the car with me."

That made him chuckle. "Would you have introduced him to me?"

"Absolutely not." She stood up and held out her hand for the empty plate. "Are you finished?"

"Yes, with everything except for this." He held up the Cellophane wrapper that contained a fortune cookie. "We should probably open it and see what it says."

There was only one cookie, since there had only been one order of food. He wasn't even sure why he'd mentioned it, except that he couldn't remember a time he and Nata had shared a meal together. Not without her brother or someone else being there. He was loath to bring the time to an end for some reason. Maybe because she had called him for help, rather than another friend or her brother.

The slight frown she'd carried all evening disappeared. "If it says something about being unlucky in love I'm going to be seriously ticked." Then she stopped. "I'm sorry, Adam, I wasn't directing that at you."

"It's okay." He'd already been unlucky in love, not once but twice. Not much could be worse than what he'd been through on either of those occasions. "There's not much chance of it predicting my future with any accuracy."

He helped her clear the table, carrying the cookie with them into the kitchen.

"You're never planning on getting married again?"

"Nope. Once was more than enough."

"But what about that big family you said you wanted?" Natália didn't look at him, making short work of scraping the plates and setting them into hot soapy water she'd prepared a few seconds earlier. "Not everyone is like Priscilla."

He didn't really want to discuss his ex. Or children. Or hear Nata say he could very well find someone amazing, if he gave women a chance. "Do you want me to make coffee?"

"Yes, please. The grounds are in the cabinet to your left."

"No fancy pod system?"

"I prefer to do things the old-fashioned way. It helps me appreciate it more."

Adam wasn't going to even touch that one. Because he could think of at least one thing that he preferred to do the old-fashioned way as well. And it didn't involve coffee. Instead he got busy measuring out the grounds and filled the machine with water. He'd only had one beer, but somehow his head was a little fuzzy, as if he'd spent the night at the bar. Maybe it was just everything that had happened: the distress call, those thugs at the *yakisoba* place, finding out that she hadn't had a date after all.

Within ten minutes they were in the living room with a tray, two coffees and the lone fortune cookie between them. Natália settled on the couch, and he set the tray on the table and lowered himself beside her.

She picked up her mug and took a deep sip of the contents, wrapping her hands around it and holding it close to her lips. Her eyes shut for a second. "Perfect. Thank you."

"I aim to please."

Those words came out all rough-edged, loaded with a meaning that had nothing to do with coffee. He purposely cleared his throat, to make it seem like that was to blame and not his own damned inner processes that had been running rampant all day.

He picked up the fortune cookie and tossed it in the air, catching it with a flick of his wrist and shoving his open palm toward her. "I think you should do the honors."

It definitely shouldn't be him. Not when he was suddenly aware of every move she made…of every glance she angled toward him. Of those damned panties that he knew lay just beneath her sensible clothing. Down that path was madness and irresponsibility. And self-destruction.

Natália's brown eyes met his for a second and then

she set her mug down and plucked the fortune cookie from his palm. Her lips twisted to one side. "Chicken."

Yes. He was. And he was okay with that label. It was better than some of the angry accusations he was currently throwing at himself.

The crinkling of plastic seemed louder than normal. He set his own coffee down as he waited for her to finish opening the package. Then it was in her hand. "We'll split it."

She broke the cookie in two and handed him the half without the little slip of paper sticking out of it. Then, gripping the fortune with her thumb and forefinger, she teased it from its home. Popping her half of the cookie in her mouth, she turned the paper over so she could read it.

Her jaws suddenly stopped chewing, her eyes widening in something akin to horror.

"What?" he asked. "It's not predicting one of our deaths, is it?"

He didn't really think it was, but the color was seeping out of her cheeks. "Do you want me to read it?"

Her mouth went back to working on the food, moving in jerky starts and stops before her throat moved and she swallowed.

Something was bothering her. "What does it say, Nata?"

She licked her lips. "It's stupid. I should just throw it away."

Maybe she should. But now he wanted to know what was on it. What she thought was so terrible that she didn't even want to voice it aloud. It was nonsense, right? Then why was he suddenly worried that his past might be rising up to find him?

"Either read it or give it to me."

"Fine. You want to know what it says? I'll tell you." Her chest heaved as she took a deep breath and then blew it out audibly. "Don't say I didn't warn you."

Her head bent as she leaned closer to whatever was written on that paper. "'Soon you will meet and kiss someone special.'"

The words ricocheted through the room, bouncing around as his head tried to make sense of them. Then they registered, and he laughed in relief. "That's what you were so upset about?"

"Well, I know it's stupid, but it's a little embarrassing, don't you think?"

"No, I don't think." He slid his fingers over the side of her cheek. "I did meet you at that restaurant. And I'm at least a little special, aren't I?"

"Well, of course."

He leaned sideways and kissed her cheek. "See? Painless. That wasn't embarrassing, was it?"

"No, I guess not." She smiled.

"Your turn, since the fortune was for both of us." He presented his cheek to her.

The second she touched her lips to his skin, though, he knew he'd made a huge mistake in asking her to reciprocate. The kiss hit him just beside his mouth, the pressure warm, soft and lingering just a touch too long. Long enough for his hand to slide to the back of her head, his fingers tunneling into her hair. Then, before he could stop himself, his head slowly turned toward the source of that sweet heat until he found it. Leaned in tight.

Instead of her pulling away, he could have sworn the

lightest sigh breathed against his mouth. And that was when he kissed her back. Face to face. Mouth to mouth.

It was good. Too good. He tilted his head to the side, the need to fit against her singing through his veins. He captured a hint of the coffee she'd drunk, and the wine, his tongue reaching for more of the same.

He forgot about the meal, the fortune cookie…everything, as the kiss went on far beyond the realm of the words "platonic" and "friend" and into the hazy kingdom where lovers dwelt.

Every moment from this morning until now seemed to have been spiraling toward this event.

A soft sound came from her throat and the fingers in her hair tightened into a fist, whether to tug free or pull her closer, he had no idea. Then her mouth separated from his and she bit the tip of his chin, the sharp sting jerking at regions below his belt, a familiar pulsing beginning to take over his thoughts. If he didn't bring this to a halt now…

Somehow he managed to let go of her hair and place both of his palms on her shoulders, using the momentum to edge her back a few inches. Then a few more.

"Nata…we can't do this." The words didn't seem all that convinced. "Sebastian would kill us."

His friend would approve of him using his name as a weapon. At least in this case.

Brown eyes blinked up at him. "Why does he have to know?"

"If you think he wouldn't find out, you're wrong." He kissed the corner of her mouth, trying to force a playful edge to the act. "Let's not take that fortune too seriously."

Her gaze went from warm to cool in the space of a

few milliseconds. "I wasn't taking anything too seriously. But maybe you were."

Hell, maybe he was. Maybe that was behind the need to claw his way back to reality. A reality he wasn't enjoying all that much right now.

"Nope. I just don't want anyone to get the wrong idea."

There was silence for a second or two. "I'm taking it that that person wouldn't be you."

His disastrous youth came to mind. All the more reason not to ruin a good friendship over a stupid impulsive move. Like kissing Natália? "No, it wouldn't be me."

"And you're arrogant enough to think I would fall down and bawl my eyes out if you say you aren't attracted to me?"

No one had said anything about being attracted to her. Obviously he was, although he was smart enough not to let his thoughts stray too far in that direction. At least not often.

He tried to soften his words. "I can't imagine anyone who *wouldn't* be attracted to you, Nata. You're beautiful and kind. Everything a normal man could want."

"You forgot to mention my uncanny ability to see through bullshit."

He had not forgotten that, which was why he'd wanted to end the kiss before she read through it and saw something very different. She'd always been able to read people, even as a teenager. Maybe because of all the medical professionals she'd been through. With a maturity that often far outweighed her years, she had known when someone was trying to placate her or when they were telling the raw, unvarnished truth.

Thank God, though, that she hadn't been able to tell how shocked he'd been by his reaction to that kiss. And if he had his way, she never would, since he wasn't likely to repeat his mistake.

"Your brother, unfortunately, tends to see things that aren't there."

"Do you honestly think I am going to go running to him and tell him we sat in my apartment and made out?"

Made out. Hell, the woman didn't know the meaning of that word, because had he gotten that far, Natália would have been flat on her back on the sofa and there would have been a very different outcome. *Graças a Deus* he'd come to his senses in time.

"No…" He dragged a hand through his hair, trying to figure out a way to explain this that didn't get him into even hotter water. "So we'll keep this strictly between us."

Her mouth twisted sideways. "Do you want me to pinkie swear?"

"Not necessary." Besides, he didn't want to touch her again. Standing to his feet, he motioned toward the coffee table. "Can I help you clean up?"

She stood as well. "No, I've got it. I guess I'll see you tomorrow at the hospital."

With that, Adam headed for the nearest escape route: the front door. "Thank you for dinner."

"Thank you for rescuing me."

Adam heard a weird note behind the statement. "You're welcome. My friend texted that he should be able to get to your car sooner than he thought. It may be back by tomorrow morning. I can come by and pick you up for work, if not."

"Thanks, but I've got it."

He frowned. "Call me if it hasn't been delivered. I'll need to check on its progress." He wasn't trying to contradict her or irritate her any more than necessary, but he'd been the one to call the repair shop and have her car towed away. The least he could do was make sure it arrived safely back at her place.

She reached around him and opened the door. "I will. Or I can call Sebastian."

"Do you really think that's a good idea?"

Up went her brows. "Do you really think *this* was a good idea?"

"It wasn't all bad, was it?"

"No. Dinner was great."

Meaning kissing him had not been. He could call her a liar—hell if she hadn't kissed him back—but what would be the point? Maybe it was better for them both to just leave things where they were.

They gave each other a quick goodbye, then Adam stepped through the door and waited until it closed and the deadbolt engaged before heading back to his own car. Yes, putting this behind them was the smartest thing. He could only hope that Natália threw that damned fortune from the cookie into the trash and forgot about tonight…and everything leading up to it.

"We kissed."

Natália said the words in a pseudo-whisper, even though she and her best friend Maggie Pinheiro were alone in the exam room. Married to a family friend, Maggie and Natália had hit it off from the moment they'd met at the couple's wedding four years ago. Maggie, her husband Marcos, Natália and Sebastian all worked at the same hospital, in fact. And now Maggie was pregnant. Very pregnant.

"You kissed who?"

Natália shook her head, suddenly remembering that she hadn't seen Maggie in the two days since she'd had Adam over to her apartment and locked lips with him. Thank God her car had been delivered the morning after, so she hadn't needed to call him and ask him for anything else. It was all too humiliating. Not only having to confess that she didn't have a date but kissing the man like a hungry piranha finding its first good meal after the rains came.

Women loved Adam and the man knew it. He had to. She saw the looks they gave him in the hospital corridors.

"Adam Cordeiro."

"The orthopedic surgeon?"

Maggie was an American who'd come over to Brazil on a special exchange program and who'd ended up staying after she married Marcos. Although she was fluent in the language, she still had a charming accent and periodically stumbled over an unfamiliar word or phrase.

"Yes."

"Aren't he and Sebastian good friends?"

Natália crinkled her nose. "Yes. We all kind of grew up together."

"I bet that was awkward."

"It was horrible."

Maggie's eyes widened as she sat on the table, waiting for her obstetrician to get there. "The kiss? I always thought Dr. Cordeiro was kind of cute."

"Says the woman who is pregnant with another hottie's baby."

Her friend's hands smoothed over her round belly. "Oh, believe me, I am not looking to swap partners."

"Adam is not my partner."

"I would hope not, if he's a terrible kisser."

Natália's eyes closed for a second before she looked at her friend again in exasperation. "That's the problem. It wasn't a horrible kiss. It was a good kiss."

"I thought you just said it was bad."

This time she laughed. "No. Not the kiss. That was phenomenal. The horrible part was that it was Adam and not someone else."

"You don't like him?"

She dropped into the chair across from the table. "He's like a brother. Well, more like he sees me as an annoying little sister. He only kissed me because the fortune cookie told him to."

"What? Okay, Nata. You have got to slow this train down a little bit. I have no idea what you're talking about."

"Well, I certainly hope not because that would mean everyone else at the hospital knows what happened."

"Including your brother?"

Natália groaned and leaned forward in her chair, rubbing the scar hidden beneath her white lab coat. Images of her teenage years and the way everyone had coddled and protected her came to mind. Including Adam.

"Don't even talk about Sebastian. Adam was more worried about him finding out than anything else." She quickly gave her friend a summary of what had happened between her and Adam, zeroing in on how she had kissed him on the cheek, only to have him suddenly swoop down and cover her mouth with his. It had been...magical. And horrible. And...confusing.

Maggie slid off the table and came to sit on the chair next to hers, making sure her hospital gown was firmly covering her thighs, Natália noticed. Her friend had scars of her own from where she'd self-harmed many years ago. "So, did you want it to be different than it was?"

Did she? Natália had no idea really. Did she want Adam to be attracted to her?

Hadn't he said that any man in his right mind would be? Yes. Which meant he was just giving her a logical excuse for that kiss. Logical, though, meant that he didn't see his reaction to her any differently than his reaction to any woman he found attractive.

So how many women besides his ex-wife had he kissed the same way he had her?

Was she kidding? This was Adam she was talking about.

So that number was way more than she cared to imagine.

"It would be far too complicated between us. He is as irritating and bossy as Sebastian. He doesn't see me as an adult."

Maggie covered her hand with hers. "I don't think that's quite true. If that kiss was anything like you say it was, he definitely sees you as an adult. Even if he doesn't want to admit it."

"You think so?" The question was rhetorical, she didn't really want an answer. Or did she?

"I do." Maggie stood and wiggled her way back onto the exam table. "And if this baby keeps putting off making an appearance, his little brother is going to be all grown up with children of his own."

Natália tensed for a moment before forcing herself to relax again. This was one of her best friends. And if anyone deserved to have a healthy, happy baby, it was her.

"You still have six weeks before your due date."

Her friend groaned. "Do not remind me. I am ready to pop."

With that, the conversation thankfully returned to Maggie's pregnancy and how far behind her friend was in decorating the nursery and making room for the pile of baby clothes she expected to amass at the baby shower Natália was throwing for her. "You can't have the baby before the shower."

"How about as soon as it's over?"

Natália laughed. "Yes. As soon as it's over I will personally drive you to the hospital."

She could only hope that the party and all the preparations leading up to it would help take her mind off of a certain handsome orthopedic surgeon.

Or else she was in big trouble.

CHAPTER THREE

ADAM CAREFULLY WASHED the exposed femur of all visible dirt in preparation for debriding. A motorcycle accident earlier this afternoon had resulted in Katia Machado's bone being forced through her skin and clothing as she slid along a dirt road. As a result, small bits of gravel and red clay had been ground into the wound. The warm, moist atmosphere of his patient's body would provide a haven to all kinds of pathogens, including tetanus. He needed to make sure the injury site and everything inside was pristine by the time he closed her leg back up.

Examining his incision to make sure it was large enough, he began the complex process of undoing all the damage Katia had done to her leg. Kind of like he needed to do with Natália?

Fixing that problem wouldn't be as cut and dried as the surgery he was now doing. What had come over him? He hadn't drunk that much. Neither had Nata. And yet they'd both acted completely out of character. And he'd behaved almost as irresponsibly as he had when...

He gritted his teeth to stop the flow of recriminations. "Suction, please." Beads of perspiration gathered on his upper lip in the air pocket beneath his surgical mask, but he didn't stop to blot them, not wanting to further the risk of contamination to the wound.

He and Nata were eventually going to have to sit down and talk this through, or that ill-fated kiss would hang over their friendship and ruin it. He didn't want that to happen. And he had been aware enough to realize that Natália had had a little crush on him when she'd been a teenager. Thank God that stage hadn't lasted long. Then those brown eyes had fixed themselves on someone her own age and off she'd gone.

There's only six years between you, Adam.

It might not seem like a big deal now, but when he had been twenty-three and she'd only been seventeen and still in the midst of her battle with osteosarcoma and the resulting surgery to remove a large section of the bone in her arm, it had been impossible.

It was still impossible, and not because of the age difference. There were a whole lot more factors in play now. And it was just not worth it. Nata knew the happy-go-lucky boy who'd hopped from one girl to another back then. She did not know the cynical, jaded man he'd grown in to.

Or maybe she did.

He could only hope. He wouldn't have been good for her back then. And he certainly wouldn't be good for her now.

As soon as the suction cleared away the blood and fluid that had gathered in the tissues, he used a gloved finger to explore further back, making sure everything was tight and secure, no sign that her bone had ripped through any other tissue. Using a squirt bottle, he rinsed the area again, the loupes he wore magnifying everything and helping him spot anything foreign as the water carried it out.

Too bad those special glasses couldn't help him peer into Nata's head and help him repair what he had messed up. Instead, he was flying blind and every word he'd spoken in her apartment afterwards had seemed to make things worse.

He knew she'd hated the way he and Sebastian had treated her like cracked glass, afraid the slightest knock would cause her to shatter into a thousand pieces. She'd surprised both of them, not only by *not* breaking but powering through her whole ordeal with a lot more grace than he might have done. And she'd come out the other end a beautiful and mostly confident woman. There was still that scar that she kept hidden. Brazilian women liked their clothes and when it was hot, those clothes were designed to help keep them as cool as possible. And Adam had never fully understood why Natália had wanted so desperately to be a neonatologist when she couldn't have children of her own. Or maybe it was because of that.

He avoided that floor of the hospital, because it might not hurt Nata to work there, but it caused a kind of pang in his gut when he thought about her cuddling those babies every single day—especially knowing the awful truth about himself.

Dragging his thoughts back to the job at hand, he inspected his work and made sure everything was as absolutely sterile as he could and then motioned to his assistant. "Let's line up the bone, so I can set the pins." Danielle moved to the knee, while Adam stayed where he was, handing his instruments to one of the nurses. Tugging the bones in opposite directions, they were able to maneuver them so the broken ends joined back together. Then, with Danielle keeping everything in place, he quickly drilled the pins into the bones.

He knew where he'd gone wrong with Nata. He just didn't know how to rectify his mistake. Not without insulting her. Or, worse, hurting her feelings.

Hell, what if they'd spent the night together? He'd have to do something a whole lot stronger than hurt her feelings if that was the case.

Yeah, things could definitely be worse than they were. The only thing to do was finish this surgery and find Natália. Then together they could come up with a game plan on how to handle this whole thing. Either that or he'd better turn tail and run for the next big city. And if there was one thing Adam didn't do, it was run.

Propping the tiny form up on her shoulder, she stared at the familiar figure standing outside the viewing area. Adam? Here in the neonatal intensive care unit?

She could count on one hand the number of times he'd been down here. Actually, on two fingers. He'd come to visit her floor exactly twice. She'd been up to Orthopedics lots of times. She had friends up there. She guessed Adam didn't have any friends in her department. Except for her, that was.

Unless they were no longer friends.

Her heart shot down her throat, lodging somewhere in her abdomen. Was he here to tell her that he wanted nothing to do with her?

He motioned at the interior of the room in an unspoken question. *Can I come in?*

More than anything she wanted to shake her head and tell him there was no trespassing. Not on her turf and not in her heart. But she also wanted to know what he wanted.

She mouthed a single word, "Yes."

Her palm smoothed over the tiny back of the pree-mie, letting the almost weightless form anchor her in place. Coward that she was, the baby also formed a shield that she could keep between her and Adam. Not that she had any reason to fear he would jump her in the preemie unit. Or anywhere else, for that matter. He'd made that perfectly clear.

She held up fingers one at a time to give him the key code that would let him into the locked area, a new se-curity feature to prevent any unauthorized person from gaining access to the babies or any of the supplies. Three weeks ago they'd had an angry family member try to abduct one of the babies. Luckily a nurse had seen something suspicious and called Security. The person had been apprehended as the baby slept on un-aware. No one had been harmed, but the hospital had made some changes to prevent anything like that from happening again.

Maybe she could do the same with her heart: in-stall a code that would prevent intruders from gain-ing access to it.

Like Adam?

That man had probably decoded lots of those locks, from what she'd seen.

Within a minute, he had made it past the door and stood over her. "I haven't been down here in ages."

Ages was an understatement. And she had no idea what brought him all the way over here now. But she had a feeling she wasn't going to like whatever it was.

And if the damn man apologized, she was going to blow a fuse. "So why today?"

"I'm sorry I—"

She held up a hand. "*Meu Deus*. Don't even."

"Don't even what?"

"Don't you dare apologize."

Up went one side of that firm mouth, a crease in his cheek making itself known. "I was going to apologize for interrupting your work, but if it irritates you that much, I'll have to say I'm sorry more often."

She wasn't sure what to say to that. Her hand stopped its stroking motions for a second, until the baby shifted, reminding Natália of her presence. She feathered her fingers down the tiny back and patted her gently. This was actually the nurse's job, but Natália came down here every chance she got to cuddle these tiny ones. Wishing for something that would never be?

Maybe. But it brought her comfort in some unfathomable way.

"Speechless?"

"Worried is more like it. Is everything okay?" A sudden thought hit her. "Sebastian?"

Adam went over to the far wall and pulled up a second rocking chair, moving it over to where she was sitting. "He's fine, as far as I know. But I did come here to talk to you about him."

All of a sudden he wouldn't meet her eyes.

"I don't understand."

"I don't think he would be happy with either of us about what…happened. I want to figure out how to present a united front."

"United? I thought we already did that. I'm not

going to tattle on you, Adam, if that's what you're worried about. We're not children. Not any more."

The days of telling on each other were long gone.

"I know we're not. I just don't want to put you in an awkward situation. Or make you feel like you have to lie to keep from saying anything." His glance went from her to the baby and something dark slipped through his eyes before disappearing. "Would you mind putting her down for a minute?"

"Is she making you nervous?" She'd never thought of Adam as not liking babies, but he seemed distinctly uncomfortable by the newborn's presence. Or maybe that was a result of the whole situation. Whatever it was, Natália obliged, getting up and carefully placing the baby back in her environmentally controlled unit. "Better?"

"Yes, thanks."

Normally, on her break she would have gone from patient to patient, trying to give them some contact that didn't involve machines, but it could wait until she wasn't staring at the face of a man she'd practically devoured on her couch. She went back to her seat, her hands clasped in her lap, and looked him in the eyes. "Is this visit really about me, or is it about you trying to stay on good terms with my brother?"

"Maybe a little bit of both. I made a mistake. I'm trying to undo it."

There it was. The second worst thing he could have said—an apology being first on that list. Her reply stung as it made its way past her lips. "It was a mistake we *both* made. We've already agreed it's never happening again. There is absolutely no reason for Sebastian to even ask about it. Unless you give him a reason to."

"I wasn't planning on it."

"Then there you go. It's all good."

Adam's hand went to the arm of her rocking chair. "Is it? All good, I mean?"

"Between us?" Her heart ached. Because he'd been worried about her having to lie to Sebastian, when it was really Adam she'd be lying to. "Yes. It's all good."

"I'm glad, because if anything came between us…" His index finger reached over and stroked the sleeve of her lab coat, sending a shiver down her spine. "Well, I wouldn't be happy."

"That makes two of us." And there it was, the unvarnished truth. Had she really been naive enough at one time to think that she could have a fling or date with him without any repercussions? Without it changing their relationship? Maybe she had back then, but she was older and wiser now. She wasn't like Adam, able to sleep with woman after woman and then go on as if nothing had ever happened. If they had gone past kissing, it would change everything. For her at least. So she had to make sure it didn't.

She tried to reassure him the best she could. "It'll be okay, Adam. It was just a tiny blip on the radar."

Something pounded on the glass outside, making her jump, while Adam cursed under his breath.

When she looked up, the person they'd just been talking about was standing outside, staring in at them. She hurriedly glanced toward Adam to find a muscle in his jaw working. "What's he doing here?"

"I have no idea." She held up a finger to tell her brother she'd be there in a minute. "You don't have plans with him?"

"No."

"Nossa." Surely he couldn't have figured anything out. Unless her brother and Adam used the same mechanic, but she knew Adam well enough to know that he'd been discreet. "What do you want to do?"

"You might start by letting him in." He smiled at her, but there was a tension behind the expression that she didn't like. "The longer we sit here, the guiltier we look."

"We are guilty," she muttered half to herself. But she got up from her chair and went over to the door, Adam following her. Signaling to the nurse at the main desk to come and take her place, they exited the glassed-in room.

As soon as they got out the door, Sebastian grinned at his friend. "Having a baby, Adam?"

Heat poured into Natália's face, and she knew herself well enough to know that she was beet red.

"Of course not. Why would you think that?" Adam's voice was tight. Angry-sounding, actually.

"Because you're sitting in the nursery."

"That doesn't mean I'm going to start a family anytime soon. When I do, it will be something *both* parties agree to."

Natália cringed. Was Adam sending her a veiled hint? Surely he remembered that she couldn't have children. Or maybe he was making sure—in front of a witness—that she knew he wasn't interested in her in that way. Well, he could have saved himself the trouble.

Sebastian held up his hands. "Whoa. I was kidding, *cara.* I actually came to ask for a consult on a patient who's due to arrive in the next hour or so from Rio Grande do Sul." Her brother glanced her way before giving her a second—harder—look. "Are you okay?

You look a little sunburned or something. What are you two doing sitting in the nursery, anyway?"

Her brain went into overdrive, words tumbling over themselves. "My car broke down a couple of days ago, and Adam helped me out. He was just checking to see if the shop got my vehicle back to me without any problems."

"Why didn't you call me?"

"I tried." *Graças a Deus* that she'd started to dial his number when Adam hadn't answered right away.

He seemed to think for a moment. "I was… Wait a minute, where the hell was I?"

"I don't know. I wasn't there." She plastered a smile on her face, although she found nothing even remotely amusing about the situation.

"So is your car okay?"

"Yep, it was the starter, just like Adam thought it was. It's as good as new." She didn't tell him about the two *moleques* that had harassed her or how Adam had arrived just in the nick of time. Or about the fortune cookie. Or that damned kiss.

Her brother rubbed the back of his neck. "Thanks for stepping in and helping her out, Adam."

"It wasn't a problem."

She was thankful he didn't expand on that answer.

"What do I owe you?"

That made her scowl. "You don't owe him anything. It was my car, I'll take care of it." She wasn't going to admit that she had already tried to get Adam to take money for the tow and repairs, and he'd refused. If anything would make Sebastian take a closer look, it was that. There had been so much turmoil in their household that the siblings had quickly learned to take care of any problems between the two of them, never asking for help. Since Sebastian was the same age as Adam, he'd gotten a job long before she had, helping her buy clothes and other necessities. She'd always meant to do the same for her brother now that they were adults, but he wouldn't hear of it. Of course.

"Don't get all huffy, Nata. I was just trying to help."

"I know, and thank you." She knew he was anxious to get back to work, but she was nervous about him and Adam going off together. He could say something he shouldn't. "Is there anything else?"

Sebastian eyed her again, a slight frown between his brows. "Why are you so grouchy all of a sudden?"

"I'm not. It's just been kind of a crazy day."

And not just today. But the craziness from her apartment was spilling over into her job now. Not good.

Adam broke in, "What did you need help with, anyway?"

"I have a *gaúcho* coming in who was thrown from his horse and fractured his leg. Only he swore that something in his leg snapped first and caused the fall rather than the other way around."

"So why are you handling it, instead of Orthopedics?"

Sebastian was an oncologist, so she could see why Adam was asking.

"Because the cowboy was right. They did an MRI to see how much damage the fracture caused and found… a problem."

Natália stiffened at the way her brother had punched out those words. As if he'd been about to say something and then changed his mind at the last second. "A problem. As in a growth?"

"Yes. Possibly." He glanced her way. "That's why he's headed up here."

Adam's soft curse said it all. He knew exactly what she'd been thinking. Because he was thinking the very same thing.

"How bad is it?" she asked.

"Bad. He might lose the leg, if it's what I think it is."

"Osteosarcoma?"

Natália was living proof of how that word could change the course of someone's life. She'd been lucky. They'd been able to do a limb-salvaging surgery that landed her with an internal prosthesis rather than an amputation. It had still rocked the foundation of her world—the chemo, the surgeries, and the fear that it would come back. The fact that she could never give birth to children. Ever. No one had thought to harvest eggs from her when her cancer had first been discovered, and the poison they'd had to give her to save her had killed off the potential for babies.

Her fingers went to her sleeve where the scar was hidden before realizing both Sebastian and Adam were staring at her.

"Are you okay, *lindinha*?" her brother asked.

"I'm fine." Why did she always end up having to say that to everyone? "Can they do the same surgery I had?"

Adam answered. "It depends on the size of the tumor and what shape his leg is in. If the blood supply to the bone below the break has been compromised or damaged by the trauma of the fall, it may not be possible."

Her throat tightened. "Try. Please." She knew exactly how proud the *gaúchos* from that region were.

Their livelihood depended on them being strong and robust. A cowboy without a leg... Well, he would adapt. He would have to, if it came down to that, but what if the leg could be saved? Shouldn't they at least consider the option?

"I'll look at him, Nata, but I can't promise anything." Adam hesitated. "You know the conditions have to be just right for it to work."

She was well aware that the stars had aligned in her favor, although she hadn't felt quite so lucky at the time.

"It's why I came up to find him, sis. I want to do everything possible to save the leg. From what I've heard, the man gave the other hospital a very hard time, threatening to walk away if they even considered taking it." He sighed. "It's not going to heal. The break probably happened because the tumor ate through the bone until it could no longer stand up to the day-to-day stress that riding put on it."

"They're sending him here because the country knows that Hospital Santa Coração is the best there is," she said. "It's up to you guys to prove them right."

Her brother grinned. "Well, thanks for not putting any pressure on us."

"Can I see him?"

He shook his head. "I don't think that's a good idea. At least not now. I want to take this slowly. Give him a chance to process things without..."

"Without seeing a living example of what he'll soon be going through?"

"That's not what I was going to say."

Maybe sensing that things between Natália and her brother were about to grow heated, Adam took a step forward. "I want to examine him before anyone jumps to conclusions. Test results have been wrong before. I don't want to alarm him unnecessarily if it turns out that he doesn't have a tumor after all but a simple break."

There was no way Sebastian would have come looking for Adam unless he was pretty sure the man had osteosarcoma. But maybe the orthopedic surgeon was right. It wouldn't do any good to alarm the patient or, on the other hand, hand out hope, if it wasn't going to be possible to do the surgery. And seeing her with an arm that was still attached to her body might do just that.

"Okay." She straightened her limb as far as she could, needing to assure herself that everything was still okay. "But will you keep me updated on how he's doing?"

Sebastian dropped a hand on her shoulder. "Are you sure you want to know?"

"If something good can come out of my own experience then, yes, I want to know."

She had joined a support group with her brother's help once her own surgery was completed, since she didn't want to place any more stress on her parents' already strained relationship. Sebastian had shielded her as best he could from what was going on, but Natália had been no fool.

"Okay, how about if I let you know once I've examined him and Adam has had a chance to weigh in? Whether or not you can help will depend on what we both think is in the best interests of the patient."

"I understand. But you'll let me know."

"Yes. We will."

So much for avoiding Adam, like she'd toyed with. Here she was offering to help on one of their cases. But she couldn't let her own petty fears stop her from helping someone else. If this *gaúcho* found himself in the same situation that she'd once been in, she would swallow her fears and push ahead. Just like she'd had to do as her own treatment progressed. She'd never felt totally alone because she'd had Adam and Sebastian to talk to.

Maybe this cowboy had his own support system. It was very possible that he wouldn't need her at all. But if he did, Natália wanted to make sure he had someone. And if she had to work beside Adam to do that, then she would.

No matter how hard it was.

Or how emotionally dangerous it turned out to be.

CHAPTER FOUR

"OF COURSE I can be there. Did you say thirty minutes?"

A week and a half after she'd first learned about the *gaúcho* with the broken femur, she found herself speaking to Adam on the phone. She did her best not to think about how their fortune cookie had predicted they would kiss or how it had come true.

"I can try to get the patient to reschedule the appointment if it's a problem."

Okay, so he didn't sound very happy to have her on the line. Maybe Sebastian had put him up to it.

"No, I'll be able to take off." She hesitated. "Is he resisting having surgery?"

"Worse. He's refusing treatment of any kind, which is why I think he's calling the team in. Sebastian tried to talk to him about using chemo to shrink the tumor, and that's when he demanded to see everyone involved with his treatment."

Her heart caught in her chest. She remembered those days far too well. Even though she was a teenager when her tumor had been discovered, she'd freaked out, saying she'd rather die than lose her arm.

And thank God she hadn't thought about babies back then, or she might have refused treatment as well.

"He'll change his mind. Sometimes people just need time to process things."

"I don't know. He's pretty proud."

"But if you and Sebastian talk to him, he'll see how important this is." Even with the infertility issue, she was very glad to be alive.

There was a sigh on the other end of the phone. "We've both tried. So far he's not budging."

"I'll be there in thirty minutes." What did she think she could do that his treatment team couldn't? She wasn't sure. She only knew that if she didn't try, she would never forgive herself.

"Thank you, Nata."

The warmth in his tone was unmistakable. Where at first he'd seemed reluctant, brusque even about her getting involved, he now sounded grateful.

"You're welcome. I'll see you in a little while."

With that she hung up the phone, staring at it for a second as if she wasn't sure the exchange had really happened. But it had.

She hurried through the remainder of the time, finishing up a few little details, and then signed out and told her colleagues where she was going. It had been a quiet shift on the NICU ward.

When she arrived in the oncology ward, she found Sebastian waiting for her. "Adam told me he'd called you. I wish he'd asked me first."

So it wasn't Sebastian who'd asked for her. "Why, so you could have told me not to come?"

"No, but I hate the memories it's going to drag up for you." Her brother paused, stretching one arm behind his back until his shoulder joint made an audible pop—something he habitually did to relieve an old high school *futebol* injury. "What's going on between you and Adam, anyway? Ever since your car broke down, he's been acting strangely."

He had? "Nothing. Why?"

"He's been almost as grouchy as you. Did you two have a fight or something on your way home?"

Relief swept through her. She was afraid he was going to suspect something far less innocent than a quarrel. "No. But maybe you should ask him and not me. It's probably something work related."

"I did ask him. He told me to mind my own business."

Relief turned to shock. "What?"

"Exactly."

"I'm sure it has nothing to do with me." She chanced a quick grin. "And maybe you *should* mind your own business, did you ever think of that?"

Her brother's eyebrows cranked skyward. "Spoken by someone who is waiting to talk to a complete stranger about his business."

"There were people who did the same for me when Mom and Dad couldn't. Or wouldn't. They wanted to pretend none of it was happening." And it was true. They'd avoided talking to her about her disease whenever possible. Except for behind closed doors when there had been raised voices, her dad telling her mom something so horrible that Natália had had difficulty processing it at the time. Even this many years afterwards, he had no idea that she'd overheard him. But when Natália had drawn in on herself, a teacher at school had coaxed her to confide about her cancer and her feelings about it. That woman had been instrumental in changing her attitude, which had been fatalistic at best—suicidal at worst. Without her intervention the outcome might not have been nearly as good.

"I'm sorry you had to live through any of that, Nata. I just don't want Adam to be harassing you into helping with patients every time you turn around."

"He didn't harass me. And this is the first time he's ever asked me to step in on a case. Are you seriously against me being here?"

"No," he admitted with a sheepish smile. "It could help. I just don't want to see you put through the wringer emotionally."

Overprotective to the end. Just like he always was. Only Natália was sick and tired of him and Adam still treating her with kid gloves. She had lived through hell, yes. But it had made her stronger, not weaker.

"I want to be here, Sebastian. If I didn't, I wouldn't have agreed." She hesitated. "Where is Adam, anyway?"

"He's already in with the patient."

"And the rest of the team?"

"They're waiting on us to call them. Adam wants to give you a chance to talk to the man first."

She nodded. "Then let's get to it, shall we?" She fidgeted with the left sleeve of her light sweater, making sure she hadn't rolled it up too high.

Sebastian pushed the door open and waited for her to walk through it.

Her eyes sought out Adam before flitting to a middle-aged man lying on the exam table. "Hello."

Lean and wiry with a shock of salt and pepper hair and a couple days' worth of whiskers on his jaw, there was a brittleness to him that worried her. He wasn't used to being sick, that much was obvious, and from the stiff set of his mouth he was in considerable pain. His leg was encased in white *gesso*, the cast probably just there to keep the bones from shifting rather than to promote healing. Because there would be no healing of this leg. Not in the traditional sense.

Adam moved to stand beside her. "Mr. Moreira, this is Dr. Texeira. She's Dr. Sebastian Texeira's sister."

"Sister and brother, huh? They let you work on the same patients?" The man's grizzled chin barely moved as he spoke. "That seems kind of suspicious, if you ask me."

Natália spoke up. "I'm not part of your team, but Adam—Dr. Cordeiro—asked me to come up and visit with you."

"Why?"

"Because I know first-hand what you're going through." She kept her voice soft, but made sure there was no trace of pity in it.

"Really?" He cocked his head and studied her with hard eyes. "I don't see how that's possible. Unless you have the same thing I do."

"I did."

He blinked then his glance went to her legs as if looking for an obvious prosthesis.

"You won't find one," she said.

"Then we have nothing to talk about."

Adam rubbed the back of his neck. "Just hear her out."

"Don't need to. I already know what I want to do. I'm going home."

"You can't. Without treatment you will die."

"I'd like to see you or anyone else at this hospital try to stop me. I'd rather be dead than be without my leg.

The other hospital said they'd have to take it." He gestured toward Sebastian, who was standing by the door. The stubborn set of Mr. Moreira's chin was probably there to disguise his fear. "Even you said there was no guarantee I could keep it."

Natália stepped into the patient's line of sight to force him to deal with her. "Did they tell you about the possibility of limb-salvaging surgery?"

"Yes," said Adam. "We've already been through this."

The irritation in his voice was plain—not at her but at his patient. She could understand where he was coming from. On the surface it seemed ridiculous to allow cancer to take your life when it could be cured. But until Adam had walked a mile in the shoes of someone who'd been there, he could just keep his damned annoyance to himself.

She shot him a glare. "Maybe he should hear it from someone who's had the surgery."

Up went Adam's brows. Oh, he needn't have bothered claiming he had no idea what she was about to say. She had no illusions as to why he had brought her up here from the NICU. She focused on the patient instead. "I've had the surgery."

"I don't believe you. You don't walk with a limp or anything."

"It's true. The surgery wasn't on my leg, though." Natália tried to make her words as sincere as possible. "They found osteosarcoma in my left arm when I was a teenager. I'd had pain for a while, and by the time they discovered the cause, the tumor was quite large."

The patient's eyes went to her hand and then traveled up to where her forearm was hidden by the sleeve of her sweater.

She glanced at Sebastian and Adam. "Will you guys give me a few minutes alone with him? I want to—"

"If you think I'm going to change my mind because of a pretty lady with a fancy degree, you're wrong. If I can't ride a horse and do my job, I won't have the surgery. Even if it puts me in a hole in the ground."

"But what if you could still do things like ride and work cattle?"

"Natália!" Sebastian's curt use of her name held a wealth of warning. He didn't want her to make promises that couldn't be kept when his patient finally got to the operating table. Which would only come after several grueling rounds of chemotherapy to shrink the tumor.

Her brother could have saved himself the trouble. She wouldn't give his patient anything more than the truth—and tell him her own story. But didn't this man deserve to hear about a successful outcome? Yes, she'd had to give up her dreams of being a neurosurgeon due to her dexterity issues, but she was still a doctor. She'd had to make some changes, but she was no longer sad about it. She loved her job. And if she couldn't have children, surely it was the next best thing: to help thousands of little ones get off to the best possible start.

Mr. Moreira needed to know that if things went well, he wouldn't be resigned to sitting on the sofa for the rest of his life. She knew how hard these cowboys worked and how much of their identity was wrapped up in their jobs. That she could understand. She was built the exact same way.

She took a deep breath and then touched his hand.

The man was a complete stranger, and yet she understood what was going on with him more than she understood Adam, who she'd known almost her entire life. "Tell them you'll talk to me."

The sun-weathered stretch of the man's throat moved as he swallowed. "Okay. I'll listen, but I won't make any promises."

"I'm not asking for any." She sent a pointed glance to Sebastian and Adam, since neither of them had budged from their spots. "Gentlemen?"

Adam was the first to push through the door, holding it for Sebastian, who gave her one last scowl. "We are going to have a discussion later." Then they were gone, leaving her to either perform that miracle they were looking for…or walk away in defeat.

Adam waited until the door was closed. "Do you think she can do it?"

"You know my sister. She is nothing if not mule-headed."

He leaned a shoulder against the wall. "We're looking at a year's worth of difficult treatment. And that's if everything goes according to plan."

"I know. Anything can happen in a year. Or even in a few weeks. As you well know." Sebastian eyed him. "Speaking of a few weeks, is there something you'd like to tell me?"

"Excuse me…?"

"You've been an ass for the last week or so. You even skipped out on our beer night yesterday. I was hoping you had a ton of girls squabbling over you and keeping you up until all hours like you used to. Meaning you're finally over what happened with Priscilla?"

Adam's jaw tightened into a hard knot. What he didn't need right now was a reminder of those days of playing the field, thinking he was invincible...that nothing bad could touch him. It had. His marriage had borne some of the brunt of that. He'd wanted lots of children almost immediately, maybe to assuage his guilt.

Hell, and then he'd had to go and kiss Natália. Which was exactly why he'd canceled his weekly trip to the bar. If he'd known his friend was going to make such a big deal about it, though, he would have gone and drowned the hell out of his sorrows.

"There is no girl—or girls—and Priscilla is over and done with. It's been a busy week at the hospital, that's all."

"Really? I asked Nata if she'd noticed anything, and she gave me some weird-ass answer."

"Weird? In what way?" Oh, hell, had she said something about him walking in on her in the exam room? Or worse?

Sebastian turned and looked him in the eye. "You would tell me if there was someone, wouldn't you? I worry about you. About Natália too, for that matter."

"I don't think she would appreciate you grilling her about her love life the way you're hounding me."

"I'm not 'hounding' anyone. I'm just being a good brother. And a friend." He smacked the back of Adam's head, like he used to do when they were younger. Except today he didn't find it funny.

Kissing Natália had been a one-off occurrence. He didn't want Sebastian or anyone else finding out about it. His friend hadn't exactly hinted that he should stay away from his sister, but he could read between the lines.

Or maybe those lines were from *his* book and not Sebastian's. It didn't matter. It was never happening again. Both he and Natália had agreed on that. Anything else would be idiocy. And a sure-fire way to ruin his friendship with both Natália and Sebastian. It wasn't worth it.

"I think what happens with your sister is her business." And that had *not* come out right.

"I just don't want her getting hurt. If I found out that someone did just that, I might have to…"

The implied threat raised his hackles. "You might have to what, exactly."

"My fist might have to find that person's face."

The words were even enough, but he'd turned up the volume a bit.

"Natália is all grown up. You know that, right?"

"I do. But I'm still her big brother." Sebastian shook his head as if to clear it, then one side of his mouth lifted. "Damn, sorry about that. I'm preaching to the choir, since you're practically her brother too."

His friend was right on one count but, oh, so wrong on the other. His behavior over the last week had not been that of a brother. Not even close. And Natália *had* had that girlhood crush on him. Had he taken advantage of that to get what he wanted?

Hell, he'd wanted a whole lot more than a simple kiss. Not that there had been anything simple about it. He gave the best response he could think of at the moment.

"I would never knowingly allow Natália to be hurt."

Sebastian nodded, dropping his hand from Adam's

shoulder. "I know that. I just would hate for anything to—"

The door opened and the woman herself appeared. In the process of rolling down her left sleeve, her eyes shot fire. "You two yahoos know that these rooms are not completely soundproof, don't you?"

Adam shifted and forced a laugh. "Eavesdroppers never hear anything good about themselves, haven't you heard? I certainly didn't listen to what *you* were saying in there."

"Maybe because my voice wasn't raised. What were you two fighting about?"

"We weren't fighting." This time it was Sebastian who spoke, a conciliatory tone to his voice that he'd used on his sister more than once. Wrong move. Natália had never taken kindly to someone trying to pat her on the head.

"Cut the act. We have more important things to talk about." She motioned toward the door behind her. "I think *your patient* has something he wants to tell you."

She was right. What was going on with their patient was life or death. Unlike the petty discussion he and Sebastian had been involved in. "You're right, Nata."

Her eyes softened for just an instant, before she glanced back at her brother and jerked her chin a little higher. "That goes for you, too."

"Seems to me that you always win these arguments."

"Not always."

Once they were next to the patient's bed, she put her hand on the man's arm. "Tell them what you told me."

Mr. Moreira glanced up at each of them. "She tells me I might not lose my leg." His mouth twisted. "At least not all of it. I know you already explained it but, well, she helped me understand."

Thank God the man had said "might." Sebastian had been worried about Natália painting pictures of flowers and clear skies. It sounded like she'd chosen her words carefully.

"If things go the way we hope they will, there's a possibility that we can insert a prosthetic device inside your leg rather than go with straight amputation."

"You'll take just the bone and replace it with a metal rod. Is that it?"

Sebastian stepped a little closer to his sister. "That's a simplistic explanation but, yes, it's what we see as a best-case scenario."

"And the worst-case scenario?"

"I think you already know what that is."

The man nodded. "Yes. I do. Talk to me a little more about this leg-saving surgery. What happens exactly?"

Adam went through the process as quickly as possible, while giving a global summary of the pros and cons.

"And it would be strong? This metal piece?"

"Stronger than your actual bone. That's not to say that it can't tear away during a bad accident."

"Or a fall off a horse?" Mr. Moreira's hand went to the spot where the cancer had eaten away the bone in his leg.

"Yes." Adam wasn't willing to sugarcoat it.

"Hell, my last spill was bad enough that my leg could have snapped without there being any cancer involved."

"I heard it was pretty serious." Adam had seen quite a few broken bones caused by riding accidents over the years. But there were inherent risks in everything. In short, living itself was a dangerous affair.

"This…probos…what was it called again?"

"Prosthesis."

He waved away the word like it wasn't important, his attention going to Natália. "I'll be able to use my leg the same way I always have?"

"Almost," she answered. "Sometimes there are limitations. For example, I can't completely straighten my arm. Only about this much." Extending her joint as far as she could, she demonstrated her range of motion. She lacked about ten degrees from getting the limb completely straight. "But with your upper leg, it would be different. From what I understand, the tumor doesn't involve the knee or hip joints, so your prosthesis would just make up for the bone lost in surgery."

She glanced at Adam as if looking for confirmation of what she'd said.

Sebastian spoke up before he could. "Your tumor is in the central portion of your femur. I'm hoping we won't have to touch the knee at all."

"This is your sister?" Mr. Moreira jabbed his thumb at Natália.

"Yes."

"And you would do this surgery on her, if she had my type of cancer?"

Sebastian wouldn't be the one doing the surgery at all. Adam would. And the thought of having Natália go under his surgeon's scalpel made a roll of nausea go through him.

Thankfully he didn't have to answer the question. His friend did it for him. "Yes, I would recommend the same procedure. Don't forget I was there as she went through the entire process. It was hard, but she's strong. Probably as strong as you *gaúchos* are."

The patient laughed for the first time. "We are a pretty tough breed."

Natália gave his arm one last squeeze and then let him go. "You would have to be careful, and it'll be a while before they know your exact limitations, but I haven't heard either of these doctors mention a reason for not riding a horse. I lift weights regularly to keep my bones strong enough to support my prosthesis. Your job is naturally weight-bearing, so you might not even have to do that."

"I don't know what weight-bearing means, but if you mean it'll take hard work…well, hell, that's about the only thing I know how to do."

"So you'll agree to treatment?" Sebastian took his tablet from the pocket of his coat and scrolled through a couple of screens.

"Yes. On one condition."

The oncologist frowned, his finger poised over his device. "What's that?"

"Your sister seems to be a straight shooter—kind of like my wife was. So I want to be able to talk to her. During my appointments. And before you start carving up my leg."

"I don't think that's going to be—"

"She's been through this. She'll know what's normal and what's not. She'll tell me if I need to start worrying, if I've read her right."

"It's okay, Sebastian." She stopped whatever her brother had been about to say with an uplifted hand. "I'll be here. And, yes, both of these men can tell you I'm pretty blunt."

Pretty blunt? The woman had as much tact as an elevator car with its cables cut.

Adam lifted a brow. "You don't want to get on her bad side, that's for sure." The last thing he wanted was to have Natália looking over his shoulder at every turn. But that wouldn't happen for a while. She'd be looking over her brother's for the first several months until chemo was completed. A lot could happen between then and surgery, but to wish her away would be to hope for a bad outcome for his patient, and Adam wouldn't do that. He would just have to power through it. Somehow.

"I have to agree with Dr. Cordeiro on this one. My sister is something else." Sebastian clapped Adam on the back. This time the gesture didn't carry any undertones other than friendship.

"Tell me where to sign then. The sooner this is over with the sooner I can get back to my *tereré*. This hospital doesn't even serve it."

Adam chuckled. "You probably wouldn't want it if they *did* serve it. It wouldn't be like what you can get back home."

Made by infusing a mixture of herbs called *erva mate*, *tereré* was popular among the cowboys and in several parts of Brazil and Paraguay. The passing of the *tereré* cup around a campfire had come to symbolize friendship and camaraderie. Since dozens of people might drink from the same flared metal straw, Adam could see why the hospital would frown on serving the chilled beverage.

"We might be able to find you something, though." Adam's family had originated from southern Brazil, and while his parents had been perfectionists who'd criticized their son for most of his choices, they'd passed on a love of their culture—like *mate* and *tereré*. So, he knew where to find the packaged herbs here in São Paulo. And the ornately carved gourds and straws were pretty ubiquitous.

He glanced up to find Natália's brown eyes on him, a soft smile playing on those luscious lips. His body sent a signal to his brain, which sent back a response, beginning a dangerous process.

Sebastian cleared his throat, looking from Adam to Natália. "I'm not sure Santa Coração will let you bring that in."

Damn. His friend hadn't missed that glance. Adam was going to have to watch himself like a hawk.

And not a sensory-deprived hawk either, because that would just make things worse.

"What the hospital doesn't know won't hurt them."

"No, but it might hurt you." Sebastian handed a form to Mr. Moreira along with a pen.

Was he imagining things? Or was there a hint of a threat behind those words? If so, Adam wasn't going to take the bait. He was just going to let it sit there and rot.

"A risk I'm willing to take." In fact, as big a mistake as kissing Natália might have been, he wouldn't go back and undo it, even if he could. He might not be willing or able to repeat it, but he had found himself reliving it in his head. Over and over. And each time her lips found his, the memory got sweeter.

Sebastian gave an irritable shrug and took the clipboard back from his patient, glancing at it to make sure he had everything he needed. "I'll take these and get the process started. Don't stay long, you two. Our patient needs his rest."

Our patient.

His, Sebastian's and now Natália's. All he could see was them going round and round and round in circles. How this was going to work, he had no idea. But he and Natália had better figure out how to collaborate so that Mr. Moreira didn't have to suffer for their stupidity. That meant no more kissing her…or picturing the way she'd looked in that exam room.

But if she kept throwing him glances like the one she'd given him a few minutes earlier, that was going to be damned near impossible. So he'd have to give her a reason to be mad and stay mad.

All he had to do was come up with something they would both believe.

CHAPTER FIVE

"What do you mean I have to promise not to say anything negative to our patient?" Natália could not believe he had just stood there and told her to basically lie to the man. She was so not having it!

"As you know, a patient's attitude can affect the outcome so I would prefer that you—"

"Paint a yellow brick road and not crap in the middle of it. Is that it?"

Adam shut the door to the exam room and then crossed his arms over his chest. "Nice image, thanks for shouting it down the hallway."

"It's the one that came to mind. Sorry if it offends your delicate sensibilities. Some of us have learned to take negative comments and deal with them."

"Such as?"

"Never mind."

"Maybe you shouldn't be involved with this case after all. Especially since Sebastian is breathing threats about going after anyone who hurts you."

Her breath caught with an audible pop that he had to have heard. "Why? Did you say something to him?"

"No, I think it was a general statement. You said you heard it."

"I heard Sebastian say something about punching someone. He wasn't threatening *you*, was he?"

Adam's hands went to his hips, thumbs hooking over the waistband of his pants. "No. But I don't want to give him any ideas."

"Such as? It's not like we're involved or anything." And the man had made it clear that they never would be either.

"No, but if you insist on staying on this case, we'll have to be around each other—a lot more than normal—and…well, Sebastian might draw the wrong conclusion if he sees us conferring in an exam room."

Conferring? Was he talking about when he'd burst in on her unannounced? That was hardly a planned meeting.

"That's ridiculous."

How humiliating this must be for Adam, having to make sure it didn't look like he was playing around with the little sister. Nothing could be further from the truth. The only thing that had passed between them was a momentary flare of lust. He would have reacted the same way to any other woman who had flashed her underwear at him.

You didn't flash them, you dope. It was an accidental exposure, like when you forget to go behind the screen when performing an X-ray.

Something about that thought made her laugh.

"I'm glad you find this whole thing so amusing."

The laugh rolled back inside her. "I don't. Is that what this is about, though? You want me to drop off the case to make this easier for you?" She paused to regroup her thoughts. It would make it easier. For both of them. That didn't make it the right thing to do, though.

"I'm sorry, Adam. That's not going to happen. This isn't about me. Or you. Or even Sebastian and his psychotic need to protect someone who *does not* need protecting. It's about a patient whose life could depend on us figuring out how to play nicely together."

A muscle pulsed in his cheek a time or two before going still. "You're right. I reminded Sebastian of that very thing."

"Thank you."

"Anyway, my thought wasn't to have you lie to our patient, but just to emphasize the positive rather than dwell on the negative."

"I walked through this, Adam. That in and of itself has equipped me to see things that someone else might not be able to. I lived through the fear, the surgeries, through the horror of someone hinting that it might be easier if I were just…gone."

The words came faster and faster, and she had to bite her lip to staunch anything else that might slip out. Why the hell had she said that last thing? She'd never told anyone what she'd overheard her father say in a fit of anger. *God!*

"Que…?" He gripped her arm. "Who said that to you, Nata?"

"It doesn't matter."

"Was it Sebastian?"

"No, of course not. Why would you even think that?"

He cocked his head, grip tightening slightly. "It would explain why he is so overprotective. Maybe he's working through some kind of guilt complex."

The way he said that made the hair at her nape stand at attention. "It wasn't Sebastian. And it was a long time ago. I don't even know why I mentioned it, except to say that I think I can help on this case. Please let me."

Adam released his grip, hand sliding down her arm until the tips of his fingers touched hers. "I hate that we're having to ask at all. Sebastian mentioned it might dredge up painful memories. Are you sure you're up to that?"

There was no way to answer that, because she didn't know.

His fingers slid higher, tickling her palm as they wrapped around her hand and squeezed. "You're stronger than anyone I know, Nata, and I can't imagine what this world would be like if you weren't in it. Whoever said that to you should be hung, drawn and quartered."

"He didn't mean it. Not really. It was a really tough time in my famil—"

"Hell, you can't be serious. If it wasn't Sebastian… Your *father* said that to you?"

"No. Not to me—he would never do that. He said it to my mom. I just happened to be on the other side of the door. You said it yourself: 'Eavesdroppers never hear anything good about themselves.' I think he felt helpless, and it just exploded one day. It's not the first time someone has talked about me when I was in the next room."

"Me and Sebastian."

She answered with a nod. His thumb trailed over the back of her hand. "I'm sorry, sweetheart. Sebastian and I were both being asses for having that discussion there."

"You were asses for having it at all. My personal life is none of your business. It's none of Sebastian's business."

That crooked smile that used to make her tremble

shifted into place. "It's kind of hard to stay completely out of it when I was in the room, participating in it." His grip tightened. "Or don't you remember?"

She remembered everything. The pressure of his mouth on hers, the rough sound of their breathing as the kiss deepened. The way parts of her softened... moistened...hoping for things to end a very different way.

Damn, she would have let him make love to her that night, she was so far gone. And yet Adam hadn't been anywhere near that point. He'd been able to move away with an ease that drove the wind from her lungs and sent heat pouring into her face.

Still, Sebastian had no right to question her choices as long as she wasn't hurting anyone.

Or was she? Wasn't she hurting herself by letting her emotions carry her down dark roads?

Yes. But one small mistake did not a ruined life make.

They'd stopped before it was too late. And they were both fine. Their friendship was still intact, even. It might be straining a bit at the seams, but it had at least lived to tell the tale. And if they'd gone further than they had?

She didn't know.

What she did know was that she wanted to help Adam and Sebastian with this case. "When exactly will he start treatment?"

"At this point, the sooner the better, since that fracture is going to have to be addressed."

"My arm never broke. It just hurt like the devil, which is why my parents took me in to have it checked out." She rubbed the area that lay just beneath her sleeve. "Thank God they did."

His fingers traveled up to where her hand was, his light touch sizzling across her senses in a way that was not good. Hadn't she just lectured herself about not letting him get to her?

"I've only seen your scar a couple of times," he murmured. "Did you show it to the patient?"

Natália swallowed as the air in the room got even thicker. "Yes. He needed to see it."

"And if I needed to see it, what would you do?"

If she thought she'd been imagining the change in him, his low words would have made a believer out of her. Was this because of what she'd told him about her father? Maybe. Because there was suddenly an intimacy between them that was almost palpable.

She breathed the words. "I would show it to you."

"Show me, then. Please, Natália."

Lord, she was suddenly standing on shaky ground, trying to find her footing. It wasn't as if he'd asked her to undress, and yet he might as well have. She showed her scar to almost no one outside her doctors. Sebastian had seen it, and her parents, of course. But outside her family? Not so much. She hadn't been a fan of flashing it around. Her mom had said she should be proud of it—it was the scar from a battle she'd won. Natália, however, had always seen it as a sign that her body had let her down. A stupid belief.

But she wanted to show Adam again. And she had no idea why.

Her sweater had three-quarter-length sleeves. She wasn't going to take it off, that was for sure. Been there, done that…in the opposite order.

As she stood there, trying to figure out how to go about it, Adam captured her wrist and held her arm out from her body. "May I?"

She had to settle for nodding, because the air now seemed stuck in her lungs and no amount of pushing would get it to budge.

Gently, he reached for the sleeve to her sweater and rolled it over and over, until it was up past her elbow, revealing the stark white scar along the inner side of her arm. She was among those unfortunate souls whose skin lost pigmentation wherever it was injured. She'd always hated that it hadn't blended in better as it healed, but instead it sent up a neon sign announcing its presence.

Which was part of the reason she kept it covered up.

Mr. Moreira had been surprised by how small it was. Just under six inches, it still looked huge to her. She'd warned him that his scar might be larger, due to the fact that his tumor was on his leg. "That don't matter. I don't spend my days laying around a beach trying to get one of them suntans. And if it helps me keep my leg, I don't care if it's twenty inches long and ugly as sin." His words had made her smile.

Adam's thumb slid up to the spot and then touched her, a bare whisper, but it ignited her senses even further. "It's dainty. Feminine. Like you."

Dainty and feminine? Her scar?

Okay, when he touched her like that, he could call it anything he liked. Her eyelids fluttered closed, while Adam continued to explore, moving up past her elbow joint to where the scar ended. Then he headed back down, gliding along the line with aching slowness. Her breathing hitched for a second before resuming.

"This scar means you are still here. Still making a difference in people's lives. In my life."

God, how could those simple words light up her insides like a torch? But they did.

And his touch...

She swallowed.

"Nata."

It was coming. She knew it was. Because it was exactly the same way he'd said her name on the night he'd kissed her.

Her eyes reopened to find him leaning over the site. And then his lips found it, and she gasped as the heat of his mouth moved over her cool skin.

Her free hand went to the back of his head, her fingers curling in his hair, not wanting him to move away from this spot. Yet she knew he would. Knew he wasn't going to make love to her in an unlocked exam room. But, oh, how she wanted him to.

If he stopped this time, she was going to be crushed. But what choice was there?

She didn't know. Couldn't think. And Adam seemed in no hurry to walk away from her.

And she was in no hurry to ask him to stop.

Then his arm was around her back and he was yanking her to him. Down came his mouth, covering hers with an urgency that matched what had been building inside her for the last couple of minutes.

Winding her arms around his neck, she leaned fully into him, coming up against the vivid effect she was having on him.

The feeling was mutual.

His hands glided down to her hips, securing her in place while his lips left hers and trailed along her cheek until he reached the side of her neck. When his teeth scraped the skin, it sent a shudder of need arcing through her.

Locked door or not, she wanted him. Right now.

Maybe he sensed what she was thinking, or maybe he was thinking the same thing himself, because he wrapped an arm beneath her butt and hauled her up against himself. Then walking toward another small door just off to the side, he opened it. Moving inside the tiny space, he did the unthinkable: he locked the door.

The bathroom. She hadn't thought of that, but it would work. Right now, she didn't care where they went. She spied the "pull for help" cord and a quick smile went through her. She'd better try to remember that was there. The last thing she wanted was for twenty people to come tearing down the hall to see what was wrong.

"Turn around."

She blinked up at him, then his hands were back on her hips, urging her to turn away from him.

They were going to do this. They were really going to do this.

When his fingers moved to the hem of her skirt and slid up the backs of her bare thighs, she couldn't prevent herself from leaning her torso slightly forward to give him more access. He took the invitation and ran with it, reaching higher until he found the elastic waist of her underwear and pulled them down with a quick decisive movement that made her moan.

"Shh." His lips went to her ear. "I'm going to need you to be very, very quiet, Nata."

Quiet? Was he kidding? She wanted to cry and scratch and beg, and make him take her quick and hard.

Cool air whispered across her butt and she heard the soft snick of a zipper being lowered. She licked her lips, her eyelids slamming shut in anticipation. "Don't worry about a condom. I can't get pregnant."

There was silence for several long seconds. Just as she began to worry, his teeth nipped her earlobe hard. "Shh...remember?"

His hands covered her breasts, and even with her thin sweater and bra separating them, her nipples tightened in response, sending fire straight down to her center. Lord, at this rate, she might explode before he even got to the main event.

"You're gorgeous, Nata. If we had time, I would kiss every last inch of you. As it is..."

His whispered words trailed away as he used his upper body to coax hers forward until she was bent at the waist. Reaching around to the front of her, one hand slipped between her legs and found that sensitive bit of flesh which was already pulsing with mad heat. She started to moan again and then remembered his warning and bit her lip—hard—to prevent any sound from escaping.

A knee touched the back of one of hers and nudged it sideways, urging her to spread her legs. She did. Quickly. Eagerly.

And then his flesh slid down and forward until he found just the right spot.

Do it. Please.

His hips surged forward. Hard. Until he was fully inside her. He stayed there, holding himself in that position with a delicious pressure that sent a jolt of something through her. She waited for him to move. To do anything. But he didn't.

She shifted slightly, wondering if something was wrong. He shifted with her.

"Um-uh. Too easy."

"What?"

"I'm not going to move, and you're going to come."

The words were simple enough, but they didn't register for a second or two, but when they did…

No! She wanted him to repeat that first hard thrust. To take everything that had been building up inside her and make it go off in a delicious explosion.

She tried edging forward, but he matched every move with one of his own, so that there was no back-and-forth friction. None. Just that steady pressure inside, his arm now wrapped around her waist.

She was dying. Wanted him to touch her. Anywhere. To release the floodgates and let her go.

"Adam—"

"Shh. Give it a minute."

A minute? She wanted satisfaction now!

The pressure morphed, and her senses, on high alert for any type of movement, went crazy. It didn't come. But her mind imagined it a thousand different ways. Pumping furiously into her. Sliding with aching slowness until she could stand it no longer.

The pressure.

Her insides quivered. Tensed.

Ah. Wait! That was it. She squeezed her inner muscles again, feeling his whole length as she did.

He bit her earlobe, as if rewarding her for what she'd discovered. She tightened around him, the luscious sensation making her quicken the pace, while that nub at the juncture of her thighs reacted with a short spasm.

Yes!

She bent slightly more to change the angle and clenched those muscles again and again, his breathing growing ragged as she experimented with different ways of gripping him. Tighter. Longer. Harder.

"*Deus*… Nata…"

Close. She was getting so close. If he touched her, she would go off in an instant. But she didn't need him to. That pressure against her cervix had made her super-sensitized. She clutched and squeezed, the earth beginning to spin at light speed. Whirling, tilting, pulsing, until…

Her body convulsed, her nervous system hijacking her thoughts and stealing away all voluntary movement. And then Adam was thrusting madly, muttering words that made no sense at all as she hurtled through the stratosphere, heading for someplace she didn't recognize.

He pumped and pumped, until his frenetic pace of a few seconds ago began to gradually slow, the tilting world righting itself as he drew to a halt. His arm tightened around her waist, holding her in place, maybe to keep her from falling. Or maybe to keep himself from keeling over too.

A huge wave of lethargy washed over her, carrying her slowly back to terra firma. The place where she'd started. And she'd never felt so…complete.

He'd done it. Adam had made love to her.

Never in a million years would she have imagined it could be like this. And…

And, oh, Lord. She was in trouble.

She'd been worried about losing his friendship over a kiss? What was going to happen now? She squeezed her eyes shut, trying to figure some logical way out of this that would put them back to where they should be.

It was just physical. Simply a much-needed release of tension after an incredibly difficult week. Then there'd been that patient. And the admission about her father. Strong emotions were bound to bring out some male/female urges. It was natural.

Normal.

Really? *Really?*

Her brain went into overdrive, sucking down energy at an enormous rate as she tried to find an escape.

But there was nothing normal about what had just happened between them. Suddenly, she was very, very afraid. Was this why he'd wanted her to keep quiet? So he could picture himself here with someone else? Someone who wasn't like a kid sister?

That thought made her squelch inside.

"Adam?"

She wasn't sure if she was asking him if he was okay, or if she was looking for reassurance, but she needed to hear his voice.

"Give me a sec, okay?"

His voice was still rough, but this was not the same sexy, gravelly tone he'd used seconds earlier. He was trying to figure out how to get away from her.

Suddenly, it was Natália who was struggling to get away, to force him to pull out. He moved back in a hurry, separating them, and she reached down and grabbed her panties with jerky movements. Anything to get out of this room. Out of view.

Within seconds, she was dressed, her skirt pulled back into place as she rushed through the door. The last thing she heard as she fled was Adam's voice calling to her, telling her to wait.

But she couldn't wait. Wasn't sure she'd be able to face him ever again. So she wouldn't try. At least not today. And maybe not tomorrow.

She would give herself as long as it took to get this whole damn encounter out of her mind. And, more importantly, out of her heart.

CHAPTER SIX

WHY HAD SHE offered to have the baby shower at her house?

Because Maggie is your best friend, that's why.

Plus she'd been so busy with the last-minute preparations that she'd barely been able to think about that disastrous encounter with Adam.

Right. Keep on telling yourself that, Natália.

Truth be told, she'd barely been able to think about anything else. But at least the shower allowed her to put off the really hard questions, like *why*…and *what now*.

Pushing aside some streamers that had drifted in her path, she made her way over to Maggie, who was seated in a chair. The mom-to-be's face glowed with health and happiness, her hand laid across her belly. She was pretty sure her friend had no idea that she was rubbing small circles over the bump as if her baby were right there instead of still tucked inside her body.

She dropped beside her friend and forced a bright smile. "Having fun?"

"Yes, thank you so much! We still have quite a few things left from Marcos Junior's birth a few years ago, but it's fun to celebrate each child." Her hand stopped rubbing. "We weren't sure we were going to be able to have another baby."

A pang went through her heart. "And now look at you."

She'd told Adam they didn't need a condom because, unlike her friend who'd had a little difficulty getting pregnant a second time, Natália had no illusions about her chances of having a baby. They were non-existent, her eggs killed by her chemo treatments. Her smile wavered.

"Hey, are you okay?" Maggie looked into her face.

"I'm fine."

"I don't think so." Her friend wrapped an arm around her. "I'm sorry. I know this can't be easy. It's why I was reluctant to let you throw me the shower."

What wasn't? Knowing most of the women in this room had children? She shook off the pang of self-pity. This wasn't like her. She'd made peace with that part of her life a long time ago. So why was she suddenly going all melancholy?

"I'm okay, Mags. Really. I'm happier for you than you could ever know. If anyone deserves a healthy happy pregnancy, it's you."

"You deserve it too, honey. And I'm sorry…" She took a deep breath. "Why do you work in the preemie unit? Doesn't it hurt?"

Her friend knew about her situation. The scar on her arm seemed to ache all of a sudden.

"Sometimes." She shrugged. "But I love babies. If I can't have them then this gives me a way to love them. I can't imagine a more fulfilling job."

"But—"

"No buts." Natália turned and gave her friend a kiss

on the cheek. "No feeling sad or sorry or anything else. I have a wonderful, fulfilling life, with the best friends a girl could have. I can't imagine anything better."

Not even an accidental pregnancy? Caused by a single slip-up?

And maybe wrangle a certain orthopedic surgeon into a proposal?

No. Not how she wanted things to happen. She and Adam were not a match made in heaven. He wanted kids. Lots of kids. Sebastian had told her that was what had broken up his marriage to Priscilla: she didn't want kids and he did.

Maggie stretched her back. "Well, you'll be godmother to this little one too, right?"

Godparenting was serious business in Brazil, and although Maggie wasn't native to the country, she had embraced her life here. And she and Marcos were unbelievably happy and in love.

Which was what Nata wanted when she finally found someone.

If. *If* she found someone.

"I would be upset if you didn't ask." She gave her friend's hand a squeeze. "Did you guys finally decide on a name?"

"I think so. Carolina is the top pick at the moment."

"I love it!"

Just then a couple of squeals came from somewhere on the other side of the room, followed by some laughter. Since she was sitting next to Maggie she couldn't exactly figure out what was going on, but as long as her guests were having a good time...

Ding-ding-ding. Ding-ding-ding.

Someone was ringing what sounded like the kind

of bell found on the counter of a hotel lobby. What in the world…?

"Hey, everyone, can I get your attention?"

She still couldn't see what was happening, but since alcohol had been banned from this gathering because Maggie wasn't allowed to drink, it couldn't be anything bad. Maybe they were ready to open the gifts.

The noise died down, people turning toward the speaker. A basket appeared in front of her. "Take one and write your name on it, please."

The woven bowl had a bunch of red cutouts in it. Only after she'd taken one out did she realize it was a pair of lips. "What's this?"

Maggie took a pair too. "This looks like fun. What did you do, Nata?"

"I didn't do anything, and this doesn't look like one of the games I planned."

The woman with the basket, a nurse from the neonatal department, laughed. "A few of us got together and planned a very special event." She winked at Maggie and then handed her a permanent marker. "Write your names on them, please."

When she balked, Maggie grabbed the pen and wrote her name on one of the cutouts and then took Natália's and did the same, before dropping the pen back into the basket. The nurse flounced away, headed for her next victims.

"I don't like this."

Maggie patted her hand. "It's fine."

Something about the way she said that made Natália glance suspiciously at her friend. "Wait. Is this *your* doing?"

"Maybe." Maggie laughed. "I may be pregnant, but I'm not dead."

"What is that supposed to mean?"

"It means that we have some very hunky men working at our hospital. Several of them are unattached."

The bell began dinging again. "Okay, everyone have a seat, please."

People wandered to scattered chairs and the couch, the sea of heads slowly receded, revealing…

"Oh, my God."

Across the far wall were a bunch of men. Only they weren't alive. They were cut out of some kind of poster board or something. She recognized most of the faces. Doctors from various wards had been propped up, the headshots from a hospital pamphlet pasted onto bodies with bare muscular chests. They all wore the same pair of red board shorts. And nothing else.

Natália gulped. There in the middle of the grouping was Adam's face. She glanced at the pair of lips in her hand.

Oh, this wasn't good. Not good at all. But since Maggie had evidently had a hand in it, it wasn't like she could override her colleagues and demand they stop at once.

"So," said Marissa Cleo, the ringleader and also a doctor. "You've all played pin the tail on the *burro* at some point as a kid, right?"

The question was met with a bunch of nods and a few whistles.

"Well, we have a very adult version of that game, just for us girls, called Pin the Lips on the Surgeon."

More laughter ensued. Marissa talked over them.

"Quiet down, ladies. Let me give you the rules and then we can get down to business."

The "rules" were as bad as she'd feared. There were blindfolds involved. And the double-sided tape she hadn't noticed on her set of lips was to be used to secure them to one of the doctors on display. Panic flooded her system. She squashed it down.

Okay, no need to have a stroke. She searched the row of men and found the oldest of the bunch, a neurosurgeon who, although in his late fifties, was still very much a silver fox. But at least he was on the far left hand side of the pack, and since Adam's cutout was on the right, there was no danger that she would somehow put her lips on his...anything.

"And now for the final rule. After each person has kissed their doc..." More laughter. "We are going to mix up the contestants. No fair, choosing your favorite ahead of time."

Damn!

Maggie suddenly stood to her feet and headed across the room. "Just a minute. I need to make a slight adjustment." She went up to the cardboard cutout of her husband and picked it up, laying it over her shoulder, shooting a mock glare at Marissa. "I don't know how he got mixed up in this group of single men, but he is most definitely taken. And no one's lips are going to land on my man, except for mine."

A chorus of *aww*s went up around the room. If only she could march over and snatch Adam's image and say the same thing—except for the "her lips" thing. Because she did *not* want her lips to wind up on him. If they were going to shuffle the cutouts in between players then she would just make sure she went high.

As in aim for the hair. A sisterly kiss on the head. Or even on the wall behind them.

Oh, that's good. She could do that. Since the heads were all pasted onto the same cutout, they were all the same height. She was safe.

"The first contestant is the party girl herself. Come on up, Maggie." Marissa grinned. "Although since you've taken your husband off the docket, that means you might end up cheating on him with one of our other handsome colleagues."

"Oh, no." She took her lips and placed them on Marcos's smiling face. "I am off the docket as well."

Everyone except for Natália found that hilarious. She was no longer laughing or even smiling as person after person played the game.

Adam had his first hit. Someone's lips landed on his left shoulder. She cringed. Another person's landed in the middle of his chest. On his eyebrow. Just like the old days when he'd shown up at events with a different woman on his arm.

Suddenly she didn't feel quite so special. Or that their time in that bathroom was any different than a multitude of other quick encounters.

She swallowed. Maybe it was a good thing that she hadn't seen him—even in passing—over the last two days. And right now she didn't care if she never saw him again.

"Natália, come on up."

She shook her head, trying to get out of it. Marissa nudged her with her shoulder. "Come on, it's just a game."

No, it wasn't. But unless she wanted to explain what

it was that made it feel so deadly real, she would have to play along.

Trudging up to the front, she let herself be blind-folded and spun around three times, knowing that there was some mad shuffling going on up front with those cutouts.

Aim high. Very high.

"Okay, Nata, walk straight ahead."

The lips in her hand, she shuffled her feet, edging to the left and hopefully away from the line-up of men. Hands went to her shoulders and righted her path, then stopped her at a certain point.

"All right, girlie, kiss your man."

Damn. Her sense of direction was all screwed up, but this could still work. She just needed to raise her hand as high over her head as she could and… She jabbed the lips onto the first thing she came in contact with and hoped for the best. The laughter was instantaneous and…too raucous to mean anything good. Reaching her hand forward to see if she could tell where they had landed, she felt something flip out of her pocket. Whatever it was hit the tile floor and made an all too ominous cracking sound.

Adam knocked on the door. He'd spent the last two days trying to figure out a way to do this that didn't involve apologizing. His head was a mass of conflicting emotions and snatches of memories. Of Nata…and him…and that damned bathroom.

He was eventually going to run into her at the hospital, and that was the last place he wanted to have this kind of discussion. So here he was. Standing outside her door. Getting no response.

He knocked again. Harder this time.

A second later, the door was flung open and sounds of wild laughter thumped him in the chest. A woman he vaguely recognized stood there, her eyes suddenly going wide. "Um...hello there."

He'd better come back later. "I didn't know Natália had company. Sorry I'll come back another—"

Against his better judgment his glance went past the woman and he frowned. The room was packed with people. Females. There were pink and blue balloons everywhere and... Men?

Not men, exactly. They looked like life-sized ad posters of some type. And he—oh, hell—he knew them. All of them. A woman at the front was just taking off a blindfold and reaching down to scoop something up off the floor, grimacing at whatever it was.

And the woman at the door waved wildly and then pointed at him. The laughter began dying away until the room was silent. The person with the blindfold turned toward him.

Nata.

He should just turn around and walk away, but something made him step into the foyer of her house.

Her eyes met his and the blood drained from her face, her head swiveling back toward the row of men, one of which was being held directly in front of her. His face was on it, but those bulky muscles were definitely not his. The woman dropped the cutout and inched away from it.

Suddenly there was a choreographed rush of movement as women began gathering their belongings and saying their goodbyes as they filed out of the door. Nervous laughter and smiles accompanied the mass exodus. Someone muttered an apology as they went past.

He could see why.

Through it all, Natália hadn't moved a muscle. She stood right where she was.

Then it was just him. And her. And...was that Maggie? Yes. Natália's friend had gotten up and was standing beside her. Before he could say anything, Maggie held up her hand to stop him. Which was funny, because he was pretty much speechless right now.

"Just so you know, this wasn't Natália's idea."

What wasn't? The party—which looked like one part baby shower, one part bachelorette party.

He glanced again at the cutouts, peering closer and noticing there were shapes—*were those lips?*—pasted on various parts of the men.

He focused on the one of him. There were five pairs of lips on it, each with someone's name scrawled across them. They were on his shoulders, his neck, his forehead, except for one pair. The pair labeled *Natália*. They were pasted squarely on his...

Oh, hell.

A shot of pure sensation hit the real-life part of his anatomy. He did his best to squash it, even as he heard a loud gasp. It wasn't Natália who made the sound but Maggie, and she was looking at the floor where a puddle had formed.

"Okay, guys. No more time for chit-chat." Her face was now as pale as her friend's. "I'm still four weeks away from my due date. And I think my water just broke."

Adam stood next to Natália in the hallway of the maternity wing as they waited on word about Maggie. He was feeling kind of shell-shocked after the crazy turn of events. First their frenetic session in the bathroom and then the baby shower.

He'd called himself every name in the book as he'd zipped himself back into his pants two days ago and had gone after her, but by the time he'd reached the bank of elevators, it was too late. Every door had already closed. He'd figured he should leave her alone for a day or two, so that's what he'd done.

He'd gone to her apartment with thoughts of rectifying his mistake, only to come across that surreal scene.

Why had she placed her set of lips on him? And why there? That did not sound like Natália at all. Unfortunately he'd never gotten the chance to ask her.

What the heaven, hell and every other place had he been thinking, dragging her into the restroom like that?

Something about Natália sharing the horrible thing her father had said about her and then willingly exposing her scar to him had ignited a slow burn in his gut that no amount of cold water could put out.

A ding from the elevator shifted his attention off his own problems. Until the doors opened, and exiting the car was the last person he wanted to see right now.

Sebastian. He'd managed to avoid his friend over the last couple of days as well. In fact, he'd hoped to have things straightened out with Natália before seeing him. That hadn't happened.

He headed straight toward them. "How is she?" he asked.

"We don't know anything yet." The worry in Natália's voice was obvious.

He wanted to put his arm around her, but didn't

dare. Especially not with her brother standing in front of them.

"What are you doing here, Adam? I didn't think the rumor mill worked that fast."

She saved him from having to think of a plausible explanation by taking a step forward with her eyes narrowed. "That's kind of a rude question. Why does it matter? Maybe we were making out in one of the exam rooms when a nurse burst in on us and told us what happened."

Sebastian just stood there for a second, and then glanced his way. "Excuse me?"

Natália's face flamed with color, and she half stepped in front of him. "I'm joking. I was joking."

"Not funny, Nat. I think you owe Adam an apology."

The irony in those words struck him right between the eyes, since that's what he'd stopped by her apartment to do: apologize. Try to explain what had come over him, although there actually was no explanation for that. However, he had wanted to promise that he would never let anything like that happen again. And then he'd seen multiple lips plastered to a poster board cutout that sported a picture of his face.

He still hadn't received an explanation about that, and wasn't sure he wanted one. All he wanted was to keep his friendship with both Sebastian and Natália intact. Was that even possible at this point?

He and his ex-wife had been friends before they'd started dating. That friendship had been demolished over the course of their marriage. He did not want that to happen with him and Natália. The only way to fix things was to somehow dial back the clock to a time before he'd seen her in those silky underthings. That sudden shot of lust had been not only unacceptable, but despicable. He had to start thinking with something other than libido.

"I'm sorry, Adam. I don't know why I said that," she said.

He knew exactly why she'd said it. Because the best way to throw Sebastian off track was to hand him something so totally outrageous that no one in his right mind would believe it.

Adam said the only thing he could. "Don't worry about it."

Only he was worried. Very worried.

Sebastian's posture relaxed, even though his brows slid an inch or so higher on his forehead. "So how is Maggie?"

"They're going to take the baby. She's in surgery now."

He glanced toward the waiting room behind them. "And Marcos?"

Adam had met Marcos Pinheiro through Sebastian and Natália when they'd been teenagers. Maggie's husband had to be worried sick.

Natália nodded toward the doors at the end of the corridor. "He's with her. The baby is almost a month early, but when we got here, her blood pressure was so high they had to act fast."

"I'm sure it will be fine." He wasn't sure if he was trying to reassure Natália or himself. Because nothing else felt fine right now. He and Natália would eventually have to figure out how to move forward from this point. But he did not want that conversation to take place in front of her brother. Or in front of friends who were hoping their baby was going to be okay.

"I'm surprised you're not in there, Natália." Her brother glanced back at her.

"They already had a team in place, and since Maggie and I are good friends they thought that it was better if I stay out here."

There had been a little bit of a verbal skirmish about that with the obstetrician, but Nata had given in and agreed to let the on-duty staff handle it.

Just then the doors opened and a man in blue scrubs headed their way. Ah, Marcos.

Natália hurried forward. "How are they?"

"They're both fine. We have a little girl. Carolina Linda Pinheiro. She's amazing." His smile was genuine, even if it seemed a little shakier than he remembered.

"And Maggie? You said she's okay as well?"

"They're still waiting for her blood pressure to come down a little bit more, but they think the worst has passed."

Sebastian clapped his friend on the back. "Great news, *cara*. Your text message didn't give me much to go on. And then I tried to call Natália but it went straight to voicemail. Luckily she was already here."

"I dropped my phone, unfortunately." She pulled the device from her pocket and displayed the front, which had cracks radiating out from the center. "I can't even get it to power up."

"How does that even happen with protective cases nowadays?"

She shrugged. "I was in a hurry. It flipped out of my pocket when I was at the baby shower."

She hadn't said anything about breaking her phone. But he remembered seeing her pick something up off the floor. Right after she'd planted those lips on him. Someday, he would get that image out of his head. But right now his body was posing a question and waiting on a response. Well, that was an easy one to answer.

Never. He was never having sex with her ever again.

Maybe he would actually believe that at some point.

While Sebastian and Marcos continued to talk, Adam moved beside Natália, who had her lab coat back on, the sleeve pulled safely down her arm.

"Hey." He touched her hand. "You okay?"

Her head turned sharply in his direction. "Yep. It's been quite a week. But I'm still in one piece."

"Except for your phone." He took the device from her and studied the damage. "I know a guy—"

"Kind of like the guy you know who can fix cars?" She wrinkled her nose in a way that he recognized. Not quite rueful but not angry, either. "I think I'd better take care of this one myself. It's safer that way."

"Safer?"

"Never mind. Sorry for telling Sebastian we were making out. He has been impossible lately, and I didn't want to give him any ideas."

"About us?" He smiled. "Smart girl. I think it worked."

"Yeah, because no one in their right mind would ever suspect you would go after someone like me."

He reeled backward in shock at the soft conviction in her voice. "What the hell would make you say something like that?"

"Something like what?" Sebastian and Marcos had turned back toward them.

Natália's teeth came down on her lip, and he could

imagine her mind racing to think up something that didn't give them away.

"She's worried she won't be able to convince Mr. Moreira to continue with his treatments."

"What?" Sebastian frowned. "You did a great job with him from what I could tell."

"Thanks." She tugged at her sleeve. But the gesture that Adam had once found endearing gave him pause now. Was she really that self-conscious? Surely that wasn't why she'd said that about no one believing he would go after her.

Something else he would have to talk to her about. He looked at her, trying to see her through eyes that hadn't known her for most of his life.

He couldn't. She was beautiful. Truly gorgeous, but there was so much more to Natália than her looks. She was kind, feisty, and she would fight to the death for someone she cared about.

So why did she think he couldn't be attracted to her? Because of the way he used to chase party girls?

"Who is Mr. Moreira?" Marcos was staring at them, lost as to what they were talking about.

"He's a patient. Natália has been trying to steer him in the right direction. He has the same thing she once had."

"Osteosarcoma?"

Sebastian nodded. "It was kind of a godsend that he fell into our laps. He didn't want to do treatments at all…he'd convinced himself that his life was over."

"I can't think of anyone more equipped to help with that than Natália." Marcos smiled at her. "Maggie loves her like a sister. Speaking of which, the reason I came out here is that she wants to see you."

"Is she up to it?" Natália took a step away from him, and Adam didn't like the way that made him feel.

"She wants a second opinion on the baby, and she's pretty insistent when she sets her mind on something."

Kind of like Nata. Only she hadn't set her mind on him. At least not for long. "I know someone else who is as well." Sebastian gave his sister a quick hug.

"I also believe in clinging to reality," she stated. "Not that that has anything to do with Maggie or little Carolina."

But it evidently had something to do with him. Maybe she was sending him the same message that he'd meant to give her. That he was sorry for what had happened, but knew better than to think that it should—or would—go any further than it already had.

In that case, he agreed completely.

They still needed to talk. But not this very second.

As Natália walked away from him for the second time in the last half-hour, he knew he was going to have to chase her down once again. Not now, but soon.

Because of all the things he might stand to lose, Nata's friendship was the one thing he couldn't afford to leave behind. Not without at least trying to make things right.

"She's perfect, Maggie." Natália's exam echoed what the attending neonatologist had said. Carolina was tiny, but the steroids they'd administered had sped up the development of her lungs, so she was breathing on her own with just a boost of oxygen to carry her through.

Her friend had no idea that she'd given Nata the escape route she'd been searching for out there in the waiting room. The last thing she wanted was to talk about their little rendezvous in the bathroom, or what Adam had seen at that baby shower.

That shower had been the wake-up call she'd needed. No matter how much she might wish things were different, they weren't. And they would never be.

So why had she ventured outside some of those known boundaries?

Because she'd wanted to. There was no other explanation.

And it was so ridiculous. She couldn't have kids, and she knew Adam wanted them. Desperately. He'd told her so once, when he'd been drunk out of his mind. That was a reality that she knew couldn't be flouted. No matter how hard she might try, the end result would be filled with heartache and disappointment.

Maggie's hand touched hers. "Are you sure she's okay?"

"I wouldn't lie to you." Natália might lie to herself, but she would never tell Maggie something that wasn't true. Not about something so important. "Marcos Junior has a perfect baby sister."

"I'm so glad." Maggie's head fell back against the pillows. "When my water broke at the shower, I was sure something was wrong. And then they rushed out of the room with her as soon as they delivered her."

"The doctors just wanted to make sure she was okay. It's a normal precaution with a preemie."

"I know. It's just different when it's your own baby, you know?"

She smiled, even though she didn't know. Not really. "I can imagine. Especially when you're not exactly sure what to expect."

"I know what I'm supposed to expect. But knowing and truly believing are two different things."

Yes, they were. Natália knew there could be nothing between her and Adam. But her mind was having a hard time getting her heart to co-operate.

On the day Adam had found out about his wife's cheating, he'd gotten so drunk that the bar had called Sebastian's cellphone. When they couldn't reach him, they'd called her. Natália had been forced to go to the bar and plead with Adam to let her drive him home.

She'd somehow gotten him up to his apartment and into his bed, tugging off his shoes and his slacks. Unbuttoning his shirt and sliding it over his broad shoulders had made her swallow. She hadn't been able to stop her fingertips from trailing down his arms...over his biceps, until she'd held his hands in hers.

He'd shifted on the bed and wrapped his arm around her, pulling her down until she was lying against him. She'd stayed there for several minutes, absorbing the feel of him.

"I'm so sorry, Adam."

Bleary eyes had looked at her without really seeing. "She doesn't want my kids. Or me, I guess." Natália could barely make out the slurred words. His fingers had slid behind her head, drawing her closer until her lips were within inches of his. "But you will, won't you, *minha* Nata? You'll have my babies. Lots of them."

Her breath had caught in her chest in a horrible spasm, the physical pain sending her wrenching out of his arms and out of the room. She'd leaned against the wall in the hallway, her cheek pressed hard to the cold plaster surface, suddenly furious. Angry at Priscilla for hurting him. Angry with Adam for choosing his wife instead of her. And blindingly furious at fate for not allowing her to give Adam as many babies as he wanted.

"Natália, are you okay?"

She shook herself back to the present. "Yes, of course. Just thinking about all the fun things you and Carolina are going to do someday."

Her friend studied her for a moment. "Does it bother you that I had Marcos Junior and now another baby?"

"Oh, honey…" She shut her eyes and tried to banish the specter of the past. When she opened them again, she smiled. "I already told you. I have never been so happy for anyone in my life. You deserve this. Both you and Marcos do."

Maggie's hand slid into her own. "Thank you for being here for me."

"I wouldn't be anywhere else."

It would be okay. She and Adam were both under a lot of stress with their jobs, it had probably just gotten the better of both of them. But nothing was going to happen between them again. It was one thing to leave pretend lip prints on the man's cardboard board shorts at a baby shower. It was another thing entirely to have her real-life lips pressed against his real-life flesh.

"That means a lot." Maggie glanced up at the monitor where her blood pressure still hovered just a touch higher than it should. "Why can't Carolina be with me?"

"You already know the answer to that. They need to make sure she's stable and stays stable. And you need to get some rest so that your meds have a chance to kick in and make everything return to normal."

If only there were some meds that Natália could

take to make everything return to normal. But there weren't. Only time could do that.

Marcos, who had been in the middle of a treatment meeting when he'd gotten the news about Maggie, popped in to say that he had to go finalize things. He promised to return as soon as he could. Maggie had told him to do what was best for his patient. The tenderness in the kiss he'd dropped on his wife's forehead made the backs of Nata's eyelids prick.

Her friend was so very blessed. Thankfully Maggie knew it. It had taken her and Marcos some time to find their way, but the love the two of them had for each other was obvious to everyone around. They were lovers who had become friends. Too bad it didn't work the other way around. But it didn't. Not for her, anyway.

Maybe someday Natália would find a love like that. She just had to start looking in places that weren't so close to home—and which didn't include a certain hunky orthopedic surgeon.

For her sake. And everyone else's.

CHAPTER SEVEN

ADAM GLANCED DOWN the long conference table where the members of Mr. Moreira's treatment team had gathered to talk about timetables and who would be in charge of planning each segment of their patient's journey back to health. He wasn't exactly sure what he thought about Natália attending this particular meeting, but Sebastian wanted her here. She'd spoken with their patient on more than one occasion and since they had all agreed that she would help keep him motivated, Adam couldn't very well ask to have her taken off the team. Not without answering some very difficult questions.

Questions that could put him in an awkward situation to say the very least.

As if sensing his eyes were on her, Natália picked that very moment to glance over and catch him staring. Her brows went up, then her attention shifted to the current speaker: Sebastian, who was talking about the chemo regimen he hoped to begin this week. They'd gotten the okay from the insurance companies and, thanks to Natália, from the patient himself. The only thing left to do was set the exact date.

"So what does everyone think about next Wednesday for starting dose one of the methotrexate?"

The treatment regimen was the one most often used for this type of osteosarcoma.

"Sounds good," Adam said. "Standard protocol?"

"Yes, unless we're not getting the results we want. If that happens, we'll re-evaluate."

A hand went up from farther down the table. Natália was asking for the floor.

Sebastian nodded in her direction. "You have something to add?"

"I'm just curious as to what 'standard protocol' means in this case."

"It means that there is a narrow window, and we want to follow what has worked for the largest segment of patients."

"He's worried about being sick and not appearing himself to the people he loves. Especially his daughter. Since she's a nurse, he knows he won't be able to hide much from her."

Leave it to Natália to think of something other than objective facts. But it made sense. Her area of expertise wasn't as cut and dried as oncology and orthopedics were. On the rare occasions he'd ventured down into NICU, he'd witnessed her tenderly holding those babies as if she could love them back to health. And maybe she could. It didn't work that way in his specialty. Cuddling his patients wouldn't mend broken bones. It certainly wouldn't cure Mr. Moreira's osteosarcoma. Or could it? Hadn't Sebastian told him he had seen miraculous recoveries in patients who—according to every statistic—should be dead?

And the way Natália had coaxed their patient to

give medicine a chance… She'd spoken from the heart and used her own experience to give the man a sense of hope. Without her, this treatment team probably wouldn't be meeting to discuss treatment at all, but rather issuing discharge papers.

His eyes caught hers again as Sebastian asked, "What exactly is he afraid of? Losing his hair?"

"He's afraid of not being seen as the man he perceives himself to be."

"He's not going to be that man. At least not for a while. But it's temporary. His daughter and those who know him can help by not treating him as if he's at death's door."

Natália stiffened in her seat for a second, and Adam could pretty much imagine what was going through her head. Her family—and Adam—had treated her exactly like that during most of her treatment. Sebastian was still overprotective of her even now. He'd seen that first-hand.

Had they been wrong?

Maybe, but they'd all just been kids at the time. They'd only wanted to help and had done so in the only way they'd known how. Sebastian had done his best to shield Natália from their parents' fights—at least from what his friend had shared and what Adam had witnessed on several occasions. It had made his friend hard and bitter in some ways.

Then again, so had Adam's divorce. It had made him cynical in ways he'd never imagined when he'd been young and in love.

Growing up as the only child of emotionally distant parents had made Adam crave companionship, needing something to ease the gnawing loneliness. He'd tried to combat that by jumping from girl to girl, with disastrous results. One of those girls had gotten pregnant and he later learned that she'd chosen to terminate the pregnancy. He'd never told anyone about it, but that event had impacted his life in ways he never could have imagined. And it still did.

When Priscilla told him she didn't want children after all, he'd felt that same helpless despair of finding out that the child he thought he was going to have would never come into this world.

He'd done what his parents had done when they'd been disappointed in him. He'd withdrawn emotionally. And Priscilla had gone elsewhere for companionship. Just like he had in making friends with Sebastian and Natália. He couldn't even blame her. Not really.

He remembered getting drunk afterwards. Vaguely remembered Natália helping him up the stairs. Undressing him. Thank God he hadn't been in any condition to do anything that night, because the scent of her hair had tickled his senses, getting into his head and lodging there long after he woke up the next morning.

He'd stayed away ever since. At least until recently.

He glanced at Sebastian, wondering if he'd seen his sister's reaction, but if he had, he'd hidden it well.

Sebastian's voice smacked him back to reality.

"I agree with you, Natália. Maybe someone should mention it to the daughter. Adam?"

"Um, no. I'm no psychologist. That sounds like an area better handled by another department."

This time Natália smiled. "I'm in complete agreement. On both counts. Maybe you should start inviting his daughter to some of these meetings and have a counselor available if she or Mr. Moreira needs to talk."

"That's a good idea. Thanks, Natália."

"I just know it might help for the family members to figure out how to deal with their emotions and fears. I don't know if his parents are still alive or not."

Sebastian studied her for a minute. "Again, thank you. I'll take it under advisement."

Something in his attitude had shifted between her first comment and her second, and Adam thought he knew what it was. Their parents was a sticky subject for both Natália and Sebastian. Neither of them spent a lot of time with their folks from what he'd seen over the years. The three of them—Adam, Natália and Sebastian—had spent a lot of holidays together. At least until he'd gotten married. Funny how they hadn't picked back up on that habit once his divorce had been finalized.

Maybe because of those blurred drunken memories.

And after what had happened between him and Natália a few days ago, he couldn't see her opening Christmas presents with him around a tree.

He'd tried to catch her alone several times, but she'd always been in a hurry to do something. He got it. She didn't want to discuss what had happened. But they needed to. Otherwise things were going to continue to fester.

As soon as this meeting was over, he was going to try to intercept her and ask her to go someplace where they could be alone.

Like another exam room?

Hell, no. He'd gotten into trouble twice by being alone with her in one of those. No, it needed to be a public place, where they didn't have to worry about being overheard by anyone they knew.

He thought he knew the perfect place. Now all he needed was for Natália to agree to go. And to keep Sebastian from seeing them head off together. The last thing he wanted was for an already complicated situation to become an unbearable mess.

Wasn't it already that?

No, not yet. But if it kept going at its current rate, it was going to arrive there any day.

Natália accepted the chilled *coco verde* from the vendor with a smiling "Thank you," waiting for the man to chop the top off a second coconut and push a straw through the opening. He then handed it to Adam. She took a sip, sighing as the slight sweetness of the liquid washed over her tongue. This park was one of her absolute favorite places to go. Had Adam remembered their trips here or was it just a coincidence that he'd suggested coming?

A large dog pulling his owner on a skateboard whizzed past them on the bike path. Nestled in the heart of the urban sprawl that was São Paulo, the Ibirapueira Park was a green oasis in a sea of concrete. She hadn't been here with Adam in years, although she and Maggie came here from time to time to get some exercise. At least before her friend had gotten pregnant a second time and could no longer run.

She knew what he wanted to talk about—had done her best to avoid coming here. Having a broken cellphone was great for avoiding awkward conversations. But Adam had been quietly insistent, and since Sebastian had still been in the conference room at the time, she hadn't dared refuse, afraid that she'd draw attention to them if she did. So here she was. And nothing had changed. She'd hoped as a few more days passed, her emotions would settle down and that things would go back to their normal state—the same advice she'd given Maggie right after Carolina had been born.

Evidently they hadn't. For her or for Adam. Although maybe he just wanted to make sure she hadn't gotten the wrong idea. If he even suggested it, she might jab him with her straw and...

And what? Run away? Like she had in that exam room?

Yeah, that had been really brave of her.

Well, running away hadn't worked. And sweeping it under the rug hadn't worked. What was left?

How about talking like rational human beings, the way Adam seemed ready to do?

Not that she had a choice. She stopped and thought again. Maybe she didn't have a choice, but couldn't she at least make sure this discussion happened on her terms rather than standing there waiting for the ax to fall?

So as soon as he had his drink and they'd started walking down the wide asphalt path, she took a deep breath. "So I'm here. What is it that you want?"

His eyes darkened for a second before they left hers and moved over the scenery before them. "I think you already know what I want to talk about."

"Probably, but what I'm not sure of is why."

"Excuse me?"

She plowed forward. "It happened. It was a mistake. It won't happen again. Am I getting warm?"

"You always did cut to the chase."

"I'm blunt, remember? I don't believe in wallowing in sentiment."

"And yet you worried about how a patient might feel as he loses his hair, as his vitality sinks to an all-time low."

Natália swallowed. He'd seen right through her—just like he always had. There had been times during her treatment when she'd used bravado to mask her vulnerabilities. It had seemed to work. Then Adam would come along and hold her hand. When she'd yank it away with a scowl, he'd simply hold out his open palm and wait. Without fail, Natália would place hers in it once again.

"That's different."

"Is it?"

"Come on, Adam. Exactly what do you want me to say? We had sex. I liked it. I think you liked it. But that doesn't mean things have to become all weird between us, or—"

"I liked it."

"What?"

"You said you *think* I liked it. I was simply agreeing with you."

She toyed with her straw, glaring at him. "Are you making fun of me?"

"No. But we can't just slap the truth down on a table without taking a scalpel to it. It doesn't work that way. We have to try to fix this thing. Because things *have* become weird."

"I know."

He gestured to a bench under a tree, waiting until she'd sat down before joining her. "We've known each other our whole lives. After my divorce, I—"

"Oh, God, don't even go there." This was what she'd been afraid of. Getting lectured on how he was never going to get married again so not to get any strange ideas. "If you think I'm expecting some kind of romantic proposal, you're worrying for nothing. You are the last person I see myself settling down with. You—you're like a brother to me."

Okay, so that was stretching the truth a little.

His mouth opened and he started to say something, before swearing loudly.

"Adam!"

"A *brother*? Is that what you said? Are you seriously going to put me in that box and close the lid on it? Because, honey, that box never existed. And even if it did, we blew the lid off it in that exam room."

A muscle pulsed in his jaw. He set his drink down on the bench next to him and leaned closer, his voice deadly soft. "Let me get this straight, Nata. When we were in that bathroom, and you squeezed and squeezed and squeezed until you got yourself off… Well, that was something you would have done with a brother. Maybe even Sebastian."

Okay, now he was angry, and she wasn't even sure why. "Of course not. That's disgusting."

"Hell, I'm not sure what we are to each other, but one thing I do know. There is nothing remotely brotherly about what I wanted to do to you in that room. About what I want to do right now. What I want to do every time I'm around you."

She sucked down a breath, not caring that it sounded like an asthmatic wheeze. "Y-you do?"

"Yes, which is why we are going to think this thing through, if it kills both of us. We need to figure out why we shouldn't keep having sex and then stick to that plan." He pressed his forehead to hers, fingers sliding over her cheek. "So what I need from you is one good reason why we shouldn't go back to my place and do it even better than last time."

Was that even possible?

Okay, that was neither here nor there. He was muddling up her head so she couldn't think straight. "Because it makes things weird."

"Too vague. Give me another reason." He scraped his cheek against hers, his voice lowering. "Because right now all I can think about is the way your scent is filling my head with crazy thoughts."

"W-we work together."

"No, we don't, Nata. We work at the same hospital. There's a difference. Try again. This time make it good."

He was right. Oh, Lord. When he was pressed up against her like this, all she wanted to do was straddle those lean hips and ask him to do all kinds of naughty things to her. Maybe there was no good reason to stay apart. Should they just throw caution to the wind and go back to his apartment?

But wouldn't that be compounding one mistake with another? And this one would be a whole lot more deliberate than their impulsive foray last week. They would have to get up from this bench, drive several miles back to his place, go up the elevator and then get to the good part. They would have time to think. To have second thoughts. To change their minds.

It would kill her if he did that, so rather than open the door to that possibility, she said the one thing that she knew would knock this train off its track.

"Sebastian." The word whispered from her lips in a shaky voice. "We can't...because of Sebastian."

If she had balled up her fist and let it fly as hard as she could against that square jaw of his, she doubted Adam could have looked any more appalled.

A sickly white line formed around his mouth and the muscle that had been jerking in his cheek went totally still.

He stood. "You're right. That's a great reason. I'll take you home." And without looking to see if she was following him, he tossed his coconut into a nearby trash receptacle and started walking.

Her stomach bubbled up with nausea, and suddenly she was afraid she had done something that couldn't be repaired. Something far worse than sleeping together had been. She couldn't let him leave like this. Not without trying to wield that scalpel he'd spoken of. She threw her own drink away and hurried to catch up with him, grabbing at his arm and pulling him to a halt. "I'm sorry, Adam. I shouldn't have said that."

He gave a laugh that was devoid of humor. "Oh, yes, you should have. I asked you for a reason, and you gave it to me."

Did she really want to do this?

"No, it wasn't, because in the end, this has nothing to do with Sebastian."

"I'm not following."

"Take me back to your apartment, Adam, and I'll explain it to you."

He stared at her, brows together, a stormy look in his eyes as they raked across her face. "I don't think that's a good idea."

"Really? Because a few minutes ago you sure as hell did."

"That was before you found the single reason why we shouldn't."

"I know, and I'm sorry." She let go of his hand, sending her fingers trailing up his arm instead, until she reached his shoulder. "We shouldn't. I know it. You know it. We don't need to come up with plans or anything else. We just *know*."

She hesitated, trying to drum up the courage to actually proposition him. "But that doesn't mean I don't want to. Desperately. I want to go with you. Please."

For a tense second she thought he was going to turn her down flat. They stood there, neither one moving for what seemed like an eternity. Then, instead of spinning around and walking away again, Adam encircled her wrist and carried it to his mouth, his gaze never leaving her face. When his lips touched her skin, the chill from his drink sent a sharp pang through her. *Deus!* She wanted that mouth on her. On her wrist. On her breasts. Everywhere.

Right or wrong, she didn't care.

"You're sure?"

"Yes."

Still holding her hand, he headed toward the park's exit, towing her behind him with quick steps, and she knew she was going to get exactly what she wanted.

And it couldn't come soon enough.

His fingers itched to wander. But they couldn't. Not yet. Not in the car as he drove toward their destination. Instead, he placed his palm just above her knee, letting it skim upward until it rested midway to where he wanted to be. The pressure behind his zipper was insistent. Reckless. His hand squeezed her thigh, thumb scrubbing at what he already knew to be incredibly soft skin. Skin he intended to explore in depth. Only this time there would be a bed. And any number of surfaces that would work a whole lot better for what he had in mind than a tiny hospital bathroom. Although that had been pretty damn good.

But this was going to be…

His erection jerked at all the delicious possibilities. But first they had to make it back to his apartment alive.

And right now she was killing him, because her hand was tucked under his ass. It wasn't doing anything, but he knew it was there. It was torture. A very, very good kind of torture.

Just a few more minutes and they would arrive at their destination. He wasn't going to ask her again if she was sure. He trusted her to tell him if she wasn't.

Hell, he'd taken her to the park to tell her they shouldn't sleep with each other again, and what did he do? Proposition her the moment they were alone.

His hand slid a little further up, only to have her fingers cover his. "Any more of that, and we won't make it back to your apartment."

"Worried about my driving?"

"No. Worried about making you finish what you started."

"I always finish what I start."

She laughed, her head leaning back against the headrest, eyes closing. "Right now you're in danger of finishing it—finishing me—before I'm ready."

"Last time I made you work for it. This time I intend to do all the work. You can just lie there and…enjoy."

"Oh, no. I enjoy taking an active role." The hand beneath his butt squeezed, almost sending him through the roof.

Natália had always been outspoken and bold, but the thought of that boldness carrying over to this area of her life made his mouth water.

"If that's the case, I'm the last person to try to put a stop to it."

She leaned over and nipped the side of his jaw. "Even if you tried to stop me, you wouldn't be able to."

"You think not? I could. With ease."

"I'd like to see you try."

Fifteen minutes later they were in his apartment and Natália was squirming on his bed. "No fair, Adam."

He leaned closer, sliding his lips over hers. "You never should have issued that challenge, *querida*."

"Untie me. Please." She pulled against the two belts that held her arms apart.

He eyed her for a moment. "Are you claustrophobic?"

"If I say yes will you let me go?"

"I think you just answered my question. So that would be a no."

Instead, he unbuttoned his shirt with quick fingers, letting the material fall open before lowering his hands to his waistband. "Another belt. Hmmm, where should I put it, I wonder?"

"In your closet," she said, glancing over at the closed door.

He unbuckled it and tugged. It slid free with a whisper of sound. Coiling it, he laid it beside one of her feet, a silent hint of what he'd like to do with it.

Natália squirmed again. "I want to touch you."

"You will." He unzipped his jeans, watching as her

mouth parted, her tongue swiping across her lower lip. He smiled. "Not that kind of touch."

This time, she frowned. "You're taking all the fun out of it."

"Remind me to ask you how much fun you had tonight. Later."

He didn't take his pants off right away. Instead, he climbed on the bed, legs on either sides of her hips, ignoring the belt for now. Then he slowly undid the buttons on her shirt. He wouldn't need to take it off completely as long as he could slide it…like so. He peeled the edges apart until her torso was bared of everything except for her bra. "Look at that. It fastens in the front as well. Lucky me." He flicked the catch open with one finger.

He really was lucky. He had the most beautiful woman he'd ever laid eyes on in his bed, wriggling with need. For him.

His hands slid up and covered her breasts. Natália arched her back and moaned.

Hell, yes.

He pushed up her left sleeve, exposing her arm and that white line where a surgeon had replaced her bone with a metal rod. He leaned down and pressed his lips to it. That mark didn't define who she was, but it was beautiful because it meant that she was still here on this earth. That was enough to fascinate him. Dragging the tip of his tongue from the bottom edge all the way to the top of the scar, he couldn't seem to make himself move away from it, kissing it again and again.

"Adam…"

Thinking at first she wanted him to stop, he glanced at her face. She was looking back at him, not with the unease that he expected to see, but a heat that blew him away. He lifted her arm so she could see. "This drives me wild." He kissed it again. Softly. Tenderly.

This time she did try to tug it away from him. "I've never liked people looking at it."

"It's an inspiration. You are a walking poster child for limb-salvaging surgery." His thumb rubbed over the site. "But I like it because it's a part of you. What makes you unique. Special."

And she was special. And beautiful.

A weird feeling surged up inside him, catching him off guard. He forced himself to take several deep breaths to banish the sensation.

What the hell was going on here? He didn't know, but it was his signal to get this show on the road. He fingered the waistband of her pants. "Ready for these to come off?"

"More than ready."

Getting back off the bed, he peeled the garment down her legs, folded it and put it on the nearby dresser. Then he ran his palms up her thighs, the way he'd wanted to in the car, until he reached the bottom edge of her panties. He didn't take them off right away, though. He gently ran his thumbs over the strip of cloth that covered her most private parts, finding heat and moisture there that set his world ablaze. "Damn. I want you so bad I ache."

"Then take me."

He swallowed and tried to will back the wall of need that was bearing down on him. But it was too heavy. Too overwhelming. Off came her panties.

He hadn't actually gotten to look at her the last time. That had to be why his desire suddenly seemed so much sharper, so much more impossible to deflect with random thoughts of sports or surgical procedures.

So much for tying her legs apart and slowly having his way with her. It was more like she was having her way with him. And nothing about it was slow.

He hadn't packed a condom. Hadn't dreamed they would end up here this afternoon, but Natália couldn't have children, right? He hadn't been with anyone without a condom since he'd found out about the pregnancy. Even during his marriage he'd always used protection. "I don't have anything with me."

She frowned for a second. "You don't need anything. Remember?"

Something about the way she said it almost made him pause, before he decided it was all in his head.

Stripping down the rest of the way, he stretched out on the bed and tried to enjoy each moment as it came rather than try to dissect it or make sense of it. She was here. That was all that mattered right now.

He nibbled her chin, her lips, not giving her time to really kiss him back, before he moved on to new territory—her jaw, her neck and lower. He licked a spot on her collarbone. He wanted to mark her.

Something small. Intimate.

Just between him and her. But she would see it in the mirror over the coming days and remember exactly who had put it there.

He sucked the skin hard.

Natália's moan shot his libido through the roof. He released her, kissing a soothing pattern over the area.

There wasn't time to do everything he wanted. So he chose the big things, leaving subtlety for another time.

Another time?

Don't think about it.

Nuzzling the underside of her breast, his mouth made a quick trip up and over the top, including the nipple in his journey. He did the same for the other breast.

Her hips arched. "Adam. I'm waiting."

And he was going to make her wait a little longer. Just a little.

"Almost there, *querida*."

He dipped a tongue into her belly button, drawing his nose along her abdomen until he reached the hard bone that marked the edge of the universe. To leap past it was to land in the place where dreams were made. Pure heaven. He didn't have to test to see if she was ready, his senses transmitted all he needed to know.

Moving back up and over, he braced his elbows on the bed on either side of her breasts, legs on either side of hers. "Open for me."

They did a sinuous little dance, where he placed a knee between her thighs as she spread her legs wide. His other knee came down next to the first so that he was kneeling. Down where his hands could cup that gorgeous ass and lift it high, lining it up.

With a whispered, "Yes, do it," she braced her feet on the bed and held her pelvis in the air.

With a quick thrust he was inside, his groan of satisfaction almost lost as his senses began to implode. His hands went to her hips, holding them steady as he pumped, the push and pull on his flesh creating an agonizing spiral that started to lure him towards its center.

He needed to hurry. One of his thumbs slid down to find that sensitive part of her, tapping gently in time with his thrusts.

Air hissed from her lungs. Not quite a moan, more like a pressure release valve that took charge when things got to be too much. He knew exactly what she was feeling. He increased his rhythm, pulling almost all the way out before driving deeper. Harder.

Her eyes closed, neck arching back as he continued to thrust.

"Ooooohhhh… Adam!" His name rushed past her lips just as he felt her go off, strong contractions gripping tight and releasing. A second later he shot into space, his nerve endings sizzling as a chain reaction started deep inside him.

He bit back a curse. It was too soon. But too late. He climaxed, pumping every ounce of pleasure he possessed into her.

Eyes squeezed shut, he continued moving, drawing out the inevitable for as long as possible, knowing he would soon come back to earth.

When he finally slowed to a halt, he was breathing hard. But, hell, so was Natália. And it was the most beautiful sound he had ever heard.

And the scariest. Because not only had he done what he'd said he would never do again, in the hazy realm of satisfaction his brain was flashing him a quiet SOS that was slowly growing—just like last time. The message was clear. When could he get more of the same?

The answer that came back shook him to his core: as soon as humanly possible.

CHAPTER EIGHT

THEY HAD BREAKFAST TOGETHER, which was strange, since Natália had not planned on spending the night with Adam at all. But once he'd released her arms from their restraints they made love again, and she got her wish to touch him.

And she had, in every way possible. Afterward, she had been too satiated to move, so she'd let him draw her close, her front to his back as his breathing slowly grew deeper. He'd fallen asleep, just like that time she'd rescued him from the bar. Only this time he wasn't drunk or muttering incoherently. And he was very aware of her presence.

She'd lain there, absorbing every nuance of his skin, his musky scent, trapping it all in the deep crevices of her brain.

She swallowed. Her childhood infatuation had not gone away after all. It stuck its head out from beneath the rock where it had hidden for all these years. Only what emerged wasn't a girlhood crush. Not any more. It had morphed into something much bigger. Something that she wasn't sure she could handle.

Natália loved him.

Loved. Him.

He'd made love to her like he couldn't get enough. Was holding her now like she was something precious. Surely that meant he felt something in return, right? They weren't supposed to have done this again. And yet here they were.

Should she say something to him? Confess her feelings?

Only if he admitted it first, because to be wrong was to be…embarrassed. Horrified. Unable to face him ever again.

As it was, she hadn't been sure how she was going to face him again anyway. Only here they were, eating a meal together. One Adam had fixed for her. French toast with strawberry preserves and whipped cream. She licked some of the cream off her upper lip. Why hadn't she known about this stuff last night? They could have had a whole lot of fun…

Scratch that. They'd had a whole lot of fun without it.

She caught him staring at her mouth. "What?"

"Nothing." His jaw tensed, and he popped a bite of his own meal in his mouth, chewing with a rapidity that gave her pause. He seemed to be in a big hurry all of a sudden.

Oh, no! Was this that awkwardness she'd been so afraid of? Was he sorry they'd spent the night together?

Should she ask?

God, she was so confused. She had never been in a situation like this before. Not even with the one man she had dated. Maybe because that man had actually talked afterward. Adam seemed intent on staying quiet and it was driving her insane.

Maybe she should break the ice. "Are you okay?"

"Fine." This time he met her gaze. "You?"

"Fine."

Well, great. That told her a whole lot of nothing.

She tried again. "What's on your agenda for today?"

"I have meetings most of the day. One with your osteosarcoma patient."

"He's not my patient. He's your and Sebastian's patient. I'm just there to help."

"His first infusion is supposed to be today. I'm hoping it goes smoothly."

"Why?" She put her fork down. "Do you think it won't? Did he get the port put in?"

"No. Not yet. He wanted to wait. So we're going to do the first treatment as a normal IV." He set his own fork down and rubbed the back of his neck.

Something was bothering him.

"What is it?"

"He wasn't talking a whole lot during our last meeting. Even with the counselor present."

She nodded. "I know. I was there, remember? He's probably in shock. I remember once I realized I really did have cancer and that it wasn't going away, a wave of panic went through me. It took a couple of infusions to get through it. Did any more of his family come up?"

"Besides his daughter, you mean? No. His wife died of a heart attack a few years ago. Right after they celebrated their thirtieth wedding anniversary. I can't imagine being married that long."

His tone had a hard edge that made her frown. Was she just being paranoid?

"Why does it matter how long he was married? I didn't have a husband or even a boyfriend, and I made it through just fine." Fine was a relative term in this case, because she'd felt a kind of detachment at home that may have been born more out of self-preservation than anything. Her parents' marriage was not like she saw with Marcos and Maggie.

Not like she hoped to have someday with her husband.

As long as that person knew she could never have his children.

She swallowed, glancing at Adam from beneath her lashes, wondering what was going on in his head. She wasn't about to ask, though, and her fantasies of waking up to find him leaning over her, stroking her brow and murmuring tender words, had just gone up in smoke.

He hadn't been in bed at all when she'd woken up. He'd been out here in the kitchen, fixing breakfast. And since he had showered and was dressed for work, she had a feeling he wasn't going to stick around for very long. Natália's uneasiness grew, and suddenly she felt at a disadvantage, since she was wearing just the button-up shirt he'd tossed aside last night. She'd obviously not packed an overnight bag and her clothes from last night had somehow disappeared. She needed to ask where he'd put them, though, before he left.

"My...um...clothes?"

"Oh, hell, I almost forgot." He nodded in the direction of a door on the other side of the stainless-steel refrigerator. "I threw them in with some laundry I had. They should be almost dry by now."

He started to get up, but she held up a hand. "Don't worry about it. I can get them. And if you have to go, I can clean up the kitchen."

"You don't have to do that." He frowned. "I thought we'd ride in to work together."

She blinked back her surprise. "I thought you had to be there soon. You're all dressed."

"I have another hour before I'm scheduled. Just wanted to be up and showered by the time you woke up."

So he wouldn't have to talk to her while naked? That wasn't quite fair, since she'd evidently been lying in a tangle of sheets without a stitch of clothing on when he'd gotten up. Her face heated. Her hair had been a wreck when she'd padded into the bathroom after crawling off that huge bed of his. She'd had to wet down the huge cowlick of her bangs in order to get it to stay flat. She'd been so afraid he'd already left the apartment that she hadn't bothered showering, had just thrown on his shirt and come sailing down the hall.

"I guess I'd better go and get ready myself, then."

He stood, picking up his plate and stacking hers on top of it. "I'll lay your clothes in the bathroom once they're done. There's a shower curtain if you're worried about being seen."

Really? He'd pretty much seen all there was of her. The sleeves of his shirt fell down past her hands when she went to move. She rolled them up, shoving them higher to keep them from sliding back down.

He stopped where he was. "Why do you hide your scar?"

She realized she had pushed the left sleeve up past her surgical scar. Since that was a whole long story that would make both of them late, she gave a shrug. "Just habit, I guess. Why?"

He looked like he might say something more, then

gathered their utensils. "No reason. Just curious." He turned away and headed for the sink, throwing over his shoulder, "There's shampoo and everything in the bathroom and a new toothbrush and tube of toothpaste in the medicine cabinet."

For the women he brought here? As soon as she thought it, she shoved it out of her head. That was none of her business. Actually, it was, in this day and age, but she couldn't imagine Adam putting her at risk. She'd only said that about condoms because she knew pregnancy wasn't a possibility. He probably used them on a regular basis when he had sex with other women.

And there it was again. That sneaky thought that made her squirm. Especially since she'd realized she was head over heels in love with the man.

Was she really? Or was this just another round of infatuation?

As much as she might hope so, she somehow doubted it. She'd known this man for most of her life. What she felt right now was light years from that juvenile crush she'd once had.

She just had no idea what she was going to do about it.

If she ignored it long enough, it would eventually go away, right? Just like those other girlie feelings had.

Like the desire to have kids?

Not a good comparison.

And she remembered the days of those softer feelings. Every time he'd brought a date by their house in those days, she would cry into her pillow at night, sure she wasn't going to survive the heartbreak of yet another girlfriend. But she *had* survived. She'd survived time and time again.

And she would survive this as well.

It was no big deal. She got up from the breakfast bar and headed down the hallway toward the bathroom and the sanctuary of the shower.

There was a light at the end of this particular tunnel. She knew there was.

She just had to be patient and keep on going—until she finally found it and followed it to safety.

"Hey, Nata, it's me again. Can you either call me or come down to the infusion room? We have kind of a situation here."

It was the third voicemail he'd left in the last fifteen minutes. He'd also called the NICU desk and asked them to have her call him back.

This was ridiculous. Normally he would just say to hell with her. If she didn't want to talk to him after what had happened last night then that was her prerogative. But their friendship wasn't the only thing at stake. There was also—

His phone buzzed. Glancing at the readout, he saw it was from the NICU unit. "Dr. Cordeiro here."

"Hey, it's Natália. Are you trying to get a hold of me?"

His mouth tightened. "Only a couple of times."

"Did you call my cell? It's broken, remember? I haven't had a chance to have the screen fixed."

He'd totally forgotten about her phone. "Sorry. You should have let me take it in."

"Probably. Right now, though, I have a twin set of preemies I'm trying to get settled in. What's so urgent?"

Adam wasn't the only one dealing with a life or

death situation, evidently. "Anything I can help with? Besides your phone?"

"Do you have any experience with newborns?"

The dryness in her voice made him smile. "Only if they have broken bones."

"Actually, one of the twins has a broken clavicle."

He cringed. "Ouch. They normally heal on their own, though, right?"

"Yes, sorry. I wasn't being serious."

He should have realized that. "Are they okay?"

"They will be. I just wanted to monitor them for an hour or so before looking at my calls. So what's up? Why are you in the infusion room? Isn't that Sebastian's domain?"

Not really, since it was normally the nurses who tackled that particular task. Although there was normally a doctor in close proximity in case something went wrong during one of the chemo treatments.

"Yes, but this is a shared patient."

"Mr. Moreira?" Her answer came back quickly enough to let him know that she'd already figured out why he was calling.

"Yes. He's having second thoughts about treatment. Again."

"As in about the internal—wait, the infusion room. He's thinking of not even having chemo? Has he decided to go for amputation instead?"

"No, he's thinking about going home. Pulling out. Taking his chances."

"Oh, no! He can't do that." The fervency in her voice didn't escape him. "Give me another half-hour to make sure the twins are okay and to round up another doctor to oversee their care, and then I'll be down. He won't leave before then, will he?"

"I wouldn't have called at all, except he's been asking for you."

"I thought we agreed that I would help with this case. Where's Sebastian?"

"It's his day off, and I'd rather you not go running to him about it right now."

"Afraid I might spill the beans about last night?"

"No." He tried to figure out exactly why he didn't want Natália to call her brother. Did he want to be the person who saved the day here? To impress her? No. Not when a patient's life was at stake. "I just want to see if I…if we can handle this on our own first. If people go running to Sebastian every time a patient was scared or wanted to leave, he would be at the hospital twenty-four seven. He needs some downtime as much as you or I."

"You're right, of course. Okay, keep him there and I'll be there as soon as I can."

The phone went dead before he could even say goodbye. Damn. He was not ready to face Natália again. Not yet. Last night had done a number on him in more ways than one. Instead of driving her home from the park, he'd practically held her prisoner in his bed.

Well, the belt thing had been more of a joke than anything, but then he'd pinned her against his body as he'd gone to sleep, something he had not planned on doing.

At first he'd dismissed it as being too tired to rouse himself enough to get up and take her home. But he could have just admitted that and then gone to sleep on his side of the bed while she went to sleep on the other side. His bed was certainly big enough to do that. But he'd wanted to touch her. To be skin to skin with nothing between them.

His thumb had brushed across her scar as they'd lain there in the dark, and a strange lethargy had stolen over him that had nothing to do with exhaustion. It had been an emotional stillness that wanted to freeze time and stay in that moment forever.

But he couldn't, and to think like that was to invite tragedy.

Natália was everything that was good and kind—and she always had been—while he...

He'd just been tired. That was all. By the next morning he'd figured out how to handle things. First he'd faced her on his own terms, with his clothes firmly attached to his body. Although seeing her in his shirt had almost undone everything. He'd almost dragged her back down that hallway and started things up all over again.

Her clothes had been in the dryer, exactly what had he expected her to come out dressed in?

Well, he'd kind of hoped her clothes would be dry by the time she woke up. He'd done his damnedest to make sure that happened. The next best thing had been to keep the breakfast bar between them and suggest she go shower as soon as she'd finished eating. It worked. She'd trailed down the hall, that fine ass of hers swishing from side to side with each step. He'd actually come out from behind the counter, and then he'd gripped the edge of it with one hand and willed himself to let her go. Even when the sun had streamed through the window at the very end of the hall, rendering the shirt she wore almost invisible.

Okay, so that was then, and this was now. How was he going to handle this next encounter?

With a professionalism that he was going to drag up from somewhere in the depths of his black soul.

Once he'd located it.

Then he was going to concentrate on his patient's well-being and leave the emotional histrionics on the other side of the door.

Just as he started to head for the nurses' desk, the elevator doors opened and the woman herself appeared. That was a whole lot less than the half-hour she'd asked for. He glanced at his watch, irritated to discover he'd been standing there mooning after her for almost fifteen minutes.

He wasn't mooning. He was...*considering*.

He met her halfway, motioning her to the side away from anyone who might be listening. Natália waited until he drew to a stop.

"Fill me in on what's going on." She paused. "I promised Maggie I'd be there to see her off a little later. She's supposed to be discharged sometime today."

"That was quick. She and the baby are doing okay, I take it."

"Yes, they're doing better than expected, thank God."

"Hopefully this won't take long, then." He ran through Mr. Moreira's list of concerns. "They're pretty much the same things he talked about when he initially came in."

"It's normal to be afraid before the first treatment. I was."

"Yes, but it's not normal for the patient to ask to leave before even attempting treatment, unless they know it's pretty much hopeless. His case isn't. He has a great chance for recovery, if he'll just see it through. Otherwise…"

Natália leaned against the wall and looked at him. "Is his daughter still here?"

"Yes, she's already tried to convince him to stay. He won't listen." He shook his head. "She was so upset she had to leave the room. He's pretty torn up about it all—hates that she's been dragged into this at all."

"Even though she's a nurse, I'm sure he doesn't want her to see him when he's at his weakest. I understand that all too well."

He swallowed. Had Natália felt like that? "You were never weak, Nata. You were—and still are—one of the strongest people I know."

Her cheek dimpled, sending a ripple of something through him. "You're only saying that because I beat you at arm wrestling with my bionic arm."

"I let you win." Hell, he'd missed this light-hearted banter with her. Things hadn't been the same between them for the last couple of weeks.

"Ha. Easy to say after the fact." She nudged him with her shoulder and then tilted her head and smiled at him. "This is good, isn't it?"

He wasn't sure if she was talking about their joking together or if she was hinting about wanting things to continue. And he actually didn't care. Because right now…it *was* good. "Yes." He leaned down to kiss her cheek.

"Were you serious about knowing someone who could fix my phone screen? I'm worried about it not even turning on."

"Yep, I have a friend who works in the IT department here at the hospital and does repairs on the side. I can run it down there, if you want. I can at least see what he says."

"Would you mind? My day is crammed with patients and I don't know when I'll be able to get downtown to the store." She reached in her pocket and handed it to him.

"You got it. Do you have a landline at home?"

"Yes." She scribbled down the number for him.

"I'll let you know what he says."

"Thanks, Adam. I really appreciate it." She smiled at him once again and said, "Okay, let me go see our patient."

When he started to walk with her she shook her head. "Alone. I think it'll be better that way. I don't want him to feel like we're an attack team coming to badger him into something he truly doesn't want. And if he really doesn't, Adam, we'll have to respect his wishes. We can't force anyone to get better if that person fights us every step of the way."

He wasn't sure he agreed with her on that account. If Natália developed cancer in the future due to the immunosuppressant action of the chemo, and she tried to refuse treatment, Adam would fight her tooth and nail.

"We'll have to agree to disagree on that subject."

She frowned for a second at him before turning away and heading into the infusion room, following closely behind another patient.

He knew she wanted him to stay out, but he couldn't prevent himself from walking over to the glass rectangle in the door and peering through it as she went over to sit beside their patient. Mr. Moreira was no longer in one of the infusion "recliners", as Adam liked to call them. Instead he was sitting in the corner in one of the visitor's chairs.

He watched as Natália talked to him over the next several minutes, motioning to her own arm at one point. He had no idea what she was saying, but her face was serious. Mr. Moreira had yet to say anything, but he nodded or shook his head a couple of times in response to whatever she said to him. Glancing up, her eyes met his in the window, and she gave a slight frown as if worried that he might come bursting through that door.

Adam stepped aside to let another patient through, a young man who couldn't have been older than thirty, his head covered in a black beanie cap. His eyebrows and lashes were long gone, and he was paler and thinner than he probably used to be. But the second he moved into the room several patients gave him a wave, and he sat down, seemingly not bothered at all as they pushed a needle into the PICC line in his chest to start whatever infusion the doctors had ordered.

He then lay back in the recliner, chatting and laughing with those around him. The times that Adam had been down to this room, he'd always been surprised by the strength and determination on display here. Patients got to know each other, encouraged each other, cheered over successes and mourned together over terrible losses. But through it all most of them never lost hope.

When he glanced back over at Natália and Mr. Moreira, she had him on his feet and had coaxed him over to speak with the newcomer. She soon had him seated on the recliner next to the man. Their backs were to him, but it was obvious that the other patient was sharing his story. Natália knelt beside him, not worrying about pulling a chair over. In another five minutes, one of the nurses had appeared beside Mr. Moreira and he let her hook up an IV and tape it to his forearm.

A wave of pride mixed with something else surged through him. She had done what he hadn't been able to. What Sebastian hadn't been able to.

Because she had lived through what this man would soon be facing.

"Are they having any luck with Papai?"

He started at the feminine voice that had sounded from beside him. When he glanced over, Adam found Mr. Moreira's daughter, Sara, standing next to him. Tall and slender with intelligent eyes and a compassionate smile, he imagined she must look a lot like her late mother.

"Yes, I think so." He moved over to let her look through the window.

"*Graças a Deus*. He was dead set against this an hour ago."

Yes, he had been. But he also knew that Natália was hard to shake off once she'd put her mind to something.

Like making love to him?

Oh, he may have felt in charge that last time, but she could have said the word and he would have stopped in his tracks.

Sara murmured, "I don't believe it."

Adam did. And in that moment he knew why his stomach had been in knots for the last couple of weeks and why his heart started racing every time he saw Natália. He was in love with her.

Not like the love he'd had for his ex. That had been passion and not much else. He'd known Natália, on the other hand, his entire life. He knew her character. Knew her likes and dislikes. Knew some of her fears. And he knew her strength of character.

Well, hell. He should have recognized it long before now. And maybe he had in some deep pocket of his being. But he'd also been too busy seeing her as someone to be protected and cared for. Not a woman to be reckoned with.

A woman who could somehow convince a patient to try, when no one else could reach him. Natália was a living, breathing miracle.

So what did he do about it?

He wasn't sure she even felt the same way about him.

And if she did? Did he even deserve her? He'd done some awful things in his life. Had played free and easy with love and sex and ended up changing someone's life forever. Did that mean love wasn't in the cards for him?

He didn't know. But one thing he did know. He needed to decide one way or the other.

Soon. Before it was too late, and the chance was gone forever.

CHAPTER NINE

"I DON'T KNOW what you mean." Natália cuddled her friend's baby close to her chest and stared into the elfin face, trying to avoid looking Maggie in the eye.

"A couple of weeks ago you told me that you kissed Adam Cordeiro, and now you suddenly don't want to talk about him?" She paused. "He's a good man, honey. I don't want to see him or you get hurt."

"You sound like Sebastian. I've already gotten a lecture from him. He came by my apartment late last night looking for me, since he couldn't get a hold of me on my cellphone, and I wasn't home to answer my landline."

"He didn't leave you a voicemail?"

Natália wrinkled her nose. "He said he left seven of them actually. But since my cellphone was broken, I never saw any of the missed calls."

"It's a wonder he didn't send the police after you. Marcos says Sebastian has always been a little over the top."

"A little?"

Maggie wormed her way into a pair of yoga pants. "Ugh. I swore I would never wear a pair of these in public, but since I don't have anything else that will fit right now, I don't have a choice. What happened to your phone anyway? I wondered why I couldn't get a hold of you."

"It fell out of my pocket at the baby shower when my lips were on Adam's… I mean, when I…" She stared down at the baby sleeping in her arms.

"I see." Her friend's voice held a wealth of meaning. "From the color of your face, I take it that your lips have really been in some of those other places."

"You can't tell my brother. He would go ballistic."

Was it really because of Sebastian's "over the top" attitude, as Maggie had put it? Or was she just afraid to face up to what was happening between her and Adam?

Maggie's brows went up as she reached for her blouse and buttoned it up her front. "I don't know anything *to* tell him. You're being awfully secretive about all of this."

"Only because I don't know what 'this' is yet. I mean I care about him, but it's been crazy lately."

"Did you sleep with him?"

The blunt words said in Maggie's cute American accent took her aback. She wasn't used to her friend being so direct. That was *her* realm. "Yes. But no one knows but you. And I'd rather they didn't. Not until I figure out where all of this is leading."

Maggie came over and hugged her from the side, laying her head on her shoulder for a second or two. "I'm sorry. I haven't been much of a friend or I would have realized something was going on long before now."

"It's okay, it hasn't been 'going on' for very long." She forced a smile and jiggled the newborn, who had started grunting. "Besides, you've been a little busy with things of your own."

Marcos had gone to install the baby seat in the car and was then supposed to return to pick them up. Marcos Junior was being cared for by another friend.

"We need to set a date for you to come over and talk, when my hubby isn't around to overhear us."

"There's nothing to talk about. At least not yet. I think Adam and I are still trying to figure out where to go from here. I don't want to keep falling in bed with him if nothing is going to come of it."

"Did Sebastian ask you where you'd been the night he tried to call you?"

"Yes."

"And what did you tell him?"

Natália bit her lip for a second. "I told him I spent the night at a friend's house. It wasn't really a lie. Adam and I are friends."

Or were they? Nothing had been quite the same. Although he'd seemed a little more at ease when she'd met him at the infusion room. They'd actually joked like they used to. And he was supposed to either call her with news about her phone or if she was really lucky and his friend was able to fix it right then and there, he was going to drop it off at her apartment a little later. Already her belly was sending up signals that his wanting to stop by had to be a good thing. Otherwise he would have just said he'd give it to her tomorrow at work.

Did that mean he wanted to be with her again? Or was he just being nice?

"A little more than friends, from the sound of it." Maggie frowned and stuffed the rest of the baby's things into a new-looking diaper bag. It was huge. She tried not to think that she would never carry a bag like that. Or that she and Adam couldn't ever…

Did he still want biological kids with whomever he chose to love? Or had his drunken statement been just that? Ramblings that meant nothing?

Maybe she should figure out a way to get a subtle question in about it. He knew she couldn't have kids, and yet he'd slept with her anyway. That had to mean something. Right?

"Yes, a little more than friends. But whether or not we should be together isn't something I've thought about."

"Well, maybe you should start thinking about it. Does he care about you?"

"Yes, of course." She stopped and made a sound. "I know he cares about me as someone he's known for a long time, but as far as relationships go… I don't know."

"I don't think Adam is the type of man who would just jump into bed with someone that he—"

Marcos opened the door, holding a baby carrier. "All done, *meu amor*." He glanced from one to the other. "Did I interrupt something?"

Natália realized her face was red hot. But at least he hadn't heard his wife talking about Adam jumping into bed with her. "No, I was just enjoying cuddling this little one. Carolina is a sweetheart, like her mother."

Smiling, Marcos went over and put his arm around his wife's shoulders. "She definitely doesn't get her good looks from me."

Was he kidding? Both Marcos and his brother Lucas were drop-dead gorgeous. Then again so was Adam.

She swallowed, looking at the pair across from her. They were so in love, even after four years of marriage. Would she ever find that with someone? She rubbed the sleeve of her left arm against her hip, making sure it was still pulled down over her elbow. Smiling, she moved toward the couple holding out the baby. "I'm sure you guys want to get her home to her big brother."

Marcos set the carrier down and took the newborn from her. "I want to get Maggie home and let her get some rest. She's had a difficult couple of days."

"Stop fussing. I'm fine." Maggie started to reach for the carrier and gasped, slowly straightening. "Okay, maybe my C-section has left me a little sore."

Her husband let out a couple of choice words, making Maggie giggle. "Watch it. We have little ears now. Although I think it's kind of sexy to hear you cuss in Portuguese."

With a snort of what sounded like exasperation, he squatted down and carefully laid the baby in the carrier, fumbling with the buckles for a second until he finally figured out how to get her secured.

"Mmm…a man with a baby is even sexier."

Another pang went through Natália's tummy. Adam would look wonderful holding their child. Tears pricked her eyes unexpectedly and she had to turn away for a second while the pair threw a couple more quips back and forth.

By the time she composed herself and faced them again, Maggie sent her a soft smile. "I think he cares. You just have to figure out if this is what you want."

Maggie was right. She could stand around wishing for children and second-guessing things for an eternity.

But in the end she had to decide if she and Adam had a shot at happiness. And if they did...

She needed to have the courage to confront him and see if he could live without having biological kids.

And if he couldn't? Well, she'd been down some difficult paths and learned that she was strong enough to withstand quite a bit.

But a broken heart? Was she strong enough to withstand that?

She had no idea. But there was only one way to find out. And like Mr. Moreira, she had to make a decision—or maybe she should start asking for a sign. And then be willing to accept the consequences. No matter what they were.

Adam paused outside Natália's condominium and drummed up the courage to ring the bell. She already knew he was on his way, because the doorman at the complex had alerted her to his presence and buzzed him into the lobby. But that didn't make it any easier to push that button.

He had her newly repaired cellphone with him. Once his friend in the IT department had powered it up, the man had given a quick whistle. "Your lady friend is one popular woman."

Adam could have corrected him on the "lady friend" terminology, but it was more trouble than it was worth. Besides, he wasn't entirely sure that the shoe didn't fit. It was part of the reason he'd decided to drop off her phone in person, rather than simply hand it back to her at work.

"Why do you say that?"

"The same man has called her like a bazillion times."

A chill went over him. Natália couldn't be involved with someone. She would have told him, right? Wouldn't have slept with him if she had a boyfriend.

Yes, of course she would have told him. This was Natália he was talking about. Not his ex-wife. Or even him, in his younger years.

It was none of his business who had called her, but he couldn't stop himself from looking when his friend held the phone up for him to see.

The name Bastian with the number twenty-three in parentheses made him sag in relief. It was what Natália often called her brother. He swallowed. And if some other man had called her that many times?

Hell, he didn't know what he would do.

It was then that he knew he had to get this matter settled once and for all. Either they were going to dive in and take a chance on each other or they were going to go their separate ways. Which was why he was standing here on her doorstep, finger poised over her doorbell.

It also meant he had to tell her the truth about his past. Not an easy thing to contemplate, much less do.

Taking another quick breath, he pressed the buzzer, hearing it ring out loud and clear from inside her place. He expected her to yank open the door right away. Instead, the seconds ticked away. Five. Ten. Twenty. Thirty.

Finally she appeared in the doorway in a white gauzy top and slim-fitting black jeans. Her bare feet stood in stark contrast to the dark wood floor.

He didn't think he'd ever seen her so casual. Not in a long time, anyway. Well, she'd come out of his bedroom dressed in just his shirt, but that was different. She'd had on regular business clothes before he'd taken them off her.

Those pale feet fascinated him. Picturing her padding around like that inside of her apartment made him want to know what else she did in the privacy of her own home.

"May I come in?"

"Oh, yes. Of course." She stepped aside to let him enter. "Sorry."

"I brought your phone. The IT guy was able to fix it." Did he tell her about her brother trying to call her repeatedly? Somehow that seemed a little bit like snooping now that he was standing in front of her. He decided to just omit that bit of information. If his friend hadn't said something, he wouldn't have looked at the screen or tried to figure out who had called her. His ex-wife's infidelity had evidently sown a seed of distrust that carried further than he'd thought. So he pulled it from his pocket and handed it over. "He said it's almost dead, though."

"Oh, okay, I'll plug it into the charger." She went off down the hallway, calling over her shoulder, "What do I owe him for fixing it?"

"Don't worry about it."

She came back a few moments later. "Did you pay him anything?"

He frowned. "I said don't worry about it."

"I want to reimburse you. It's not right for you to pay for it."

"Can we talk about something else for a minute?"

She stopped. Looked up at him. "What is it? Mr. Moreira?"

"No, this has nothing to do with him." He shoved

his hands into his pockets. "It has to do with us. Or me, that is."

"Us?" A wary look came over her face. Not a promising sign. Maybe this was a bad idea.

Screw that. He had to get it out in the open. Rip it off like an adhesive bandage. Otherwise the unfinished business would hang over his head.

"First of all, I care about you, Nata. I would never purposely do anything to hurt you. You know that, right?"

"Oh, God." She turned away and headed toward the sofa—dropped onto it. "Here it comes."

Hell, this was definitely not the way this scene had played out in his head. Still, he had to follow it all the way to the end. He went and stood over her. "What is that supposed to mean?"

"If this is where you give me the brush-off, you can save it. I'm a big girl. I can play big-girl games as well as the next woman."

Exactly what kind of games was she talking about? The kind that Priscilla had played? The chill that had gone through him before crawled back down his spine with an ominous slither. "You're going to have to enlighten me, since I'm not a woman."

"I mean I can sleep with a man without it necessarily ending in marriage—or even a relationship. Have a fling here. Have a fling there."

He'd done the same thing once upon a time, but hearing it come out of Nata's mouth made…

"Have a fling here. Have a fling there." He repeated the words, counting to ten as he did. A muscle in his jaw kept time with the numbers as they slid by. "Is that what we're having, Nata? A fling?"

"Isn't it?"

Her tongue inched out to moisten her lips, and a weird buzzing started up in his head. Heaven help him if it didn't bring with it all kinds of thoughts that were better off left where they were.

A fling. Seriously? None of the flings he'd ever indulged in had ended up with him holding a woman deep into the night. Or caring about what she thought or felt.

But one of them had ended with a pregnancy.

Somehow that thought made him really angry. He'd come here to confess his sins, and she was worried about how to label their relationship?

Maybe she was the one who needed to be enlightened. To understand exactly what a true fling looked like. "I don't know. Why don't we find out?"

He stripped his shirt over his head in one quick move, tossing it over the back of her couch.

"Adam? What are you doing?"

"Isn't this what you wanted? A fling here...a fling there? Or did I misunderstand?"

"Well..." She blinked a couple of times. "I guess I'm still not sure what we're talking about."

"We're talking about sex, in its simplest form. If that's what you want, I can give it to you. I've been there, sweetheart, more than once. I know exactly how the game is played." His fingers went to the button on his jeans.

She stood in a rush, her chin going up. "You think I can't engage in a little meaningless sex? I might surprise you."

"Then, *minha querida* Nata, surprise me." He reached out and gripped her arms, drawing her toward him, some of his anger giving away to baser emotions. His head came down and captured her mouth, body coming to life when her arms snaked tight around his neck, holding him with a fervor that matched his own.

There was no time for formalities. Or foreplay. He was already on fire.

Reaching down, he cupped her butt, bringing her hard against him. When he lifted her up onto his hips, her legs clung, back arching.

Hell, yes. This was what he was talking about. They could discuss relationships later. There was no way she could be this wild for him without it meaning something.

So he would just go with that.

In a small corner of his mind a warning sounded. He ignored it, thrusting his tongue past her lips and going in. She encircled him, sucking him deeper. Still supporting her, he carried her over to the wall beside her door and ground against her, wondering how to get his zipper opened and her pants down without letting go of her.

The warning sounded again.

He dismissed it, reaching again for the front of his jeans. Natália's arms suddenly left his neck and started frantically pushing against his chest.

Before he could fully register what was happening, the door to his right snapped open. Both of their heads cranked to the side.

Nossa Senhora do céu.

There stood Sebastian. He stared at them for a second as if not sure what he was seeing.

Then his hand landed on Adam's shoulder, yanking him backward, dumping Natália onto the floor with a thump. She'd just shouted her brother's name, only to have the hand on his shoulder shove him again. His heel caught on something and down he went, flat on his ass.

He was up in a flash, his fists going up in a defensive posture.

"Adam, no!" Natália scrambled to her feet and put her hand on his chest. "Don't."

"I trusted you." Sebastian stepped around her and from the cold words and the angry gleam in his eyes, Adam knew he was in deep trouble. And there was no explanation known to man that was going to stop it.

"How dare you come into my home without knocking?" Natália was shaking with anger and embarrassment. Worse, her brother was acting like a lunatic, stalking around the room throwing obscenities around like it was his everyday speech. It wasn't. Sebastian rarely cursed. Rarely showed any kind of emotion at all. A trill of fear went through her. Not for her own safety but for Adam's.

Her brother turned and fixed her with a look that could have frozen lava in its tracks. "I wouldn't have had to if you'd answered your damn cellphone."

"It was broken. I told you that."

"I just called the carrier and told them it was an emergency. They tried ringing it themselves and said it seemed to be working just fine."

"Wh-what was the emergency?"

"That I haven't been able to locate you for two nights in a row. I was worried." He turned around and shot a look at Adam, who had buttoned his jeans and pulled his shirt back over his head. She couldn't believe this was happening!

"I was at work today. It isn't like I disappeared off the face of the planet. Why didn't the doorman call up?"

"He damned well did. You didn't answer that either."

Natália only heard the interphone go off right before Sebastian burst into the room—it was why she'd tried to push Adam away. Maybe it had rung before that, but she'd been a little busy at the time.

"I'm sorry."

Adam stepped forward. "You have nothing to be sorry for." He turned toward Sebastian. "You are way out of line, here. Your sister has a right to her privacy."

"You have a right to her privacy too, evidently."

"You need to dial it back a notch."

"Really?" Her brother's volume went up. "I come in and find my best friend—who is half-naked, by the way—doing his best to nail my sister to the wall, just like he's done with a thousand other girls. So tell me again why *I* need to dial it back a notch?"

The ugly image of that cardboard cutout with all of those lips stuck to it came to mind. Was her brother right? Was she just one more girl in a long line of girls? Maybe that's where this had come from...he was glad not to have to act any more. She'd been worried about whether or not he would care about her infertility when she should have been worried about something else entirely.

She'd asked for a sign. But, please, God, this wasn't the one she wanted.

She glanced at her brother, trying to make sense of things. "Sebastian, please. Please, don't do this."

Adam took another step forward, hands still rolled into fists, knuckles white. "Your sister is right. We are going to sit down and talk about this like civilized people, so I think you need to lower your voice before something…happens."

"Happens? As in you trying to take me down?"

"There won't be any trying involved." Unlike her brother's, Adam's voice was deadly quiet.

Natália's breathing, which had never quite gone back to normal from Adam's kisses, began getting a familiar stuck-in-her-lungs sensation with the air she inhaled getting harder and harder to expel. The beginnings of a panic attack. Oh, no. Not now. The last time this happened had been back when…

When she'd overheard her dad say it would be better if she were gone.

She sucked down another painful breath and fought against the raging tide that was threatening to pull her under. Adam glowered at Sebastian, who was still throwing out angry words, but now they all ran together into an indistinguishable roar of sound.

Unless she acted quickly, they were both going to be witness to her horrible breakdown. She struggled to pull in enough air to do the deed.

"Stop it! Both of you! Just. Stop. It." She yelled the words at the top of her lungs.

Her world went silent for several long seconds, and she saw stars. Then she realized it wasn't because she was about to pass out but because both men were now staring at her, their faces tense—Sebastian's with concern and Adam's with… She couldn't tell. His eyes were dark emotionless pits.

Her own eyes stung with tears. She didn't want her brother to be right. But his words were gaining traction in her head, replacing all the bright hopes she'd had an hour ago.

She stood straighter.

"I want you both to leave." Another breath wheezed into her lungs.

Her brother reached out a hand, but she lurched backward to avoid it. "No."

He tried again, his voice softening. "*Olha, querida*, I overreacted, and I'm—"

"Just stop." If he said anything else, she was going to burst into tears in front of both of them. "You need to go. I'm safe, as you can see. We'll t-talk about this later. But not now. I just want to be alone."

"Natália."

"I am warning you, Sebastian. I want you out of my house. Now."

"I'm sorry."

She didn't say a word, just went over and pulled her front door open. "I'll call you tomorrow."

Her brother's eyes closed, a muscle working in his jaw. When his lids parted, there was a sadness in them that cut her to the core. "Don't hate me."

"Never."

He looked like he might say something else, but then he turned and went out the door, pushing the button to call the elevator. He didn't look back at Adam to see why his friend wasn't following him out.

She actually had no idea why he was even still in her apartment. What did he think was going to happen now? That they were just going to take up where they left off?

Well, he was wrong. So very wrong. Unlike him, she had no clue how the game was played. But she'd obviously been living in a dream world where rainbows lined the skies and leprechauns waited at both ends, flipping coins to everyone who happened by. Reality wasn't like that at all. At least not for her.

Once the elevator swallowed Sebastian, she turned to Adam. And then, looking him in the eye, she took a shaky breath and pushed out the hardest words she had ever spoken.

"You were right, Adam. This was a fling. At least for me. I wasn't sure before, but I am now."

"What?"

She lifted a shoulder in a half-shrug. "Maybe I needed closure on an old childhood crush, I'm not sure." She pressed her palms flat against her legs to control their trembling. "If it helps any, you were as good as I painted in my fantasies. Thanks for explaining the difference to me. Let's see: sex in its simplest form, have I got that right?"

Adam's face had drained of all color, his jaw a ropy mass of muscle. "Something like that."

At least her breathing was back under control, even if everything else felt like it was spiraling away from her.

She stretched her lips sideways in what had to look more like a macabre death mask than anything resembling a smile. "I figured after what happened with your wife that you would be gun shy about relationships. I guess I was right."

There was silence for the stretch of a few seconds. Then he laughed, but there was no humor in the staccato burst of sound. "Yes, Nata, you were right. You were very, very right. Thank you for the wake-up call. And the booty call. It's been a while since I answered one of those."

Something about the way he said that planted a niggle of doubt in her head. She hesitated, hand still gripping the edge of the open door. "You said you came here to tell me something. What was it?"

She held her breath, hoping beyond hope that he was going to walk over to her and take her in her arms and tell her that she'd made a mistake—that they both had. That he loved her and didn't care that she couldn't have children. That he didn't need twenty women, or even ten—that he just needed her.

He stood there, staring at her for a long time. "It doesn't matter. Your brother was right. About me. About the way I was." He gave a half-shrug. "So, yeah, whatever...we had going on, it wouldn't work. Thanks for helping me see that."

Disappointment froze her in place. But she didn't have time to sit there and process his words, or even think about him having sex with the next faceless woman that came along. Because he was already tucking his shirt into his waistband with short jerky movements and scooping up his car keys and cellphone. Then he walked past her and into the foyer.

Her heart threatened to splinter into a thousand pieces. She turned to face him. "So that's it?"

"I think so." He wouldn't meet her eyes, simply pushed the button to call the elevator. When it finally arrived, he stepped in. Only then did he look at her. "I'm sorry, Nata. Truly sorry. For everything."

Then the doors slowly slid shut and took him out of sight…and out of her life.

CHAPTER TEN

NATÁLIA WENT THROUGH the next two weeks in a haze. Sebastian had called her at least a half dozen times the day after she'd ended things with Adam. She'd finally answered the phone and accepted his apology, but the words had felt heavy and wooden. She could tell he was worried about her, but there was nothing she could do about that. In time things would get better.

Hopefully he and Adam had made their peace, but she didn't dare ask, because even the thought of Adam was enough to send her spinning into a vat of misery. She couldn't eat. Could hardly sleep.

But she had to somehow climb up and get back to the business of living. She had gone her whole life without being in a relationship with Adam, so she could do it again. Somehow.

Thank God she'd never told him she loved him. That would have made this so much more unbearable.

More? Was that even possible? How could it be more unbearable than realizing that making love with him hadn't been merely as good as her fantasies? Those few hours with him had stripped the fantasies down to mere caricatures. The reality was flesh and bone…and love.

She would never get over him. She knew that for a

fact. But she could still live a fulfilling life. She just had to figure out how to go about constructing that life.

Surely she could meet someone else. Be content with that person.

There was a tiny voice of doubt that rose up each time she allowed herself to think along those lines.

Forget it.

She went into the nursery in her unit and checked the babies and charts to make sure they were all okay. One by one she studied their tiny faces, some of them with ventilators breathing for them, others with oxygen tubes under their nostrils. All of them, though, had one thing in common. They were fighting for a life that would eventually take place outside a hospital bed. Just like she once had. And hopefully they too would find their place with people who loved them.

Speaking of fighting for life, maybe it was time to pay Mr. Moreira a visit, since neither Sebastian nor Adam had contacted her about the patient's progress. She checked the schedule she'd been given about his infusion times, then she drew a deep breath. He had one today, which meant he was probably down in the room right now.

Clocking out, she made her way to the oncology unit and peeked through the rectangle on the door. Sure enough, he was there in a recliner that faced her, his daughter seated next to him, holding his hand. He laughed at something she said.

She should leave. He looked like he was doing fine.

Just then his glance crossed her path and then returned to her with a frown.

Too late.

He waved her in. Oh, well. She plastered a smile on

her face. She would just keep her troubles to herself. The last thing he needed was someone coming in and unpacking their sadness in front of him.

Sliding past the door, she walked over and shook his proffered hand. "Just came to check to see how you're doing."

His daughter stood. "Do you want to sit with him for a while?"

"Oh, I don't want to intrude."

The young woman studied her for a minute then her father spoke up. "It's not intruding. Sara needs a break anyway, don't you? Why don't you go to the cafeteria and grab some coffee and a *coxinha*? Look out over the park for a half hour or so?"

"That sounds like a good idea." Sara turned and gave her a quick hug. "Thanks for all you did."

Dropping a kiss on her father's weathered cheek, she said, "I'll be back in a little while. Do you want anything?"

"I want a lot of things. Some of them out of my reach."

Natália could relate to that. The thing she wanted most was firmly out of reach, but she smiled as Mr. Moreira's daughter blew him another kiss as she went out the door.

"You're a very lucky man. Sara seems like a sweet woman."

He glanced at the IV bag next to him and sighed. "Yes, her mother and I couldn't have asked for a better daughter. She brought us much joy, especially since she was the only one we could have."

"Oh?" An ache went through the pit of her stomach. At least his wife had been able to have a baby.

"My wife almost bled out. They were able to revive her, but they had to take her…female parts to save her."

Normally she would have smiled at how some of the toughest men were unable to say certain words, but this hit too close to home. Natália's uterus hadn't been removed, but the eggs that her uterus would have housed and protected had been rendered useless by her chemo.

She decided to change the subject. "How long were you married?"

"Thirty years. She was our rock. I didn't think I was going to make it when she died."

Natália touched his arm. "I'm so sorry."

"Don't be. We had a lot of happy years together." He eyed her. "So, is this a social call? Or are you here to give me another pep talk?"

"I don't think you need one, do you? You look like you're doing fine. Any side effects from the chemo?"

"None that I can't handle."

She could well imagine the man could endure anything that came along. He'd survived his wife's death. The fact that she could only have one child. And now cancer. She touched her sleeve.

He nodded at her. "You're the reason I'm sitting in this chair."

At first she thought he was blaming her for something in the chemo treatments, then she realized he was talking about the fact that he'd stayed. "You have a lot of reasons for sitting in that chair, and the most obvious one just walked through that door a few minutes ago."

He gave a nod of agreement. "What about you? You have just the one brother?"

"Yep." Thank God for that. She didn't think she could handle another overbearing sibling.

"And that other doctor. He's your boyfriend?"

She swallowed. "Adam? No. He's just…a friend."

Not really. Not any more.

"But he was more."

She looked into his gray eyes and realized he saw a lot more than she'd given him credit for. "I thought so at one time. But…" She gave a quick shrug, glancing around. No one was paying any attention to them. In fact, the infusion chair on the other side of her was empty.

"But?"

"Adam…" How did she explain it so that it didn't make him look like a jerk? "I…" She took a deep breath. "It's a long story."

"I'm going to be in this chair for a couple more hours, and if I know Sara, she won't come in until she knows we're done talking."

It would probably be unprofessional to talk about his doctor in front of him. "I don't think I should say anything."

He patted her hand. "I have learned over the years that there is no better listener than a steer. They don't talk back and they are very good at keeping secrets. The more I work with them, the more I value those two traits. I won't think any worse of your doctor friend. Or of you. You can tell me."

She did just that, words pouring out in short, jerky phrases. Some of them were things she'd never dreamed she would ever talk about. Especially not with a stranger. Her infertility. Her crush on Adam. Her cancer.

How she was so afraid no one would ever love her.

All through it, he listened without saying anything.

When she'd finished, he nodded. "My wife and I grew up in the same town. We knew the same people. We were childhood friends. We were so close that we never really looked twice at each other. Until I was an usher at a friend's wedding and had to escort her down the aisle." He smiled. "I remember she had on the prettiest purple dress, all lacy with these skinny little ties up the back. I had never seen her show that much skin. Ever. I was kind of tongue-tied. And then I looked down at her feet and saw the tips of her old beat-up boots peeking out from under the fancy dress."

He shifted in his seat. "Just like that, I was in love."

"That's beautiful."

"No, it wasn't. Not for a while." He cleared his throat. "I had never been interested in a serious relationship until that moment. And Isabela didn't want to believe that I could change. I had to convince her. It took three years of my life. But it was worth it. If I'd given up... Well, I wouldn't have the memories I do, or my sweet daughter."

"You were right to keep trying."

"Yes. I was." He shifted his shoulder where his port was. "When she had her heart attack, I kept hoping she'd make it. It couldn't be happening, not to my Isabela. And when she died... I buried her in those boots from that wedding thirty years earlier. She would have wanted that."

Natália dashed moisture from her cheeks. His love for his late wife was evident in every word he spoke.

"Not many people find that kind of love."

"I think they would, if they just took a closer look when the unexpected happens."

"Like what?"

"Like seeing cowboy boots under a formal dress." He smiled and patted her hand. "Like the unexpected passion in the kiss of a friend."

Like she and Adam had shared? But that was different.

Or was it?

"I don't think he wants a relationship with me. Not really."

He held up a finger. "You don't *think* he does. But do you know?"

She searched back through that last terrible conversation when Sebastian had accused him of treating her like one of the many girlfriends that he'd had over the years. Except she'd never really given him the opportunity to finish his sentence when he'd first walked in the door. She'd assumed, and then had gone on the attack. Just like the distinction Mr. Moreira had made, she'd "thought" she knew what he was going to say. But she hadn't known.

"No, but I think it's too late to do anything about it."

"It's never too late. It took me three years to convince my Isabela to be my wife. Surely you can at least spend a few days or a few weeks. Until you no longer 'think' but you 'know'."

Two weeks had already gone by, and she was still not sure what had happened between her and Adam after Sebastian had burst in on them. One minute they'd been kissing like there was no tomorrow and the next she'd thrown him out of her house. And like Mr. Moreira had said, she could hypothesize and rationalize all she wanted, but until she "knew" she would never be able to lay it to rest.

"What should I do?"

"What do you think you should do?"

"Talk to him?"

He glanced down at the simple gold band on his hand. "It's a very good starting place."

Natália leaned over and hugged him for several seconds, noticing that Sara was peeking in the door. She nodded at the woman, motioning her to come in. "I've taken up enough of your time. Can I come back again, though?"

"Yes." He gave her hand a squeeze. "Please do. I want to hear where your journey leads you."

"Thank you."

"You're welcome. Now go and find him. If he's as smart a guy as I think he is, you'll come back with some good news."

Natália didn't know about that, but what she did know was...she had to at least know. One way or the other.

Adam studied the fractured bone displayed on his computer screen for what seemed like the thousandth time. An open break, the little boy's collarbone had come through the skin after a bicycle accident. Every time his eyes traveled across the film, he remembered Natália telling him about the twins and how one of their clavicles had snapped during delivery. He'd told her at the time that there was nothing you could do for them, those breaks just had to heal on their own. That was normally the case, but here was concrete evidence that that wasn't always true. Sometimes they couldn't just spontaneously heal. They needed a little help from a surgeon.

What about what was broken inside him? Would it heal on its own?

If not, then he was kind of like the nursery rhyme, because there hadn't been a surgeon invented yet who could heal that kind of break.

He still wasn't sure what had happened. But Natália's words had found and gouged at every insecurity he carried around inside him.

Dammit! She'd as much as said she didn't love him. That she'd been putting her old childhood crush to bed. His lips twisted at the double meaning behind those words.

To hell with it. If she wanted to pretend there had been nothing more than lust between them, then let her. It wasn't like she'd given him much of a choice.

One of the nurses poked her head into the room. "Dr. Cordeiro? Someone is here to see you."

It had to be one of his patient's parents. He'd told them he'd be back with a decision in a few minutes. Time to get his act together and give them some answers. "Send them in."

"Them?"

"Whichever person it is."

The woman's brows went up. "Oh, okay."

She withdrew from the room.

Adam stared at the break again. Okay, so he would have to open it up and give it a good wash with sterile solution to rinse away any grit from the road. Then fashion a plate to hold the ends of the bones together...

"Adam?"

He froze. He knew that voice, and it sure as hell wasn't the voice of either one of the boy's parents. Swallowing, he slowly turned around.

Natália stood there in her hospital gear, the pink scrubs sporting teddy bears and green frogs, a totally incongruous pair that somehow fit her to a T.

"Hey." His head spun through possible reasons for her visit. "Mr. Moreira? Has something happened with him?"

"No, not really. I sat with him for a little while yesterday. He gave me some good advice."

"He did?"

"Yes." She came in and closed the door behind her. His teeth ground together. The last time they had been in one of these rooms alone, it hadn't ended well. Well, it had, but it had been the first in a progression of incidents that had finally come to a disastrous conclusion in her apartment. "Aren't you going to ask me why I'm here?"

"No."

Her eyes widened, and he thought for a moment she might turn around and leave. But then she sucked down a deep breath and came over to look at the computer screen where his patient's bone was on display. "Wow, what happened?"

"Bicycle accident. He was hit by a car."

"Oh, I'm sorry. You'll have to operate?"

"Yes." What was going on? Surely she hadn't just stopped by to discuss a random case. Maybe he'd just give her what she wanted. "Why are you here?"

She turned away from the screen and gave him a stiff smile. "I'm glad you asked. I came to talk to you about our…fling. I think I know what happened, but I'm not absolutely sure. And until I am, I can't let it rest."

"Dammit, Nata. Haven't we already done this once? Do you think I didn't understand what you said?"

"No, I know you did." She licked her lips. "But I came to tell you that I was wrong. It wasn't a fling."

He inserted every ounce of sarcasm that he could into his voice. "No? What was it, then? A tryst? An affair? A..." he counted on his fingers "...two-and-a-half-night stand?"

She flinched and was silent for several seconds. "No."

Okay, he was lost. If she wasn't here to rub salt in his wound, what was she here for? "I give up. What was it, then?"

"I'm not sure. But what I do know is a fling is temporary. It has a beginning...and an end." She paused again. "I don't want the end."

His head was spinning, and a flash of hope went through it before he extinguished it again. "But it did end. So how is it anything else?"

"Did you love any of those women you slept with in your past?"

Oh, hell, no. He did not want to go there. But what choice did he have? "No. Not until Priscilla, and probably not even then. I don't understand what that has to do with anything, though."

"You came to my apartment to tell me something, and I cut you off. What was it?"

He searched his head for some cynical answer, but couldn't find one. He decided to go with the truth. Because once he did, she would be out of that room in a flash.

"I got a girl pregnant when I was in high school."

Her face registered shock and then something else. "You what?"

"Yep. Remember Sebastian saying that I slept with

thousands of girls? Well, I didn't, but I slept with enough. And one of them became pregnant."

She blinked, and then dropped into a chair. "Do you know where the child is?"

"There is no child. She had an abortion. I didn't know about it until afterward."

"God, Adam, I had no idea. I'm so sorry."

"Yeah, me too. I can't imagine what that girl went through. What her parents went through. But it knocked some much-needed sense into me." He leaned against the wall, crossing his arms over his chest. "I never told anyone. Not even my parents."

"But you wanted to tell me that night. Why?"

"Because…" He couldn't bring himself to finish that sentence.

"You didn't love her."

"No."

"Do you still sleep around like you did back then? Like Sebastian implied back at my apartment."

"Nope."

She fingered her sleeve. "You know what I think? I think you have a scar, Adam, and you wanted to show it to me. Something you keep hidden from everyone. Just like the one I keep hidden."

"A scar?" He had no idea what she was talking about.

Then she said in a small voice, "Do you know why I cover up mine?"

"Because of what your dad said? Or reminders of what you went through?"

She rolled up her sleeve and looked at the puckered white mark where a surgeon had once sliced her arm open and performed a miracle. "No, it has nothing to do with either of those. This scar should make me happy. Should remind me of how lucky I am. But it doesn't."

"Are you afraid of the cancer coming back?"

She blinked, maybe thinking about her answer for a moment. "If I'm honest, yes, I am, and that's something that you need to consider as well."

"Because?"

"Because it might affect your answer."

"I didn't realize you'd asked a question."

"I'll get to that in a minute." She drew a finger down her scar and stared at it. "Do you know what I think of when I look at this?"

"No."

"I think of how it changed my life forever. How I can't have children. How my dreams of being a neurosurgeon will never become a reality. And, yes, I think about how my cancer might come back." She gave a soft laugh. "I used to lie in bed and wonder what I did to deserve what was happening to me."

He took her hand and tugged her sleeve back down. "You didn't do anything to deserve what happened to you. Whereas my 'scar', as you put it, was very much my fault." His voice trailed away. "I'd always had trouble getting emotionally involved with people, and after I heard about the pregnancy it just made things worse. I couldn't bear the thought of hurting someone else. And when I finally did try to connect—with Priscilla—I found I still couldn't. Not really."

Not until Natália. And then he'd gone and wrecked that too.

She stood to her feet. "That brings me to my question. I showed you my scar because..." She hesitated for several long seconds. "Because I love you. Your answer to what I say next determines where we go from here. Why did you want to tell me about what happened all those years ago?"

His head went fuzzy for a second, sorting through the words and then rewinding them.

She loved him?

"Are you serious?"

Her brows went up. "Serious about which part?"

"About loving me." His heart leaped into a crazy rhythm, half-afraid he'd imagined the words.

"Oh, yes. I have for a long time, I think. I was just too afraid to tell you."

This time he didn't try to resist. He pulled her into his arms and held her as tight as he could, hoping this wasn't all in his imagination. "I wanted you to know my secret for the exact same reason. I love you, and I wanted to tell you what happened between us was never just about the sex. Not for me."

He kissed the top of her head. "When you started talking about flings, I saw red and wanted to give you a taste of the man I was back then. To show you there really was a difference. That I had changed."

Natália wrapped her arms around his waist and snuggled close. "Really? Because I kind of liked that taste."

"You did, huh? I'll have to file that little bit of information away and save it for a rainy day." His hand slid down her back, coming to rest on her hip.

"So what do we do if Sebastian never comes to terms with the fact that we love each other? I can't have him pulling me off my wife every time he sees us."

"Your...your *wife*?" She leaned back to look up at him.

He grinned. "I don't think Sebastian will accept anything less. And neither will I. Will you marry me?"

She placed a kiss in the center of his chin, her lips warm and lingering. "Oh, yes. I will. And as far as Sebastian goes, I've already had a long talk with him. I told him I love you and that that wasn't going to change."

"And what did he say?"

"Well, he didn't exactly give us his blessing, but he promised not to punch you the next time he sees you."

Adam fingered his jaw in mock fear. "No punching. That sounds promising."

"It's a start." She walked her fingers up his chest, sending a jolt of electricity through him. "I also told him he's never to barge into my house unannounced again, if he doesn't want to find us in a compromising position."

Adam choked back a laugh. "You told him what?"

"You heard me."

"Hmm...so there are going to be compromising positions in our future, are there?"

"Absolutely. Lots of them, in fact." Her fingers reached his chin then stroked along his jaw. "One of them involves being tied up with scarves."

"I think we've already lived out that particular fantasy."

"Uh-uh, I don't think so. Because in this particular scenario, the person who is restrained isn't me. It's you."

A certain part of his body was beginning to like this topic of conversation. "Oh, it is, is it?"

"Yes. And you're begging me for mercy. Over and over."

He cupped her face and kissed her long and hard. "I'm asking for it now."

"Why is that?"

"Because I still have to meet with this boy's parents." He nodded at the computer screen where the image of a broken bone stared up at them. "And perform his surgery today. I'll be busy for the next several hours."

Natália smoothed back the hair from his forehead. "Don't worry. I can wait several hours. I can wait for an eternity, in fact. As long as I *know* that you'll be there at the end of that wait."

"Oh, I'll be there. You don't have to worry about that. Today. Tomorrow and forever. I love you, *querida*."

"My cancer could come back someday."

"That day isn't today." He smiled at her. "And if it does, we'll face it together."

"And children?"

"Don't you get enough of those in your line of work?"

Her fingers stopped stroking. "I do. But what about you?"

"I just want you, for now. We can worry about the rest when it comes along. There are a lot of kids who deserve a set of parents who will love them unconditionally. I think we could give that to one or two."

"Yes," she breathed.

"Let's go, then. I'll go talk to my patient's parents

and get that little boy put back together. And then we'll go back to your place and, first and foremost, lock the door. And then we're going to delve a little deeper into that fantasy you mentioned."

"Hmm, I've been thinking. What's the difference between a fantasy and a dream?"

He stopped for a moment and looked down at her beautiful face as the answer came to him. "A fantasy is something that is never quite real. No matter how hard you reach for it, it evaporates. But a dream..." He smiled. "A dream can come true, if you're willing to work, and fight...and believe. You, Nata, are my dream."

"And you, you are mine. From now to all eternity."

EPILOGUE

NATA'S WHITE DRESS fluttered in the breeze as she stood behind the huge house in the Brazilian state of Rio Grande do Sul.

Right in the heart of *gaúcho* country.

It had taken a year from the time they'd professed their love for one another, but both she and Adam had felt waiting to get married was the right thing to do.

Sebastian had come around. Kind of. He was still oddly broody, but he'd seemed to realize that this was how it was going to be. He'd only said one threatening thing to Adam, and it had made her smile. He'd warned him not to hurt her or he would more than match that hurt.

It was a promise that would never come to fruition. Neither one of them would purposely hurt the other. She knew the man she was marrying. Really knew him. He was good and kind and stronger than anyone she'd ever known. And for the first time she wore a sleeveless dress, letting the world know that she was no longer afraid. She and Adam had broken down that barrier. Her parents were there, but Natália hadn't wanted the traditional giving-away element to be included in her ceremony. She wanted to stand on her own as Adam's equal. And he'd been all for it.

The rest of the wedding party gathered around her. All except for Adam, who would be there shortly.

Maggie had helped her with her hair and make-up and now sat with Marcos and their children in the front row, along with his brother Lucas and his family.

Then Adam emerged from the house along with Mr. Moreira, who had his daughter supporting him on one side and Adam helping him on the other. He'd gone all the way through his chemo treatments and had received his internal prosthesis a month ago. He was still regaining his mobility but was getting steadier and stronger as the days went on. Doctors predicted that he would be back to riding horses in another few months.

He'd insisted that the wedding take place at his ranch, and since he'd been the one who'd given her the courage to talk to Adam, she owed him more than she could ever repay. He was going to be Adam's grooms-man, with Sebastian taking the role of best man.

Adam finally stood by her side after helping Mr. Moreira sit in a nearby chair. Sebastian stood next to Sara, staring straight ahead as if not sure where to look. One of the ranch hands, who was also the chap-lain for the large sprawling operation, waited in front of them, ready to begin.

Her left hand was soon enveloped in her husband's as the ceremony started, although it was kind of a moot point. Religious ceremonies were not binding as far as marriages went in Brazil. Instead, they'd stood before a justice of the peace a few weeks ago and taken care of the legalities. So really they were already married. She would have been just as happy to skip this part, but Adam had wanted to profess in front of God and witnesses that they belonged to each other. So here they were.

When they got to the exchanging of the rings, Adam took her hand and slid the slim gold band over her finger and repeated his vows. She did the same when it was her turn.

Then came the passing of the *tereré*, the longstanding *gaúcho* tradition that Natália had wanted incorporated into their ceremony. Mr. Moreira handed the ornately carved gourd with its silver trim to his daughter, who carried it up and handed it to Adam. He offered the first sip to Natália, holding the straw toward her and gazing into her eyes as she drank from it. Then she gave it to Adam. The cup went to Sebastian next and his eyes narrowed slightly as he held it so Sara could sip.

Then it was off moving from person to person, and Adam took advantage of the distraction and kissed her. Long and deep, until the guests' attention came back to them amid cheers and laughter.

The chaplain pronounced them husband and wife.

There was music and food, with most of the ranch joining in the festivities. Mr. Moreira had one of the bunkhouses—the smallest one on the property—scrubbed and decorated for them to spend the night in.

Their very own rustic honeymoon suite.

Natália couldn't wait to be alone with him. And from the way he danced with her, arm snuggling her close as they swayed from side to side, he felt the same way. They would get there. When the moment was right.

It was that whole being willing to wait that Mr.

Moreira had talked about. She knew now it wasn't the waiting that was important. It was the prize at the end of that wait that made everything worthwhile.

And this man—who rocked her nights with love and filled her days with happiness—was definitely a prize worth waiting for.

* * * * *

Look out for the next great story in the
HOT BRAZILIAN DOCS! *series*

FROM PASSION TO PREGNANCY

*And if you enjoyed this story, check out these other
great reads from Tina Beckett*

RAFAEL'S ONE-NIGHT BOMBSHELL
THE NURSE'S CHRISTMAS GIFT
TO PLAY WITH FIRE
(HOT BRAZILIAN DOCS! *Book 1*)
THE DANGERS OF DATING DR CARVALHO
(HOT BRAZILIAN DOCS! *Book 2*)

All available now!

FROM PASSION
TO PREGNANCY

BY
TINA BECKETT

MILLS
BOON

Published in Great Britain 2017
By Mills & Boon, an imprint of HarperCollins*Publishers*
1 London Bridge Street, London, SE1 9GF

© 2017 Tina Beckett

ISBN: 978-0-263-92664-4

To my babies.
You may not be little anymore,
but you will always hold my heart in your hands!

Books by Tina Beckett

Mills & Boon Medical Romance

Hot Latin Docs

Rafael's One-Night Bombshell

Christmas Miracles in Maternity

The Nurse's Christmas Gift

The Hollywood Hills Clinic

Winning Back His Doctor Bride

Hot Brazilian Docs!

To Play with Fire
The Dangers of Dating Dr Carvalho

Her Playboy's Secret
Hot Doc from Her Past
Playboy Doc's Mistletoe Kiss
A Daddy for Her Daughter

Visit the Author Profile page
at millsandboon.co.uk for more titles.

PROLOGUE

TWO THINGS CAME to mind as Sara Moreira stood behind the bride-to-be.

One: she was grateful her boyfriend hadn't waited until her wedding day to ghost her. Instead, he had left in the middle of the night. No response to her texts. No returned calls. He'd just disappeared into the ether.

And two: Dr. Sebastian Texeira looked as gorgeous in a tux as he did in a lab coat.

More than gorgeous. Even when he slid a finger behind his bow-tie and tugged as if his collar were ten times too tight. Something he'd done repeatedly during the wedding, looking none too happy with the proceedings.

Why was she even noticing that? Wasn't she supposed to be knee deep in her own woes, not worrying about someone else's problems?

Her tummy tightened as she took in the broad chest and narrow hips. Wow, evidently her devastation hadn't reached the more primal regions of her brain.

Dr. Texeira's glance shifted with shocking swiftness and—*yikes!*—caught her staring. The second time he'd done that. His mouth kicked up to one side, sending her errant stomach diving feet first into a dark pool.

What was wrong with her?

This was his sister's wedding, for heaven's sake. She needed to keep her eyes to herself.

Besides, this man was way out of her league. Even further than the guy she'd imagined herself in love with. The man she'd cried bitter tears over a month ago.

Or had that just been wounded pride?

"Up here, please?"

Sara's attention snapped back to the minister. He'd asked something and was staring right at her.

Céus. Was she supposed to be doing something? Straightening the bride's train? Vacuuming the red carpet that covered the dusty ground of her dad's ranch? Lying down and dying of embarrassment?

The last option was a definite possibility.

A sense of hysteria began building in her chest before Dr. Texeira snagged her gaze once more, lifting his right hand and waggling his little finger. The glitter of a diamond band appeared. What the...?

Oh...ring! She was supposed to give Natália the groom's ring.

But where was it? Her mind went blank in an instant.

A few giggles came from behind her. Oh, Lord, she couldn't believe this was happening.

The good doctor came over to her. "Here." He reached for the bouquet she held. Tied to one of the ribbons was the errant ring. With a few quick twists, he teased it free of the knot.

"Give me your hand," he murmured.

She jerked it back in a rush.

"I'm just going to give it to you."

"Oh." Feeling like a fool, she opened her hand, and

the sizzle of cool fingers brushing across her palm made her suck down a couple of breaths. She handed the ring over to Natália as if it were coated with poison.

It might as well be.

She looked back across the aisle to where he had retreated.

Okay, the man was now watching her with open amusement. Her lower lip jutted slightly, then froze when his gaze dropped to her mouth.

Mini-frissons of heat overtook each of her limbs.

Was she getting heatstroke?

What had her father been thinking, inviting members of his cancer care team to have their wedding at the ranch?

Dr. Texeira had been part of that team. And Sara had spent the better part of last year at his hospital during her dad's treatment.

And now Antônio Moreira was well again. *Graças a Deus*. She could feel his presence in the small group of people seated behind the wedding party.

Once they'd left São Paulo and returned home, she'd never expected to see the hunky doctor again. But here he was. And her thoughts were not the kind she should be having at a friend's wedding.

He'd looked at her mouth. She was almost sure of it. Except when she gathered the courage to glance through her lashes, she found him staring straight ahead.

She'd imagined it.

Just like she'd imagined him leaning toward her and…

"You may now kiss the bride." The minister's proclamation whipped that thought from her head and sent it spinning away.

The pair at the front of the makeshift chapel turned toward each other, their happiness almost palpable as they came together for a long, long, *long*—she counted down the seconds—kiss that had her attention sliding back toward the best man.

She gulped.

Not her imagination. He was definitely looking at her. Then the bride and groom broke apart and swept down the aisle, leaving them behind. Dr. Texeira pivoted, his shiny black shoes unscathed by the red dust that covered every inch of the ranch. He held his right arm toward her.

Oh! She was supposed to go down with him.

She settled her hand in the crook of his arm, trying to calm her rattled nerves. "Nice wedding, huh?"

"Yes. *Great*."

Hmm, that word didn't ring true. In fact, she was pretty sure he was lying, which was odd considering the fact that it was his sister who had gotten married.

She frowned. "Is everything okay?"

"Hmm. I just see someone I'd rather avoid." He glanced down at her. "Mind cutting through that section of chairs on our way to the reception?"

Maybe he was ghosting someone too.

Without waiting for a response, he towed her between the rows of organza-draped seating to their right.

"I think we're supposed to be following the bride and groom."

"Humor me for a second. We'll get there." Only there wasn't a trace of humor in his voice.

Who exactly was he trying to evade? When they

reached her dad's huge barn, which had been converted into a reception hall for the big event, she led him to one of the side entrances. The massive sliding door stood open, and a drape of gauzy fabric had been interwoven with twinkle lights, a slight breeze making them wink in and out like stars against the growing dusk. "We can sneak in this way, if you want."

"Perfect, thank you."

Thinking he was just going to abandon her there at the door, she was shocked when he cupped her elbow and ducked through the curtains, eyeing their surroundings before moving toward the table set aside for the wedding party. The same frothy organza that graced the chairs and all the entrances had been tossed over it. Placed on a wooden platform lined with more tiny glimmering lights, Sara had to go up three steps to reach it. Natália and Adam were already seated. The bride glowed with happiness, while the groom gave Sebastian a pointed look. "I wondered if you were taking off before the toasts."

"No."

The answer was short and curt, and he cut around the table and went to Natália, whispering something in her ear. She gave a quick shrug and glanced out at the guests. "There was nothing I could do. They insisted."

When Sara peered out at the tables, which were filling with guests, she saw a lot of strangers, so Natália could have been talking about anyone.

Just then, a small group with stringed instruments began playing, a fiddler stepping forward to set up a lively melody that drowned out Sebastian's response. And, of course, there were only two more chairs at the table. One for Sebastian. And one for her. Right next to each other. There were even little printed cards with their names on them.

Unfortunately, those seats had been placed next to the groom, so she didn't even have the luxury of turning and engaging Natália in conversation for the entire evening.

Did it matter? It shouldn't.

She should just sit back and enjoy Sebastian's company.

Except he made her just a little nervous. Because he was a city man like her ex?

Big deal. It was one night. She'd survived much worse.

He sat down next to her, his arm brushing her bare shoulder as he did. A shiver went through her.

Yep. Nervous.

One of her dad's rugged ranch workers, looking out of place in formalwear, brought a tray with four champagne flutes. His hands gave him away. Gnarly with calluses he grinned at Sara as he moved down the table and handed her a glass. "You look great."

"So do you, Carlos."

He then turned to Sebastian, his tray outstretched. Sara was unable to suppress a smile when the doctor took the proffered drink with a frown.

"You don't like champagne?" she asked after Carlos move away.

"I was hoping for something a whole lot stronger."

He had to lean close to make himself heard, and his shoulder bumped hers again. This time she went with it, not even attempting to put any distance between them. Instead, she focused on that point of contact and allowed herself a tiny forbidden thrill. He'd never know.

"Something stronger? At a wedding?"

"Especially at a wedding." The wry humor behind those words came through loud and clear.

"Drink enough of that stuff and it will probably have the same effect."

"So would cough syrup."

This time she laughed. "Okay, so champagne really isn't your thing. If you want something fast and to the point, you can always head to the Casa de Cachaça afterwards. I can show you where it's at."

Why had she said that? Maybe because he was so obviously unhappy about someone in attendance. And his "especially at a wedding" comment resonated with her.

Boy, did it ever.

At least her ex hadn't shown up tonight.

She scanned the guests again. Maybe Sebastian had an ex who had. Could that have been what he and Natália had been discussing a few minutes ago?

"*Cachaça* sounds like a good choice." Sebastian set his fancy flute beside the plate. "In that case, I'd better hold off on those so I can drive us there."

Us? An even bigger and more forbidden thrill cut through her belly. Well, she *had* just offered to show him where it was. He must have taken that to mean that she would be drinking with him.

If she was going to correct him, now was the time. Instead, she set her own glass down next to his.

Didn't she deserve to drown her sorrows? She had always been about playing the good girl, and look where that had gotten her: abandoned and forgotten.

Couldn't she, for one night, do something daring? Something a little out of character?

She didn't have to work in the morning. And if she was honest, having a man like Sebastian take an interest in her was highly flattering.

Not that he had. Not really.

The sound of spoons clinking against glasses began to filter up to their table, growing in volume until it almost drowned out the music. Right on cue, Natália and Adam turned to each other and kissed. Murmured to each other.

She glanced at Sebastian. Not even a hint at a smile. Wow, something really was wrong.

Just then an older gentleman at one of the center tables stood and lifted his glass high, sweeping it from side to side as if trying to gain everyone's attention. The music stuttered, then faded to nothing.

The guest gave a toothy grin, staring up at them. "I'd like choo propose a toast. To my darrrrling girl and her new husband."

The voice slurred its way through the words, and the woman next to him tugged on his sleeve, urging him to sit down. Sebastian's hands curled into fists on the table, and he turned to Adam and Natália. Her friend seemed frozen in time.

"Do you want me to ask him to leave?"

Adam nodded at him, but Natália laid a hand on his arm. "No. It's okay. Mom will get him back under control. If she can't…"

The groom leaned over and kissed her cheek. "Just say the word, and I'll take care of it." He then glanced at Sebastian. "Can you propose your toast now, to get everyone pointed in the right direction? Then we'll get the dancing started. Hopefully that will circumvent any more problems."

"Sure thing." Picking up his own glass, he made a tall and imposing figure as he went to stand behind Adam and Natália's chairs. "Can I have everyone's attention, please?"

The whole barn went silent. He waited a second or two longer, and Sara was pretty sure he leveled a glare at the man who'd made the previous toast.

"I've known these two people for a very long time." A couple of chuckles came from the tables below. "And while in all those years I never dreamed this would happen, I'm happy for them. Genuinely happy."

His gaze softened, and he put a hand on Natália's shoulder. Tears gathered in her eyes as she mouthed, "Thank you."

Sebastian continued. "And while I gave them a hard time of it for a while, I can't think of two people more deserving of happiness. May you have many years of it." He raised his glass. "To my sister and my best friend. Cheers."

Sara remembered to grab her champagne just in time to take a sip along with everyone else. Adam stood, and he and Sebastian embraced.

Then the groom held out his hand to Natália. "Dance with me."

They made their way down to the floor where thick wooden planks had been fitted together to form a dance area. The music started back up, taking on a slower, more intimate tone that was perfect for the couple's first journey around the room. Adam swept his new bride into his arms and smiled down at her.

It was beautiful. *They* were beautiful.

Her dad had made the right decision in having the wedding here, despite her earlier reservations. Sebastian sat back down, and only then did she realize he'd never lifted his glass to his mouth after giving his toast. Had he not meant what he'd said?

Struggling to find something to say, she settled for, "Nice job."

He gave that wry smile that jerked at her tummy muscles. "Would you believe I wrote the words on my palm so I wouldn't forget them?"

"No."

She'd seen those hands, and there was nothing on them except a light, masculine dusting of hair. Neither had there been anything on them when his fingers had brushed her palm in a way that had shattered her composure.

His smile widened. "Well, I probably should have. I think that concludes my duties as best man. I am more than ready for that *cachaça*. Do you want to stay for the rest of the reception?"

She had a feeling his real motivation in wanting to leave was to avoid the toast maker from a few minutes ago. The same man he'd been trying to evade earlier? It had to be his father. Or stepfather, if she was reading the signs correctly.

Did she want to stay? He was obviously giving her an out.

She should take it and run.

And do what? Sit here all by herself while the happy couple—and everyone else—celebrated all around her?

No. She deserved a little bit of fun too, especially after all she had been through in the last several weeks.

"I'm not really interested in staying. Besides, I need to show you where the place is, remember?"

He studied her for a minute. "Are you sure? I probably won't be in any condition to drive you home afterward."

"Don't worry about me. I'm a big girl, and this is a very small town."

"Let me tell Adam I'm leaving, then. I'll be back in a minute."

She had a feeling he wanted to make sure his friend could handle things with the older man, if they got out of hand.

A minute later, he was back beside her chair. "Okay, he cut me loose."

They ducked out of the same entrance they'd come in at. By now, it was dark, the lights from the barn spilling out onto the ground. When they reached the parking area, he stopped in front of a sleek silver sports car.

"Are you sure you want to ride with me?"

There was something loaded about that question. The memory of his shoulder pressed tight against hers rolled through her mind, along with a warm, prickly sense of need.

This was a man who could help her forget the ache of loss in a way that no amount of champagne or Brazil's famed sugarcane alcohol, *cachaça,* ever could. If she dared to let him.

And suddenly she realized that's exactly what she wanted. To forget. For a few hours. Or an entire night. Whichever one he was offering.

"I'm very sure. I'll ride with you."

He paused for a second, then leaned down and

brushed his lips across hers, the briefest of touches that left her trembling and wanting more. So much more.

When he opened the passenger side door, he murmured, "Buckle up, Sara, because if I'm reading this correctly, things could get very, very bumpy before the night is over."

She sank into the plush leather seat and clicked her seat belt into place, yanking it tight. "Is that a promise?"

"It is now." His fingers feathered across her cheek and were gone. "And I never go back on my word."

It was all a blur.

Sebastian Texeira's arm stretched to the side and found…nothing. Sitting up, he scrubbed his fingers through his hair and glanced at the pillow on the bed next to him.

She was gone. Not even the indentation of her head remained. Should he be relieved or upset?

He wasn't sure of anything right now.

Deep purple curtains hid the view outside. And the same gaudy color was splashed with a generous hand throughout the room.

Damn. A motel.

But it had been the closest place to the bar. Not an accident, obviously.

He groaned and fell back against his own pillow. He hadn't even had the decency to take her to a respectable place?

The motels in his country were all used for the same thing. Cheap encounters at a cheap price. Normally the place where affairs took place.

The type of place his dad would have holed up for a few hours.

His father had been the reason he'd been hell bent on getting away from the wedding as soon as possible. He'd had no desire to talk to his parents. And that toast his dad had given had been cringe-worthy.

What he hadn't expected was for Sara Moreira to offer to go with him. Or to climb into the taxi beside him as he'd headed for this place. Which meant his car was still at the liquor joint.

He swallowed and closed his eyes. Except as soon as he did, images of the frantic press of mouths and bodies moving deep into the night flashed behind his eyelids. He snapped them back open.

He lifted the purple bedspread and peered underneath.

Still naked. Damn.

Where were his clothes? He scanned the room.

There. On the dresser. His formalwear was neatly stacked and folded.

Relief was beginning to outweigh regret and the throbbing in his head. It was easier this way. She obviously didn't want to be found here with him. And that was fine with him. He'd rather her dad not find out about this at all. Although Antônio Moreira was no longer his patient, it could still prove to be awkward.

Climbing out of bed and stalking toward the bathroom, he showered quickly, using the tiny bottles of products he found on the counter. They were untouched, the seals intact until he opened them. She'd left in a hurry, evidently.

He finished and toweled off, his nerves beginning to settle as he padded back into the bedroom.

It was okay. Yes, he'd had a few too many drinks. Yes, he'd shared a couple of hours at a motel with a beautiful woman.

That this was not his normal behavior didn't matter. What was done was done.

The shock of his sister and his best friend deciding they were "in love" had still not worn off, almost a year later. He'd kept thinking it was just a phase, that they would get over it. They hadn't. And as of yesterday they'd sealed the deal. They were married.

He shook off the thoughts, snagging his clothes from the dresser and jerking them on. He should have at least thought to bring along some jeans to change into.

Grabbing his wallet from the heart-shaped nightstand, his lip curled in disgust at the gaudy furnishings, an over-the-top nod to what the room was designed for, from the cheerful wicker basket of condoms on the dresser to the...

His gaze jerked back.

Condoms.

And three torn Cellophane wrappers.

He blew out a breath. At least they'd been protected. Both he and Sara were free and clear. And that's the way he intended to keep it.

No weddings or rings in his future—he was strictly a best man kind of guy. Although as he'd held that ring over Sara's hand, he'd had the weirdest sense of déjà vu. Only here in the motel room, there was no 'déjà' and no 'vu'. There was only him.

No wife. No children.

And "for as long as he alone shall live", that was exactly the way it was going to stay.

CHAPTER ONE

Four weeks later

"WE'VE FINALLY HAD someone respond to our request for a nurse. It looks like your mobile screening unit is a go after all. We still need to discuss the start-up costs, though."

The slums of Brazil weren't the most desirable place to work, and yet Sebastian had hoped for more than just one taker so he could choose the most qualified individual. Especially since the memo had been sent out to hospitals in various states of the country.

He sat back in the chair and regarded Paulo Celeste, the hospital administrator. "The costs are all listed in the dossier. I know we have a couple of ambulances that are out of commission. If we could use one of those, it would cut costs tremendously. I'm donating my time, of course, so that will help as well."

His trip to *gaúcho* country had brought more than just a wedding and a night in a motel, it had once again emphasized the need for screening services in areas where medical facilities were few and far between. Even in the state of São Paulo, there were rural locations that were difficult to access. And then there were the *favelas*. Hospital Santa Coração had a clinic in the slum down the hill, which was run by Lucas Carvalho. But if the mobile unit was up and running, they could go into some of the other areas as well.

The hospital administrator opened a folder on his desk. "So basically a portable ultrasound machine and some blood draw equipment?" The man peered a little closer. "And, of course, the nurse. She is willing to settle for the stipend listed as long as we provide her with lodging. Check and make sure there's a place available in the hospital housing division."

"Okay. And if there's not?"

The administrator made a sound in his throat. "We can't afford to rent her an apartment in the city." He shuffled through a stack of files on the right-hand side of his desk. "She's from a little hospital in Rio Grande do Sul. No local relatives. Her father was a patient here a while back, and she's anxious to do an *estágio* in oncology. With the hiring freeze it's a little tricky…but if there are no units in the hospital you could always consider housing her yourself." The man gave him a sly smile.

"I don't think so." That was all he needed. He'd just hope there was something available. "The hospital bigwigs would probably frown on that kind of arrangement."

"I *am* the bigwig, but yes. It was a joke. Professionalism is the key, especially in this kind of situation."

"Of course."

Wait. He flipped through his own mental file drawer. Rio Grande do Sul—wasn't that where his sister's wedding had taken place a month ago?

"Who was the patient?"

"I'd have to check. The daughter's name is Sara Moreira."

A stream of shock zipped up his spine. He knew exactly who that was.

Tall with legs that wouldn't quit, and expressive eyes that reflected every single second...

Deus, it couldn't be.

She was applying for the job?

"Does she know who the request came from?"

Paulo's head tilted. "It came from Marcos Pinheiro, since he's the head of oncology. Why?"

What was he supposed to say? "Oh, remember that whole *professionalism is key* thing? It's already gone way beyond that."

And boy had it. Several times. In multiple positions.

He swallowed hard. That was probably the dumbest move he'd ever made. And if he admitted to it here and now, his project was dead in the water. She hadn't been a nurse at his hospital at the time, so there had been no problem. Right?

When Paulo started to hand him the file, he waved it away. "I know who she is."

He wanted to tell the man, hell, no, he didn't want her. Standing next to her at that wedding had made something in his gut churn to life, just like when he'd worked her father's case. After a few drinks, things had gotten out of hand, and the rest was history. A crazy sensual history he was better off forgetting.

But if he said he wasn't willing to accept this particular nurse, he would have to explain why, and that could make for a very awkward conversation. It could also mean the death knell for this project, since no one else had responded to their request. Was he looking a gift horse in the mouth here?

He'd certainly enjoyed kissing that mouth.

He took a deep breath, hoping he wasn't making a huge mistake. "I can give her a try and see if she works out."

The administrator shook his head. "We'd need to be able to offer her three months, minimum, and six months is what she prefers. She wants the experience, Sebastian. She can't get it in less time than that. Take it or leave it."

In other words, his pet project was resting on the answer to this one question.

The question was could he keep his hands to himself for that long? Yes. Some mistakes did not bear repeating, no matter how pleasurable they had been at the time.

"Sure. Why not."

He could handle six months of anything. After all, he'd lived in a household that had been pure hell during the time Natália had been undergoing her cancer treatments. He'd never told his sister what he'd found out about their father. And seeing the jerk at her wedding had made a slow boil start up in his gut. It had been part of the reason he'd dragged Sara to the bar that night. To avoid having to interact with the louse that had cheated on his mother and made her cry, who had said terrible things about his sister when she'd been ill.

The folder slid back to Sebastian's side of the desk. "Take this down to Human Resources, then, and tell them that I'm okaying the transfer." The man tapped his pencil on the paper in front of him. "But I'm keeping six months as the maximum, and I'm holding you to these figures. So, keep the costs down as much as you can."

Time for a little last-minute haggling. "I want to be up and running in a week or two."

"A week or two? The ambulance needs to be painted at the very least. I don't want anyone mistaking it for an emergency vehicle, especially if you're taking it into the *favelas*." His lips tightened. "And no narcotics of any kind are to be carried onboard, understood?"

The *favelas* could be dangerous places on a good day, and if someone thought that they could find drugs inside it would be a recipe for a disaster.

"Understood. I'll make arrangements for the painting." He wasn't going to tell the administrator he already had a body shop lined up. A friend of a friend who was giving him a huge discount on the job.

"If this goes well, it will be great PR for the hospital. So make sure everything runs smoothly. No snafus, got it?"

"I understand." And if there were snafus with Sara? What if she expected to take up where they'd left off at the motel, once she found out she'd be working with him? Although the fact that she'd disappeared before he'd woken up made him think she wouldn't. There'd been no sexy good mornings. No breakfasts in bed. Just an empty motel room.

There would be no snafus. Sebastian would do everything in his power to make sure they were able to work together. As long as she was okay with keeping things purely professional.

And if she wasn't?

Then she might very well make his life difficult. Or at least his job.

So he had to make sure that didn't happen.

No matter how hard it became. At least for the next six months.

Sara was elated. Even though part of her had been dreading this trip for the last week.

Would she run into Sebastian? It had been five and a half weeks since they'd found themselves at that motel together. But they'd both had far too much to drink. He probably didn't even remember that night. Not that she'd waited around to find out.

What did it matter? She had the job! Carrying her small suitcase up the walkway toward the huge modern hospital, she felt like she was coming home. She'd spent almost a year of her life at this place while her dad had undergone treatment—first chemo, and then surgery to replace part of his femur with an internal prosthesis, a surgery she hadn't even known existed before they'd come here. That was when she'd realized how insulated her little world was.

Her dad's care had been first class. His doctors had saved his life. And Natália, the neonatal doctor who had shared her personal story of surviving the same type of cancer, had infused him with the will to try. Sara really believed that. The two had become fast friends over the course of their time there. And if she had to face Natália's brother at her new post, well, she would grit her teeth and bear it. He hadn't tried to contact her since that night, but that was understandable, since she'd been the one to sneak out at the crack of dawn.

Her stomach gave a twinge of nerves, the butterflies she'd felt for the last week developing wings of steel as they flapped around her belly. Her dad was worried about her being this far away from home, but at twenty-six it was well past time she found her own wings and flew away. Even if they were waging war inside her at the moment.

She was pretty sure that in the big city men made love to women and then went on about their lives—wasn't that how things were depicted on television? Thank God she'd never told her father what had happened that night. He would have been firmly against her coming here if he'd known, and it might tarnish his perception of Sebastian. Instead, Sara had simply told him that she'd spent the night with a friend after having one too many drinks.

And she had.

Pushing a buzzer at the entrance, she gave her name to the person who answered. The glass door promptly clicked open and she pushed through it, wiping Sebastian Texeira from her thoughts. At least for now.

The service entrance was well lit, the marble fittings she remembered being in the main corridor were echoed even here. Employees were treated well. You could tell by the care put into the details. They probably had to attract and keep the best talent in the country, so they treated them right. And now she was here. Among the best of the best. A place she'd never thought she'd be. The fact that it was only temporary made her determined to get as much as she could out of the experience. Maybe she would learn something she could introduce to her own hospital back home.

She swung into the door marked "Administration", where she was supposed to meet some of the members of her team. As soon as she entered the room, however, she stopped, her heart stumbling for a beat or two. Sitting in a beige leather chair, one ankle propped on his knee, was the person she had just shoved from her mind. The wings in her belly turned into chainsaws, slashing at her innards and turning them to mush.

"What are you—?" She tried again. "I'm sorry. I'm supposed to meet someone here."

A someone who isn't you.

His long legs uncurled as he stood upright. And he was much taller than she remembered, her neck having to tilt to look into his face, unusual for her. Of course, when you were horizontal, differences in heights didn't— *Stop it!*

"I'm assuming that person is me."

"Excuse me?" Shock streamed through her, washing away the saws, the wings and anything else that might still be cruising around inside her.

"Not who you were expecting?" His lips thinned, face turning grim. Other than that, not a hint of emotion flickered through those dark eyes. No "Hello, nice to see you again," or "How have you been?"

So that's how he wanted to play this. He was going to pretend he didn't know her. Or maybe he wasn't pretending. Maybe it had meant so little to him that he could just lock it away and hurl the key out into the universe. Something she should be doing as well. Maybe people here in São Paulo were like the hospital: cold and clinical. Wiped clean of anything that didn't belong. Where she came from things were very different. She'd been a willing participant in his little game, so she was going to have to live with the consequences.

She'd wanted this job, had practically gotten down on her knees and begged her little clinic for the opportunity to come once she'd seen the ad go up on the staff bulletin board. So she'd better get over it or she was going to ruin everything.

"You're in charge of the screening program?"

"I am. Partly because of your father."

Her brow furrowed. "I don't understand."

"He made me realize that not everyone recognizes symptoms of illness before they're advanced. I want to help change that by going into the poorer communities and working with people who wouldn't normally come to the hospital."

Her dad had made that happen?

And what about what had happened between her and Sebastian? Should she bring it up?

Why? So he could sit there and wonder if she was hung up on what had happened over the course of a few hours?

No way. If he could act like it hadn't happened, then she damn well could too.

"I'm grateful for this opportunity."

"That's good. Staff at Hospital Santa Coração are already stretched thin. I couldn't ask anyone to take this on pro bono."

"I wasn't aware this was an unpaid position. My understanding was that the *estágio* brought in a stipend. They quoted me a figure." How was she going to support herself if she didn't get paid?

"You're right. It does. You were the only one to apply for the position…" He nodded toward another man in the room that she'd just noticed. That person's eyes were studiously fixed on some document in front of him. "Did you want me to say no?"

He could have. He could have turned her down flat.

She swallowed. He'd said she was the only one who'd applied for the position. So, was she the only one who had raised her hand when he'd been looking for a sleeping partner at the wedding as well? The thought made her feel physically ill.

Doing her best to choke back the sensation, she drew herself up to her full height. "I guess you said yes."

"And so did you." His voice was soft as he said it, his glance studying her in a way that made her tummy ripple.

"Yes, and so did I. I actually thought I'd be working with Dr. Pinheiro, though." So what if they'd slept together? It wasn't like she'd had any expectations of that night other than what had happened.

But a motel? She'd never in her life set foot in one of those establishments and if anyone she knew found out...

They hadn't. She'd crept out early in the morning, while it had still been dark and had asked the desk to call her a taxi, unable to look anyone in the eye. But she'd made it. And the experience had changed her in a way she didn't quite understand.

She'd gotten over her ex-boyfriend once and for all.

"Marcos is the head of oncology. He signs all the request forms for the department. But this project is all mine."

That made her swallow. She would be working with him? Only with him? If she had known that ahead of time, she might not have applied.

The other man looked up finally. "Sorry, I wasn't trying to ignore you. Dr. Texeira has found you a studio apartment in the hospital. Is that okay? Or would you prefer to make other arrangements?"

Like maybe get on the first plane out of here?

"The apartment will be fine, thank you. It doesn't make sense to try to look for something else. I won't have to worry about transportation to or from the hospital this way."

Besides, the rents in many parts of the city were so high she wouldn't be able to afford it on what she'd be making. And although it was comparable to her salary in Rio Grande do Sul, the amount wouldn't go nearly as far here. A thought occurred. Would she have to travel to get to wherever they were going to do the screenings?

"Is there a metro that goes from here to the screening site?"

"No. We have a mobile unit. We'll leave from the hospital together."

"Leave? Together?" Okay, the way she'd separated the words gave them an entirely different meaning from his simple statement.

If he'd heard it, he ignored it, because he didn't hesitate with his answer. "The hospital is converting an old ambulance for us. We'll go to where our patients are, instead of waiting for them to come to us."

The reality of the situation was creating a buzzing noise in her head. She had been told what the job opportunity was and had jumped at the chance. But then again, she hadn't known at the time who she would be working with. And if what he was saying was true, they would be working together much more closely than she'd been expecting.

She'd assumed they would bump into each other periodically. Had even steeled herself for that possibility.

Get a grip, Sara! If it were any other doctor you wouldn't have batted an eyelid.

But it wasn't. It was Sebastian, a man she'd made passionate love with. Surely the hospital didn't approve of workplace romances.

The incident had happened before she knew she was coming here, so that didn't count, right? And since it was never going to happen again, it was a moot point.

And it *was* never going to happen again, even if Sebastian wanted it to. Although right now he looked all business. It didn't matter. He might be able to play loose and easy with relationships, but Sara really wasn't built that way, as was obvious from the way she kept obsessing over the same topic.

"Like you said, that will make it easy, then. I take it you live close by."

He gave a half-smile. "Close enough."

And what was that supposed to mean? She had no idea, but the sooner she got away from him the better. "Well, I guess I have some paperwork to fill out?"

"Yes." He scooped up a file that was on a nearby table. "I have it right here. We can go over it together."

Perfect. That was all she needed, to have to sit next to him and have him go over things. But she'd better get used to it if she was going to take the job. Because if what he'd told her was true, she was going to be sitting next to him day after day.

Until either the job was done. Or she was.

CHAPTER TWO

THE VEHICLE WAS PERFECT. But not too perfect, given where they'd be working.

Once an ambulance, but now painted a cool silver to reflect the fierce Brazilian heat, it was fully outfitted and ready to go. The hospital's name was not emblazoned on the side, for fear that it would be a target for thieves who were looking for illegal drugs. In fact, there were little nicks in the paintwork and a dent marred one side. A picture of two hands, palms outstretched, was painted in muted colors. Nestled inside them were the words "Mãos Abertos." The name was fitting since the hospital saw it as opening their hands to those in need. Below the hands was a mobile number that would ring through to a special cellphone that Sebastian would carry. Word would get around quickly about what the old ambulance did, and hopefully it would become a symbol of hope.

"What do you think?" he asked Sara, who stood a few yards away.

"It doesn't look like a normal ambulance."

"The hospital didn't want it to. Besides, I'm hoping to take away some of the stigma—the fear of the unknown that comes with emergency vehicles."

Like the time his teenaged sister had been hauled off to the hospital in a flurry of red lights and sirens, while he'd been left at home with his ailing grandmother, wondering if he would ever see her again. Her cancer diagnosis had devastated everyone. But she'd pulled through, thank God. It was one of the reasons Sebastian had gone into oncology.

To help people like his sister. He'd always felt that if she'd been diagnosed earlier maybe she wouldn't have had to have an internal prosthesis in her arm. It was another reason why this mobile unit was his heart's desire.

"So what will we do, exactly?"

"We'll do things never attempted before." Only when her teeth came down on her bottom lip did he realize how that sounded. He was doing his best to keep his cool, but failing miserably. He cleared his throat. "We'll do screenings and teach people what to look for in themselves. We'll check for enlarged thyroids, breast lumps, do pap smears, look for skin cancers. If we find something suspicious, we'll refer them for testing."

"To Santa Coração?"

That was one of the sticking points. Their hospital wasn't part of the public sector, so the administrator would probably balk at them sending dozens of people their way. But Sebastian was already building relationships outside his hospital. Lucas Carvalho, who ran a free clinic inside one of the larger *favelas*, worked with a public hospital as well as Santa Coração. Lucas had agreed to partner with him and use the mobile unit as a springboard to expand his clinic's reach. It was the perfect way to get started. Hopefully as time went on, Lucas could use this as a means to garner donations and grants from outside agencies, since he and his wife traveled with relief groups quite a bit.

"The sister hospital Dr. Carvalho works with is called Tres Corações. They're willing to take up to fifty patients a month."

"Fifty?" Her eyes widened. "You think we'll refer that many people?"

"Probably not. It depends on how many are willing to be screened. The whole 'ignorance is bliss' attitude is the scourge of most health-care professionals."

"Ignorance is death." Her voice was soft, maybe remembering what Sebastian had once told her father when he'd tried to refuse treatment. Thank God the man had changed his mind—all thanks to his sister's willingness to be vulnerable and share her own story with him. It was exactly what Sebastian was hoping would happen with this unit.

Sara pulled her hair over one of her shoulders, catching the long dark waves together in one hand, the ends sliding over the curve of her breast. It was something he'd seen her do at Natália's wedding as well—he'd been fascinated by the way she'd kept twisting those silky locks. It had taken his mind off his best friend marrying Sebastian's sister, something he still had trouble wrapping his head around.

She twisted the rope of hair tighter. Nervous habit? He wasn't sure, but with her crisp white shirt and dark skirt she was the epitome of a professional nurse, but not quite what he was looking to put forth when they ventured into the neighborhoods. But he wasn't quite sure how to broach the subject without appearing to be dictating what she should and shouldn't wear. It was just that climbing in and out of the back of the ambulance was going to be difficult enough as it was, and it was Sebastian's hope to appear casual and approachable—engender trust where there was normally suspicion.

His gaze traveled down to her feet, where a hole at the toe of each shoe allowed a glimpse of pink sparkly polish, something that didn't quite fit in with the rest of her attire. She'd had the same sparkly polish on at the wedding. He'd kissed each of those gorgeous toes of hers...

Her hair not being pinned up was another of those little idiosyncrasies. Maybe that's what was with his continued fascination with it. His eyes traveled back up her bare legs.

He definitely didn't want men ogling them as she got in and out of the truck.

Like he'd ogled them that night? And was still ogling them?

No, he was simply trying to decide how to best bring up the subject of their attire.

He'd worn jeans and a dark T-shirt today.

Her fingers twisted the rope of hair yet again and a corresponding knot in his throat formed and then squeezed shut. He swallowed to loosen it. "Do you want to see inside the vehicle?"

Time to get this show on the road and Sara out of his thoughts.

She nodded, moving around to the back with him. When he opened the doors and pulled down the steps he'd had installed for their patients, her brows went up.

"Maybe this isn't the best thing to wear out on runs." She released her hair, the locks tumbling free as her palms ran down the smooth line of her skirt.

Okay, here was his chance. "I think the more casual we are the better, if that's okay. I want people to see us as allies rather than as authority figures. It's why we put a few dents and dings in our vehicle."

She seemed to think about that for a second. "That makes sense. I *guess*."

Her slight hesitation over that last word made him frown. "I'm not sure I follow."

"Will people take us seriously?"

Professionalism was one of the things impressed upon students in medical school, and it was probably the same in the nursing sector. But he'd seen from Lucas's own practice in the *favela* that his friend had fit in and become a fixture in that community. He almost always wore simple, even slightly tattered jeans. Maybe it wasn't his clothing that did it, though. Lucas had been born in that very same *favela*. But Sebastian thought it went deeper than that, and he hoped to be able to build on Lucas's success. Maybe they could be an example to other doctors who would then give their time and talents in other communities. Sebastian had taken a trip into the Amazon several years ago and had worked with a medical missionary who'd traveled to villages providing free health care. It had impacted him deeply.

Almost as deeply as his sister's cancer journey.

And his parents' simmering anger toward each other. And how he'd always felt the need to shield Natália from it.

He guessed he'd done something right, since she'd fallen in love and gotten married. Too bad he'd been the one to see all the ugliness first-hand. It had soured him on relationships and made him suspicious anytime a woman started wandering a little closer than he wanted.

Like Sara?

Totally different situation.

"I would hope so." He climbed the metal steps that led into the back of the truck. "We also have a ramp we can use for people who have trouble climbing stairs. Do you want me to slide it out?"

Her pink lips curved, activating a dimple in her right cheek. "I grew up on a ranch, remember? I'm actually a tomboy at heart, so wearing jeans will be a welcome relief. I can manage."

Okay, so much for wondering if she was going to be upset about not wearing scrubs or skirts. When her dad was being treated at the hospital, she'd always worn sleek tops and fashionable slacks. And at the wedding she'd looked like every man's dream.

And she'd been his for a single heady night.

As for tomboy, he wasn't sure he'd ever seen her in jeans. But now that he thought about it, the description might not be so off the mark. It was there in the loose-limbed way she walked. In the slight twang to her words. Maybe she'd felt she had to dress to match the hospital's fancy decor.

Sara put her first foot on the bottom step, the narrow skirt tightening and exposing a pale knee. Her skin was fairer than that of most of the women he knew, maybe because Rio Grande do Sul had a large contingent of people with German ancestry. Her hair was dark, though.

"Okay, so a handrail might be useful for women who come for screening wearing skirts or dresses." She paused.

He got the hint, reaching a hand toward her. Her fingers wrapped around his, and she made short work of the other three steps, coming to stand within inches of him. He released his grip in a hurry. "Point taken. I'll have one installed."

Anything to avoid having to touch her each time she went up or down those steps. Something about the way she stood in front of him...

An image flashed through his head of a woman straddling his hips, laughing down into his face at something he'd said, his words slurring slightly due to the amount of alcohol he'd consumed. The sensation of being squeezed. Soft hands with a firm grip, just like hers had been a second ago.

His brain went on hyperdrive.

What was wrong with *him*?

Then, almost without volition, the words came out. "Why did you leave that night?"

Something in her eyes flashed, and she suddenly grabbed for the metal edge of the ambulance's door opening.

Afraid she might fall out of the back—or turn and flee—he wrapped an arm around her waist and turned them both ninety degrees, the narrow aisle providing precious little room between their bodies. But it also meant she couldn't run away.

"I have no idea what you're talking about." Her face had gone white.

Maybe she didn't even remember the events of that night. Except something about the way those words had shot out of her mouth said she did. Along with her horrified expression. A stab of regret speared through his gut. He remembered most of it. But her leaving without saying goodbye bothered him somehow. Had he done something awful?

His jaws clamped together for several tense seconds while he tried to figure out what to say to make this right. He came up empty.

"I think you know exactly what I'm talking about. Are you okay?" Realizing his arm was still around her, he let it drop to his side.

Right on cue, her chin went up as if daring him to say anything further. "I'm fine. My father doesn't know, though, so I'd prefer you not to discuss it with him or anyone else. We both agreed it was one night. No strings. No regrets."

So why was he feeling a whole lot of that right now?

That warning about not discussing it was completely unnecessary, though. He wasn't about to go trumpeting it to her father, or to anyone else for that matter. "I would rather keep it that way as well."

His head was reeling, still trying to blot out the more explicit images from that night. As drunk as he'd been, he should remember a whole lot less than he did.

"You still didn't answer the question. Why did you leave?"

"Um—because I wanted to. I would just as soon forget it ever happened."

Maybe he really had done something horrible at the end? Passed out on her? Thrown up? Been unable to perform?

No. He could remember each of those performances in stunning detail. Three encores, to be exact. And nothing horrific in any of those memories.

And could there be a more self-centered list of

things to be worried about? He didn't think so—except for one glaring issue.

"We used…" he forced himself to spit the word out, changing the term at the last second "…protection. So we're covered, right?"

"You don't remember?"

He wasn't sure what she was asking. *Merda!* He did not want to be having this conversation.

"Yes, but we'd both had a lot to drink. I wanted to make sure." And if that wasn't the lamest excuse ever.

"We're good. There's nothing to be worried about."

But he was, for some unfathomable reason. He tried to find the cause—decided to settle for the truth. "I wasn't that thrilled that my sister was getting married." He shrugged. "I never saw it coming, actually, and when she fell in love with my best friend, I was… Well, I acted like a jerk."

"Do tell." The dryness of the words made him laugh.

"Shocking, I know."

Her dimple appeared again. "Not so much."

He took a deep breath, the urge to reach up and touch her sliding through him. He forced it back. "I'm sorry I dragged you along on my little joy ride of misery. Believe it or not, I don't normally drink. Or seduce wedding guests."

Mainly because his father had done a lot of that. His parents had battled relentlessly all during his sister's illness. He'd finally realized they didn't love each other—his dad's dalliances proved that beyond a shadow of a doubt. They had simply been staying together for their children—more specifically for Natália, because of her illness. It was one reason Sebastian had basically sworn off marriage and children. What if it didn't last? Would he follow his parents' example and stay in a miserable marriage because of any offspring he might have? They'd already been expecting him when they'd got married. He knew that for a fact. Sebastian, like most children, was attuned to whether his parents loved and respected each other—or when they didn't.

"You didn't have to seduce me. I wanted to go. Even though, I've never…" her smile faded "…spent the night at a motel with someone I barely know."

A few more curse words tumbled around in his head. Had she been a virgin?

Before he could ask, she shook her head. "No, not because of that. I just don't normally go to motels. Especially not with a stranger."

Neither did he.

They knew each other in a superficial way because of her father, but for all intents and purposes she was right.

"Hell, Sara, I'm sorry. I have no idea what—"

She stopped his words with a raised hand. "Don't. It's over and done with. Let's just do our jobs and keep the past where it belongs—in the past."

Much easier said than done. And if the flashes of memory kept replaying in his head every time they worked together?

Well, he would just do what she'd suggested and put it behind him. Except Sara was standing in front of him looking too beautiful for words. A shaft of sunlight ventured in through the open door and touched the hair over her left shoulder, infusing the strands with gold. The sight tugged at something inside him.

"You're right. I'll try not to mention it again. Or even think about it." Those last words came out rough-edged, and he knew they were a lie. He'd already been thinking about it. And his body was torturing him with whether or not they might be able to do any of those things again.

No. They couldn't.

"Neither will I." Her voice was soft. Almost a whisper. As if she sensed the turmoil that was chewing up his gut and was answering it with some of her own.

Not good. Because his gaze slid to her lips. Came back up to her eyes, where he saw it. The slightest shimmer of heat beneath the cool brown irises.

"We'll put it behind us."

"Absolutely."

"Starting right now."

"Yes." The tip of her tongue peeked out, moistening her lips before darting back in. He wanted to follow it. Find it.

No, this was not good. Only it had been. Far too good.

He gave a pained groan.

"Sara?" His palms came up and cupped her cheeks, relishing the cool softness of her skin against his.

"Yes."

There was no question mark after that single word. No "Yes? What do you want?" It was more like she'd breathed, "Kiss me. It's what we both want."

It had been what they'd both wanted on that fateful night.

He wanted it to happen again, his body already responding to the stimuli of having her this close. And it was too much.

Tilting her face, he met her halfway, his mouth covering hers in a way that muttered, *Home. Finally.*

Even though it wasn't. It was merely a stopping place.

But, damn, the burst of steam that zipped through his veins erased that notion in a split second. He suddenly didn't care about stopping places or anything else. Instead, he shifted so that the angle was perfect.

And it was. Her lips were warm and giving and the tongue that had played peek-a-boo with his senses a second ago was back, coaxing him to sneak away with her, luring him just like those sirens of old. Without hesitation he ducked inside, finding heat and wetness that shoved his body further down a forbidden road, a growing pressure behind his zipper impossible to ignore.

Sara's hands went behind his back and slid upward until they curved around his shoulders, her body coming into full contact with his.

Maybe she felt the same sudden urgency that he did.

It was only when one of his hands left her face to pull the door next to him shut, only to have it bounce off something with a loud *clang,* that he realized how far gone he was. How far gone they both were.

Their lips came apart at exactly the same time, Sara being the first to come to her senses, uncurling her arms and pushing at his chest.

He released her and tried to take a step back, but his butt hit the metal counter behind him, stopping him from retreating any further.

Her mouth was pink and moist, lips still parted as she drew in several breaths.

He glanced to the side to see what had happened with the door and realized the metal steps had stopped it from closing.

Graças a Deus. Because otherwise…

What exactly would he have done? Tossed her onto that counter and made love to her? In the hospital parking garage?

What the hell had he been thinking?

He hadn't been. That was the problem. Just like the night of the wedding. He'd been operating off pure lust.

Gripping that very same metal counter, he tried to get his bearings. Saying he was sorry was going to be met with angry words. But what else could he do?

"I take it that wasn't what you meant by 'putting this behind us'." She tossed her hair back over her shoulder.

"Not exactly. No."

"So what do we do? I worked hard to get this *estágio*, and I'm not going to let a little thing like this make me run home with my tail tucked between my legs."

A little thing like this? This was pretty damn huge in his book. He never mixed work with personal stuff. Ever. It was just the shock of being alone with her again. But it stopped right here.

"I would never ask you to go home. You're here, and so am I. This project can't go forward without both of us, so we are going to have to figure this thing out. Fast."

"And how do you propose we do that?"

"By making sure we are alone as little as humanly possible."

She blinked. "Isn't that a little unrealistic? We'll be driving around together in this thing—alone—in order to do our jobs."

Maybe, but right now it was the only way. Because his head was still wrapped around the taste of her, the scent of her hair, the sounds of her breathing as they'd been fused together. "If you can think of a better option, I'm all ears."

And mouth. And raging hormones.

She bit her lip. "I can't."

Neither could he. He was appalled that his body had responded with an immediacy that had yanked him from that fully-in-control-but-fake-as-hell persona he liked to cloak himself in. It had exposed the true Sebastian Texeira. And he didn't like it. At all.

"We can still do this. We have to do this. Otherwise I might as well turn this mobile center back over to the hospital and forget I ever asked for the funds to try."

"Which means there would be no reason for me to stay in São Paulo." Her eyes sought his. "The hospital wouldn't keep me on?"

"I could talk to them and ask—"

"No. I want to do this. I need to do this."

"Why?" He wasn't quite sure what had driven her to come here. She'd probably made more money in Rio Grande do Sul.

"When my dad was sick, I realized how isolated my little hospital was. Doing things the same way as they'd been doing them for decades. I want to make a difference."

"I'm sure you already have."

She shrugged. "Maybe, but I saw the effect you, Natália and Adam had on my father. I want to be a part of something like that. To take back new ideas and ways of doing things." She motioned around the inside of the truck. "This is exactly what I've been looking for. And I'm not going to let an embarrassing lapse in judgment stand in the way of that. Neither one of us should, if you're as serious as I think you are about doing this."

"I am."

"Then let's focus on that, okay?"

She was right. He knew she was.

The only thing left was to get his body to agree to forget this "lapse in judgment", as she'd put it, had ever happened.

Only he knew that was going to be almost impossible.

So he was just going to have to pull that cloak tighter and pretend. And hope to God that Sara never saw the truth.

CHAPTER THREE

Six weeks.

That time frame rattled around in her head over and over as she sat in the cab of the truck beside Sebastian.

Stress. A change of jobs.

Working with a man she'd slept with.

Slept. With.

Those two words linked arms with the other two words and began to dance a little jig in her stomach. Right beside the butterflies that had never left.

Six weeks.

She couldn't be. They'd used protection. All three times.

Oh, God.

"Have you ever visited a *favela*?"

The question slid past her before turning in a smooth circle and coming back at her. "I'm sorry?"

He glanced at her with a frown. "I asked if you'd ever been to a *favela*."

"Yes." She blinked back the growing fear. "I think all cities have some kind of slum. There was one a few miles from our house. It was fairly safe—run by a group of women who decided to fight back against the image that all *favelas* are dangerous, drug-infested places. They had to give the okay for anyone new to move in."

"This one is not like that. It has had—and still does have—a drug presence. You'll need to be on the look-out for any unusual activity."

She was. Only that unusual activity wasn't happening outside the windows of the mobile unit. It was happening deep inside her body. And there was a sense of panic that said the unthinkable could very well be reality.

But it couldn't. It was—while not impossible, it was highly unlikely.

Except hadn't she read recently about a spate of condom tamperings across the country? A fad where kids dared each other to go into stores unnoticed and stab pinholes in packages? It had caused an uptick in unwanted pregnancies. And STDs.

Deus. STDs. An even stronger spurt of alarm went through her.

Surely she was safe. The condoms had been provided by the motel. There were quality control checks. There had to be.

At a *motel*?

Those establishments were gorgeous on the outside with their high walls, beautiful signs and manicured landscapes. But the elegant facade hid what really went on behind the entry gate. Sex. Lots of it. Mostly between people who weren't married—or who were, but not to each other.

It's okay. You're overreacting. It's an easy thing to check.

Except she had to endure the entire work day before she could get to a *farmácia* to buy a pregnancy test.

She realized he was waiting for a response. "Don't worry. I'll make sure I'm aware of my surroundings. Aren't we going to your friend's clinic?"

"No. We may at some point, but Lucas has already set up a couple of appointments at people's homes. One of them is an elderly lady who rarely leaves her house and can't make it to the clinic. The other appointment concerns a child."

"A child? We're doing screening on a kid?"

"Yes. He's evidently had a lump in his neck that's been there for a while."

"An infection?"

He glanced her way again. "We can hope so."

A reminder that there were more important things out there than her churning stomach right now. She would do well to remember that.

They reached the entrance to the *favela,* and Sara smoothed her palms over her dark-washed jeans. It seemed so strange to not have on her normal scrubs or business attire. It felt like she was simply going out to visit friends. Only none of her friends lived in a neighborhood like this one.

Ramshackle homes made of plywood boards hastily nailed together to form a box were scattered around. Some of the "nicer" places were constructed of bare clay bricks. None of them had seen the business end of a spackle float or a paintbrush. Roofs were either blue tarps held down by more of the same crude bricks or clay tiles. The roads were the same red clay. It could have been a neighborhood on the red planet, it was that foreign-looking to Sara.

He thrust a piece of paper at her. "Does your cellphone have GPS?"

"Yes." She glanced at the address and then reached into her purse for her phone. Then she made short work of punching the address in and waiting as the service pinpointed their location and looked for the destination.

"In thirty meters, turn right onto Viscaya, then turn left."

The neutral computer voice did more to calm her nerves than anything else that had happened today. The voice wasn't worried. About anything.

She shouldn't worry either. It was just an upset in her hormonal system. That was all. She relaxed back against the seat. She was here to do a job. A role she was comfortable with. Or at least should be.

Sebastian concentrated on navigating through the narrow streets, their truck seeming huge compared to the bicycles and motorcycles parked at odd angles. For the first time she was glad they'd played down the appearance of their vehicle.

"Have you been to many of these?" she asked.

He didn't seem like the type of person who popped in and out of a slum on a daily basis.

What about a motel? How many of those had he been to?

This is ridiculous. Stop it already!

"I've been to a few. And I've covered for Lucas at his clinic several times when he was on vacation."

"And you've never had a problem?"

"No. Despite the drug problem, *favelas* have a kind of internal code on who is and isn't welcome." His hands tightened on the wheel. "I guarantee if we came in here with a police car, the reception would be very different."

She swallowed. He must have sensed the trickle

of fear that went through her because he continued. "Lucas has made sure people know who we are. They've already had eyes on us, but no one has given us any grief."

"They have? I haven't noticed anyone."

"And you probably won't." Up went his brows. "Are you sorry you came to São Paulo yet?"

Was she? Actually, she wasn't. "No, I'm just trying to be aware of my surroundings, like you asked me to be."

"Great."

"So whose house are we going to first?"

Neither of them had mentioned what had happened a week ago in the back of this very vehicle. As the hospital finished outfitting the mobile unit, Sara had unpacked and tried to get settled, dreading having to actually go out with him and receive patients. But it was either that or admit defeat, and she wasn't one who gave up. Not easily anyway.

Her phone gave another set of instructions, listing the next street as their destination.

"We're going to the shut-in's place first. She has a lump in her breast."

That surprised her. Not the part about the lump but about them tackling that kind of screening. "I don't remember seeing a mammogram machine back there."

Not that she remembered seeing much of anything outside Sebastian's face and the feel of his mouth on hers.

And that was a very inappropriate thought.

"We don't, but we have portable ultrasound equipment."

"You can tell from that?"

He gazed at the row of houses, slowing down slightly. Some of them had numbers painted on them in crude lettering, but some of them didn't. "I can't tell if something is malignant, not with any certainty. But I can tell by the way it registers on the ultrasound what kind of lump it is. We want to see a fluid-filled pocket rather than a solid mass. It won't be definitive, but without being able to force anyone to go to the hospital for check-ups, it's the best we can do. It has a pretty good track record."

"How old is the patient?"

He nudged a couple of files toward her. "She should be in here somewhere."

"Name?"

"Talita Moises. I think she's seventy-eight."

Flipping through the names on the tabs, she found the patient without much difficulty. But when she opened it, there were no neat, computer-generated forms inside. Instead there was a wrinkled piece of paper that looked like it had been torn from a notebook. The patient's name, age and complaint were scribbled on it. "We're not going to keep actual records?"

"Yes. But we'll only do up paperwork for patients we actually treat. Some of them might refuse to be seen. I have a micro recorder that I'll use to take notes. I'll have it transcribed later."

Was that going to be part of her duties? A lot of times nurses acted almost like secretaries, entering diagnoses and listing findings.

"Um, okay."

"You won't have to do that, if that's what you're worried about."

"No, not worried at all. I'll do whatever you need me to do."

Including carrying his child?

The thought entered her head unbidden and her face became a scorching hot mess.

He glanced sideways at her. "Are you okay?"

"Hot flash."

One side of his mouth tilted. "A little young for that, aren't you?"

When this man was around, she wouldn't put anything past her body. She'd had sex with him, for heaven's sake. Something she was still having trouble accepting. She'd only slept with her boyfriend after months of dating.

"We live in Brazil. I think everyone is subject to them from time to time."

His grin tipped higher. "Indeed."

With that, he shut the engine off. "I'll get the equipment."

"I'll go up and ring the bell."

"No. You won't. We don't go up to any doors unaccompanied. We do everything together."

Yes. They had.

She gulped. *Céus.* She'd better stop with all the double meanings. "Is that really necessary?"

"It is. You never know who is going to open that door."

"And you would do what, if some crazed drug dealer appeared brandishing a gun?"

"I would try to talk my way out of the situation."

"And you don't think I could do that?"

His fingers covered hers for a second, the warm grip slightly tighter than necessary. "Yes, I think you could do that. It's just safer—for both of us—if we stick together."

Sara was all for staying safe. Which was why she'd handed him a second condom when the time had come. And a third.

Why? Why are you insisting on thinking about this?

"Okay. I'll help you carry the equipment, then."

As they both climbed into the back of the truck, Sara took the opportunity to look around this time. A metal counter along one wall held an assortment of containers that were wedged into holders so they wouldn't spill all over the place. The standard tongue depressors, rubbing alcohol and cotton balls were all neatly tucked away. And it looked like beneath the counter there was a— She fingered the metal edge of whatever it was.

"Yes, it's an exam table, in case we need to look at someone or draw blood."

"There's barely room in here for us as it is. How are we going to work around something like that?"

"It's gurney sized. It'll be a tight fit, but we'll manage."

Damn. Her brain wasn't even going to try to tackle that one. "Okay, and the ultrasound machine?"

"Right inside that blue box."

A tackle box thing was clamped to the wall, a wooden peg supporting the machine's handle. "Wow."

Sara was seriously impressed. "How many things can we screen for?"

"A lot. Especially if we can draw blood from our patients. We have a mini-fridge just beneath the legs of the pull-out exam table where we can store samples until we get them back to the lab for testing."

A spurt of pride went through her, erasing all the little quivers of fear she'd had ever since she'd climbed back into the truck with him. They could actually make a difference here. Just like she'd hoped. All she had to do was keep her mind focused on that fact, and off a certain handsome doctor. Not an easy task. But she could do it. She knew she could.

"What do you want me to take?"

"I'll take the sonogram machine and laptop so we can view the images, if you'll reach under that cabinet and grab the red soft sided bag. It has the lubricant for the wand and some other items we might need."

She wrapped her fingers around the handle on the only cabinet in the place when he stopped her. "Here's the key."

She took it, noticing the lock. "I thought you said we weren't carrying anything with narcotics in it."

"We're not carrying much of anything, but there are syringes in there for blood collection. Sometimes it's better to keep temptation behind lock and key."

Yes. It was. Too bad she hadn't thought of that the night of Natália's wedding. She could have locked her heart up and thrown away the key.

Although her heart hadn't been involved in that little encounter, right?

No, just parts of her body. She hoped nothing more than those pleasure centers had been activated that night.

Carrying that thought with her as they hauled their equipment up the dirt walkway, she asked, "Is she not mobile enough to come out to the truck?"

"I don't know. But I didn't want to take any chances.

The only thing Lucas left me was that piece of paper, which is sometimes all the information he has."

He raised his hands and clapped three times. Doorbells were reserved for people in wealthier areas. In poor neighborhoods—actually, even at Sara's dad's house because of the migrant workers they often hired—they still gave that staccato series of claps to announce their presence. Even though they'd had a doorbell ever since she could remember.

The door opened and a tall gangly boy with dark eyes appeared. *"Quem é?"*

"We're here to see Dona Talita Moises. Lucas Carvalho sent us. Is she home?"

"Sim. Minha avó está por aqui." He motioned them inside, instead of calling his grandmother to the entrance, which surprised Sara. Maybe they weren't as wary of strangers here as Sebastian claimed.

They went into a living room, and then she immediately saw why they'd been summoned inside. A frail woman with a shock of gray hair sat on a stained floral chair. She wore a blue checked house dress, and unless one of her legs was tucked beneath her… It wasn't. It was missing. She swallowed, remembering her father's cancer and what could have happened if they hadn't been able to get him in for an appointment at Hospital Santa Coração. He could have been sitting on a chair very much like this one.

No, he wouldn't have been. Because he would have refused treatment. A die-hard cowboy whose entire existence was measured in how many kilometers he'd ridden that day, he'd somehow had the notion that his life wouldn't mean anything if he couldn't ride his horse or work his cattle. But people had survived much worse than that and found ways to make their lives count.

Sebastian was already introducing himself and Sara to the woman. Talita Moises' shrewd eyes took in their appearance, making her very glad that she was wearing clothing that didn't scream money. Not that she had that many expensive pieces, but even the little she did have were far beyond the means of this household.

She reached out to shake the woman's hand, finding Ms. Moises' grip tight and unyielding. So much so that she couldn't simply pull away from her. Instead the woman studied her. "You are his wife?"

Her brain stumbled over the question for a second before realizing that—

"No!" The denial bounced around the room with such force that Sebastian's head cranked around to look at her. She softened her voice. "I'm a nurse. I just started at the—at this job." She wasn't sure if Sebastian wanted the name of the hospital announced to everyone, since it could be seen as a symbol of the chasm between this community and neighborhoods that were able to afford the insurance necessary to go to a place like Santa Coração.

The woman grunted a sound that could have been an affirmation or a protest, she wasn't sure which. But at least she'd released her death grip on Sara's hand. For some reason the woman made her nervous, and it had nothing to do with where she lived.

"Lucas Carvalho spoke with you about us coming?"

She nodded and then motioned her grandson to make himself scarce. He left the room, the snapping of his flip flops across the tile floor the only sound for a minute or two. And then it too was gone.

Sebastian sat across from her. "How can we help?"

"Well, I found a… I found a bump on…" Her hand made a circling motion over her left breast. "I've already lost my leg. I'm not sure I want to lose anything else."

"No one said anything about losing something. We're just here to check on it, if you're okay with that."

The woman's head gave a snapping nod. "I have diabetes. Maybe that's what's causing it."

Sara didn't want to tell her that it was doubtful that blood sugar issues had caused a lump in her breast. But the loss of her leg? Probably. It could also complicate surgery, if it came to that.

"Have you been undergoing any treatment?"

Talita's laugh came across like the sound of crumpling tinfoil. "Gave myself a shot in the leg every night. Except it didn't do much good. One of them is still gone."

Sara was out of her depth here. She had no idea what to say or do. Was the woman saying she no longer even tried to control her blood sugar levels?

Maybe this hadn't been the right move after all. What exactly did she think she was doing by coming to São Paulo?

It's your first case. Don't judge everything by just one patient.

That last phrase had been pounded into her head during nursing school. But it was hard not to. In a hospital setting she could slip into a familiar role that everyone expected her to play—and she played it well. So well that stepping outside that box made it hard to breathe—to think, let alone come up with some kind of comforting words.

Because if the woman did have cancer, could it even be treated?

Unlike her own chaotic thoughts, Sebastian went through a calm series of questions that had to be second nature to him. Or maybe he was just inured to the heartbreak of a cancer diagnosis. Somehow, she didn't think so, though.

Sebastian cared.

For his patients, at least. The women he slept with? Well, that was another matter. Big city men were no different than men where she came from except people tended to make a bigger deal out of things, since the pool of available dates was much smaller.

Maybe that was why her ex had been able to slip away without a twinge of conscience. He was from one of the larger cities up north, but had come down to help her father with several cattle auctions. Once those were done? *Poof!* Just like a genie retreating back to its bottle.

Her parents' marriage, on the other hand, had been rock solid. No hint that they'd had to settle for whomever had been available.

That was because they'd fallen in love.

Something Sara had once hoped to do. But right now she was resigned to being alone.

Her hand went to her stomach when it gave an odd twist. Oh, God, if she was pregnant, she wasn't going to be alone for long.

Really? She would be more alone than ever, because there would be no one to share her burden.

Her dad would. But Sebastian?

"Sara, could you help Ms. Moises strip out of her blouse and bra, please?"

And just like that, she was back on duty. Maybe Sebastian had sensed her unease and misread the cause of it. Whatever it was, she was just glad to have something to do that didn't involve thinking about everything that could go wrong but probably wouldn't.

Besides, this woman's life was far more important than anything she was currently worried about. "Of course."

"I'll get set up over in the corner and then bring the machine over on the portable gurney. Let me know when you're ready for me."

Thank goodness the grandmother had shooed her grandson to his own room and told him to stay there for an hour or until she called. "Let's get this over with," she grunted.

It was as if the woman was resigned to her fate. Kind of like Sara had been moments earlier. But who would take care of Talita's grandson if she gave up? "What's your grandson's name? He seems like a nice boy."

"His name is Jorge. And yes. He is." The woman sighed as she unbuttoned her blouse and dropped it from her shoulders. "His mother—my daughter—died of a drug overdose five years ago. So I've been doing my best to raise him. But really he helps me more than I help him."

"I very much doubt that. Does he go to school?"

"He's in his fifth year. His grades are some of the highest in his class." The pride in her voice was evident.

"Thanks to your help, I'll bet."

Ms. Moises reached around to unhook her bra, but hesitated, her hand going to her left breast. "There's a hole…"

A hole. Oh, Lord.

That was bad. If it *was* cancer and had broken through the skin…

"Wait right here for a minute, okay? I want to see if the doctor needs anything."

What Sara really wanted was to warn him that he probably was not going to need the ultrasound machine after all. She went over to where he was arranging the equipment.

Careful to keep her voice low, she said, "Whatever it is has turned into an open wound."

A soft curse met her ears. Before he could say anything, she hurried to finish. "I—I want to let her maintain as much of her dignity as possible."

"Agreed. Good job, by the way." His gaze softened. "Okay. I'm going to need you to go back to the truck and get me some gauze. We may need to transport her."

"She's raising her grandson. I doubt she'll let us take her anywhere."

He gave her a sharp look. "You suggest we just leave her here?"

Sara wasn't sure what she was suggesting. "No, I'm just not sure—"

"Go get the gauze, and I'll talk to her."

Her sense of nausea increased tenfold. She was already screwing this up and she hadn't even been on the job for a week yet. Then his hand landed on her shoulder. "You're doing fine."

She sucked down a calming breath and glanced into his face. "Thank you."

By the time she got back with gauze, saline solution and some antibiotic ointment that they had on the truck, Sebastian was on a stool in front of their patient. On his face was a look of fierce concentration. The woman's bra had not come off yet. Maybe Sebastian had been waiting for her return, since a male doctor normally had someone there with him when examining a patient.

She threw a small protective cover on the table next to the woman's chair and then set the items she'd brought on top of it.

"Okay, are you ready?"

Talita nodded, the thin set of her lips showing just how tense she was.

Sara snapped on gloves and then helped the woman peel the bra away. "I'm going to go slowly, if that's okay. I don't want to damage your skin."

"I think the damage has already been done." Talita looked up at them. "I'm not worried about me. I'm worried about Jorge. If I die…"

Her voice trailed away, but it was obvious what she had been going to say. It was exactly the same thing that Sara had thought.

"Let's not worry about that now," said Sebastian. He nodded at Sara to go ahead.

Carefully she eased the layers away to reveal a hole the size of a small coin on the outer edge of her breast, right where her arm would lie. It could be due to infection. Or, worse, cancer.

Sebastian shoved his hands into his own set of gloves and examined the wound, palpating the tissue around the area. He didn't say anything, but Sara could almost see the wheels turning as he tried to sort through possibilities. "I want to go ahead and set up the ultrasound, but I want to disinfect the skin and cover the wand so there's no transfer. We'll also change into new gloves."

Transfer. So he did suspect there was at least some kind of bacteria inside the tissue, or else he was going with an abundance of caution. She could only imagine what would happen if their mobile center became contaminated by MRSA or one of the other multi-drug-resistant bacteria. While he prepped the patient for the procedure, he asked Sara to set up the machine. Thank goodness she had done a pretty long stint inside the maternity ward at her hospital, so she at least knew the basics of getting it ready. She calibrated it to the tissue depth that Sebastian shot off to her, and laid the components on the sterile pad, ready for Sebastian to use.

Fifteen minutes later, he ran the transponder over the woman's breast while Sara did her best to engage her in conversation, hoping to keep her mind off what was happening. She learned that Talita had become a widow at the young age of nineteen and had been left to raise her and her husband's only child—a daughter named Marisa. She had worked three jobs to try to support them but, having been raised in a *favela* herself, she'd found it almost impossible to rise up out of the narrow streets. And now she was raising her grandson all by herself.

Sebastian interrupted them. "Did you have any kind of procedure done on your breasts?"

"Procedure? Like what?"

"Breast augmentation, maybe?"

"Aug—what?"

"Did you have them enlarged?"

The woman's eyes grew wide. "No, of course not. I could never afford such a thing."

"I could have sworn…" His brows were pulled together. "Did you ever have anything injected into them?"

"No, I haven't—" Suddenly her teeth bit her lip for several seconds. "Many years ago when I was a young woman there was this party some girls talked about. I was very self-conscious about how slowly I was developing... I was very small back then, even after having my daughter.

"A priestess—a *Mãe-de-Santo*—said there was a safe and easy way to make them grow. She could do it right there inside her house. I went along with it because some of my friends were going to have it done. She gave us each a large shot. One on each side. I don't know what it was—other than it really hurt. But she was right. It instantly made us bigger."

Sebastian shot a quick glance her way. "Silicone."

She'd injected silicone into her breasts? And someone had told her it was safe?

Sara knew that what appeared safe and easy wasn't always. In fact, it was something she was having to learn all over again.

"You think the silicone had something to do with this?"

"I've seen a couple of cases of sclerosing lipogranuloma that mimicked cancer."

"Sclerosing lipogranuloma? I've never even heard of it."

Talita tilted her head. "I don't have cancer, then?"

"I don't think so. I want to get you into a clinic where we can check for sure, but silicone—or another substance—injected directly into tissues can sometimes cause a bad reaction. Kind of like globs of fat that turn into lumps. They can sometimes get infected."

"But that was so long ago."

"It sometimes takes decades before the reaction is enough to be noticeable. And it doesn't happen to everyone."

Sebastian put down the transponder wand and set about bandaging her up. "I want to check to be sure. It might still require surgery."

"No. No surgery."

Sara touched her arm. "Jorge needs you. You said it yourself."

"Would they lop them off? Like my leg?"

Sebastian nodded to Sara to help her get dressed. "It depends on how widespread the problem is. You could eventually develop more of these. Or none. But if you get them taken care of, you can live a long life. Finish raising your grandson. I think you both deserve that."

The woman rubbed a palm across her eyes with a forced casualness that belied far deeper emotions. It was as if Sebastian had just given her back her life. And maybe he had. At the very least, he'd replaced fear with hope. Just like he'd done with Sara's dad.

And glancing over at this enigmatic surgeon, she couldn't help but wonder if he had done the same for her, only in reverse. What had started out as hope for a new job, a new beginning, and a chance to help people like her dad was slowly being swallowed up by fear. The very real fear that Sebastian Texeira might have unintentionally changed her life forever—and the fear of his reaction if it ended up being true.

CHAPTER FOUR

His new nurse was late to work. Already.

Not a good omen for their future work relationship. He and Sara were supposed to spend one day a week out in their mobile clinic. The rest of the time she did work in the oncology ward at the hospital, which was where she was supposed to be today.

Had she decided it was all too much for her and thrown in the towel? Leaving without so much as a goodbye? She'd done that very thing after they'd spent the night together. It hadn't seemed like her back then, it didn't seem like her today. Then again, people had surprised him before.

Like his dad with his philandering. Or Sebastian's playboy best friend settling down and marrying Natália.

Could she have left?

Her first day spent in the mobile unit had been a kind of trial by fire with Talita Moises and the little boy with a swelling in his neck. The swelling had turned out to be an inflamed lymph node. All in all, he thought everything had gone well. To an oncologist, any day that brought news of survival was a good day. They had connected Ms. Moises with the doctors at

Lucas Carvalho's hospital and things were underway for scheduling surgery. One that might not mean the removal of her breasts. Even if it did, she would live.

Definitely a good day.

So where was Sara?

A niggle of worry settled in his gut.

Just as he was getting ready to check to make sure he'd read the schedule correctly, she came hurrying around the corner, her fingers fiddling with her hair, which was in a high ponytail. Relief warred with irritation. She was due at work and she was worried about how her hair looked?

She stopped directly in front of him, her eyes not quite meeting his. "Sorry. I know I'm late."

"You are." He wasn't about to admit he'd been envisioning her scrambling to catch the first flight home. "Most people around here will tell you that I'm a stickler for punctuality."

"Something came up."

"An emergency?"

"Yes. No." Her face was flushed, beads of perspiration lining her upper lip.

His relief morphed into genuine concern. "Is everything okay?"

She still wasn't looking at him. "No, it's not."

"Your father?"

Although Antônio Moreira's cancer treatments were over, something could always go wrong. Or there were accidents. And since he was a cowboy, there were any number of things that could happen.

"He's fine." Brown eyes met his with a jolt before closing. Reopening. "Is there someplace we can go to talk?"

"Are you quitting the hospital?" Maybe he'd been right after all.

"I'm not sure. I just really need… I really would like to talk to you."

"Let's go to my office." If she had a problem with him, he should be sending her down to Human Resources or to the hospital administrator, but he wanted to hash this out face to face. Why would she quit? She'd only just gotten there, and even though they'd almost kissed in the back of the mobile unit, she'd given no indication that it made a difference. So what was going on?

He led her down a short hallway, opened the door to his office and motioned her inside. Rather than taking a seat behind the desk, he stood in front of it, resting his right hip against the solid surface, suddenly sure he needed the extra support. "So what's this all about? Does it have something to do with your reasons for being late?"

"Yes. I was… I haven't been feeling…" She stopped, her hands squeezed together in front of her. "I'm—I'm pregnant."

There was silence in the room for about five seconds before a slurry of something ugly oozed through his head. She was pregnant? He could have sworn she wasn't the kind of girl who slept around, but maybe he was wrong. Or, worse, maybe sex with him had been an effort to make a boyfriend jealous.

"Does the father know?"

She blinked a couple of times before her gaze hardened, lips thinning dangerously. "He does now."

He tried to process that and failed. "And he wants you to quit, is that it?"

"I don't know. I haven't asked him yet." Her chin went up. "Do you want me to quit?"

"I'm not the one you should be asking. But I'll certainly understand if…" His words faded away as a little thought in the back of his head appeared out of nowhere. He stared at her, willing her to be a mirage—for this whole meeting to be some kind of sick joke.

"You'll certainly understand if what?" Her face was stiff, quiet—almost as if a sculptor had carved a gorgeous image and then encased it in a block of ice.

The hatching thought grew into an adult-sized idea within a few more seconds. "What exactly are you trying to say, Sara?"

"Haven't you figured it out yet?" Her hands were still clasped, knuckles white. "I am pregnant. And you—you are the father."

Father. *Father?*

Uh, no. That isn't right. Can't be right.

Nausea roiled through his gut, spinning in all directions until he was no longer sure what was what. He gripped the desk beside him. "I'm the what?"

"You heard me. I'm pregnant." She licked her lips. "And there hasn't been anyone else. Not since that night."

"Are you sure?"

Her brows went up. "Am I sure there hasn't been anyone else? Pretty damned sure. I think that's something I would remember."

"What's that supposed to mean?" He didn't know why he even asked that question, so he squelched anything that might have followed. But they'd used—

"But that's not possible. I sure as hell found the evidence of protection in that room."

She opened her purse and pulled out a pink stick. "I have some evidence too."

A pregnancy test. On the little readout was a pink plus sign as plain as day. "It could be a false positive."

"Would you like me to show you the other five tests? I can go get them from the apartment."

"*Santa Maria*. No, that won't be necessary."

"One of the condoms must have failed. Or something. Maybe we were one of the victims of whoever has been going around stabbing holes in condom packages. I take it you didn't inspect it before using it."

No, he hadn't inspected it. At the time he'd just been happy that his memories would include safe sex.

Only no one who played with fire was ever truly safe. And Sara was fire. And, at the moment, ice.

"I'm pregnant. I'll do a test here at the hospital as well, if you want, but I really didn't come here to tell you that."

"Are you kidding me? The words 'I'm pregnant' just happened to fall out of your mouth and land on the floor?"

"Oh, I meant to say it. The other thing is this. I'm clean. I've only been with one other man in my life—and he didn't stick around for long."

The pain of those words tore at him, erasing some of his horror. But sticking around wasn't always the best thing that someone could do.

His father, for example.

Yeah, he'd stuck around, but he'd gotten some on the side as well.

She licked her lips. "Are you clean? If there's any doubt, I need to know now."

He laughed. As if dropping a bombshell like being

pregnant wasn't enough, now she wanted to know if he'd shot anything besides his sperm into that condom? But if anyone should understand it should be him. In medical school they'd stressed that STDs needed to be reported and partners traced, if at all possible. Sara was trying to do the responsible thing.

So the pregnancy angle was just a little sidebar to the real issue? Would she have even told him about the baby if she hadn't been worried about whether or not he'd given her something?

He didn't even want to think about that.

But pregnant?

Dammit. Lightning really could strike twice. He'd been an unplanned child. And now he'd repeated history with Sara.

"I'm clean. I get tested once a year at the hospital because I work with immunocompromised individuals." He jerked his shoulder to the side to make it crack. The sharp sound was followed by a quick rush of endorphins. An old *futebol* injury had turned into a bad habit. One he couldn't seem to break.

"I should know that. Sorry."

His brain tried to make sense of things, but right now that subway train was rushing past at speeds that caused his head to swim. "You're sure. You're pregnant."

"Do you want to say it a couple more times?" She heaved in a deep breath and then let it out so fast that it sent tendrils of her hair flying to the sides. "Listen, I know this is a shock. It is to me too. But I couldn't live with myself if I didn't at least inform you."

"Inform me." His thoughts wavered. So she'd

planned on telling him even without the STD angle.
Although... "Are you thinking of terminating?"

"No! I wasn't. I'm not." She paused. "I'm sorry if
that makes you unhappy. My dad once told me I was
an unplanned pregnancy, and I ended up being the
only child they could have. I just can't. I won't. So I'm
asking you again. Do you want me to quit my job?"

His parents' bitter marriage came to the forefront
of his mind. His folks had stayed together because of
him and, later, Natália. They'd as much as admitted it
on several occasions. He'd sworn that was never ever
going to happen to him. And yet here stood a woman
who told him she was expecting a child.

Because of him.

Suddenly he was faced with a horrible decision that
really wasn't a decision at all. He knew what he had
to do.

"No, Sara, I don't want you to quit. I..." Words suddenly rose up from the abyss, unbidden. Maybe it was
an old protective streak left over from when his sister
had been sick. Whatever it was, they tore out of his
mouth before he could stop them. "I'll help support
you. And the baby, of course."

Support her? As in with money?

Sara's chest burned as she stared at him in disbelief. Oh, hell, no.

"Are you kidding me, Sebastian? I don't want your
money. I'm insulted you would even say that to me."

"Then why did you come? Do you want a proposal?"

The muscles in her abdomen tightened until she
could barely breathe. "What is wrong with you? When

I get married, it's going to be because I love someone. Not because I'm pregnant with his child."

A cord of tension appeared in his jaw.

"I'm trying my best to do the responsible thing here. If I fathered a child, I certainly want to help take care of it."

"If?" A chill went through her. "You did. And the responsible thing would be to sit down and calmly work through where we go from here, as far as this job goes. If my being here will make it too awkward for you, then I'll move back to Rio Grande do Sul."

And take the baby with her. She left the words unsaid, but they hung in the air nonetheless. Only it wasn't just her baby. It was his too. And her conscience wouldn't let her just keep working with him without telling him the truth. She could have. It would have been so easy. When her condition became evident, he would just assume that the baby was someone else's. He probably wouldn't even have asked. In the end, she couldn't bring herself to be that dishonest.

"Why even tell me? Why not just leave and not look back?"

"Is that what you wish I had done?"

He turned away, going to stand by a large window at the back of his office. From where she stood she could see several apartment buildings fanned out into the distance. A sky-high office with a gorgeous view. This man was so far out of her league it wasn't even funny.

And they'd made a baby together. Tears gathered behind her eyes.

"No. It isn't what I wish you'd done."

He wished it hadn't happened at all. He didn't say it, but he might as well have.

"Don't worry, I'm not asking for anything. I don't *want* anything. I just thought you deserved to know."

He turned around to face her, putting his hands on his desk and looking across it at her. "It's my child too, Sara. If you're keeping it, I'm serious. I'll assume responsibility for it." His cool clinical tone dashed away any urge to cry.

Her heart became a chunk of granite, continuing to pulse and push blood through her system but refusing to feel. "Please, don't think you have to do that. Lots of women raise children on their own. It happens all the time nowadays."

"It's my child too." The repeated phrase was a little softer this time. A little less clinical. "Don't try to keep me out of its life."

That took her aback. Far from telling her to get away from him or, worse, just throwing money at her to assuage his guilt, he was saying he wanted to be a part of the baby's life. Marriage or no marriage.

"No, of course not. I just assumed you wouldn't want anything to do with it."

He gave a rough snort. "You don't know me very well, then. I practically raised my little sister because our parents—let's just say they weren't exactly the doting type. My dad cheated, and Natália's cancer diagnosis ended up being the only glue that held them together."

That shocked her into silence for several seconds.

"I'm sorry. I had no idea." Why was he even telling her this? Her parents' marriage had been the exact opposite. They had loved her with an all-encompassing type of love. And they *were* the doting type. They doted on her. And on each other. She couldn't imagine anything sadder than to grow up in a home devoid of that kind of love.

Sara wasn't so sure her parents' kind of love existed any more. Her runaway boyfriend was a case in point.

"It's not something I talk a lot about. I'm not even sure why I told you, except to say that I don't want any child of mine to go through life not knowing that he or she is loved."

"He or she will be. By me. And by my father."

"But not by me, is that it?"

"I won't try to keep you out of his or her life." That would be making one mistake into an even bigger one. She just wanted to make sure that's what Sebastian wanted to do. She couldn't bear the thought of him being a part-time dad and then at some point down the road deciding it wasn't for him and walking out of his child's life. Like her boyfriend had done to her. No, if he was going to do that, he could just forget about it. "But think carefully about it. Because once you decide, there will be no going back. It wouldn't be fair to the baby."

"I don't need to think about it."

She shook her head, a steely determination she hadn't known she possessed coming to the fore. Or maybe her maternal instincts were already kicking in. Whatever it was, she felt a fierce protective drive that wouldn't be denied. "Oh, but I insist. Take a couple of weeks. Or, better yet, a month. Think about it. Weigh the pros and cons of all that will be involved in a lifetime of parenting. And then get back to me with whatever you decide."

He came around the desk and took her by the shoulders. "I don't need a month, Sara. Or even a day. I am telling you right now. I want to be involved in this child's life."

"Are you sure?" Suddenly she was backpedaling like crazy.

They stared at each other for several seconds, and then Sebastian's grip softened, his gaze dropping to her mouth before coming back up.

"I've never been more sure of anything in my life."

A shiver went through her.

Céus! What did she think she was doing, handing down ultimatums? He was a city man, well versed in the comings and goings of relationships, just like her ex. To him, she probably seemed like a country bumpkin. And right now, unlike what she'd just told him, she did indeed want to go back in time. To six weeks ago and a certain wedding, actually. If she could, she might have made another choice. And she certainly would have brought her own damn protection.

Except what was done was done. Whether she liked it or not.

And now she was going to just have to stand back and accept the consequences.

Lucas Carvalho's clinic was in the heart of the Favela do São João. The addition of the tiny healthcare post had added a measure of hope to a desperate population. And, actually, Lucas had named the clinic to reflect that: The Star of Hope Clinic. Joined by Adam Cordeiro, Sebastian had driven here to meet up and get some inside information on the residents and hopefully figure out the biggest areas of need. Adam was already donating a couple of hours a week to the staffing of the clinic. They were scheduled to go out and get drinks together after the meeting.

To tell his friends or not to tell them. That was the question. He was still on shaky ground where Adam was concerned. His sister seemed happy, though, and that was all that mattered. Or it should be.

Adam parked the car in front of the whitewashed little building. The red dirt of the favela—splashed up by rainfall and street traffic—stained the bottom half of the clinic. Even so, with its flower-filled planters that hung beneath each window, the building was cleaner than most of the others in the neighborhood. The greenery and the cheery hand-lettered sign had to be the work of Lucas's wife.

Adam turned to him, pausing with his hand on the door latch. "Just so I'm sure, is everything okay between us?"

Sebastian had been silent for most of the trip from the hospital, and he knew he hadn't been acting quite like himself for the past several months. Time to make amends, if he could. "Yeah, it's all good. Sorry about being such an ass about everything."

"I would have wondered about you if you hadn't gotten in my face. I never saw myself as good enough for Natália."

"You're perfect for her." He sent his friend a forced grin. "But I know where to find you if that silver perfection ever tarnishes."

"Not going to happen, bro. I'm pretty crazy about the woman. Someday you'll meet the right one and understand exactly what I'm talking about."

Hardly. But that made his decision. He wouldn't say anything about Sara's announcement. Not yet. Not until he absolutely had to. "Like you said, 'Not going to happen, bro.'"

Adam rolled his eyes and stepped out of the car. "I seem to remember saying almost the exact same thing. And now look at me."

Lucas met them at the door. Great. Another happily married friend to contend with.

And if Sara had said she wanted a proposal, would he have given her one? He didn't think so. It would have been for all the wrong reasons. Just like his parents.

"I heard you got Dona Talita worked into the schedule at Tres Corações," he said. "I appreciate that."

Lucas stood aside to let them through the door. "Not a problem. She'll have surgery in a couple of weeks and a follow-up with an endocrinologist to get her blood sugar level back on track. I appreciate you making her a priority. She wouldn't have gone on her own."

"Sara Moreira, the nurse working with me in the mobile clinic, had a lot to do with it."

"Well, whatever the reason, it's great news."

The inside of Lucas's clinic was just as simple as the outside. White plaster walls and white tiles were all easy to disinfect. The space had been divided into three small areas: a spartan waiting room with plastic chairs lining the walls, a small but efficient exam room, and a tiny office that he could see from the waiting area. It contained just a basic metal desk. From what he understood, Lucas took the laptop that held all his patient information with him when he left the building to keep anyone from having a reason to break in and steal anything. Actually, his friend had made it so there was very little to steal. Some cotton balls and tongue depressors maybe, but he kept most of his equipment in tubs that he loaded in and out of his van whenever he was here.

If only Sebastian could load and unload his problems like that. Just tuck them out of sight until he was ready to deal with them again. Only he didn't feel like he would ever be ready to deal with a certain unexpected "problem".

And he damned himself for even thinking of it as a problem. It just hadn't been planned, the way he liked to do with most of his life. A product of having to care for his sister and act as referee for his parents' arguments. He was an expert at compartmentalizing.

Only how did you compartmentalize a child?

Or his or her mother?

You didn't. At least not in a way he was accustomed to.

"Is the clinic open today?"

Lucas shook his head. "Not today. Sophia has finally convinced me that I need to take a day or two off each month to 'recharge my batteries', as she put it."

"A day or two a month? I should say so. That's where I come in, I assume."

"Yes, if you have time." He pulled three of the white chairs from their spots along the wall and dragged them to the center. He motioned them to sit. "Adam is already working two hours a week. I don't want you to feel like you need to be at the clinic itself, since I know you're going to be putting the hours in with the mobile clinic. If I could just plan it so that the clinic is closed on the day the mobile unit is here, that would be great. I can send you cases, if you want, like I did the last time."

"That works for me. In between patients, then, I

could park by the clinic and if someone has a need they can just stop by. That way it'll be easy to find me."

Adam glanced his way. "Maybe you should have a key to the clinic and just meet patients in here?"

"I'd rather keep things as simple as possible, actually. I'll email you information on any patients I see, just like I did with my first two. It will make your record-keeping easier, I think. And I'll know where everything is inside the truck."

"How are things going with Sara, by the way?" Adam asked. "You two getting along? You seemed to be making eyes at each other at the wedding. Or was that just my imagination?"

Great, he'd been hoping no one had noticed.

"Your imagination. There were no 'eyes'. Or anything else involved. Sara and I have only been working together for a week. We'll see how it goes in a few more. But hopefully any possible issues have been resolved."

Except for one.

The bombshell she'd dropped earlier in the day still seemed unreal, like it had happened to a different Sebastian in an alternate universe. He didn't do things like get drunk and get women pregnant.

Only he hadn't set out to get her pregnant. Even drunk, a little part of his head had tried to do the right thing by protecting them both.

Instead, he'd failed.

Lucas glanced at him. "What issues?"

"Just a little lovers' spat." Adam said it with a grin, but the words hit Sebastian just the wrong way.

"We are not lovers." The words came out half growled.

"Whoa." Lucas's brows shot up. "I'm pretty sure Adam was kidding."

"Sorry." He popped his shoulder joint and sighed. "It's been stressful trying to get the hospital administration fully on board with the mobile unit. If you knew how many hoops I've had to jump through to get this up and running, you'd be buying me a drink—or five."

"If that's what you need, you got it." Adam slapped him on the back.

No, it wasn't what he needed. What he needed was a way out of his predicament. One that had both him and Sara coming out of it unscathed. Once she started showing, and people started asking questions…

Talk about hoops. Somehow he didn't think Paulo Celeste would approve of Sara suddenly expecting his child right after going to work for the hospital.

Dammit, he hadn't even thought about that. Until now. Surely it was no one's business.

But people were curious. They were bound to ask. And the truth would come out, even if he didn't want it to.

He hadn't technically broken hospital policy that he knew of, since Sara hadn't been working for the hospital when she'd gotten pregnant. And if he'd known about it before she'd come to Santa Coração, he would have vetoed them hiring her. But he hadn't known. Neither had she.

Or so she said. What if that's why she'd wanted to come to the hospital? Because she'd already known about the pregnancy?

No, she'd been genuinely shocked.

"Drinking's what got me into this mess."

"What mess?" Both men were now staring at him.

It was then that he realized the words hadn't gone with the conversation at hand. Talk about letting the cat out of the bag. They were going to find out. Better that it came from him than from the hospital grapevine. And maybe they could give him some advice on how to handle things.

"Sara's pregnant."

"Sara?" Lucas frowned. "As in your new nurse, Sara?"

"Yep."

"Wow, she didn't reveal this at her interview? It's going to be pretty damned difficult to replace her, isn't it, when she goes on maternity leave? When is she due?"

Sebastian did some quick mental calculations and came up blank. "Subtract six weeks from nine months."

"Six weeks." Adam planted his elbows on his knees and leaned forward. "That's back when Natália and I got married, so let's see… Do not even tell me."

It was now or never. "I think I just did. We'd both had a little too much to drink and things got—out of control."

How lame did that sound?

Lucas's gaze sharpened. "*You're* the father?"

"It would seem that way."

Adam shook his head, patent disbelief on his face. "What was it you said to me in the car a few minutes ago? 'Not going to happen'?"

"It's not. We're not. It was an accident."

"Is she going to keep it?"

Lucas's question was innocent enough, but it raised the hair on the back of his neck. Hadn't he asked her the same thing, though?

"Yes, she's going to keep it."

"Well, congratulations. I think."

"Yes," said Adam. "Congratulations. Sometimes things don't go as planned. I'm proof positive of that. But they tend to work out the way they were supposed to."

Not for his mom and dad. Not for Natália either, in getting cancer. But there was no way he could say that.

"We'll see."

"Are you going to keep working with her?"

Sebastian gave a shrug. "What else can I do? If we tell anyone, things could get messy. Worst-case scenario is that she'd be asked to leave the project."

"Because of that? Even if she is, surely there are other jobs at the hospital."

"We're currently on a hiring freeze, according to the hospital administrator. Unless someone quits, we can't hire any additional personnel, because of the economy tanking. Sara was already the exception to the rule. I imagine the other local hospitals are in the same spot."

"I know Tres Corações is. Damn, that puts you in kind of a touchy situation, though, doesn't it?" Lucas propped a foot on his knee.

"Touchy is how he got into this."

"Oh, you're a funny, funny guy, Adam." He knew his friend was trying to lighten the atmosphere, but right now there was nothing anyone could say or do to make this any easier. In truth, Sebastian held both his future and Sara's in the palm of his hand. He'd spoken the truth. If he let Paulo know, the man might start worrying about corporate sponsors and turn sour on the whole Mãos Abertas project. Sara would probably then be let go because of a lack of other job positions, and

Sebastian himself might receive an unwelcome lecture on maintaining professional appearances.

And with the mobile clinic being an experiment, he could very well sink its chances for continuing into the future. All because of a single error in judgment.

Sara was going to pay for it, and so was he. But he would be damned if all of the patients who'd stood to be helped by this endeavor would pay.

So he would just have to do his best to keep this thing under wraps. Starting with Adam and Lucas.

Then, he somehow had to convince Sara to keep her pregnancy a secret for the next several months. Or else ask her to go back to Rio Grande do Sul before anyone at the hospital got wind of the situation.

Even if she hated him for it.

CHAPTER FIVE

"I ALREADY TOLD YOU. I'm not planning on telling anyone. At least not right away."

When Sebastian had called her into his office this morning, she'd expected him to maybe try to get her to agree to let him support her again.

Not a chance. He'd obviously seen the error of his ways and had decided on a different tack. Just shove his future child under a rug to keep the scandal from messing with his stellar reputation.

She should be glad and take that as evidence that he'd never gotten anyone else pregnant. Until she'd come along.

Instead, an oppressive weight of exhaustion came over her. Probably due to the early changes in her body from her pregnancy. She thought of something.

"I won't deny this baby prenatal care. And I'm not sure how you can keep it a secret if I'm seeing an obstetrician."

The pencil he'd picked up from his desk tilted back and forth between his thumb and index finger, the speed increasing. "I'm not asking you to not get medical care, I just…" His glance went beyond her as if he was thinking things through.

So he hadn't thought about that angle either. "Natália is a neonatologist, maybe she can help."

"In other words, you're willing to share the news with your sister as long as it benefits you." Her voice was flat. So he could dictate who knew and who didn't? To hell with that.

He shifted in his chair, the pencil in his hand going still. "This situation isn't easy for anyone."

"'Anyone' being?"

"Why are you so angry?" The pencil dropped onto the desk.

"I'm not. You just went from not caring if anyone knew to keeping it a complete secret."

Up went his brows. "I never planned on sending out birth announcements, so I don't know where you got that idea."

He'd started out by asking to be a part of this child's life. If that wasn't sending out an announcement, she didn't know what was. Or had he forgotten about that?

Since she couldn't think of a witty response, she clamped her jaws shut and willed them to stay that way. He stared at her for a few seconds.

"Do you want to go home?"

"I'm not sick. At least, not at the moment." She'd felt a couple of twinges earlier, but a pack of *água e sal* crackers had taken care of that.

"I don't mean to your apartment here at the hospital. I'm talking about Rio Grande do Sul."

A ripple of fear went through her, and she pressed her spine against the back of her chair. "Are you threatening to fire me?"

"What?" His eyes shut for a moment, fingers going to the bridge of his nose and pinching. When he looked up again, his gaze had softened. "Hell, no. I'm not threatening you, Sara. The hospital has been cutting costs for a while. That means no extraneous personnel."

"But the mobile clinic…" Was he saying they'd decided to do away with her job?

"Is an experiment. It's not guaranteed to continue. If there is the slightest glitch along the way, they could scrap the entire project."

A glitch. As in her pregnancy. Oh, Lord. She put herself in Sebastian's shoes for a second. A new nurse was hired to work with the illustrious Dr. Texeira and came up pregnant with his child soon afterwards. At the very least it would raise some eyebrows. Not many hospitals would tolerate questionable behavior on the part of its staff, especially if it affected its reputation. Even if the hospital wasn't affected, Sebastian could be. Especially if the news came out at just the wrong moment.

"I'm so sorry, Sebastian. I swear I didn't know about the pregnancy before I got here, or I never would have come."

"I believe you. The timing just—"

"Sucks."

One side of his mouth went up. "That's one way of putting it."

"I don't want them to squash the project." Which was a surprise, because a few days ago she had been wondering if she could even do this job. And then she'd seen what had happened with Talita Moises. Without the mobile clinic, she might never have sought treatment. And she probably would have died of an infection, somewhere down the road. Yet now she had a good chance of survival.

All because of the clinic.

"I don't either. But you're right. It's not worth risking your health or that of the baby." His fingers sought out the pencil again. "I'm sorry to say that Adam Cordeiro and Lucas, the doctor who runs the favela clinic, already know. It came out during a meeting. They won't say anything, but the wider the circle gets of those who know— and they will know—the harder it will be. Natália has to know at the very least. Any pharmacist who fills a prescription will know. Ultrasound technicians. The list goes on and on."

"I'll move to another hospital."

He shook his head. "As big as São Paulo is, most of the doctors know each other, and the pool of hospital administrators is even smaller."

"So what do you want me to do? Do you *want* me to go home?"

She couldn't believe she had even asked that question. It might be the easiest solution, but it wasn't what she wanted in her heart of hearts.

"Not unless that's what you want."

She leaned forward and put one of her hands on his desk. "I don't. I really think I could do some good here."

"I think you could too. I'm toying with an idea, but you probably aren't going to like it."

"I don't understand."

"I asked you if you expected a proposal when you first told me. A question to which I got a resounding no." He covered her hand with his own. "But think about it in the bright light of day, Sara. It's the perfect solution. There are several husband and wife teams that work at the hospital. If we did it quietly, and I told the hospital administrator that we had already been 'involved' before you came up here, no one would be the wiser. It would be the truth, to a certain extent."

She swallowed, finally understanding. "You want to get married. Why not just tell the administrator I'm pregnant? Surely this has happened before."

"Maybe. The administrator stressed that things needed to stay professional between us. And since you're here doing a temporary *estágio*, it may be misconstrued as my taking advantage of my position."

"But you didn't. There has to be some way to explain all of this."

"If you can think of something, I'm all ears."

She racked her brain, but came up empty.

Sebastian squeezed her hand. "If you really want to stay here, I think it's what's best for the patients."

"So you'll make a noble sacrifice."

"No. I've never claimed to be noble." He blew out a breath. "I'm trying to help. To figure out a way that not only keeps the Mãos Abertos program up and running but also keeps you from losing your job."

"I'll go work at another hospital in the area."

"I already checked. The answers were all the same. No one is hiring. A lot of the health-care sector is operating in the red, and that situation doesn't look like it's going to improve anytime soon."

He'd already checked. Had already thought of sending her away to a different hospital to save his own ass?

No, he'd said it was to keep her from being sent home. She could only imagine what her dad would say. Actually, knowing her father, he'd probably travel up to São Paulo and give Sebastian a piece of his mind—if not worse. She'd been planning on keeping the baby

a secret from him, at least for a while, so why was it
any different that Sebastian wanted to keep the situation quiet?

It wasn't any different. It just hurt that he didn't
trust her not to say anything. Realistically, though, if
she stayed the whole six months, she was eventually
going to show—and the secret would be out. And he
was right about the list of people who would know once
she started prenatal care.

But to get married because of it?

"I can't see myself marrying someone I don't love."

"And rightly so. I've seen where that can lead and
it's not pretty. This would just be temporary. For maybe
a year or two until well after the baby is born and your
estágio is over. Then we get a quiet divorce. Just like
lots of other couples."

Did he even hear himself? Her parents had been
married for a long, long time, and they'd been happy.
It was what she'd once hoped for herself. So to go
through a sham of a marriage seemed disrespectful to
her mom's memory somehow. And yet what else could
she do? Abortion wasn't common in Brazil, but even
if it was, she wouldn't choose that route. She wanted
this baby.

There were several other married couples, he'd
said—some of them probably had children—so they
would just blend in with the crowd, was that it?

Maybe he was right.

He'd said it himself, this wouldn't be forever. And
she certainly didn't have a boyfriend any more or even
a distant prospect that could give her the cover story
Sebastian wanted her to have.

"A year or two is kind of ambiguous. If I agree to

this—and I haven't said I would—I would want to have a definite time frame so there are no misunderstandings on either side." Not that she expected Sebastian to fall head over heels for her and refuse to give her a divorce. No, it was more as a reminder to herself that he wasn't promising her roses and forever.

Sebastian's head cocked to the side. "How about we split the difference and say eighteen months, then? Can you stand to carry my name for that long?"

"Our situation wouldn't be any different than it is now, would it? Just a fake marriage to keep our situation from ruining everything."

"The marriage would have to be legal, that's the only way any of this will work." He frowned. "And the situation wouldn't be any different, but your living arrangements would."

"I'm sorry?"

"Don't you think it would look kind of odd for a married couple to live in separate apartments?"

"I'm not sure… You want me to move in with you?" Surely that wasn't what he was saying.

"My apartment is big. You would practically have your own place with a few minor adjustments."

"How minor?" She was rapidly losing control of the situation. Was she actually thinking of going through with this? Of marrying a man who was practically a stranger?

Her mouth twisted. That certainly hadn't stopped her from sleeping with him. From carrying his child.

He'd said he wanted to be involved in the baby's life. What better way than to have said baby living under his roof for a few months after it was born? Except her *estágio* was only listed as being for six months. Was he inviting her to stay past that date? Maybe it was better not to ask.

"There are two bedrooms." He paused. "They share a bathroom, though. There's another one down the hall, but it's not a full bath. We'd have to work out a schedule for showering."

A shared bathroom. She could only imagine hearing the water running in there as he took his shower and picturing him naked. With water streaming down his...

She gulped. That was no minor adjustment. She would have to invest in earplugs. Or something. "There are locks on the doors, right?"

Up went his brows. "Afraid I might try to sneak into your room while you're asleep?"

The thought of that made something in her tummy shift sideways. She covered it with a laugh.

"Of course not! I just don't want to walk in on you when you're in the bathroom."

"Yes, there are locks, Sara. Strong enough to keep out even the big bad wolf."

He might have meant it as a joke, but his words hit far too close to home for comfort. Because in that particular story the big bad wolf only wanted one thing. To devour Little Red Riding Hood. And he would do anything it took to get her.

Only Sebastian didn't want her. Not really. He just wanted to make sure his clinic stayed in business. And that she wasn't sent packing—although that was probably all part and parcel of making sure his pet project continued operating. Either way, she should be grateful. And she was. He was risking an awful lot for her.

The least she could do was listen to his proposal and give him an honest answer.

"Tell me exactly how you expect all of this to work."

A week after making his crazy, impulsive suggestion, Sebastian found himself in a courthouse, reciting words that meant absolutely nothing to him. Worse, he was promising that he would keep to those words. Natália was there as a witness, although she had tried to talk him out of it several times. "This is too fast, Sebastian. It doesn't feel right."

It didn't feel right to him either. But once he'd decided, and Sara had agreed, there was nothing left but to go through with his scheme. As stupid as it now seemed.

Sara had asked that her father remain out of the loop. At least for a while. Once she got through her first trimester, when most miscarriages happened, she would tell him. As if getting married in secret would go over any better with him than it had with Natália.

This was seeming less and less like a good idea and more like a recipe for disaster.

Unless they could keep it together and do exactly what he'd said they would do: stay together until the baby was born and then for nine more months after that. When he broke it down like that, it didn't seem like such an eternity.

Who was he kidding? It already seemed like an eternity.

Wasn't it a small price to pay, though, to continue saving lives in the *favelas*?

Sara took the ring from his sister with a smile that

wavered just slightly. That was okay, because everything inside him was wavering. And not just slightly, either.

Taking his hand in hers, she slid the thin band onto his ring finger. The ring he'd placed on hers moments earlier glittered an accusation at him. What would his child think of this once he or she was old enough to understand?

The same thing he'd thought when he'd found out the truth about his parents' marriage.

Hopefully he and Sara would exit this arrangement as friends, if nothing more. That was more than he could say for his mom and dad.

He glanced at Sara's face as she parroted the words the justice of the peace spoke. Her eyes were somber and unhappy.

Hell, he had practically forced her into doing this. He should have just asked her to go home. Oh, he'd blathered on about the project and it being canceled—and that was important. It was. But he'd also realized that if she left, he might never even see his child. There'd be no reason for her to seek him out. Especially if he'd sent her packing back to Rio Grande do Sul. And that killed him.

She took a breath, hesitating just a brief second longer than necessary. Sebastian gave her hand what he hoped was a reassuring squeeze, since he couldn't ask her if she was okay.

She did look at him then and returned the pressure.

A sense of relief went through him. He wasn't quite sure why—maybe he'd needed a little reassurance himself.

Then the stranger pronounced them husband and

wife, inviting Sebastian to kiss his new bride. Natália glanced at him, brows raised in challenge. Fine. She thought it was too fast? That he was having second thoughts? He'd show both her and that smug official.

Cupping Sara's face in his hands and registering her slight gasp of shock as he did so, he lowered his head and planted his lips on hers. Only her mouth was a little sweeter than he remembered. A little more pliable. A lot more, in fact. If he hadn't known better, he might almost believe she was…

Returning his kiss.

He blinked, pulling back in an instant—somehow managing to fake a smile as he leaned down again and kissed the tip of her nose. There. Playful. That's how he would get through all of this. She was the mother of his child, but she was not his lover. He could treat her like a distant relative or a…

His glance went to Natália and a rock dropped to the pit of his stomach. No, what he felt for Sara was nothing like the easy affection he held for his baby sister. It was more like the uneasy yearning that happened when he was around his mother and father. A wish for things to be different. Not good.

Natália came over and hugged his new wife, while sending him another silent glare over her shoulder. She mouthed, "This is wrong." Then she turned around and left the room. Well, there was nothing keeping her. She'd already signed the document that made all this legal.

But legal didn't necessarily make it right.

His plan was to talk to the hospital administrator as soon as they moved Sara into his house. He wasn't quite sure what his angle was going to be yet, because the man would undoubtedly ask if this was why he'd been so eager to start the project.

And then Sebastian would remind him that he'd been pushing for a mobile unit for the last two years. And it only made sense that he'd want to share something that was so important to him with those he loved.

Loved. That was a laugh.

The justice of the peace shifted, maybe sensing that the atmosphere in the room was darker than it should have been.

Sara saved him from trying to make small talk by glancing up at him. "You ready to head out?"

"Yes." He thanked the government official, and they walked out the door and into the blinding light of midday. He held a hand over his brow to shade his eyes, looking for his car. "That wasn't as bad as I thought it would be."

"Wasn't it?"

Sara's voice had a sad quality to it that he didn't like. Had he really done the right thing? Natália didn't think so.

"Hey." He took her hand and stopped her. "It's going to be all right. Eighteen months will go by fast. And you'll have the baby to worry about soon enough."

"I know. It just seems dishonest somehow."

She and Natália were evidently reading from the same play book.

"Not dishonest. Just necessary."

The glare from the sun kept him from seeing her expression.

"Do you really think the administrator is going to buy our story?"

"He should, if we put on a united front. I'm pretty

sure he's not going to fire one of the hospital's two oncological surgeons." He hesitated. "Would you be willing to roll part of your salary into mine? I can make up the difference. But if Paulo Celeste thinks he stands to gain something from the arrangement, he'll be much more likely to overlook any slivers of doubt. I'll talk to him."

She blinked. "Shouldn't that be 'we'?"

"I think it will be easier if I do it alone."

Pulling her hand away, she shook her head. "It's my life too. You talked about presenting a united front. How can we do that if I'm not even there?"

"He's been known to yell." Something that always made Sebastian distinctly uncomfortable, since his parents did that routinely.

"I'm a big girl. I think I can handle it."

She might be able to, but could he?

"If you're sure, I won't try to stop you."

He saw a flash of something that could have been teeth. "You can ask my father how easy it is to stop me once I have my mind set on something."

"That bad, huh?"

"The worst. He says I'm more stubborn than a steer during cutting and branding season."

"I have no idea what that even means."

She tilted her head and gave him a look. "No? Where I'm from, everyone knows what that means. I'm sure you city guys have a similar expression."

"Not really." Especially not since that sassy little look she'd just sent him had arrowed straight down to his groin. Probably remembering that kiss a few moments earlier.

"Sure you do. 'More stubborn than…'" She gave a little hand flourish that told him to fill in the blank.

Cornered, he forced his sluggish brain to think of something. Anything. "More stubborn than a V-fib that refuses to be converted."

"Okay, I'm not sure I like being compared to a deadly arrhythmia."

She was right. It was a stupid comparison. And a stupid game.

"Let's just go get your stuff and move it over to my apartment. And then tomorrow we'll tackle telling the hospital administrator."

"Are you sure you don't want to wait a few weeks? Until we see if the pregnancy is even viable?"

"Someone is bound to mention you moving out of the hospital apartments. And then it will be harder to explain away."

"I guess you're right. I just hate lying to people."

"Let's just concentrate on what's true, okay? It's true that we got married, is it not?" He turned and started walking back toward the car.

"Yes."

"It's true that you're moving into my place, right?"

"Um—yes." She caught up to him a few yards later. "But we don't love each other."

"When was the last time you asked a newly married couple if they loved each other?"

"Well…never."

He unlocked the passenger side door and waited until she climbed inside. "That's right, because you just assume they got married because they fell in love. The hospital administrator will assume the same thing. I doubt he'll even ask."

"I hope you're right."

"Don't worry. As soon as I mention combining incomes, the dollar signs in his eyes will block out any objections he may have. He might even be happy for us." Sebastian carefully omitted the fact that he planned on making up the difference in her salary and putting it aside in a special account. And if she was able to carry the pregnancy to term, he would sock money away into a college fund. That news could wait until they started their divorce proceedings, though.

"And if it doesn't?"

"Then we'd better have an alternate explanation ready."

All he had to do was think of one. Between now and tomorrow morning.

CHAPTER SIX

Nossa! SARA COULD see why the condominium building was called the Vista do Vale, because the scenery from the twenty-fifth-floor balcony was spectacular. Sara had never been inside an apartment this luxurious. It certainly didn't feel like it was situated in a valley from where she was looking. After living her entire life in her parent's one-story house on the ranch, she felt kind of queasy about how high up they were. Or maybe that was her pregnancy. Honestly, it was probably a little bit of both.

"Where did you say the fire escape was?" She called back to where Sebastian was setting her two large suitcases on the polished marble floor of the foyer.

He came through the double sliding glass doors that opened to an outside living space. A space that was almost as big as her whole nurse's apartment at the hospital.

"I didn't, but see that platform hanging over there?"

"Where—? Oh, no!" She'd noticed the contraption hanging a few floors below them. Panic went through her system, the queasiness growing exponentially.

"Relax, Sara. I'm kidding. They're in the process

of polishing and repairing the tile on this side of the building."

"In that?" No one in their right mind would stand on what appeared little more than a wooden platform with a thin line of metal railing encircling the outside. Even as she looked, it seemed to sway in the breeze. Her nausea spiked. There was no way she would go out in something like that.

She could tell the difference, though, in the cobalt tiles that had been polished and those that had collected years of dust and grime from the city below. Even the "before" view, though, oozed opulence and wealth.

"The company has many years of experience in this work. They know what they're doing."

She glanced down again, and then backed away, only to bump into Sebastian, whose arm went around her to brace her. The warmth of his touch soothed her rapidly fraying nerves. "Seriously, we could get out if there were a fire, right?"

"There are stairs, in case the elevator goes out."

"Have you ever had to use them?"

"I have. More than once."

"Deus do céu." She pressed both palms against her stomach. "Why?"

He turned her around to face him, hands still on her shoulders. "Hey, are you okay?"

"I think so. I just didn't think this would all be so…" She couldn't find the right word, so she settled for waving her hand to encompass the inside of his condominium. "How long have you lived here?"

"Not long. I moved here about a year ago."

"And you've already used the stairs more than once?"

His thumbs trailed over her collarbones as he peered

into her face, as if seeing something that worried him. "I was kidding. I only went up and down them for exercise when I knew I wouldn't have time to go to the gym."

Her whole body sagged closer to him. "Well, you could have said that right away."

"I had no idea you were afraid of heights."

"I've never really had a chance to test out whether I was or wasn't. I think the tallest place I've ever been was the waterfall at Iguaçu."

"You really only notice the height out here. Inside, it just feels like a regular living space."

Regular living space? Was he kidding? There was nothing "regular" about his apartment. "I'll take your word for it." As much as she tried to keep her voice neutral, even she could hear the ironic overtones behind her comment. Besides, that continued brushing movement of his thumbs was beginning to warm her up in ways that worried her.

Maybe he read her thoughts, because he grinned and put his hand under her elbow. "Come on back inside, and I'll show you where you'll be staying. Since you're such a fan of heights, maybe I'll take you to the observation deck of the Banespa building. You can see a lot of the heart of the downtown area from there. You can even see this building from it."

Groaning, she let him lead her back inside. "Are there stairs there too?" She could see this being a common litany for her time in São Paulo.

"There are, but we'll want to take the elevator. Once we reach the thirty-third floor, we'll have to go up two flights of stairs to get to the deck."

Okay, so the fear was still there, but there was also

a glimmer of excitement. Maybe it was from the gentle way he'd calmed her fears out on the veranda. Or because he wanted to take her to see parts of the city.

He's probably joking, Sara. You don't need to take any of this too seriously.

Because doing that could make for a whole lot of heartache. Especially since her wonky hormones were making her feel a little off—a touch lovey-dovey about everything—as it nurtured those maternal instincts. She had to remember that none of her emotions were trustworthy at the moment. And Sebastian would be horrified if he thought she was looking down the road and picturing them as an old married couple.

Not that she was. Even if the way he'd looked at her a few minutes ago had made her want things she couldn't have.

Good thing they had set up some ground rules.

"Well, we'll see. With the mobile clinic and your regular rounds at the hospital, you'll probably be too busy to do much of anything outside of work."

"We have to eat lunch or dinner sometime." He threw a glance over his shoulder as he headed toward the foyer.

"We?"

"We'll be working most of the same hours, and we're newlyweds, remember? It stands to reason that we would want to eat together from time to time. Like Adam and Natália do. Or the other married couples who work at the hospital."

"The two couples who were at your sister's wedding. They both work at the hospital as well?"

"Kind of. Marcos does, as you know. You'll be seeing a lot of him around the oncology department. And

his wife, Maggie, works there as well. Lucas and Sophia do quite a bit of relief work in poorer parts of the
country, and of course Lucas runs the clinic in the
favela we were at the other day. But, yes, it seems that
Santa Coração is a breeding ground for romance, my
sister included."

Okay, so if he had caught the irony in her earlier
words, she had definitely caught a hint of sardonic de-
rision in his tone.

"You disagree with people falling in love?"

"I don't disagree with their decisions. I'm just saying that I tend to be a little more skeptical. I've witnessed some train-wreck marriages that never should
have taken place."

Was he talking about theirs? This whole sham had
been his idea, not hers. Maybe he was already regret-
ting having suggested it. Or warning her not to get too
attached. He needn't bother. Maybe she should try to
reassure him on that point.

"Train wrecks have to be lifted off the tracks at
some point. They're not permanent."

"Sometimes there are extenuating circumstances
for them to linger." He reached down and picked up
her luggage, no longer looking at her.

Oh, God. He *was* talking about them—about her
pregnancy. Maybe she should have insisted on a prenup to make him feel better about everything. And
here she was acting like a starstruck teenager about
his apartment and the city in general. No wonder he
was nervous.

"Hey." She caught at his arm, the biceps tightening beneath her touch. "Stop for just a minute, please."

Sebastian set her luggage down and turned to face

her, his eyes a dark molten mass of—anger? "What is it?"

She took her hand off him in a hurry.

"If you're worried about me trying to extend our arrangement, don't. I'll sign a prenup or a contract, if you want. It's not too late for either."

"What are you talking about?"

She shrugged, needing to look away from those huge pupils. "I'm talking about this farce. I didn't want to do it in the first place, remember, and I only agreed in order to—"

"No. I'm sorry." His hands went to her shoulders once again, gaze softening. "I wasn't referring to you at all. I know you didn't try to trap, coerce or whatever other words you think are rattling around in my head right now. I'm talking about my folks. They haven't been the greatest example of marital bliss. Natália and I both know they stayed together for our sake. And now they just—stay together, probably because they've been married for so long. But they're not happy. I don't remember them *ever* being happy."

"How awful." She tried to switch gears, but all she felt was a huge sense of relief, mixed with sadness. "Surely they must love each other. Some couples just show it differently." Her dad was a good example of that. He had always been a man of few words, but he had loved his wife deeply. So deeply she didn't know if he would ever marry again.

"I don't think the word 'divorce' is used as a weapon in most homes. I was surprised when Natália decided to get married at all. Especially as quick as it was."

"They seem very happy. At least from what little

I've seen. Natália and I are friends. Surely she would have mentioned something if there was trouble in paradise."

"I'm sure they're fine. I just wonder how long it can— Forget it. I shouldn't have mentioned any of it."

She reached up and covered one of his hands with her own. "Yes, you should have. It helps me understand how hard this whole situation is for you. But we don't hate each other. At least, I don't hate you."

One side of his mouth went up and his fingers tightened their grip on her shoulders before he let go of one and caught her hand. "You probably should. I keep telling myself I should have checked those condoms when I put them on, but I wasn't quite myself that night."

"Neither of us were. Knowing about your parents helps me understand. And I don't hate you. I hope we'll come out of this as friends."

"Hmm—friends." His smile slid just a bit higher. "That can be a loaded term. My sister and Adam started out as friends. Look what happened with them."

This time he was joking. She should be elated that they'd gotten everything out in the open, but there was this vague sense of loneliness rolling around inside her. "Not all friends become lovers."

His thumb stroked over the palm of her hand, sending a shiver through her.

Careful, Sara.

"No, they don't. But former lovers can become friends, don't you think? We just have to make sure we don't go on any more drinking binges."

They were in trouble, then, because the low thrum of his voice was as intoxicating as any liquor. And his thumb, still scrubbing across her palm in a soft back and forth motion, was making her nerve endings tingle in spots far removed from her hand. Was he doing that on purpose? If so, she should tell him to stop. Except it felt good. Intimate in a way that rough, grabbing hands could never be.

"Well, since I'm not allowed to drink until after the baby is born, there's nothing for either of us to worry about."

Right?

"Nothing at all." Sebastian's voice deepened, laced with a tension she hadn't heard since—

That night at the bar. Right before he'd swept her off to that motel.

Deus! It had to be her imagination. She was letting it run wild. If she just tugged her hand, he would release her and all would be right with the world.

But even though her brain tried to tell her arm to slide backward, it stayed right where it was.

Okay, Sara, try something else. Hurry!

Before she could, his mouth kicked up sideways in a half-smile that drove the wind from her lungs.

"Do you do that on purpose?" He let go of her hand, his index finger traveling up to her lower lip and making it wiggle slightly. The touch went through her like an electric shock. It took her a second to find enough words to answer.

"Do what?"

"Puff that out when you're nervous about something." He let his hand drop back to his side, although his gaze stayed put.

She sucked the errant lip back over her teeth before realizing how ridiculous that was. "No. At least I don't think I do."

"I noticed it for the first time at the wedding."

He had? Her insides quivered with heat. Was he doing *that* on purpose?

She tried to clear her throat, but it came out as a weak puff of air that sounded more like a sigh. Maybe because that's what it was. Time to change the subject. "You were going to show me the bedrooms?"

No, wait. That huskiness in her voice wasn't right. And that low pulsing in her belly—the one telling her to do strange things—had to belong to someone else.

"You lip is doing that thing again." He shifted closer. "And there is nothing I would like better than to show you the bedrooms. Except for maybe—this."

His head lowered until he was hovering just above her mouth. *"Posso?"*

Deus. Did he have to ask?

"Yes." She drew the word out, letting that *s* roll across her tongue, everything inside her screaming for him to close the gap between them and kiss her.

Then he was right there, his hand moving to cup her chin. This was no tentative, questioning touch. It was mouth to mouth and beyond, a display that said this had been just as much on his mind as it had been on hers.

She opened to him, shuddering when his tongue slid easily inside, his exploration turning into long, lazy movements that left no doubt as to where his thoughts were. *Graças a Deus*, that was a relief, because hers were in exactly the same place.

His arm went around her waist, hauling her against him, widening his stance so she fit between his legs. And, yes, that hard ridge of flesh was right where she expected it to be: cradled in the soft flesh of her belly.

The bedrooms. His. Hers. She didn't care which,

but she needed to be there. But to say anything, she would have to pull her mouth away from the sweet thrill of having him inside. And she wasn't willing to forgo that. Not yet. In fact, she closed her lips around him, relishing the groan that followed soon afterwards.

He wheeled back in a rush, separating himself so quickly that she just stood there dazed for a second.

What? No!

Just when she thought he had come to his senses, he reached down, his arm going behind her knees and scooping her feet out from under her. He gave her a little toss to settle her against his chest, leaving her to clutch at his shoulders. "Do you still want to see where I sleep?"

All she could do was give a single nod that had him striding down the hallway, past one closed door and stopping in front of another.

She licked her lips, his taste still as fresh as it had been seconds earlier. When he made no move to go inside, she asked, "Do you need me to get the door?"

"Mmm…" He leaned down and kissed her again. "No, just anticipating what's going to happen once it's open."

He wasn't the only one. But she was getting impatient, and a little afraid he might back out at the last second.

She unhooked one of her arms and reached toward the ornate silver lever, her fingers barely able to brush against it. Sebastian obliged by tipping her far enough so she could grab it. She pushed down, the latch releasing and allowing the door to swing in.

"Waiting is highly overrated."

He gave her a heated glance, chuckling. "Oh, but the pleasure is that much sharper when it finally arrives."

The words made her shiver. Did that mean he meant to draw this out?

He moved inside the room and set her on the edge of a huge bed, his presence preventing her from closing her legs. That was okay, because the way he was standing was pure invitation. All she had to do was...

She scooted closer, fingers sliding up his thighs only to have his hands grab both of hers.

"What are you doing, Sara?"

"Didn't they teach you anything in sex education class?" She gave him what she hoped was a sexy grin.

"Oh, I have plenty of education. Want to see?"

He spread her hands so they were wide apart and then bore her back onto the bed. His kiss was immediate. Almost aggressive. And her hips arched high, trying to find him.

He lifted his head to look at her. "Since you don't seem interested in slow and easy, let's go fast and hard, shall we?"

One leg spread hers even further, settling his length in the opening he'd created.

"Yes!" This time when her hips went up, they connected with him, a jolt of sensation careening through her. She repeated the movement, her pleasure centers engaging in an instant. Okay, this was good. A little too good. On her third foray around the sun she slid along him, eyes fluttering closed as she ventured closer to—

He edged away. "I changed my mind."

"What?" Her eyes snapped open.

Her reaction was met with a rough laugh. "Just kidding. Let me get my zipper down, okay?"

She sucked down a relieved breath. "No protection needed tonight."

"Oh, no? I think you might need a little."

She tried to figure out what he meant, but her brain was too clouded with wanting him. "A little what?"

"A little protection. From me."

Evidently he'd gotten his zipper down because his fingers were at the top of her waistband, undoing the button and sliding the fastener. But when he went to tug her pants down, he could only get them past her hips. Her spread legs prevented them from going any lower. "Won't. Work."

He leaned down and bit her neck. "Want to bet?"

"No. A bet isn't what I want right now."

"I think I know exactly what you want." He pushed her legs together and then hauled her pants and underwear off. Then he was back again.

Up went her hips, just like before, seeking him.

This time, he found her instead and plunged home in a rush that drove the breath from his lungs. Sweet, sweet heat gripped him, massaging the ache right out of his flesh and replacing it with a need to drive into her again and again.

Forcing himself to count to ten, he only made it to five before those sexy hips were at it once more, trying to locate the very relief he'd been hoping to delay.

Damn, he hadn't even gotten her shirt off. And maybe they wouldn't make it that far, because his muscles were starting to take on a life of their own, her movements coaxing an equal and opposite reaction from him.

Soon the pace quickened, the thrusts growing quicker,

getting wilder. Her head tossed from side to side as he hovered over her, his elbows braced on either side of her arms. Then he dove deep. Stayed there.

Her grip on him tightened. Squeezed.

Deus do céu. He wasn't going to be able to hold on much longer.

Her hips suddenly bucked up and back, her hands going to his butt, nails digging in. The sharp pain sent him over the edge, but not before he felt that blessed series of spasms that signaled her orgasm. That was it, he was off like a shot, pumping like a wild beast, his body erupting right along with hers.

He kept that ecstasy going as long as he could, until gravity stuck suckered tentacles on his flesh and began to drag him back to earth. He tried to resist, because he knew as soon as he landed, his first thought was going to be—

He hit with a bump.

And there it was. That raging, damning thought that happened every time he was around her:

How in the hell could he have let that happen?

CHAPTER SEVEN

"You're married? Congratulations." The hospital administrator barely looked up from his papers.

Okay, so this wasn't the reception he'd expected. No conflict of interest speeches or comments about there needing to be oversights.

Maybe finding out that Sara was pregnant wouldn't have been such a big deal either. Although the administrator had been known to come down on anyone who might give the gossip columns something to chew on. Some of their more conservative sponsors were pretty strict about the hospital's reputation. That included its staff.

Paulo was all about keeping things running as smoothly as possible and making sure the income and expenses were lined up in neat little rows. Sponsors and benefactors had to be kept happy.

"As of two days ago, yes." He didn't even want to think about what they'd done on their honeymoon night. In fact, that was why he was here alone, instead of presenting that united front they'd talked about. He hadn't been able to face her at the apartment. Not yet.

He'd been pretty careful to come home when Sara was already in bed and leave before she got up in the morning. That had meant taking naps in his office during the day, but it was the only way he could function.

"Good, good. Make sure the nurses' housing department knows that there's an empty apartment available. And make sure Human Resources knows about her name change for tax purposes."

Name change. He'd forgotten about that. Damn.

"Right, I will." The sooner he got out of this office the better. He was going to have to tell Sara that it went well, but maybe he wouldn't let on just how well it had gone. "Thank you."

The man waved him away, before looking up suddenly.

Sebastian tensed, waiting for the ax to finally fall.

"If you could write me up a statement on how things are going with the mobile clinic, I would like to use it for publicity. Maybe along with a congratulations announcement and a picture of the happy couple. We've had a couple of weddings over the last year or so. It might make for some good visibility for the hospital."

What the hell? Oh, Sara would just love that. And the man would probably get a big kick out of knowing they hadn't really spoken much over the last couple of days. Just some business stuff. But that would change tomorrow when they had to meet to do their rounds in the *favela*. There was no way to maintain silence when you were trapped together in a vehicle for an entire day.

"I'll check with her and see what she thinks."

The man's eyes narrowed slightly. "I would think that as a new hospital employee, she would be glad to help in any way she could."

A veiled threat? Not happening. And Sebastian wasn't about to let it slide by unnoticed.

"Would you care to rephrase that, sir?" The hospital might think it could do without Sara, but could it do without both of them? There were only a handful of oncologists that could do what he did in the field of osteosarcoma.

"I stated that badly. You're right. Ask her if she would be willing to be photographed with you for hospital publicity. We're asking our other married couples to do the same for our Valentine's Day campaign. If she'd rather not, I won't push it."

"Thank you. I'll ask her and get back to you."

With that he headed out the door.

Only to barely miss crashing into Adam.

He matched his step to his friend's. "Did Paulo Celeste try to talk you and Nata into doing pictures for some kind of wedded bliss publicity stunt?"

"Yep, he's hoping to feature all the couples in the hospital for a Dia dos Namorados ad. Why? Did he say something to you about it?"

Okay, so Paulo had been telling the truth, it wasn't just him and Sara. He could understand that since Brazil's version of Valentine's Day would be here in a few months.

"Yes, he asked if Sara and I would pose next to the mobile clinic."

"Ironic, isn't it?" His friend shot him a glance.

"What do you mean?"

"Just that after all the objections you had about me and Nata, you end up married a month and a half later. Your sister has a few reservations about how it all went down."

He gave Adam a half-grin. "I would tell you to mind

your own business, but since that seemed to be your line several months ago, I won't bother."

"Yeah, and somehow the request never made any difference, no matter how nicely I asked."

He laughed. "Nicely? I remember some pretty heated moments there toward the end."

"And who started those moments?" Adam stopped at the bank of elevators and pushed a number into the console, waiting to see which elevator assignment came up on the screen.

"I'm not afraid to admit it." He slapped his friend on the back. "I'm also not afraid to admit when I was wrong about something. Natália seems happy. Really happy. I'm glad for both of you."

"Thanks. And you, Sebastian. Are you happy?" The letter E pinged on the screen. "Don't answer that. Just know that I want the same for you as what Nata and I have."

As his friend went over to Elevator E, Sebastian sighed. Some people didn't find happiness as easily as others. He'd already resigned himself to that fate. And since history seemed to like repeating itself, he knew better than to hope that it might get any better. His best bet was to hope it didn't get any worse.

It was worse. Sara barely said a word to him when she met him by the mobile clinic the next day. He couldn't blame her. He'd avoided her for the last three days. Mainly because he didn't have a clue what to say to make things better. He'd promised himself—and her—that it was a marriage on paper only. He'd even assured her there were locks on the doors, because she hadn't trusted him to keep his hands to himself. And rightly so. Less than an hour after they'd arrived in his home, he'd been all over her.

Was that what his father had been like as he'd had affair after affair—allowing his baser instincts to run the show? Wasn't that what had gotten Sebastian into this quandary in the first place?

Droga!

He paused before starting the vehicle, even though the heat was beginning to cause perspiration to bead on his forehead. "Sara?"

"Hmm?" She stared out the window as if something out there fascinated her. Since all that was there was a bunch of parked cars, he was pretty sure she was just avoiding interacting with him. He couldn't blame her.

"I think we need to at least try to get past this."

This time she did glance his way. But only for a second. "Past what?"

Was she kidding him? "What happened the other night."

"I'm already past it. Way past."

Great. He hadn't been able to work his way through things, and yet she acted like it hadn't meant any more than... Maybe she was too worried about something else. The baby?

"Are you feeling okay? Not sick?"

"Not today."

Okay, he was a first-class jerk. He'd been worried about his own comfort, while Sara was probably downing crackers by the dozen. "Morning sickness?"

"Not today."

"Well, then, when? Yesterday, dammit?" A flash of irritation went through him. He was just trying to help—to fix whatever was going wrong with their plan—and she was shooting him down as soon as he opened his mouth.

There was no way he could survive eighteen months of the silent treatment.

She swiveled in her seat and faced him. "Why does it matter? Did you ever talk to the hospital administrator?"

"Yes, as a matter of fact. He's thrilled for us."

She paled. "Are you serious?"

"I'm sorry. I don't know what is wrong with me." He touched her arm. "And, yes, I'm serious. He wasn't upset. Just the opposite, actually. He'd like to feature us in some kind of promotion for Dia dos Namorados along with Adam and Natália, Marcos and Maggie, and some of the other married couples."

This time she laughed. Or it started out as a laugh, and swiftly changed to a weird keening sound that ended in a sniffle.

He put a finger under her chin, turning it toward him. "What's going on, Sara? Besides what happened the other night. Or is it because of that?"

"No, it's not about that at all. Well, it is, but not in the way you think."

"I have no idea what you're talking about."

"I'm talking about my dad."

His heart gave a painful thud. "Your dad? Is he okay?"

"He's fine. It's not his health I'm worried about." She closed her eyes for a moment. "He's coming to visit. Next Monday, in fact."

"What?" There was no way he could have imagined this happening. Or maybe he could have, if he hadn't

been in such a damned hurry to screw up his life. And Sara's. No more drinking for him. Ever.

"Yes, and I haven't told him. About us. About the baby. I was going to wait until I was further along, but since I'm not in the nurses' dorm any more, he is certainly going to figure something out. Because I know good and well he's not going to expect me to be living under the same roof as you."

Her father probably wouldn't be thrilled that he'd taken his daughter to a motel right under his nose either.

"We'll figure something out." When he'd thought about things getting worse, never in a million years had he imagined them getting this much worse. Not only was Antônio Moreira's daughter married, she'd married his oncologist, and she was now pregnant with that oncologist's baby. What a mess.

He started the truck, setting the air-conditioner to high as he tried to think through this thing logically. His lips twisted. An easy task, since everything about their marriage *reeked* of logic. He decided to be honest. "I'm coming up completely blank."

"I know. Me too. Barring asking you to move out of your own house, I have no idea how to fix this."

"Exactly how would me moving out solve anything?"

"I could say I was house sitting for a friend."

The muscles in his mouth jerked sideways in a smile. "Some friend, this friend."

"You know what I mean."

"And here I thought this was all about me."

Her head tilted. "What was?"

"I thought your irritation was because of what we

did. Never mind. If you think my moving out tempo-
rarily will be the best solution, I'll do it."

"No. I was kidding." She smiled. "Okay, half kidding. But we were going to tell Daddy eventually. And
someone at the hospital is bound to spill the beans.
We'll just get it over with and do it when he gets here.
We fell madly in love and decided to get married."

"In a matter of weeks. You think he's going to buy
that?" Although maybe it was better to just throw it
out there and see how he reacted.

"If I know my father, he'll probably be over the
moon. That's part of why I didn't want to tell him
right away. Well, making sure the pregnancy has time
to take root was a big part of it, but I also don't want
him to be hurt." She sighed. "He always wanted me to
find the love of my life like he did. He's going to be so
disappointed when he hears we're getting a divorce."

"He can't expect everyone to have the same kind of
luck as he did." His parents certainly hadn't. And Sebastian didn't see himself having that kind of luck either. He already knew he didn't, if this was anything to
go by. His parents had felt forced into marriage, kind of
like he had. Only in trying to stick it out, they'd made
themselves—and their children—pretty damned miserable. It looked like he really was a chip off the old
block. His dad would be proud.

"I know. I just hate being the one to shatter his illusions. I've already disappointed him once, in that area."

He wasn't sure what she meant by that last sentence,
and didn't feel like asking. "If what you said is true, he
may be so happy to meet his grandchild that a lot of the
extraneous stuff will fly out the window. Especially if
we make sure that our split is as amicable as possible."

"I hope so." She took one of the pamphlets that advertised their clinic services and fanned herself with it. "Do you think we could start driving so that the air-conditioner works better? I'm about to be steamed in my own skin."

"Of course. Sorry."

"Don't be sorry. It's just a relief to not have you flip out about this."

"Why would I flip out?"

"Um. Because not only did your one-night stand get pregnant. And not only did you marry her to save her job and your pet project, but now her dad is coming to visit and expects to see his little girl put on a happy face."

"You want us to put on a good show for him, is that it?"

"I can't ask you to do that."

He pulled out of the parking lot and onto the busy street. "Of course you can. It won't be that hard. We both have to work this week, so the only time he'll see us is when we're home." He flashed a look at her. "Damn. When we're home. He'll have to stay with us, or he's going to know something is off, which means…"

She nodded her head and glanced sideways at him. "We're going to have to share a bed again. Only this time it will be completely chaste."

He waggled his eyebrows at her. "Not necessarily. Especially since your lip is doing its cute little puffer fish imitation."

"Oh, no. That was your last hurrah, mister."

"My very last one? Forever?"

She laughed, although it came out sounding a little choked. "Hasn't it gotten us into enough trouble?"

"Yes. It has." He popped his shoulder joint to relieve the ache building in it. "But it was at least a little fun, wasn't it?"

"Maybe a little."

He had to content himself with that, because the tone of her voice gave her away. It hadn't been a "little" anything. And Sebastian, Sara, and her lower lip all knew it.

Talita Moises met them at the door. "You were right. About everything. I'm having surgery to try to scrape that silicone junk out. Or at least try to fix things as much as possible. At the very worst they'll have to remove both of them. I wasn't sure how I felt about that, but there are worse things."

She'd taken a one-hundred-and-eighty-degree turn from where she'd been last week, when she'd said she didn't want to lose her breasts.

It was kind of hard to say "Congratulations" to a woman who might be facing a double mastectomy. "How do you feel about that?"

"I should be sad, but I'm not. I'm just relieved it's not cancer. The doctor said my diabetes might cause some problems in healing, but he's hopeful. I won't know ahead of time whether I'll come out of surgery with boobs or without. The doctor said there was really no way to tell until he gets in there and sees how much damage has been done. I'll just be so glad not to have to deal with this any more that I don't really care what he has to do."

It was kind of surreal, hearing the change in Ms.

Moises' attitude toward a possible mastectomy. Of course, Sara had changed her mind as well, hadn't she—going from swearing Sebastian to secrecy about her pregnancy and their marriage to agreeing to sleep in the same bed as him the whole time her dad was here? But only as a way to pretend that they were a happily married couple.

Pretend, Sara. You need to remember that!

Sebastian glanced her way. "Have they set a date for surgery yet?"

"The doc is squeezing me into his schedule, so it will happen in two weeks."

Right after Sara's father left to go home.

The woman clasped her hands together, picking at a piece of chipped red polish on her thumbnail.

"What's wrong?" She'd seemed happy enough a minute or two ago.

"I'm worried about where my grandson will go if something happens to me."

Sara laid her hand on the woman's shoulder. "Like I told you last time, nothing is going to happen to you."

It was dumb to promise something like that, she knew it, but somehow the words just came out of her mouth.

"It might. I'm no fool. And I don't have any relatives left."

"None?" A flash of pain went through her heart. She couldn't imagine being totally alone in this world. Sara had her father. And friends back home. And she would soon have a child.

But not even Talita was totally alone. She had her grandson. "How old is he again?"

"Twelve. He'll be thirteen in two months."

"Hmm, let me see what I can do."

Sebastian sent her a warning look. He was right. But she'd already blurted it out. It wasn't like she'd promised to adopt the boy or anything. And a mastectomy wasn't brain surgery, where the outcome wasn't certain. Not that any surgery was certain. But surely it wouldn't hurt to give the woman one less thing to worry about. If worse came to worst, maybe they could house the boy while his grandmother was in the hospital.

Somehow she didn't think Sebastian would like that. And there might even be a hospital rule against it. She would have to check. But, in the meantime, she could ask around and see if anyone would be willing to look after him for a week or so.

"Would you do that for me?"

There was such hope in her eyes that Sara couldn't bring herself to say no, even though she never should have said yes in the first place.

"I will. I'll see if I can find someone, and I'll let you know."

Talita grabbed her hand in both of her own. Tears ran down her cheeks. "Bless you. And thank you. You can't know how grateful I am."

She could know. It was written all over the seventy-eight-year-old grandmother's sweet face. And she didn't care if Sebastian was glaring daggers at her. He could go stay at a hotel if he didn't like it.

Although it would be the second time in a day that she'd asked him to do just that. But there had to be some kind of compromise that would work for everyone. The last thing she wanted was for a government agency to step in and take a boy away from an obviously loving home.

She and Sebastian would be sleeping in the same bed next Monday when her father came to visit. Why not extend that a little bit, since their patient's surgery would be in two weeks, right about the time her dad went back home. It couldn't hurt to ask.

Right. She had a feeling it was going to hurt at least a little once she left this house.

If not physically then emotionally, because Sebastian was probably going to let her have it with both barrels.

But what else could she do? If the patient didn't get the surgery she needed, she might die of infection at some point. And if she didn't feel secure in thinking her grandson would be well taken care of, then she might refuse to go through with it. No, Sebastian was going to agree to this. The same way that she'd agreed to this cockamamie marriage. And if he didn't, then she was going to make sure the next two weeks were some of the most miserable of his life.

CHAPTER EIGHT

THEY'D NEEDED THE BREAK.

At least that's what Sebastian had told her. She had an idea this was more for his benefit than for hers. But it didn't matter. She was going to be traveling to the top of a really tall building. Again.

But at least there hadn't been one of those freaky window-washer contraptions strapped to the outside of the Edifício de Banespa.

Evidently people were only allowed five minutes at the lookout area and then had to leave. Even so, there was a line of people waiting to go up in the elevator. A lot of them were couples or lovers. In fact, everywhere she looked there were people linking arms or caught up in their own world. Not her and Sebastian. After the busy day spent in the *favela,* she had gone home, showered and gone to sleep almost immediately. They had the day off today, so he'd suggested they come here.

He probably just didn't want to be home alone with her. And that was a good idea. Less chance of things taking a wrong turn. Again.

"Ten people, please." The elevator doors had opened and the guard was ushering sightseers into the elevator. He counted down until he reached Sebastian. "Ten. You're the last one, sir."

"We're together. I'll wait."

And it was true. They were together, but not by choice.

Except it had been, or she wouldn't be standing in a line with this man and wearing a gold band on her finger. Her thumb went to the back of it, sliding back and forth over the smooth surface.

The guard found a single person to take the last spot. Suddenly she envied that young man. He could just go up there and not worry about a partner. Or whether he regretted taking the leap that she had. One that was changing a lot more than just her name.

Her father was coming in less than a week, and they had a photo shoot to get through before that. "It could be worse," she muttered.

Sebastian tilted his head. "What could be worse?"

"Just thinking about the timing of the photo shoot. It would be worse if my dad were here, because he'd want to see us do it."

His mouth ratcheted up. "I don't think that's a requirement for marriage any more."

"Oh!" Her face flamed with heat. "I didn't mean that."

"I know what you meant." He paused, his smile fading. "Have you thought about how you want to break the news to him?"

"No, but I guess we should sit down and make some kind of plan."

"You're going to wait until he arrives?"

"I hadn't really thought about it. Do you think I should tell him before he gets here?" How big a shock would it be to arrive and find them sleeping in the same room? Probably a pretty big one. "Are you going to tell your parents?"

His lips tightened. "No."

"Not at all?" Shock and—yes, she could admit it—a tinge of hurt came over her at the cold way he'd said the word. He'd mentioned his parents didn't have a happy marriage. Was he afraid that they would be upset over his choice? Or did he just not care what they thought?

"Not at all. They won't ever visit, so there's no reason to."

"And what about their grandchild? Will you keep that from them too?"

Just then the elevator opened and people from another group exited. "The next ten, please."

Saved by the bell. Or the elevator. They all piled in, the fit a little tighter than she expected it to be. She tried to shift her bag in front of her and ended up elbowing the man beside her in the stomach. He gave a sharp *"Mmph"*.

"So sorry," she murmured.

The doors closed with an ominous whoosh, and people jostled each other, trying to find an extra inch or two of space. Sara, on the other hand, stood stock still, too afraid to move.

A sense of claustrophobia prickled along her spine, sending shards of discomfort spiraling into her brain. It sent a message back: escape!

Only there was nowhere to run. *Deus.* Her heart rate sped up. What had she been thinking, letting him talk her in to coming here? They weren't even at the top and she was already a bundle of nerves.

She twisted around, needing to reassure herself

that he was there, as steady and calm as always. She couldn't remember seeing him frazzled. Ever. Even when she'd told him she was pregnant, he hadn't gone off at the deep end and flipped out like she would have expected him to do.

There he was. That rock-solid body and deep brown eyes.

When his glance met hers he frowned, his head tilting in question. She was being ridiculous. But when she turned back to face the ticking numbers, an arm snaked around her waist, drawing her into his narrow circle, back from the crush of people. And just like that her heart slowed its frantic pace and the buzzing in her skull turned into the lull of background noise. She leaned her head back against his chest in relief, allowing the warmth of his body to seep through her. His arm tightened further, and she slid her hands over it, afraid he might let go.

A minute later the doors opened and people spilled out onto the concrete surface of the viewing area, all of them anxious to see as much as possible in the five minutes they were allotted.

"Thank you," she said in a soft voice as she pulled out of his embrace. "It was a little close in there."

His hand slid down to grip hers. "I thought you were about to ask me to boost you up to the hatch in the ceiling."

"There was an escape hatch? Now you tell me." She grinned up at him, startled when something dark went through his eyes. His fingers released their hold.

"I always make sure there's a way out."

Was he talking about elevators? Or relationships?

Had her ex-boyfriend done that same thing? Had his escape been planned the whole time?

It was probably better not to think about that. What if Sebastian decided he wanted no part of fatherhood after the baby was born? Or when he or she was five years old? Ghosting her as easily as her ex had. After all, São Paulo and Rio Grande do Sul were several states apart. How long before the traveling back and forth to see his child became a chore, and the visits ground to a halt? Or if he chose to remarry and start another family with someone else?

The thought had her struggling to catch her breath.

Before she could walk away, though, he reached for her hand again and gripped it tight, holding her in place.

"What?"

"If you thought my apartment was high, this is even higher. How close do you want to get to the edge?"

Okay, she had remembered that, and yet she hadn't. Her body relaxed, thankful to have something else to fix her thoughts on. "How many flights of stairs are there?"

"More than you want to think about."

"Great." She took a deep breath. "Okay, how close do *you* want to go?" As long as he was holding her hand, she would be fine, right?

"I want to go all the way to the edge and back, but I'm willing to restrain myself if that's not what you want."

A shiver went over her. Why did she keep hearing double meanings behind everything? Maybe because the low thrum of his voice always gave her crazy ideas. Or maybe it was simply because she was at the top of a building, where the air was impossibly thin. Did she trust him? If he pulled her all the way to the guard rail, was she going to have a meltdown?

No. The way he'd held her in the elevator had made her feel safe. Protected. Just like the way he was holding her hand right now. Just like when he'd made love to her. "I don't want you to hold back. Let's go together."

He threaded his fingers through hers. "Okay. Together."

They walked over to the guard rail, and her free hand clenched around it.

"Still okay?"

She hadn't quite trusted herself to look yet. "I think so."

"Here." He moved around behind her and wrapped his arms around her middle, just like he had on the ride up. Her unease disappeared almost immediately.

"I love it up here," he murmured, his chin coming to rest on the top of her head.

She allowed her eyes to focus and…

Oh, boy.

The view was horrifying and beautiful all at once. As far as the eye could see, there were buildings upon buildings upon buildings.

The ranching town where she came from had apartment complexes, but nothing like these. Nothing like this gorgeous *vista*. She didn't look down. Instead, she kept her gaze pointed toward the horizon. "You said we could see Vista do Vale from here."

"Yes, the condo is…" His voice paused for a second. "Just off to our right."

She turned slightly to the right, but everything was

one jumble of shapes that seemed to go on forever. "I don't see it."

"Let me see if I can show you." He shifted until his cheek was pressed tight to hers. "It's the cobalt and white building about ten blocks out and at your one o'clock. It's one of the tallest in the group."

She looked a little bit closer, using his instructions to narrow her search, except all she could concentrate on right now was the feel of his skin against hers. She started chanting inside her head: *Cobalt and white. Cobalt and white. Cobalt and...*

There, she could see it! "It looks so small from here."

His cheek scraped across hers as he nodded, the rough edge of his whiskers awakening nerve endings she'd rather remained dormant.

"Don't forget it's located in a valley and it's some distance away. Perspective can get skewed."

Yes, it could, because with him so close that his body seemed to enfold hers, she realized it would be far too easy to get used to this. To go from thinking of their marriage as a necessary evil to something that was comfortable and...exciting.

She breathed in deeply, his scent mixing with that of the city. São Paulo seemed to have soaked into his very pores. He was as grounded here as she was in Rio Grande do Sul.

She'd do well to remember that. She'd always known her move here wasn't meant to last forever. It was to help her learn ways to help people like her father.

Neither of them said anything for a few seconds as they continued to look out over the downtown area.

She did her best to enjoy these moments and not think about the future.

"How much time do you think we have left?"

If he had said seventeen months and twenty days she wouldn't have been surprised, but he didn't. "Only around two minutes."

"It's all going by so fast." A flash of sorrow hit her right between the eyes as she realized she meant that in more ways than one. "Right now I just want to stay here forever."

The warmth of his breath made wisps of her hair flutter. "Everything comes to an end. Or it should."

The cynicism behind those words made her ache inside. "Not everything. Not life. Love. The birth of children."

"Even those things don't last forever."

"The cycle does, though, don't you think?"

"Yes. Some of them. But they're usually the ones you don't want to continue."

A small commotion on the other side of the viewing area caught her attention. A huddle of people suddenly broke apart and a young man, maybe in his thirties, staggered out of their midst. His eyes were wide and terrified, face red. He slumped to the ground almost immediately. Someone screamed, "Daddy! What's wrong?" The words were in English and a tiny girl leaned over his chest, patting his face with chubby little hands.

Without a word, Sebastian released her and jogged toward the group, leaving her to hurry after him. Even before he got there, he was taking charge of the situation. He switched to English. "I'm a doctor. What has happened?"

A woman knelt down beside the girl, trying to pull her back, but it only caused her to wrench against the restraining hands and cry even harder. "I don't know! He just suddenly grabbed his throat as if he was trying to cough." The sheer panic in her voice was unmistakable.

Sebastian leaned over the man, putting his head to his chest. "Was he eating something?"

"Just this." The woman handed him a package that said "Soja Torrada"…toasted soybeans.

"Does he have allergies?"

"No. Not that I know of." Tears started pouring down her cheeks. "Can you help him?"

In an instant, Sara was at the man's head. Every second was critical. The man's breath wheezed in partially and then went silent. He'd stopped breathing.

The woman fell to her knees beside them, clutching the child to her chest. "Oh, God, someone do something!"

"Sara, tip his head to the side. I'm going to try something."

She did as he asked, instinctively turning him to face away from the mother and daughter.

Sebastian put one hand over the other, placing the base of his palms on the man's abdomen just under his chest. Already the victim's face was turning dark as his circulation pumped unoxygenated blood through his system.

Thrusting his joined hands sharply toward the man's diaphragm, while Sara made sure his mouth was open, the first attempt yielded nothing. By this time there was a crowd around them. Even the man from the elevator was there, no longer counting the minutes. He repeated the attempt, then a third time, his compression even harder. Something flew from the man's mouth and landed on the ground a few inches away. A nut.

Sebastian had been right.

Hoping the man would start breathing on his own, alarm swept through her system when he lay lifeless on the concrete. No rise or fall of his chest, no improvement in his color. It had been less than a minute since he'd collapsed.

Sebastian put his fingers against the man's neck. "I have a pulse, but it's weak."

Working as a team, they straightened his head, the oncologist beginning mouth to mouth while Sara counted the puffs of air as they went in. When they reached seven, Sebastian paused and listened. Still nothing.

"Do you want me to take over?"

"Just count." With that, he went back to breathing for the victim.

Come on. You can do it!

She wasn't sure if she was willing the words to Sebastian or to the man on the ground.

"Seven."

Pausing again, he lifted his head.

This time there was a weak gasp, and then another. Suddenly the man took a huge gulping breath. After the third one, his eyes fluttered, but they didn't open.

His wife—if the ring on her finger was any indication—grabbed his hand. "Max! Can you hear me?"

Still a little blue around the mouth, he barely nodded, then his eyes opened, seeking the woman and child immediately. One arm reached toward them.

Relieved murmurs went up all around them. One

person clapped and several others joined in. It was a little too soon to assume everything was going to be all right, though.

The man's mouth opened, but Sebastian stopped him with a quick shake of his head.

"Don't try to talk." He glanced up at the elevator attendant, who was standing a few feet away. "We need to take him down with as few people as possible. Can you have an ambulance waiting for us?"

"Yes, of course." The man walked a few steps away, speaking into a cellphone.

Sebastian turned toward the woman. "His name is Max?" His English was fluent and easy, while Sara struggled to keep up with the strange words.

"Yes. We're here on holiday." She gripped her husband's hand. "Is he going to be all right?"

When the child whimpered again, Sebastian reached over and tugged a lock of her blonde hair, giving her a reassuring smile. "He should be just fine. Don't worry, okay?"

The gesture made Sara's chest ache. Would he one day comfort their child like this? His words from a few minutes earlier came back to her, making the ache grow. Or would he walk away from them, thinking this was one of those cycles that should end?

He glanced at her. "I want just the family and us on that elevator. The fewer people the better."

"I'm…okay." The croaked words came from the man on the ground.

"You need to go to a hospital and get checked out. We work at one not far from here." He paused as if trying to gather his thoughts. "It's for the best."

"Max, you need to go," his wife said. "Please."

He gave a short nod, not trying to say anything else.

Already he had pinkened somewhat, but Sebastian was right. They needed to make sure he hadn't aspirated anything else. Even a tiny piece of food trapped in a person's lungs could cause inflammation or, worse, aspiration pneumonia.

The girl scrambled out of her mom's grip and landed on Max's chest, her small arms going around his neck. "Daddy. I love you!"

He returned her hug, his arms snug around her back, even though it was obvious his strength hadn't completely returned.

"Let's get you out of here. Do you think you can get up, if we help?"

Max glanced up at them and gave another nod. "Think so."

With Sara on one side and Sebastian on the other, they levered him up and slowly walked to the elevator, the crowd parting around them with more clapping.

She could only imagine the fear of being in another country and going through a crisis like this. Actually, she could imagine at least a little bit. Her own crisis wasn't life or death, but she was away from the only home she'd ever known, thrust into a strange city, and then discovered she was pregnant.

And what had been the result of all of that? Sebastian had attempted a metaphorical Heimlich maneuver, hoping to avert disaster for the program. Only unlike in Max's case, where the rescue attempt had worked, Sebastian might have unwittingly thrown them into a situation that was far worse. They would find out when her father came to visit. A tough old cowboy, he had an uncanny ability to see through people as easily as he could judge a steer. He'd warned her about her boyfriend, but she hadn't listened, too infatuated with the idea of love to pay attention to the warning signs. Until it had been too late.

Would her dad realize that this was just an act?

He would be devastated, if so.

They got onto the elevator, and although he tried to wave off their help, Sara kept her shoulder wedged under Max's arm. Sebastian did the same while his wife stood in front of him, still holding his daughter in one arm. She touched his face, murmuring to him in soft tones. He nodded yes or no to whatever she was saying.

Behind Max's back, Sebastian's hand touched Sara's elbow. She leaned her head back slightly to look over at him.

"Thank you," he mouthed.

There was something in his expression that made her stomach cramp. She sent him a nod and a slight smile.

When they arrived at the ground floor and the doors opened, there was indeed an ambulance waiting. The emergency crew came forward with a gurney, while Sebastian filled them in on what had happened and what he thought the prognosis was. There wasn't enough space for all of them to ride, and the trip through São Paulo wouldn't be a walk in the park anyway because of the huge amount of traffic. But this was no longer a life or death situation, so Sebastian didn't need to ride with them. He did give Max's wife his card, telling her to call him if they needed anything while they were at the hospital.

As they loaded her husband in through the doors,

she used her free arm to hug the oncologist, whispering something into his ear.

When the EMTs helped her and her child into the back of the ambulance, Sara came up to stand beside him. "What did she say?"

His jaw was tight, and he appeared to be battling some kind of raw emotion. "She said, 'You just saved my whole world.'"

Pinpricks needled the backs of Sara's eyes. "She loves him very much."

"So it seems."

She nudged him with her shoulder. "Still think everything comes to an end?"

"I'll have to get back to you on that."

The ambulance pulled away from the building and forced its way into the snarls of traffic, siren wailing and horn giving off long blasts of sound. Then they were swallowed up by the never-ending sea of vehicles. "They should be okay."

"Glad we went up?"

"Oh, yes. And very glad you didn't boost me up to that escape hatch. We were right where we were supposed to be."

He turned and looked at her, his expression unreadable. Then he leaned down and kissed her cheek. "Yes. We were."

CHAPTER NINE

SEVEN COUPLES WERE lined up outside the hospital, each of them awaiting their turn with the photographer. And Sebastian felt like the biggest kind of fraud. Every single one of these people thought their unions would last forever, judging from the arms casually slung around waists and subtle touches. His marriage, on the other hand, had an expiration date built right into it. Eighteen months. No more. No less.

He never in his wildest dreams imagined he would marry for the sake of a child.

Unlike his mom and dad, though, he refused to linger in a marriage built on the wrong motives. He'd told Sara the truth when they were at the top of the Banespa building. Oh, in the aftermath of that choking crisis yesterday, when Max's wife had murmured those heartfelt words to him, his world view had quaked in its foundations a time or two. But the old cynicism had returned.

Ha! But that sure hadn't stopped him from coming to this photo shoot and pretending to "love the one he was with". And Sara didn't look any happier about the arrangement. She was standing with her eyes focused on the ground, not even looking at the poses the first couple was given.

He couldn't blame her. There was mushiness right and left, along with a lot of gazing into each other's eyes.

What the hell had he been thinking, agreeing to any of this? He was not cut out to smile and pretend. He was…stoic. That was how he saw himself. None of the histrionics that had gone on in his childhood home. In fact, the quieter and more invisible he became, the better it was for everyone. Especially his sister, who had been fragile for most of her teenage years because of the cancer. He'd protected her from a lot of the drama. At least, he hoped he had.

Maybe that's why he'd been so quick to jump in and offer marriage to Sara. That protective instinct had never been totally snuffed out.

In fact, it was kicking in right now like it had yesterday, when they'd talked about escape hatches and when he'd held her out on that balcony. Pressed his cheek against hers.

It had all felt too good. Too real.

But it wasn't real. He needed to remember that.

He leaned down and whispered, "We can just leave, if you want." To hell with what the hospital administrator wanted. There could just be one less picture in their precious promotional article.

"It's already too late."

At least, that's what he thought she'd said. The words had been so soft, he couldn't be completely sure.

Too late for what?

"Are you feeling okay?"

She motioned him over to the side. "Remember

when you asked me about my dad? And you asked if I was going to tell him before he got here? Well, I decided to go ahead. So I told him. About the baby. About us."

Okay, he wasn't sure what that meant. She'd told him the truth? Or she'd given him their cover story?

"He knows what, exactly?"

"Well, it would be kind of awkward for him to get here and say, 'Oh, by the way, I'm sharing a bed with the man who was your doctor.'"

Ah, okay, so that answered that. She'd told him that they were married.

"What was his reaction?"

Her head cocked to the side. "He was happy. Horribly, terribly happy."

The words "horribly" and "terribly" fit the situation. But to put them together with "happy"? That just seemed like an oxymoron. "In other words, he bought the story."

"That's what I just said."

Another couple was called to the forefront. Sebastian had no idea where they were in the queue.

"So that's a good thing, then. It should make his visit a piece of cake."

"No." She looked at him like he'd lost his marbles. "He is going to expect me to be like him and Mom. And—and—" Moisture rimmed her eyes, just like it had yesterday. Only this was for completely different reasons. And he'd caused it. All of it.

Damn! In trying to help her, he had made things infinitely worse. Which was why she'd said it was too late. It was done. And they were stuck.

Except that in eighteen months she was going to

have to go through the explanations all over again. And he doubted her father would be quite as happy.

Unless they chose to stay married.

Um, no. Then he *would* be following in a set of footsteps that he despised.

"It'll be okay, Sara. We'll figure this out." He put his arm around her shoulders.

"Sebastian and Sara Texeira?" The call cut through the air like a knife and every head turned in their direction.

Hell, could this day get any worse?

He unhooked his arm from around her and linked their hands—to keep up the pretense. "Let's get this over with," he muttered, trying his best to plaster a pleasant expression on his face. It wasn't easy when every muscle in it felt stiff and frozen.

A second later, Sebastian was seated on a little stool with Sara standing behind him, her fingers curled like claws into his shoulders.

"Can I get a smile from the bride?" The photographer's mop of black hair flopped to the side as he peered out from behind his camera.

A few seconds later, a titter of nervous laughter came from those still in the arca. Sebastian glanced up and over his shoulder to see what Sara was doing. Oh, Lord. Her lips were cranked skyward in the most unnatural expression he had ever seen. And that sexy bottom lip was nowhere to be seen.

The photographer got up and made his way toward them. "Okay, it's normal to be nervous. Maybe we'll try something without a smile."

"I'm sorry…" Sara started, only to have the man

give her a wide grin that was much more spontane-ous. A little too spontaneous, if you asked Sebastian.

Sebastian's frown grew when the photographer came up beside her, using cupped palms to tilt her head downward and to the right. "We'll just have you look at each other, how's that?" His hands kept fiddling with her pose, touching her arm here. Her waist there.

When he leaned a little too close, steam gathered in Sebastian's head.

Camera boy was beginning to really get under his skin. Did he know she was pregnant? Was he even an adult? He looked like a gangly kid from where he was sitting.

"Dr. Texeira, can you kind of peer over your shoul-der at your wife?"

He did as he was asked, seeing the nerves still alive in Sara's face. He reached up and laid his hand over one of hers to reassure her.

"Yes, that's it. Hold it just like that."

Sebastian nodded at her and tightened his grip just a touch, feeling her relax, a lock of hair falling over her shoulder. With the sun behind her, she looked soft and radiant and—beautiful.

And there was that lip. Puckered just right.

At that second, he heard the tell-tale click of the camera. It went again and again, as they stared at each other.

Her eyes. Her upturned nose.

That sexy mouth.

"Okay." The sharp clap of the man's hands broke through whatever had been holding him in place, and he blinked.

Swallowed.

Sara took her hands off his shoulders and shoved the errant lock back over her shoulder.

"Let's try something a little different."

Sebastian frowned. "You mean we're not done?"

"I want just a couple more shots, and then I'll let you pick one to take home with you." He studied them for a second or two. "Why don't we have—Sara, wasn't it?"

When she nodded, he continued, "Sara, why don't you come and sit on your husband's lap."

"Excuse me?"

"Here." When the man acted like he was going to reach for her hips, Sebastian pre-empted him by gripping them and tugging sharply. She tumbled onto his lap, her arms going around his neck to keep from careening onto the ground.

Their cheeky photographer just laughed. "That's it. Just like that. Hold it."

Sebastian's right arm anchored her in place, while the man studied them from a couple of different angles. When she whispered, "I'm going to kill you," he just smiled.

"Better that than me killing that damned photographer." He kept his voice low enough so that only she heard him.

As if on cue, the guy was back, standing directly behind Sara, tilting her head back and resting it against his abdomen for a second. The muscles in Sebastian's neck went stiff with rage. This was no longer cheeky. It was unprofessional and inappropriate. When his gaze clashed with the photographer's the man's eyes widened slightly, and he took a step back. "That should do."

He took three more pictures, and Sebastian had to

give it to the man. Inappropriate or not, he knew exactly how to play up Sara's features. With her head tilted back, the long line of her neck was on display. Her hair fell in a curtain that went past his hip, almost touching the ground. Her eyes were closed, probably from embarrassment, but to a casual observer it probably looked like she was waiting for his lips to slide over her throat. And if they had been alone, he would have been tempted to do just that. He would have bent over her and used his mouth to—

"Okay, that's it. Thank you."

Sebastian almost groaned aloud. Parts of him had woken up unexpectedly, putting him in an awkward position. Sara's back came up as she straightened and her hip pressed hard against him. Air hissed through her lips, and she jerked around to stare at him. She'd felt his reaction.

Lord, how could she *not* feel it?

Her brown eyes crinkled at the edges.

"Can you get up?" Her voice shook slightly as if holding back laughter. Oh, she thought this was funny, did she?

"What do you think?"

"I think you already are." She popped off his lap, leaving him to somehow uncurl his body in a way that didn't reveal exactly what this little photo shoot had cost him. To his surprise, Sara stood in front of him, giving him a chance to collect his senses and put his life—or rather his body—back into some semblance of order.

"If you'll go over to the computer and take a look at the shots, while I get the next couple set up, that would be *bacana*. They're right on the monitor in the order they were taken. Just select the number beside the image you like best and write it on the card with your name."

They actually had to look at the photos? Great. But at least it gave him a chance to send blood flowing back into his head, rather than pooling in his groin.

They moved over to where the camera was set up. The shots were there, just like the man had said.

"Do you have a preference?"

When he glanced over, Sara was staring out at the landscape.

He chuckled. "You might actually have to look at the screen in order to choose."

"Ugh, I can't."

So he did it for her, and what he saw took his breath away. That stilted grin picture was there, but as soon as his eyes tracked to the first posed shot, he knew the photographer had done his job a little too well. The ones of her behind him showed a loving couple gazing deeply into each other's eyes. One right after the other, the angle of the camera lens changing just slightly between those three shots. When he came to the images of her on his lap, his throat tightened.

He'd thought she was beautiful when she was standing up? These pictures were magazine-worthy. Sebastian was staring down at her, his lips curved just slightly. And she looked totally lost in the moment, carefree and happy, one of her legs lifted off the ground to help her keep her balance. He remembered those long slender calves wrapped around his waist less than a week ago.

Damn. He wanted it. Wanted her. All over again.

"This one." He tapped the monitor.

As if fighting an inner battle, her eyes swung toward the screen. Her hand went to her throat. *"Misericórdia."*

Have mercy? It should have been him asking for mercy.

"Do you think your dad will believe it now?"

"*I* almost believe it." As if realizing what she'd said, she glanced quickly at him. "You're a very good actor."

He hadn't been acting. And in the shot he'd chosen—the very first of the lap pictures—he could still see a trace of the anger in his face over the photographer's hands being on her. He was almost in a swooping position, ready to protect what was his.

Only she wasn't.

And he'd better not start wishing she was, because he was the last person she needed. She deserved someone who actually believed in love and fairy tales. Who wasn't afraid to show emotions like anger and frustration. Who wouldn't always wonder if he'd married her for herself—or because of what he'd done to her. Didn't they used to call that "doing the honorable thing"?

There was no honor in marrying for that reason.

Irritated at himself for even letting his thoughts wander in that direction, he scribbled the number down on the card. "I think we're both pretty good actors when we want to be. One more task to cross off the list."

He stood up, his body once more firmly under control, and he flipped the card onto the small stack of cards of the couples who were already finished with their photo shoot.

Well, so was he. He was finished. And *pelo amor de Deus*, he'd better damn well remember that.

* * *

They weren't the only ones who'd chosen that picture. The day her dad was to arrive, a huge publicity poster appeared in the entryway of the hospital. Perched on an easel, it proclaimed:

Hospital Santa Coração:
A place where hearts are healed—
and love is found.

And the image at the very center of the poster was their lap dance.

Heavens, had Sebastian seen this yet? She hoped not, although how could he have missed it, as he'd been called in early to treat a patient? Maybe they'd just put the poster up.

The pictures of the other smiling couples surrounded them, but it seemed the photographer had put them all in much more conventional poses, reserving the most embarrassing one for her and Sebastian. The guy had made her feel a little uncomfortable, but even worse was Sebastian's reaction to it. For a brief second, she'd wondered if he was jealous. And then there was his…*reaction*. A very physical kind of reaction. It had nudged her as she'd moved to get up, shocking her. She'd had her eyes firmly closed to block out the experience, because she'd felt a familiar tingling awareness when she'd stood behind him and he'd looked up at her with those sexy hooded eyes she loved so much.

Loved?

No, not loved. She was only thinking that because of that huge, glaring word on the poster. It was sending a subliminal message, burrowing into her brain like a screwworm.

No matter. In the three hours since Sebastian had left the apartment, she'd gotten her things and moved them into his bedroom. Thank God his bed was huge—larger than any bed she had ever seen before. She could just put a stack of pillows between them and it would be as if they each had their own island to sleep on. She would simply get dressed in the bathroom in the very unsexy garb she had purchased for just this occasion. Not that they would be tempted to do anything with her dad practically sleeping in the next room. She was being ridiculous.

Shaking herself back to awareness, she wandered over to the elevators, trying to keep her head down and hoping no one recognized her as she headed to her appointment. Although she looked totally different in that picture than she did in real life. At least she hoped she didn't carry around that besotted expression everywhere she went.

They were supposed to pick her dad up at the airport at five this afternoon. Sara had tried to convince Sebastian to just let her go on her own, but he'd insisted, saying her father would think it was strange if she arrived by herself.

"He'll just think you're working."

His brows had edged up. "But I'm not."

"But you could be."

They'd gone back and forth a few more times before she'd slumped into a chair in the living room. They'd finally compromised. He could go with her to pick up her father, but he wasn't allowed to go to the prenatal exam he'd talked her into.

She took a deep breath. It was going to be okay. Her dad was only going to be here for a week. Sebastian wanted to do a little blood work on him and check his cancer markers. He didn't expect there to be any changes, but it didn't hurt to do a quick check. "Thank you. I owe you."

He'd given her a strange frown she still didn't understand. It was almost as if she'd said the wrong thing. But that didn't make any sense. It was a figment of her imagination. Much like their marriage.

Within seconds the elevators shuttled her to the correct floor, where Natália stood waiting for her. She swooped in for a quick hug.

"Hey, *moça linda*, how's married life treating you?"

God, she felt like such a liar. This was Sebastian's sister and one of her closest friends. "Oh, you know. We're still trying to figure things out, just like any other married couple."

"Okay, then," was all she said. Natália didn't believe her—and who could blame her? As someone who was also recently married she probably saw right through the sham. Or had Sebastian already told her it was all a farce?

"Are you sure it's not too soon to do this?"

"Nope. If you're eight weeks, we should be able to see something. Maybe even the heartbeat, if we're really lucky."

She nodded, following her down the hallway, doing some quick calculations in her head. She'd been in São Paulo for… "Maybe a couple of days over eight weeks."

"I thought so. That was right about the time of my and Adam's wedding. I had no idea you and Sebastian even knew each other that well."

Squirming inside, all she could do was nod again. "We went out to get a few drinks after the wedding and things just…happened." No need to mention the reasons behind it.

"I know how it is. I have to admit I feel a little bit responsible. Sebastian wasn't himself once he found out about me and Adam. He was still acting out of sorts and moody at the wedding."

What was she trying to say? "We're both adults. He didn't take advantage of me, if that's what you're implying."

"Oh, God, no. Sebastian could be raging drunk and he would never lose control of himself."

That was funny, because Sara remembered them both being kind of out of control. Although Natália was right. She couldn't really recall many times when he'd totally lost it. Hmm. The night they'd had sex in his bedroom *could* be considered one of those times. And then when the pictures were being taken. And— It didn't matter. It was what it was. There was no wishing that things were different. They weren't and they never would be. He'd made that perfectly clear.

And Sara was fine with that. She had to be.

She decided to change the subject. "Can you do the ultrasound yourself?"

"I can. It might be better if you and an OBGYN do it, but I should be able to find something. We'll take a traditional pregnancy test as a back-up, just in case."

Ten minutes after Sara had peed into a cup, she found herself lying on a table, ultrasound wand gliding across her belly. "Let's just see if we can find little Billy."

Sara rolled her eyes, trying to act nonchalant about the whole thing. "How do you know it's not a girl?"

"I don't. Billy can be a girl or a boy's name." The wand hit a ticklish spot, making her squirm. It then went back over the same spot.

"Are you doing that on purpose?" She choked out a laugh. "Let's change places and see how well you like it."

The second the words were out of her mouth, her laughter died a hard death. "I'm sorry. I didn't mean that."

There was silence for a couple of beats, then her friend smiled. "It's okay. I came to terms with the fact that I can't have children a long time ago. Actually, we're thinking of adopting at some point."

"That's wonderful." She shifted on the table.

"Let's try the left side." When Natália changed her location, she went "Bingo" within seconds. "There, do you see?"

Her friend pointed at a small blob on the screen, then fiddled with something, moving the transponder again. "Oh, Sara, look."

"Is something wrong?" Had she found some kind of horrible deformity?

"Nothing is wrong. Your baby's heart is beating."

She stared at the monitor, straining to find what the neonatologist was talking about. Then she saw it. A tiny quick movement. Rhythmic. Continuous.

A heart.

Her own swelled, and she was afraid to look away for fear that little flutter on the screen would suddenly stop. "Is it okay?" she whispered.

"As far as I can tell, everything is perfect. You need to have a real examination, though."

"I will." She swallowed, suddenly overwhelmed. "Okay, I've seen enough. Thank you."

Natália switched the machine off and the screen went dark. She had to bite her lips not to ask her to find the baby again. It was okay.

There really was a baby in there.

Her friend wiped the gel off her abdomen and pulled the gown back down.

"Thank you." She hesitated. "Could you come up here, please, if you're all done?"

"Sure thing." She moved to stand by her shoulder. "Do you feel better now?"

"Yes, a little. Can I sit up?" When Natália nodded, Sara jammed herself upright. "I can't believe I'm really pregnant."

"You really are, according to your body. But, then, you already knew that, didn't you? It's why you got married."

She put her legs over the side of the exam table, her hands clasped in her lap. "He told you."

Rather than continuing to stand, Natália hopped on the table beside her. "He didn't have much of a choice. I was all over him about marrying so quickly."

"He was trying to protect his project, and actually protect me too. He thought maybe they would remove me from the team if they thought there was any kind of impropriety."

"Instead you ended up getting roped into the Dia dos Namorados campaign."

She examined her toenail polish to keep from having to look directly at her friend. "That was a hoot, let me tell you."

"I bet. I saw the poster downstairs. If I didn't know better, I would think you two were in love."

"The photographer somehow pulled stuff out of his hat that wasn't there. Some kind of airbrushing trick."

"With your skin, I would be very surprised if he had to do anything."

A scoffing sound came up from her depths. "I barely even know him, Natália."

"You're carrying his child."

"Last time I heard, you didn't have to know anyone at all to carry a child. There are lots of ways to get pregnant."

"Yes, there are. And yet you looked pretty darned happy to see that baby's heart beating."

"I was. I'm not sure why. I should be frantic. Or horrified." And yet she was none of those things. She hadn't had time to sit and think about it. Until right now when she'd seen living proof that a baby was growing inside her.

The only thing that horrified her was the thought of her dad figuring out that her marriage wasn't built on love but on convenience and self-interest. They'd taken the picture from the campaign and had it framed, putting it on the mantel like they'd talked about. Just something to reassure her dad that she was okay. That she *would* be okay.

And she would be, no matter what happened between her and Sebastian.

"I think my brother is a lucky man."

Shock rippled across her nerve endings. "We're not going to stay together, Natália."

"You don't know that for sure." Her friend gave her hand a squeeze.

"I do know. We set a date to divorce after the baby is born."

"Well, that's interesting." If Natália was surprised, she didn't let on. She just hopped off the table with an enigmatic smile. "Just remember. Plans change. So do people, if you give them some time."

Sara sighed and then got dressed before following the neonatologist to the door. Once there, she stopped for just a second or two and then gave a sad shrug. "Not these plans, Nata. And not these people."

CHAPTER TEN

SHE'D PUT A bunch of damned pillows down the center of the bed. Under the covers so they formed some kind of blockade.

Against what? Him?

Did she really think he couldn't just roll right over them and land on her side?

"This is more than ridiculous. You know that, right?"

Her muffled voice came from the far side of the mattress where she lay teetering on the edge. "I just didn't want to accidentally move to your side and crowd you."

"Crowd me. On a king-sized bed." Even he could hear the irony dripping from his voice. He was lying just on the other side of the barrier, but even if he stretched his arm as far as it could go, he wouldn't be able to reach her. And that was probably the point. But she couldn't stay there all night. In those long flannel pajamas in the dead of summer.

Her father's flight had been delayed twice before finally landing at almost midnight. They hadn't had much time to talk. Used to rising at the crack of dawn, the older man had dozed most of the car ride back to the condo. Once there, he was tired enough that he'd kissed his daughter and shaken Sebastian's hand with muttered congratulations.

The man hadn't asked a single question. About any of it. But he had no doubt that those would come tomorrow. Especially since they were scheduled to do blood work and a quick health check. And then he and Sara were supposed to head over to Tres Corações to meet with Talita, whose surgery had been moved up by a week. Natália and Adam had agreed to take care of Jorge until his grandmother got out of the hospital. Thank God, because he didn't think he would be able to survive having Jorge and Sara's dad here at the same time.

"I move around a lot in my sleep."

Yes, he knew she did. He'd slept with her before.

And yet as much as he was ridiculing her, he had to admit she was all kinds of adorable with her dark hair flowing across the white of his sheets. He laid an arm across the mountain of pillows. Nope, couldn't reach her. But he could tease her. At least a little.

"I had to turn the air-conditioner way up. I don't normally wear this many clothes to bed." Actually, he didn't normally wear any. The pajama bottoms were for her benefit. He didn't think she would appreciate him coming to bed naked, even if she had seen him that way before.

She gave a weird cough. "It is kind of warm tonight, although Daddy thought it was chilly in the apartment. He doesn't use anything but fans at home. It's taken a little getting used to for me as well. The hospital I worked at before I came here had air-conditioning, but it was broken most of the time."

He propped his hands behind his head. "It sounds like you loved your life there."

"I did." She rolled over to look at him. "I always loved watching my dad rope steers. He always seemed so—strong, you know?"

He really didn't, since his dad had never been someone he'd looked up to. "He's still a strong man."

"It scared me, seeing where he was a year ago when the cancer caused him to break his leg. I thought he was ready to give up."

"But he didn't."

"Thanks to you and Natália." She scooted closer to the barricade and leaned up on her elbow, her long hair just touching the mattress. Now he could reach her, if he wanted to. He forced himself to stay where he was, content to hear the sound of her voice.

It was almost—normal. Was this what some couples did every night?

"It was all Natália. She was the miracle worker in this case. Her surgery was similar enough that it made your dad think he might have a good outcome as well."

"And he did."

"Yes, he did."

She fiddled with the fabric on one of the center pillows. "I appreciate everything you've done for us. His surgery. My position here at the hospital."

He didn't like where this conversation was headed. The last thing he wanted from her was her gratitude. It made him wonder things like whether she'd slept with him the night of the wedding because she'd been trying to pay a debt.

No, she wasn't like that. And since she was a nurse, it was unlikely that she'd been indulging in a little bit of hero-worship. He'd never encouraged that with patients, and he knew the boundaries that needed to be set and kept. So what had happened with Sara?

He'd gotten good and drunk. And she'd been so beautiful, carrying an air of vulnerability that he hadn't understood. Still didn't, in all honesty. But beneath all of that lay a heat and fire he hadn't expected. It had consumed him that night. Burnt him alive.

The ashes were still glowing, waiting for the slightest breeze to tease them back to life. Even those silly chaste pajamas couldn't extinguish it. Or her attempt at a pillow levy bank.

Right on cue, something in his body stirred.

He moved, so that only the bridge of pillows was between them. "The program needed you. I needed you."

It was true. In more ways than one.

"And I needed it." She gave a heavy sigh, plumping the pillow beneath her hands. "The opportunity came at just the perfect time."

He could barely see her over that damned mountain she'd created.

"Don't you think this is idiotic? We're expecting a child together."

"It just seems kind of funny with my dad in the same house." She lifted her head a little higher to peer over the pillows at him.

"He's not right next door. And the rooms in this place are pretty damned soundproof. He couldn't hear you if you screamed the place down."

She blinked at him. "Why would I do that?"

"Guess." Parts of him lifted higher than ever. "I know exactly what you sound like."

"Sebastian!" Her voice was a shocked whisper.

"He can't hear you. But if you prefer to play it safe…"

All of a sudden he didn't want safe. He wanted dangerous. And forbidden. And the woman lying less than a foot away was even more beautiful than when he'd first laid eyes on her.

"Play it safe?"

Did he hear a glimmer of disappointment? All he knew was that he wanted to go down this road just a little further. Tease her just a little bit more.

He reached under the covers and plucked one of the pillows, sending it sailing over the side of the bed. The first brick in her flimsy little fortress—gone. "Safe—as in if we're very, very quiet, your dad won't hear us at all."

She squeezed the pillow she held tighter. "I don't remember either of us being all that quiet."

Parts of him were now pulsing, demanding he listen.

"I'm always up for a challenge." He reached over and took the pillow from her and tossed it behind him, putting them face to face. "How quiet can you be? I bet I can come without making a single sound."

Her loud gasp made him chuckle. "Oh, not good. You're already failing the first part of the experiment."

Reaching out, his fingers encircled her wrist and tugged her onto the pillows, flipping her on her back. "But I can think of a very, very good use for these. And it has nothing to do with keeping us apart and everything to do with bringing us together."

With that his head came down, and he found her mouth, taking it in a kiss that seared his own senses, even as she squirmed to get closer.

He wanted her. Father or no father. The fact that she was carrying his child made it even sweeter.

Fingers swiftly parted the buttons on her pajama top and his lips moved to the first of the pink nipples he'd uncovered. Sucking it hard, he relished the way her back arched as she pushed toward him. The tiny moan she gave turned him to molten lava, making him release his hold to look down at her. "Shh. I need this. And I think you do too."

Straddling her hips, he gathered her wrists in one hand and carried them over her head. "You do, don't you?" He whispered the words against her lips. "Need this as much as I do?"

She gave a single nod. "But please be quiet."

"I will." He stretched out on top of her and parted her legs, pressing himself hard against the heart of her, "I guarantee it. But I can gag you, if you're worried about yourself."

Sara bit her lip when he ground against her again. Then she leaned up and kissed the side of his mouth. "I won't be the one making any sounds."

"It's too late. You already did."

The back and forth whispering was intimate. Sexy. And his body was aching for her. Mouth against her ear, he slid slightly to the side, leaving just enough room for one hand to skate down her still-flat tummy and edge beneath the elastic of her bottoms. He went past her panties, and curved around until he was just where he wanted. She was hot. Wet. And he'd done almost nothing except talk.

Well, he was all done talking. Sitting up, he stripped her of her bottoms, laying her bare to his gaze.

Deus! He didn't ever remember being this hot for a woman.

His fingers moved up to her face, then captured

a strand of her hair. He drew the blunt end down her nose and across her lips, which parted. His erection twitched and strained.

"Time to make good use of these pillows." He stacked them three high, while she watched. "Now. Come here, Sara."

As soon as she got on her knees, he took her pajama top and slid it down her arms before moving behind her. His fingers trailed down her spine, curving up under arms and cupping her breasts. "So perfect." He squeezed the nipples, leaning down to bite the side of her neck. She gave a tiny whimper, not much louder than their whispered talk had been. But it was enough to tell him it was time.

"Lie over the pillows, baby." He put a hand between her shoulder blades and applied slight pressure. She obliged, her body aligning perfectly so that her hips were elevated, while her torso lay flat on the mattress. His hands squeezed those perfect ass cheeks, before moving up to grip her hips, one hand going down to release himself.

Taking a second to position himself, he found that moist heat he'd discovered earlier.

Bracing himself, he thrust home, burying himself inside her silky flesh.

That tiny whimper came again. He leaned over, pressing his front to her back and scooting his hands underneath her. One at that tight puckered nipple and the other at the nub of flesh at the V of her legs. He flicked both, pulling his hips back and then plunging forward once again. Her breath rasped in and out as he repeated the act. He couldn't hold it together much longer. Not any longer, in fact.

Changing tack, he gripped her nipple between his thumb and forefinger and began a rhythmic squeeze that matched his thrusts. He buried his lips in the hair at her nape as her whimpers grew more frantic. "I love the way you squeeze me. Like this." He tightened his fingers around her in both places, still pumping hard and fast. And just like that she fell apart around him, her body convulsing as she buried her face in the mattress and made all kinds of sexy muffled sounds. Unable to stop himself, he plunged deep and let the ecstasy take hold, pouring everything he had into her, teeth gripping the soft skin of her neck.

He was done. Completely done.

Satiated, he lay there and took stock of the situation. He heard no movement from any part of the apartment. No sense that they'd been discovered. Sara's back was soft and supple, her muscles completely relaxed.

Maybe he wasn't so done after all.

They could have fun with this. A whole lot of fun.

He pulled out, smiling as she gave a breathed protest. He licked the spot on her neck that he'd just bitten. "Don't worry. We're not finished." With that, he flipped her onto her back, hips still elevated by the pillows. "But let's try it this way this time."

With that, he lifted her to his mouth and watched as he got ready to ravish her all over again.

She loved him.

Sitting across from him at the breakfast table, she felt the same trill of fear she'd felt last night as she'd listened to him sleep. Those deep easy breaths that had spelled total contentment. How was she going to give him up in eighteen months?

Maybe she didn't have to. He couldn't have made love like that without feeling something for her, right?

"Do you want some eggs, Daddy?" She held a plate out toward her father.

Sebastian had seemed distracted this morning. Oh, he talked easily enough with her dad, but it was almost clinical. He asked questions about his health as if he were any other patient.

And she'd caught her father glancing between her and Sebastian with open speculation in his eyes.

Surely he couldn't have guessed.

"Everything looks great, honey." He took the bowl and served himself a healthy portion. It made her smile. Breakfast had always been important in their house. Her dad worked long hours and claimed he needed food and plenty of it to sustain him throughout the day. In reality, Sara thought he did it because it made her mom so happy to cook for him.

A pang went through her heart. What would her mom think of her daughter's deceit?

She would be so disappointed. She was a firm believer in telling the truth whenever possible. Everything about Sebastian and her relationship had been built on a lie. From that time in the motel, when they'd both had too much to drink and she'd been looking for a way to ease her heartache, to their marriage, to those pictures and beyond.

Only what she'd felt for that lost boyfriend paled in comparison to how Sebastian made her feel.

Unbidden her eyes went to the mantel where that photo was on display. A sense of nausea slid up from nowhere, gripping her stomach and squeezing tight. She took a bite of toast.

"Everything okay, sweetheart?" Sebastian's voice carried a question. Only it too was a lie. Sweetheart? She wasn't his sweetheart. Maybe she would never be.

She forced a smile. "Fine." She took another tiny bite, hoping the dryness of the bread would soak up whatever pool of acid was forming in her belly. She swallowed. Then gulped again when it did nothing but add to her troubles.

"I'll tell you the truth. I was mighty surprised to hear that you two had gotten married. Especially since Sara's last boyfriend was a big city man as well. Although I think that one knows better than to ever show his face at the ranch again."

"Dad!" She was horrified that he was even talking about this right now.

"What? I'm just glad to see that there are still some good men out there. And I'm sure you got married for the right reasons."

Her eyes shot to Sebastian's, who laid down his fork a little too carefully. "I think it was."

She almost snorted. Of course he thought it was. He'd been saving his project.

"Love shows up when you least expect it, though, isn't that right?" her dad went on.

This time Sebastian didn't even attempt to answer. Didn't attempt to even pretend that their marriage was based on that particular emotion. Her heart squeezed so tight she could barely breathe.

She needed to stop this. Now.

"Daddy, I think you're embarrassing him."

Her husband's eyes met hers. Cool and indifferent. As if last night had never happened. "Not at all."

"Sorry if I'm speaking too plainly. She's my only child. I want to make sure she's happy."

Happy. Now, there was a fickle word. And what a difference twelve hours could make.

"I understand."

"Adding a baby so soon will add some stress, but I know you two can work through it." Her dad smiled at her. "Your mom wanted more children, but you were it for us."

Why was he saying this? Her hand went to her belly in a protective gesture.

Sebastian saw it, his gaze hardening slightly. "Lots of people only have one child."

"Yes, they do. But it was the one thing that Dalia wanted that I couldn't give her. Even after thirty years of marriage, it was still hard for her to accept. I would have sold my soul to give it to her."

"Oh, Daddy, she loved you for you."

"I wasn't perfect. I think sometimes she just stayed with me because of you."

An odd sound came from the other side of the table. She glanced over to see that Sebastian's jaw was rigid, white lines forming on either side of his mouth.

"That's not true." She said it in a rush, trying to circumvent a disaster in the making. She remembered Sebastian talking about his parents and how they had stayed married for the sake of the children. "You two loved each other very much."

"Yes, you're right, of course." He forked up a bite of eggs and chewed for a minute or two, looking at her with a frown. "I'm sorry, this has nothing to do with your relationship. I know you'll have a long, happy marriage just like your mom and I did."

Her husband picked up his fork again and stabbed at a piece of ham on his plate. He said nothing. Didn't try to reassure her father, didn't try to reassure her. Because there was nothing he could say without tossing one more lie onto an already stinking pile.

If anything, he seemed to be studiously trying to avoid looking at either of them.

In that moment, Sara realized it was hopeless. They were not going to have a long, happy marriage. Because he didn't love her. It was never going to happen. She was pretty sure her dad might even realize that. He'd hurled those barbs like little jokes, but they'd caught at Sebastian's throat and given him a bad case of laryngitis. Maybe it was better that he didn't try to defend his actions.

Her nausea increased fourfold and her gaze returned to that picture. How carefree she'd looked in it with her head thrown back and her husband smiling down at her as if he—as if he loved her.

Only he didn't. He'd as much as admitted it.

Her eyes pricked with tears. She'd been living in a fantasy world. Oh, not at first. She'd sworn she could handle this fake marriage and all it entailed. Sebastian had sure been able to.

Her dad had it all wrong. They'd married for the worst of reasons. It hadn't even been about the baby. It had been trying to save both of their asses from the possible consequences of their actions. Consequences that might not have even come to pass. They should have just confessed and let the chips fall where they may.

And now she'd committed the ultimate sin. She'd fallen in love with the man.

And in seventeen months—if they even made it that

long—he would walk away from her without a second glance. Just like her ex had.

"Hey, you two." Her dad was looking from her to Sebastian. "Did I commit some kind of faux pas? I'm not really acquainted with the rules in the big city."

Sebastian laid his fork down once again. "Of course you didn't. I just have a big case I'm working on that has taken all my energy. In fact, if you'll excuse me, I need to get to the hospital."

"Of course." Her dad stood to his feet. "I think Sara was going to take me to see some tall building that she says will give me a great view of the city."

"The Edifício do Banespa." Her husband's glance landed on her, before skipping away. "Yes, it has a great view."

A great view. He could have been talking about any normal building. There was no mention of how he'd held her tight against him during that long elevator ride. Or how he'd pressed his face close to hers as they'd looked for this very building.

Who was she kidding? He *was* talking about just another building. Because that was all it was to him.

She had to close her eyes for a moment to fight to keep the contents of her stomach inside her. Seventeen months?

There was no way. She wouldn't last that long.

Sebastian would guess the truth long before then. Hadn't he realized how scared she'd been on that trip to the top? He would realize she loved him in a month, if not sooner.

And it would drive him away long before she was ready.

What choice did she have?

She could leave.

She could wait a week or so after her father left and then she would follow him—tell him that she realized she really had married Sebastian for the wrong reasons. He would be devastated, but he would get over it. Just like she would.

She followed them to the door, plastering a fake smile on her face that resembled the macabre grin she'd had in the first picture of the photo shoot. But nothing she tried made it look any more natural.

Because nothing about this situation was natural.

Sebastian would make a great father, and there was no way she would keep him from his child, despite her words in his office all those weeks ago.

Wow, had it only been weeks?

At the entrance, Sebastian leaned over and kissed her on the cheek, but the light touch seared like the branding iron her dad used on his steers, and she jerked away from it.

"See you when I get home," he said.

"Sounds good. Drive safely." The words had a sour taste as they came out of her mouth.

Oh, God, how was she going to sleep in that bed again after all they'd done in it?

She didn't know, but she'd better figure it out. Or else she needed to confess the truth to her dad and get out long before then.

Maybe even before Sebastian came home from work.

He closed the door behind him without a backward glance.

Yes. She and her father could just leave. Go to the

Banespa building. Look at the city, and then over lunch she'd lay it all out.

She could raise a child alone. People did it all the time. And she was positive there were plenty of people who loved someone who didn't love them back. This was her second time around that particular block.

Knowing it didn't make it any easier, though.

Her dad glanced over, his smile fading in a hurry. He wrapped his arm around her waist. "Sara, what is it?"

"Oh, Daddy…" Turning, she buried her face in his familiar shoulder and burst into tears. Between sobs, she said, "I've made the biggest mistake of my life. I got pregnant. And he doesn't love me. He never has, and we just did this to save my job and his project, and it was never supposed to be real, but now it is. And I don't know what to do."

He didn't try to put a stop to the incoherent babbling or tell her to back up and start again. He just held her as she poured her heart out to him in a long stream-of-consciousness torrent. When she finally wound down, he took hold of her shoulders and held her away from him, studying her face.

"You love him."

"Yes, but didn't you hear me? He doesn't love me back. And he won't stay with me once this marriage runs its course." She didn't go into Sebastian's parents or how he hated that they'd stayed together in a loveless, bitter union. And that's what their marriage would turn into as well: a dry empty husk. Oh, the sex might keep him coming back for a little while, but it wasn't enough to build a real relationship.

And did she really want a man to stay with her just

for the pleasure he found in her body? Bile washed up her throat all over again.

No, that was not what she wanted. And that was not what she would settle for.

So, is this the end?

Yes, it was. And she'd better get used to it, because like Sebastian had said up at the top of the Banespa building.

Everything eventually came to an end.

Even their marriage.

CHAPTER ELEVEN

"ARE YOU SURE this place is safe?"

Sebastian had a new nurse.

And no wife.

"We'll be fine. The people we're treating aren't hit men." Irritation bubbled up in his throat, most of it directed at himself.

A month after coming home to an empty house, he still couldn't believe Sara had just walked away without saying a word. And when he'd tried to call her, Antônio had answered and bluntly told him not to call back until he figured it out.

Figured what out? He had no idea what the hell he'd even done wrong.

Really?

His behavior at the breakfast table had been atrocious, but he hadn't been able to stand listening to Mr. Moreira talk about how wonderful his marriage was and watch Sara sink further and further into herself. It was all Sebastian's fault. He'd practically shoved this marriage idea down her throat and forced her to go along with it. Had basically threatened her with losing her job if she didn't.

What kind of person did that?

His father, that's who. A man who lied and cheated and went to motels to have cheap sex with women he didn't love.

Sebastian had done exactly the same thing. And he'd compounded it by lying and cheating to get what he wanted: the Mãos Abertas project.

He'd gotten it. And lost his self-respect in the process. And a friend.

A friend?

Hell, he had no idea what Sara was to him.

It didn't matter in the end, because she was gone. He'd simply told Paulo Celeste that she'd gone home to help her father for a while. He hadn't elaborated any further than that. And surprisingly the man hadn't asked questions, he'd simply assigned him another nurse. Another punch to the gut. He could have avoided all of this.

And his baby?

That was still a huge unknown. Sara had told him he could be a part of the baby's life as long as he was sure he could be there for the long haul. Well, she must have changed her mind about that. There'd been no word on how either of them were doing.

Don't call back until you figure it out.

"What's the woman's name again?"

"It's right there in the chart." He fired the words at her and immediately regretted his attitude. It wasn't her fault he'd screwed up his life. He took one breath. Then another. "Sorry. Her name is Talita, and her grandson's name is Jorge."

He turned down the narrow street that led to her house, finding the crude board fence with ease. Maybe he needed to do something about that. Surely he could spend a few hours fixing up some things around her house. And it would give him something to think about besides his sorry state.

"Someone actually lives here?"

Something about the nurse's words made his hackles rise all over again. It wasn't all her fault. Santa Coração dealt with wealthy patients for the most part. This was a foreign world to many of them—to most of the staff as well. Besides Marcos and Lucas, there weren't many people who had actually spent a large amount of time in a *favela*.

Well, if she wanted to work with him, she'd better get used to it and fast. "Yes, someone does. Do you have a problem with that?"

His grouchy attitude was back with a vengeance.

"No. Of course not."

Well, at least he'd knocked a bit of the haughtiness from her voice.

He turned off the truck and got out. This was more of a courtesy call than anything. Talita had had a double mastectomy three weeks ago. She'd healed well, and the doctors told her she shouldn't have any more episodes of lipogranuloma.

She was still working on her blood sugar, which was why they were here.

At least, that's what Sebastian told himself.

"Do you want me to bring her chart?"

"Sure. Why not."

Veronica Cantor's mouth thinned, but she didn't say anything else as they arrived at the entrance and Sebastian clapped three times.

Within seconds, the door was thrown open by Jorge, who held his fist out for a teenage version of a handshake. Sebastian bumped his own against it with a smile. "How have you been?"

Jorge looked past him at the Mãos Abertas truck, probably looking for Sara. He hadn't said anything to Talita about the break-up, and he was swiftly realizing that coming here might not have been the best idea.

"Who is it?" The grandmother's voice came from inside the house.

"It's Dr. Sebastian and some..." Jorge looked the nurse up and down and Sebastian got ready to give him hell if he said what he thought the kid was thinking of saying. But to his credit, the boy filled in the blank with the word "lady".

"Well, don't just keep them standing outside in the heat."

Jorge ushered them in, not that it was much cooler in the house. But a fan in the living room at least moved the air around enough to take his mind off the oppressive humidity.

Talita, seated on her customary floral chair, glanced at Veronica and then at him. "Where's Sara?"

"She went home." Those simple words came out of his mouth before he could catch them.

He wasn't here to check up on her. He was here to—He had no idea.

Don't call back until you figure it out.

Talita motioned her grandson over. "Why don't you take Nurse...?" She sent Sebastian a glance.

"Her name is Veronica Cantor."

The older woman nodded. "Take Ms. Cantor to see the game system Sara sent for your birthday."

Sara had sent him something? Hell, Sebastian hadn't even known it was the kid's birthday.

How did she do that? Make everyone feel special?

Until they were no longer on her radar.

Veronica shot him a glance, and he nodded at her. Talita was either going to lecture him or console him.

He didn't need to be consoled.

He just wanted to be left alone.

Ha! Wasn't that what Sara had done? Left him alone?

Dammit, maybe he shouldn't have come here after all.

As soon as Veronica and Jorge had left the room, Talita waved a hand at the ragged faux leather sofa next to her chair. Suppressing a roll of his eyes, he lowered himself onto it, but decided to go on the offensive. "How are you feeling?"

"I'm fine. How are *you* feeling?"

She'd turned it around on him, the emphasis on the penultimate word making Sebastian laugh. "Are we really going to do this?"

"Do what?" The older lady batted her sparse lashes at him.

"What do you want me to say? Sara decided she wanted to go home. So she went."

She and her father had slipped out before he'd even gotten home from work. The day after they'd made love.

Don't call until you figure it out.

That phrase had been knocking around in his head ever since that phone call.

"Why did she decide to leave?"

"I don't know."

Talita stared at him long enough to make him wince, her lips twisted in thought. "I wondered why the postmark on Jorge's present said Rio Grande do Sul. Is that where she's from?"

He nodded, not sure where she was going with this. "Her dad is a *gaúcho*."

"When is she coming back?"

This was one question he knew the answer to. "She's not."

Antônio hadn't said it when he'd called, but the intimation was plain enough.

"I'm sorry."

"Me too." It was true. He was damned sorry. And he had no idea why. It should make his life a whole lot easier.

Maybe he didn't want easier.

She was gone, so it didn't really matter what he wanted.

"Did you tell her you love her?"

"No, of course not, I—" Too late he remembered Talita didn't know the real reason he'd married Sara: so that people like Talita could get the surgery they needed.

Only the project hadn't been sunk the moment she'd left. It may not have been sunk even without marriage. Although it still could have caught up with him.

Could have?

It had. Sara had left.

He kept coming back to that. Why did it matter that she was gone?

Talita gave him a sharp look. "You didn't think you loved her, did you?"

He shook his head, not even bothering to answer.

"But you do."

His brain caught on the words. No, he didn't. He couldn't.

It was impossible, because…

There was a gaping hole where that missing word should be.

A thunderbolt struck him in the chest.

He did. He loved her.

Which was why he couldn't seem to get past the fact that she'd left him high and dry.

Don't call until you figure it out.

Was this what he was supposed to figure out? That he loved her?

"Yes. I do." He shrugged. "But I guess she didn't feel the same way."

"She married you, didn't she?"

"Yes, but only because she felt she had to."

Which was the very reason he'd been so hung up over this whole thing. Why he'd set an end date. Because he hadn't believed that a marriage built on that premise—on a pregnancy—could last.

He still wasn't sure it could. His parents' marriage had, if you could call that miserable existence something that "lasted".

Talita leaned over and looked him in the eye. "Are you that blind? The last time I saw you two, it was written all over her face. The way that girl looked at you said it all."

He frowned. "The way she what?"

"She looked at you the way my Henri used to look at me."

"How did he look at you?"

A dreamy look passed across her face. "As if I was his whole world."

His throat clogged. Wasn't that what the woman at the top of the Banespa building had said?

You just saved my whole world.

He fought for something to say that wouldn't sound cheesy or patronizing. Or hopeless. He settled for simple. "How long were you married?"

"Twenty-five years. One child. And one grandchild."

Five years less than Antônio Moreira had been married.

Had Talita really read something in Sara's expression that had led her to believe she loved him?

And if she did?

Could he actually be happy with someone—with her—for thirty, forty or however many years they lived?

Yes. He thought he could.

He and Sara were not like his parents. He couldn't remember even one serious argument—oh, there'd been little ones, but not about things that mattered. They'd laughed together, worked together—made love together.

Veronica poked her head around the corner. "Can I come out yet?"

"No!" Talita and Sebastian both said the word at the same time. The older woman giggled like a girl when the nurse retreated back into the bedroom.

"So what are you going to do?" she asked.

"Her father told me not to bother calling until I figured something out."

She leaned closer. "I think you just did."

"I think you're right."

"He's probably wondering what took you so long." She crossed the stub of her left leg over her right. "So I'm going to ask again. What are you going to do?"

"I'm going to go down there?" Why he made a question out of it, he had no idea.

"You're damn right you are. And don't come back until she believes you, you hear? No matter how many times you have to say it."

He leaned over and kissed her cheek. "I hear you, Talita. Loud and clear."

Sara slid her hands into matching oven mitts and opened the door to the stove. The casserole inside sizzled. *Escondidinho*—one of her favorite dishes. It should be making her mouth water, and although the meat pie topped with puréed manioc smelled delicious, all she felt was a rock where her stomach should be.

It had been that way ever since she'd come home.

Because she'd run away from a difficult situation without saying a word to anyone. How was that any different from what her ex had done to her? It wasn't. But it was too late to go back and fix it.

Her father had been supportive and wonderful about everything, but over the past month she'd caught him staring out the window. When she asked him what he was doing, he said, "Nothing. Just thinking."

Probably wondering how he was going to survive toddlerhood all over again.

No, her dad said he was looking forward to having little feet running all over the place, and she believed him.

Clap! Clap! Clap!

Ugh! Not again! It seemed every time she turned

around, one of her father's employees came over from the bunkhouse to ask some question or other.

It wasn't like her dad not to be out working the ranch. He still had to be careful with his leg, but two weeks ago he'd gotten a tentative okay to start riding a horse. At a walk. But he'd seemed more interested in that stupid window.

Was he worried that the cancer had come back? They hadn't had the chance to do the blood work Sebastian wanted.

She took off the oven mitts to answer the door, but her father beat her to it. Good, whoever it was could get the answer right from the source. She turned around to finish her lunch preparations, even though her stomach was still doing somersaults inside her. Just another month until her morning sickness should be over.

If that was even what this was.

The door clicked open.

"What in the hell took you so long?"

Sara's brows shot up as she took another step toward the kitchen. She'd never heard her dad greet anyone that way before.

"It took me a while to figure it out."

She stopped dead in her tracks.

Deus. She was having some kind of stress flashback. That voice wasn't real. It couldn't be. Her guilt was making her hear things.

"And have you?"

Okay, that was her father's voice. It was okay. Just her imagination. She started to walk again.

"Yes. I have."

No. It wasn't her mind playing tricks. She swung

around toward the door, but her father was blocking the view.

"Daddy?" she called out.

He glanced back and smiled. "There's someone here who wants to talk to you."

Her hand went to her throat. "Is—? Is it—?"

A man stepped around her father's form. "I hope it's *my* name you're searching for."

Sebastian. It was really him.

"What are you—? Why are you here?"

Her dad gave her a strange knowing smile. "Is that any way to talk to your husband? I think you should at least invite him in for lunch."

Lunch? *Lunch?*

She was having some kind of breakdown, and he was worried about missing a meal? He was acting like he'd been expecting Sebastian for ages.

The image of him looking out the window day after day came to her. Was this why? He'd expected Sebastian to appear?

Her dad swept past her, giving her arm a quick squeeze. "Hear him out, okay? He's traveled a long way to see you. And to say it."

To say what? That he wanted a divorce?

Deus, that's what it was. He figured if she was no longer working at the hospital, there was no reason to keep up the pretense. She should have expected this.

What she hadn't expected was for him to come in person. He could have simply sent the paperwork by certified mail or something.

Once her dad was gone—listening from the kitchen, no doubt—Sebastian closed the door then slowly made his way over to her as if—as if he wasn't sure.

This Sebastian was different from the one who knew what he wanted and went after it. Or maybe she was still trapped in that hazy dream state from when she'd heard his voice at the door.

But he was here. This was a flesh and blood man. Her dad had seen him, had spoken with him, so he was real.

She lifted her chin. Okay, then. It was time to face him and get this over with. "Did you bring the papers?"

He nodded.

Her mouth popped open to help her force air into her suddenly aching lungs. "If you have a pen, I'll sign them and you can be on your way."

He rolled his shoulder in a way that made it pop. Her eyes burned. It had been forever since she'd heard that sound—since she'd heard his voice.

"Maybe we're talking about two different sets of papers." He pulled a sheaf of documents from a long white envelope, then his eyes came up and met hers. "I want to get married. Again. In a church."

Pain ripped through her chest. So soon?

"To who?"

One side of his mouth tilted up. "Do you have to ask?"

She guessed she did, or she wouldn't have voiced the question. But he was smiling. That sexy heart-stopping twist of lips that made her insides go all gooey.

It hit her. There was only one person he would be saying that about. She hoped.

She took her index finger and curved her hand around until it pointed back at herself, her eyebrows raised to make it a question.

"Yes, Sara. You."

"You want to marry me? Why? I thought you were coming to ask for a divorce."

"I don't want a divorce."

"You don't. Is it because of Mãos Abertas?"

He set the papers down on a nearby table. "It has nothing to do with the project. It has everything to do with you."

"The pregnancy, is that it?"

Why did she keep firing questions back at him as if unable to believe his request could be related to something besides all the obvious choices? Because the only other option was...

Surely not.

"This isn't about the baby. Or the project. Not this time. This is about you. And me. I want you to come home."

Home. As if that was where she belonged.

He reached for her hands. "I love you."

"No, you don't."

His head tilted. "I think I would know."

She tried to tug free, only to have his grip on her tighten.

"Please, stop. I already told you I wouldn't keep the baby from you."

"I love you. I'm going to keep on saying it until it sinks into that pretty head of yours."

"Did my dad put you up to this?"

"No, but when I tried to call you the day after you left, he told me not to call again until I figured it out." He lifted one of her hands to his lips and kissed it. "So I didn't call. I came instead. I love you."

Maybe he was really going to keep saying it.

"Are you sure?"

"I wouldn't be here if I wasn't." He nodded at the side table. "I brought proof. Unless you don't feel the same way about me."

"I did." She blinked a time or two to clear her vision. "I mean, I do, but are you sure you really want this?"

"I'm more sure of this than I've ever been of anything." He reeled her in until she was flush against him. "Marry me."

"But what about not being able to see a relationship lasting for decades?"

"I'm out to prove myself wrong. And you're going to help me do it." His fingers sifted through the hair at her nape. "Because I already know the outcome. We're going to last for the duration."

Muscles in her body that had been tensed relaxed against him. "That could be a very long time."

"I'm counting on it." He smiled. "And on having a few more babies along the way."

"More babies?"

"Does that scare you?"

"No. It makes me happy." She believed him. Her arms went around his neck and she raised her face for his kiss.

It was the same sweet fire she remembered, and it injected warmth to her very core.

"I want a real wedding. To make a real commitment. Not because of any baby or babies, but because I want you to be my wife. My forever wife." He took her hand where her wedding ring was and slid it off her finger. At her shocked gasp he hushed her with a kiss. "Don't worry, I'll put it back on. At a ceremony, which will happen here at the ranch, because this is where it all started."

Their mouths met again. Clung. The promise of a lifetime full of love and happiness shimmered around them.

He pulled back, his lips still touching hers. "Do you think your dad would be shocked if we shared your bedroom tonight?"

"I doubt it, but that's not what I want."

When he made to take a step back she did what he had done earlier and tightened her grip. "I have something very different in mind."

"You do?"

"Mmm." She stood on tiptoe, rubbing her cheek across his. "Yes, because you said it all started here at the ranch. Well, that's where you're wrong."

"I don't understand."

"Think about it, Sebastian. Our relationship did not start here. And I want to spend the night in the place where it all began."

He stood there for a second and then his brows slowly went up.

"I see you're beginning to get the picture," she said.

"You want to spend the night at the—"

"Shh. We have to be very, very quiet." She knew he would get the reference to their shared night.

He lowered his voice to a whisper. "You want to start this new phase of our relationship in a sleazy motel? Remember, we now have a baby in tow."

"And I think our baby would say, 'Thank you very much,' don't you? Since that's where he or she got their start."

He chuckled, biting her lower lip and sending a

sharp pang of need through her belly that spiraled lower and lower.

"Do I think so? Oh, I do, Sara. I do indeed."

EPILOGUE

BABY SILAS TEXEIRA came on a stormy day.

But the one thing that wasn't stormy was Sebastian's heart. As the sound of thunder rumbled just outside the hospital, he leaned his head against his wife's, relishing her tired sigh as she whispered, "Love you."

"I love you." He kissed her cheek, his hand going to their baby's tiny back. "And I love our life."

He did. His heart gave a couple of hard beats. He'd worried so much about his motivation for staying that he'd realized he'd lost his way for a little while, almost never getting the opportunity to feel the joy that came with discovering a person in tiny bites. Those moments in time that were meant to be savored and enjoyed.

Yes, he'd jumped into marriage for the wrong reasons. But he was staying for all the right ones.

"Can I call them in?"

"Yes. Please do." She tried to drag her hands through her hair, but he stopped her.

"You look beautiful."

"No, I don't. But no one will be looking at me, anyway." She laid her hand on top of his. "He's amazing, isn't he? This little creature came from both of us."

He grinned. "Maybe we'll leave out some of the details of how he came to be, though."

"I want to go back to that motel every anniversary."

"Sorry?"

"We belong together. I want it branded on our souls, etched in our minds. The motel will just make the process fun."

"Little pitchers." He pretended to cover Silas's ears. "And I don't think it's appropriate to try to seduce me in front of a newborn."

She smiled back at him. "*Try* to seduce you?"

"Okay, so that's pretty much a done deal." He wanted her. All the time. Not because of the sex, although that had been pretty damned amazing. But because of Sara herself. She touched a part of him that no one had ever reached. And he couldn't get enough of her. Her ex-boyfriend had done Sebastian a huge favor in leaving, although if the man ever came back, he was probably going to meet the wrong end of Antônio Moreira's branding iron.

He kissed that cute lower lip. "I think we'd better let some people in here before the room starts to steam up."

She nodded, sighing as she gazed down at their child. "I guess we can share him."

"We might be facing a mob scene if we don't." He moved his lips to her cheek before forcing himself to stand up. "I'll go get them."

He ducked into the hall, and fifteen heads turned toward him in bright expectation. Marcos and Maggie, Lucas and Sophia, Sara's dad, of course. His sister and Adam.

Then his chest tightened. Because a little off to the

side was Talita Moises in her wheelchair. Jorge stood directly behind her.

Talita, who had read Sebastian the Riot Act and brought him to his senses. Her blood sugar was finally under control once again. It looked like she would be there for the rest of Jorge's childhood and into his adult years as well.

He was just getting ready to ask everyone to follow him when one of the nurses from the front desk came barreling toward them. "You are not going to take all of these people in there at once, are you, Dr. Texeira."

Funny how that hadn't been a question but a statement. This particular nurse was known to be ruthlessly protective when it came to her patients. He could understand that. He was pretty protective of Sara as well. But this would be good for her.

He wasn't above a little bargaining to get his way. Unlike his dad, though, this was for a good cause. "How about if I take them all in, but we stay half the amount of time. They'll be in and out." He did a quick head count. "I think since most of us work at this hospital, we know how important it is for patients to get their rest. And since I'm her *husband…*"

For a second, he thought she might veto even that bargaining chip, but although her lips tightened, she gave a brusque nod and glanced at her watch. "Half the time would put you at five minutes."

"Five minutes sounds perfect." He led them down the hall and opened the door. While the rest of the group went in, he waited until Talita and her grandson wheeled up next to him. Laying his hand on her arm, he lowered his voice. "Thank you. For everything."

"I could say the same for you. If it wasn't for Mãos Abertas, I might not be here. How can I ever repay you?"

"You already did. Just by doing us the honor of being here."

"That girl is your whole world, isn't she?"

"Yes, Talita, she is."

"I knew it." She leaned up and pressed her lips to his cheek. "Don't be a stranger, okay?"

"Never."

Then she and Jorge went in to join the rest of the people who were busy oohing and ahhing over the baby and Sara.

As he stared at the gathering, a burst of gratitude sizzled inside him. He was a lucky, lucky man.

He went to the head of the bed and draped his arm on the pillow above Sara's head, watching as she laughed at something Natália had said. He was rich beyond his wildest dreams and it had nothing to do with money.

"Two minutes," he said, feeling a little like the elevator man at the Banespa building.

The nurse was right, though. Sara might look perfectly content, but she was exhausted from giving birth.

Besides, he wasn't quite as willing to share her and Silas as he'd thought. These moments were precious. Irreplaceable.

"Sebastian." His wife's voice carried a chiding tone he knew all too well.

"Nurse's orders."

Natália stepped forward and kissed Sara's forehead. "He's right. We shouldn't tire you out." She gave a pseudo-whisper. "We'll come back when your bodyguard is at work."

"I work here." Sebastian's dry response wasn't lost on anyone. They laughed, but all followed his sister's lead and congratulated them and filed out one by one. Talita and Jorge lingered a moment longer.

"You have a beautiful baby there, honey."

"Thank you." Sara squeezed the older lady's hand. "I hear you're the reason I still have a husband."

"Oh, he would have realized he was being a fool eventually. He just needed a big kick in the behind to understand it sooner rather than later."

"Can I call you whenever he needs another kick?"

"No need," said Sebastian. "I have learned my lesson."

Talita smiled and put her arm around her grandson's waist. "You have to come and eat at our house, once you're out of the hospital."

"Nothing would make us happier, right, Sebastian?"

"Absolutely."

Jorge smiled. Always quiet, he nodded toward the baby. "I could show him how to do things someday. Like maybe ride a bike."

Sebastian had probably heard Jorge say maybe ten words the whole time he'd known him. And the thought of this shy, retiring boy being willing to come out of his shell in order to help Silas made something in his throat grab. He coughed, trying to rid himself of the sensation. Then he put a hand on the boy's shoulder. "Silas would be very fortunate to have a mentor like you."

"Like a real mentor?" The boy stood straighter.

"Yes. Like a real mentor. He'll need one. So you'll have to set a good example."

Talita reached up to ruffle the teen's hair. "Oh, he will. And now we'd better be on our way." With a last flurry of hugs, Jorge wheeled his grandmother from the room, leaving Sebastian and Sara alone with their baby.

He kicked off his shoes and then settled into a nearby chair, propping his feet on the bed.

"You've been awake as long as I have. You need to go home and get some rest."

He reached for her free hand and gripped it tight. "I don't need to go anywhere, *querida*. If you're here and the baby is here, this is my home."

* * * * *

If you missed the previous story in
the HOT BRAZILIAN DOCS! *series*
look out for

THE DOCTOR'S FORBIDDEN TEMPTATION

And if you enjoyed this story, check out these other
great reads from Tina Beckett

RAFAEL'S ONE-NIGHT BOMBSHELL

THE NURSE'S CHRISTMAS GIFT

TO PLAY WITH FIRE
(HOT BRAZILIAN DOCS! *Book 1*)

THE DANGERS OF DATING DR CARVALHO
(HOT BRAZILIAN DOCS! *Book 2*)

All available now!

MILLS & BOON®

MEDICAL
ROMANCE

THE ULTIMATE IN ROMANTIC MEDICAL DRAMA

A sneak peek at next month's titles...

In stores from 5th October 2017:

- **Sleigh Ride with the Single Dad** – Alison Roberts
  and **A Firefighter in Her Stocking** – Janice Lynn

- **A Christmas Miracle** – Amy Andrews *and*
  Reunited with Her Surgeon Prince – Marion Lennox

- **Falling for Her Fake Fiancé** – Sue MacKay *and*
  The Family She's Longed For – Lucy Clark

Just can't wait?
Buy our books online before they hit the shops!
www.millsandboon.co.uk

Also available as eBooks.

MILLS & BOON®

EXCLUSIVE EXTRACT

Dr Grace Forbes is reunited with old flame ER Chief
Charles Davenport – can the single dad and his adorable
twins make her Christmas wish come true?

Read on for a sneak preview of
SLEIGH RIDE WITH THE SINGLE DAD
the first book in the magical CHRISTMAS IN
MANHATTAN miniseries

But there was something else there as well.

A… twinkle…

Of amusement, laced with something else.

Appreciation maybe.

No… it was deeper than that. Something she couldn't
identify.

'What?' she heard herself whisper. 'What are you thinking?
That you'll never leave me in charge of your kids again?'

One corner of his mouth lifted into a smile that could only
be described as poignant.

'I'm thinking,' he said quietly. 'That I've spent the last three
years trying to be both a father and a mother to my kids and
keep their lives as predictable and safe as I can and then someone
comes in and, in the space of a few hours, wrecks my house
and shows me exactly what I didn't realise was missing.'

Grace's brain had caught on the comment about wrecking
his house.

'I'm sorry,' she murmured.

Charles was smiling back at her and that twinkle in his
eyes had changed into something else.

Something that was giving her a very distinctive shaft of
sensation deep in her belly.

Attraction, that's what it was.

A very physical and very definite attraction.

Maybe Charles was feeling it too. Maybe that was why he
lifted his hand to touch her hair.

'Chocolate,' he told her.

'I know...' Grace made a face. 'You might find you need to wash the boys' hair in the morning, as well.'

'It's not a problem.' Charles was touching her cheek now, his finger feather-light. 'You've got some here, too.'

Grace couldn't say anything. She was shocked by the touch and the electricity of the current it was producing that flashed through her body like a lightning bolt to join the pool of sensation lower down.

The smile on Charles's face was fading fast. For another one of those endless moments, they stared at each other again.

Fragments of unformed thoughts bombarded Grace. Memories of another time when they'd looked at each other just like this.